Books by Lisa Plumley

MAKING OVER MIKE

FALLING FOR APRIL

RECONSIDERING RILEY

SANTA BABY
(anthology with Lisa Jackson,
Elaine Coffman, and Kylie Adams)

Published by Zebra Books

RECONSIDERING RILEY

Lisa Plumley

ZEBRA BOOKS
KENSINGTON PUBLISHING CORP.

http://www.kensingtonbooks.com

ZEBRA BOOKS are published by

Kensington Publishing Corp.
850 Third Avenue
New York, NY 10022

All Kensington titles, imprints and distributed lines are available at special quantity discounts for bulk purchases for sales promotion, premiums, fund-raising, educational or institutional use.

Special book excerpts or customized printings can also be created to fit specific needs. For details, write or phone the office of the Kensington Special Sales Manager: Kensington Publishing Corp., 850 Third Avenue, New York, NY 10022. Attn. Special Sales Department. Phone: 1-800-221-2647.

Zebra and the Z logo Reg. U.S. Pat. & TM Off.

First Printing: October 2002
10 9 8 7 6 5 4 3 2 1

Printed in the United States of America

To Ethan Ellenberg,
with thanks for his savvy, his vision, and
his belief that my writing is "exceptional."
And to my husband, John,
whose love inspires me more than
he knows, every single day.

One

Jayne Murphy hadn't intended to tackle the rugged northern Arizona wilderness armed with not much more than pink stilettos, a tin of Altoids, and two hardcover copies of *Heartbreak 101: Getting Over the Good-Bye Guys*. But when she arrived at the Hideaway travel adventure lodge shortly after ten on the sunny Monday morning that was to begin her weeklong trip, it became immediately clear to her that intentions didn't necessarily mean a thing.

Reality, on the other hand, did.

And Jayne's reality included none of the things she'd been prepared for. Where were the valets? she wondered as the airport shuttle jolted to a stop in a cloud of red dust. Where were the private spa cabins? The chic outdoorsy patio for dining al fresco? The back-to-nature Jacuzzis?

In their places were a lot of boulders, a hand-lettered "parking" sign, two picnic tables beneath the trees, and a single long, low building accented with smaller outbuildings. It looked like Abe Lincoln's summer home. Like *Frontierland* come to life. Like, like—Jayne took a deep breath and fought back her panic at being thrust unexpectedly into such hardscrabble surroundings, trying hard to fit the scene into her personal frame of reference—like a grunge-meets-L.L.-Bean ad layout.

Minus the glossiness, of course.

She swiveled in her seat toward the van driver who'd transported her and her five companions from the airport in Sedona.

"Is this the gatehouse? The garage?" She couldn't keep the hopefulness from her voice. Maybe Arizonans envisioned the standard two-and-a-half-car number differently than she did. "Someone's private residence?"

He chuckled. "No, ma'am. This here's the lodge."

"The *Hideaway* Lodge?"

"The very same."

Jayne frowned in confusion. Her publicist had led her to believe the Hideaway Lodge was about as rustic as the Ralph Lauren department at Macy's. She couldn't help but feel a little misled.

"And home base for you ladies for the next week, I understand." The driver pulled out the keys and tossed them jauntily in the air before catching them. "Welcome to the back country."

His door creaked as he opened it. He jumped out, ostensibly to retrieve their luggage. That was when Jayne realized he wasn't kidding. This really was it.

Faced with the truth—that the research for her next book was going to take place here in Paul Bunyanville and that a compensatory sea salt aromatherapy rub followed by a champagne cooldown was unlikely at most—she rallied her spirits and prepared to make the best of things.

After all, there was a lot riding on this week's activities. Her whole future depended on what happened here in Arizona. And now that she'd discovered where that future lay, Jayne intended to grab every opportunity with both pink-manicured hands. Starting this minute.

"Okay, ladies." Moving into full leadership mode, she raised her voice to gain the attention of the five chattering women on the van's bench seats behind her. Simultaneously, she pulled a compact from her handbag. "This is it. The beginning of the next chapter of your life: breaking free!"

Everyone cheered. The driver, hauling bags from the storage area behind the final seat, shook his head.

"You're about to make your entrance into that new life. Compacts at the ready!" With a swift look, Jayne confirmed that each woman had withdrawn the leopard-print compact she'd been issued. "Okay . . . primp!"

Nose-tickling powder pouffed into the air, sent adrift by the force of six puffs diligently in action. Various perfumes filled the spaces between the seats. Lipsticks were passed, mouths puckered, hair fluffed. Finally, Jayne surveyed her own reflection, blew a kiss into the mirror, and snapped her compact shut. A series of echoing clicks followed.

"What's our motto?" she asked.

"If you look good, you feel good!"

The ladies' enthusiastic response made Jayne smile. Obviously, the mini-orientation session she'd held while waiting in Phoenix for their connecting flight had paid off. Satisfied, she complimented everyone on their efforts.

There was nothing better, she thought as she gave her charges a fond look, than helping people in need.

"All right, then. Let's go!"

"Yay!"

Ready or not, Jayne led the charge. Opening the van's passenger-side door, she thrust her T-strap stilettos bravely into the high-desert air. She touched the reddish dirt with her toes. She grabbed her handbag and both books she'd brought, then emerged into the sunlight with a smile on her face.

The adventure was about to begin.

Ten minutes later, the adventure had yet to begin, and Jayne was getting a little worried. Not that she meant to

show it. Her ladies' sense of confidence and well-being
depended on her, and she wasn't going to let them down.

Luckily, she'd brought enough luggage to see them
through any contingency . . . even, as was the case right
now, the mysterious absence of their lodge hosts.

The place was as deserted as a Thanksgiving swimwear
sale. No one had answered their knock at the Hideaway
Lodge's locked front door. No one had answered their cell
phone call to the number Jayne's publicist had listed on her
itinerary. No one had arrived in their driver's wake and
explained the whole mess while handing out complimentary
bottles of Evian and creatively assembled finger foods.

More's the pity, Jayne decided. She really could have
used a little nosh. Maybe some of those cream-cheese-stuffed
cherry tomatoes, or a nice mini quiche Lorraine. She hadn't
had a bite since breakfast—but with only airport food available, who could blame her? Her favorite blueberry frappe
bath gel was probably more edible than the average stuff
served up between concourses.

She'd been looking forward to the gourmet lunch she'd
thought would undoubtedly await them at the lodge. Instead,
Jayne's stomach rumbled as she traversed—yet again—the
distance between the lodge's front door and their assembly
in the parking lot.

Seated on various pieces of Jayne's hard-sided signature-
baby-blue luggage, the women all looked to her for guidance.
The game of gin rummy being played atop her steamer trunk
of shoes came to a stop.

"Still no answer."

They drooped. Grudgingly, the players resumed their
game. Although Jayne didn't know any of them well yet,
their disappointment tugged at her.

"But I'm sure it's only a matter of time. I'll see what I
can do."

For privacy, she strode into the shadow of a semicrumpled
pickup truck with its hood raised. Careful not to brush her

close-fitting baby-blue-print silk shirtdress against the vehicle's grimy exterior, she took out her cell phone and dialed. Her publicist answered on the third ring.

"Francesca? It's Jayne. Listen, about this research trip you planned—"

"Jayne! Great to hear from you! How are things in the Southwest?"

Jayne covered her phone-free ear, the better to hear Francesca speaking from her noisy Snap Books cubicle in far-away—and blissfully civilized—New York City. "They're . . . unexpected. This Hideaway Lodge is—"

"Rustic, yes? Charming? Quiet? All the things you're going to need to work on that next blockbuster for us. Don't worry about a thing. I've got every detail covered."

That was what worried Jayne. "When you said you were sending me and my workshop participants on an 'adventure travel trip' to get away from it all, I thought that was just one of those sayings. You know. Like 'instant classic' or 'wash-and-wear hair.' " She tossed her own shoulder-length tresses in frustration. "I think they actually have outhouses in this place!"

Francesca hooted. "*Those* didn't show up on the Web site picture when I was scouting locations for you."

"I think you mistook them for the guest cabins."

"Hmmm. Maybe. There *were* several of them. . . ."

Jayne didn't want to speculate on the reasons for that. "All I wanted was someplace private and serene. Someplace where my workshop participants wouldn't be bothered by reminders of the problems they were leaving behind."

"By which you mean the 'good-bye guys,' right? The ex-boyfriends."

"*And* ex-husbands, ex-lovers, ex-unforgettable one-night stands. Yes."

Jayne's gaze fell on the two hardbound books—copies of the book *she'd* actually written—stacked on a nearby boulder to give her handbag a clean spot to rest. *Heartbreak*

101: Getting Over the Good-Bye Guys was her claim to fame and the key to her newfound purpose all in one. If its follow-up workbook was going to be half as successful, she needed to make Francesca understand her dilemma.

"Most of these women have spent the time since their breakups in full phone-hovering mode," Jayne explained, "hoping to hear from Mr. Wrong again. Or dropping by their old hangouts, expecting to 'accidentally' run into him. It's self-destructive, and it's not part of my plan. So while being out of town certainly *is* part of my plan, for this to *really* work—"

"You need someplace like the Hideaway Lodge," Francesca interrupted. "It's secluded, it's quiet, and it has only one public phone—a half-hour hike from the lodge. It's perfect."

"It's deserted."

There was a verbal shrug in Francesca's voice. "The owners are a sweet older couple. They bought the place after the husband retired. Probably they're just out for their afternoon constitutional or something."

" 'Afternoon constitutional'?"

"Or something. They're expecting you, after all." Briskly, Francesca went on. "Look, we're putting a big push behind this breakup guide and workbook idea of yours. It's already on the schedule for next spring. You've got to deliver. If you have a problem with the way we're supporting you . . ."

The unvoiced alternative was clear. Jayne could practically hear her current book contract—and all the contracts she hoped would follow it—shrivel into dust and blow away. If she didn't make a success of this, she'd be back working full-time in the art department of the San Francisco advertising agency she'd taken a sabbatical from.

Even worse, her book's followers would be out in the cold. Including the five women waiting for her across the dirt ruts.

"I'll manage," she promised, crossing her fingers for luck. "Don't worry."

"I'm not worried." Francesca went over a few additional details about a possible local talk show appearance, then signed off with some encouragement about "roughing it." At the last instant, she added, "Oh, and don't worry about the hiking part either. You'll do fine. Byeee!"

Click. Tilting her head as the publicist hung up, Jayne blinked. *Hiking part? What hiking part?*

She glanced down at her shoes. Made of pink leather with three-inch heels and a tiny bow at the T-strap's juncture, they managed to say *cute* and *sassy* with nothing more than a flash of ankle. They did not, however, say *hike*. In fact, Jayne was pretty sure none of her shoes spoke Hike. Ever.

Well, she'd just have to deal with that when the time came. Until then, she had a group of breakup-ees to help: Mitzi, a waitress from Michigan; Carla, a student from New Mexico; Doris and Donna, sixty-something sisters from California; and Kelly, a data analyst from Washington State.

She gathered her things and went back to them. They looked up at her expectantly.

Sudden nervousness pushed through her, tightening Jayne's grip on her handbag and books. Who was she to offer advice to these women? She wasn't a psychologist, a psychiatrist, a therapist, or a relationship counselor. She wasn't even a bona fide expert. She was just a girl who'd had her heart broken one too many times . . . and lived to tell about it. What if she couldn't do this?

For the sake of her group, she mustered a confident smile. "The lodge owners should be back any minute." *She hoped.* "Until then, does anyone have any questions?"

Carla, a petite brunette with a pierced nose, raised her hand. "Umm, yeah. I have a question."

"Great!" Encouraged, Jayne tilted her head, ready to discuss breakup-recovery strategies, healing methods, and anything else outlined in her book. "What is it?"

"Can I borrow your cell phone?"

"Me too!"

"Me too, please."

"Me next."

"No, me, Donna!" Doris complained, elbowing her gray-haired sister. "You always get to go first."

Amid the hubbub, Jayne sat on the shoe trunk beside Carla. She put her hand on her shoulder. "Who do you want to call?" she asked gently.

Everyone quieted.

"My Paolo. If I could just, like, hear his voice on the answering machine *one* more time. I mean"—Carla glanced upward, meeting Jayne's concerned gaze—"what if this trip really works, and I'm over him by the time I get back?"

Biting her lip, she hugged herself. Mitzi and Kelly did too. Even Doris and Donna abandoned their shoving match to listen.

They were afraid, Jayne realized. Afraid of the unknown, afraid of letting go, afraid of moving forward. She understood.

She'd been there too.

"I know a part of you doesn't want this to work," she said. "A part of you wants to hang on. But if your relationship's ended, it's ended, and you have to accept that. Getting over him—whether his name's Paolo or Hank or Marty—"

Doris and Donna gave a joint telltale cry.

Jayne nodded encouragingly. "—or anything else—will be for the best. It really will."

Kelly adjusted her rectangular-framed eyeglasses. "How can you be sure?"

Jayne closed her eyes. She didn't want to get personal with this. She really didn't. But if it would help . . .

"I'm sure because I've lived it. My heart was broken"—just like her voice, when she spoke of it. She cleared her throat and went on—"not so long ago, and I got past it. I came up with some strategies that helped. Eventually, I passed them on to my girlfriends, and they helped them too. One thing led to another, somebody suggested I write them down, and . . . *voilà!* A book."

She thumped the topmost copy of *Heartbreak 101* in her hand. The women all brightened.

"You have a gift," Mitzi said seriously, popping a bubble in her gum. "A genuine knack for helping people."

Nods all around. It was Jayne's turn to brighten.

"You do," Doris said, still nodding. "Everyone in our canasta group agrees. Right, Donna?"

Her sister folded her arms. "No. Our golf club loves Jayne's book more. And you know it."

"Everyone in my dorm was like, completely green with envy when they found out I was going on this trip," Carla volunteered. "You're our hero, Jayne."

Kelly nodded. "The women in my office feel the same way. I'm lucky to be here."

Overwhelmed, Jayne looked from one woman to the next. She could have hugged every last one.

It was one thing to know *Heartbreak 101* had shot to the top of best seller lists on the strength of readers' demand. It was something else again to talk with those readers, and to know she'd really, truly helped them.

You have a gift, she remembered Carla saying, and wanted to grin like an idiot, all over again. Jayne had never had an honest-to-gosh *gift* before. Now that she did, it meant so much to her.

"But I'm dying to know," Kelly went on, giving her a speculative look, "exactly what happened with the guy? The guy who broke your heart? Who was he? What was he like? How did you meet him?"

To Jayne's dismay, everyone else chimed in, clamoring for details. How had it ended? Where was he now? How did she feel? *Tell, tell, tell.*

Finally, Jayne held up both palms, leaving her handbag and books balanced on her lap. She laughed. "Okay, okay.

At the risk of giving away terrific book-three material . . . here goes."

They all settled in. Around them, the afternoon breeze swooshed past the rocks and mesquite, and an occasional bird chirped. The setting was serene, peaceful . . . and way too "raw wilderness" for Jayne's tastes. Seriously. How was she supposed to get a decent decaf soy latte out here?

Anyway . . .

"Well, let's see. It was almost"—she paused, as though the time that had passed *weren't* emblazoned in her memory—"almost two years ago now, I guess. We met at the pier in San Francisco while I was on location for an advertising shoot. He was a photographer on assignment taking pictures of migrating whales off the coast—"

"What was his name?" Mitzi interrupted.

Jayne hesitated. Then she decided there really wasn't any reason *not* to tell them. "Riley. His name was Riley."

She barely stifled a sigh. Hearing Riley's name again—especially from her own lips—was strange. Thinking of him was even stranger. Yet at the same time, it was tempting too. A half-forgotten yearning nudged itself awake inside her, and Jayne knew she'd be wiser not to travel down this road again.

"To make a long story short, we hit it off," she said casually. "You know those romantic montages in the movies where the couple walks along the beach, laughs over dinner, and chases each other in the park? That was us. Instantly smitten. Love at first sight. Blah, blah, blah."

They smiled. Doris leaned forward. "So what happened?"

Jayne fingered the gold pendant she'd worn to fill the neckline of her shirtdress. She shrugged. "Six months later he left. That's what happened. One minute, everything was wonderful. And the next, he was gone. Just . . . gone."

"*Awww.*" The group huddled closer, patting Jayne on the shoulders. Their comfort surrounded her, freely offered even though they were still mostly strangers—strangers who'd bonded over shared loss.

Jayne felt herself weaken, felt a sting of tears at the long-lost memory of Riley's desertion, and told herself she had to get a grip. Falling back under the spell of *coulda, woulda, shoulda* wouldn't help anyone now. Least of all herself.

Besides, she was over Riley now.

She sniffed and swiped a hand over her eyes. Straightened. "It's all right," she croaked, knowing she had to set an example for them. "I'm fine now. But thanks, everyone."

Amid the comforting murmurs her breakup-ees offered, Jayne sucked in a deep breath. She stood. "I'd better . . . go try knocking on the lodge door again. Maybe they've just been asleep in there."

At ten forty-five in the morning? a part of her jibed. But none of the women called her bluff, so Jayne managed to get away. At the big plank door she pulled out her compact and checked her makeup.

Bawling over lost loves was, after all, hell on a girl's Benefit "babe cakes" classic eyeliner.

A shout from Carla carried from the parking lot. Jayne turned to see her pointing past the boulders and scrubby bushes toward the dirt road beyond. "I see, like, a dust plume! Somebody's coming!"

The lodge owners. If they were back, then she could get started—and move on to something positive too.

Jayne ran (okay, *walked quickly*—sacrifices had to be made for beauty and for stylish shoes) back toward her things. Sudden excitement shimmied through her as she gathered up her handbag and the autographed books she'd brought for their hosts.

Now that the time had come, she could hardly wait to get started. Anything was better, Jayne figured, than thinking about Riley Davis . . . and the bewildering vanishing act he'd pulled just when things had started to get *good* between them.

Two

Over the thirty-two years of his life, Riley Davis had, on occasion, hacked his way through jungles. He'd climbed his way to mountain peaks in subzero temperatures. He'd even risked his neck in white-water rapids and held his breath while skydiving. But he'd never, during all those adventures, encountered anyone more frustratingly, aggravatingly, crazy-makingly stubborn than Bud Davis.

His grandfather.

Who, at this moment, happened to be sitting in the passenger seat of Riley's battered Suburban as they meandered down the service road toward the lodge . . . driving him ape shit with every word he said.

"You are not leading this group, Gramps." Riley forcibly relaxed his grip on the steering wheel and shot Bud an earnest don't-mess-with-me look. It was tough to pull off on a man who'd once watched eight-year-old Riley cry over losing his favorite grass snake, but he gave it a try all the same. "The doctor said you need to take it easy. I'm here to make sure you do that."

"You're here 'cause you're in cahoots with your grandma," Bud grumbled. "She wants to turn me useless too."

Riley's heart softened. Putting himself in Gramps's shoes, he could imagine how helpless, how embarrassed, how—yes, thoroughly pissed off—he would feel. But that didn't mean he was going to let his seventy-year-old grandfather work himself to death. Especially if he meant to do so by leading a bunch of namby-pamby city types on a five-day adventure hike.

He glanced sideways. "You're not useless. You never will be. Those water lines near the lodge need work, and—"

" 'Water lines need work,' " Bud mimicked, making a face. "A damned plumber could do that, and you know it."

"That's not the point."

"I'm trained to take that group out. I'm doing it."

"No, you're not." Calmly, Riley steered around a pothole left by a recent rain. He squinted into the distance, where two people could be seen walking along the roadside. *"I am."*

"Hell. You don't wanna do that."

"Yes, I do."

"Bullshit. You don't care about this place." Bud's out-flung arm indicated the scenic red buttes, the creosote and cypress along the roadside—and the lodge in the distance. "Or any place, for that matter. You haven't spent more than three months straight in any one spot since you were old enough to put on your own boots."

It was coming, Riley knew. The usual reminder. The usual dig. Wait for it. . . .

"Just like your father."

Stifling a sigh, Riley glanced sideways again. He deliberated making a rebuttal. Sunlight shone through the Suburban's window, casting Gramps's lined skin and stubborn features into bold relief . . . and changing Riley's mind about stirring up trouble too.

"No point trampling over the past. It's over with" was all he said.

"Hmmmph."

Stubborn to the core, Riley thought, giving his grandfather an affectionate—if aggravated—look. Those weathered lines of his—and his shock of thick white hair—were the only visible reminders of Bud Davis's advancing years. Past retirement age now, he was nonetheless broad-shouldered, lean, and as strong as the day he'd first ascended the more than twelve-hundred-foot summit of nearby Humphrey's Peak.

On that day, though, he hadn't had two bum knees, torn cartilage in his shoulder, ever-worsening arthritis, and a trick ankle that threatened to send him careening down a canyonside someday.

"I know you want to get back to your own life," Bud said, resting his open palms on the knees that had helped betray him. "Take some of them pictures, hike into some godforsaken no-man's-land—" At this, he smiled. "For that magazine of yours. Didn't you say something about heading off to Antigua for another *National Explorer* assignment?"

"I don't remember."

Riley's gut clenched, protesting the lie. Ignoring it, he kept his gaze fixed on the two people he'd seen strolling the roadside up ahead. He recognized them.

"It's not important," he added. What *was* important was keeping safe the ridiculously bullheaded man who'd spent summer after summer watching over Riley.

Bud shook his head. "You're a piss-poor liar. You still tap your foot whenever you're telling a stretcher."

Frowning, Riley stilled his jittery brake foot.

"It's a bunch of them New Age types, I think," Bud warned further, "going on that trip you're so hot to lead. Probably, they'll have crystals and crap. Want you to burn incense on the trail and free the spirits in the red rocks."

His disgusted tone made his opinion of "New Age types" plain. "The leader, she wrote one of those self-help books.

S'posed to help women get over the men who broke their hearts."

A self-help guru. Picturing the kind of uptight, brainiac man-hater who'd be likely to write such a book, Riley made a face too. He didn't know why people couldn't just help themselves. That's what he did. And he was perfectly fine.

He slowed up just behind the walkers, who were headed in the same direction he and Gramps were, but on the opposite side of the road. Dust billowed from beneath the Suburban's thick-treaded tires. Beside him, Bud squinted through the windshield.

"Hey! Is that your grandma? And Alexis, right along with her?"

"Yep. Looks like Alexis is running away to Phoenix again."

Bud shook his head, watching the two females stride side by side. "Spittin' image of your brother, that girl is. Leastwise, on the inside. She's got a stubborn streak a mile wide."

"Wonder where the family gets that from?"

"Damned if I know."

"Uh-huh." Riley grinned and gave the Suburban a little gas. Once abreast of the pair, he let the vehicle idle and rolled down his window all the way. He leaned out and offered a wolf whistle. "Goin' my way, ladies?"

They turned. Recognized him. Blushing, his grandmother shook her head. His thirteen-year-old niece giggled—then remembered she was in the midst of her latest adolescent angst, and put on a dramatic face instead.

"Only if you're going to Phoenix, Uncle Riley. Then I'm *all* yours." Alexis cast an accusatory look at her great-grandmother. "*Some* people around here don't understand what life is like for a person who still has a *passion* for *living*."

Gwen Davis, sixty-six and still plenty lively despite the challenges of caring for a newly hatched teenager for the

duration of spring break, rolled her eyes. "What you have
is a passion for trouble, young lady. If I hadn't caught up
with you when I did, you'd have been on the back of that
man's Harley and halfway to God-knows-where by now."

"Phoenix." Alexis pouted. "That's where I'd be. Phoenix, where my *life* is."

By "life," Riley assumed she meant "the mall." It
couldn't be easy to survive shopping withdrawal without so
much as a cherry-berry smoothie and a gigantic pretzel for
comfort.

"There's nothing wrong with a little hitchhiking," Alexis
went on. "He was *nice*. He had a Tweety Bird tattoo." She
issued the ultimate recommendation: "My *mom* would've
let me."

"Your mother's a nincompoop," Bud offered, leaning
across the Suburban's gearshift. "Best thing she ever did
was divorce your dad."

Alexis's lower lip pushed forward. She crossed her skinny
arms.

"Bud." Gwen shook her head. "Not now."

He subsided and settled for hunting down his favorite
Hank Williams song on the radio. Static crackled and popped
as he spun the SUV's pre-digital-age controls.

Riley gestured Alexis nearer.

"I don't have a Tweety Bird tattoo." The tattoo he *did*
have was in a place he did not intend to share with his
impressionable niece. "But what say you and Nana jump
in here and take a ride back to the lodge with me? You can
help me break in that new group that's coming today. I'm
taking them out—"

"Like hell you are," Bud grumbled.

"He is!" Gwen insisted.

"—tomorrow for training. Since we're already late"—
Riley shot a glance at his scratched-up Swiss Army watch—
"we'd better hit it."

Morosely, Alexis schlumped to the Suburban and got in.

She sat in the backseat beside her great-grandmother, who got in next, and chewed a lock of her long brown hair.

Riley glanced in the rearview mirror. "Doesn't that ever get caught in your braces?"

His niece yanked her hair from her face. She snapped her lips closed to hide her recently installed purple orthodontia and gave him a look that definitely plugged him into the "lame *old* people who don't *understand* me" category. Riley made a mental note never to mention her braces' existence again. Even if he did think they made Alexis look cute in a gawky, tender, between-stages sort of way.

He redeemed himself by selecting a magazine from the grocery store bag next to Bud's seat. He handed it over his shoulder. "I got you something in town."

"*Cosmo!* Cool! Thanks." Glossy pages ruffled as Alexis rapidly flipped through them. " 'Fifty ways to look smokin' hot!' Number one . . ."

"Wouldn't *Tiger Beat* have been more appropriate?" Gwen asked. "I don't want to be a prude, but—"

"*Tiger Beat* is *so* fifth-grade," Alexis said, waving her half-bitten glitter-polished fingernails. "I'm a *woman* now."

Bud scoffed. "And I'm one of the Backstreet Boys."

"Ha. Good one, Gramps."

Gwen frowned, her hand hovering over Alexis's bent head as the girl went back to reading hottie tips. At the last instant, she halted the caress she'd undoubtedly been about to give and looked out the window instead. Riley put the Suburban into motion again, having decided keeping his trap shut was the better part of valor. After all, he'd been the one who'd handed over the bone of contention.

They drove farther down the road. Navigating the steep switchback climb during the final two tenths of a mile to the lodge required vigilance and a certain tolerance for dust. It also required patience, Riley learned, since his grandfather was hell-bent on resuming their argument.

"It's only a five-day trip," Bud said as though they'd

never quit talking. "With a gaggle of that how-to woman's groupies. To the lodge in Catsclaw Canyon. I can—"

"I'm doing it. End of story."

"Dammit, Riley! I said I'll—"

"The publicist who booked the trip said they'll need to stop frequently," Gwen chimed in, "to conduct some sort of heartbreak workshops along the trail. You know you'll never have the patience to settle for less than a twenty-mile-per-day pace, Bud."

His grandfather scowled. Jouncing along in the backseat, Alexis perked up. "Heartbreak workshops?"

Gwen nodded. "Yes. Apparently, that's why the author came here. To test out her new theories in private."

Riley shook his head. This just got better and better. His unwanted group was slow, new to the backcountry, fond of New Age mumbo jumbo, *and* dead set on using the quiet canyon trails to conduct open-air therapy sessions. Whoever the heartbreak book's author was, she must be a real piece of work.

"What a bunch of hooey," he said beneath his breath.

Bud heard. "See? I *knew* you didn't want to do it! I'll just get out my gear as soon as we get to the lodge, and—"

"I'll do it," Riley said quietly. Firmly.

Angling his head to loosen the tight muscles in his neck and shoulders, he pondered his future. The sooner he finished this trail-guiding job and completed the rest of the repairs he'd begun on the lodge, the sooner he could get back to the life he loved.

The vagabond's life.

Riley had sometimes joked he was one part interpreter, two parts Gypsy, and one part daredevil . . . but given his upbringing, it really wasn't much of a joke. He'd had to become all those things to survive. Now, though, he accepted and appreciated the life he'd built. However willing he was to temporarily help out his grandparents, his intentions remained clear to him.

He intended to see, to do, to conquer, and to enjoy. Not necessarily in that order.

He'd only once been tempted to alter his plans. To settle down, to toe off his boots and hang up his rappelling ropes and sample life the way a rare few did ... with someone they cared about. But although the temptation had felt nearly irresistible, the urge to stay had felt so alien that Riley had—

No point trampling over the past, he reminded himself savagely, feeling a familiar—and unwanted—sense of loss wash over him. *It's over.*

"You said the group's six women?" he asked, taking refuge in the job to be done.

Gwen nodded. Bud glared. "Hmmph."

Riley knew his grandfather would understand. Eventually. "Then I'll probably ask Mack and Bruce to come along."

On a typical guided adventure travel trip, a traveler-to-guide ratio of three to one, or even four to one, would have been perfectly acceptable. Higher ratios were safe so long as the guides knew their jobs. They meant better profits too. But the Hideaway Lodge was firmly in the black, and Riley wasn't leading this trip for the money anyway. In the midst of the "how-to junkies do the wilderness" craziness, a couple of extra guides would help keep him sane. If a shortfall arose because of his decision, he'd make up the difference himself.

"Good idea," Gwen volunteered, forced cheerfulness evident in her voice. "Since we don't have any other groups coming in this week, I'm sure Mack and Bruce would love to help out."

" 'Mack and Bruce would love to help out,' " Bud mimicked, making a disgusted face. He shifted in his seat, the safety belt chafing against his flannel work shirt. "I guess *I'll* be busy working on the water lines."

"The septic system needs work too," Gwen informed him.

Beside Riley, his grandfather put his head in his hands

and sighed. A string of muffled obscenities followed, mostly relating to Bud's opinions of ''goddamn plumbers'' and his fervent desire not to become one at this stage of his life. Riley patted his shoulder in silent empathy.

''I'm trapped,'' Bud said, shifting his bleak gaze to his grandson. ''Trapped.''

Riley didn't need to hear it twice. Trapped was exactly the way he felt right now, and he didn't like it one damned bit.

Especially once he rounded the last corner and the lodge came into view . . . along with the women waiting for them.

Baby blue. Riley would have recognized that particular shade of his favorite color anywhere. It was as recognizable as the McDonald's arches, as familiar as the color of the sky, as memorable as . . . as the only woman he'd ever known who'd actually possessed a ''signature color.''

Jayne.

She was here.

Nah, Riley told himself amid the clatter and chatter of the rest of his family getting out of the Suburban, gathering up packages, slamming their doors. *That was crazy.*

Jayne Murphy was the least likely candidate for a wilderness vacation he could think of. She wore high heels exclusively, except when she was barefoot or in bed. (And sometimes, he remembered with a grin and a stupidly fond mental flashback involving a pair of red stilettos, even then.) She ''cooked'' by nuking microwave popcorn, ripping open a packet of margarita mix, or (occasionally), pouring some Cap'n Crunch. She wore miniskirts.

Jayne's idea of wildlife was the abandoned pets she rescued (she had a serious soft spot for mutts and strays of any kind), then dressed up in petwear ensembles, complete with hats, while looking for the best new owner. Her notion of ''roughing it'' was a vacation spot with no ice machine and an unheated swimming pool. She hiked only to the nearest Nordstrom so far as Riley knew, loved nothing more than being indoors with a flute of champagne and a happening band playing nearby, and avoided all contact with anything that might make her dirty.

There was no *way* Jayne could be here. She'd sooner chew up her Macy's card, he felt certain, than voluntarily forgo her God-given right to room service.

And yet . . . somehow . . .

He peered closer. The bombshell with the ready smile and the honey-blonde hair, the "It" girl with the va-va-voom baby-blue dress and the legs up to there, the talking, laughing, guilelessly generous woman who was at this very minute sympathetically patting Bud's bum shoulder . . . *nah*.

Shaking his head, unable to move from behind the steering wheel, Riley squinted through the windshield. All around him, life went on as usual. Greenhorn adventure travelers milled around, looking apprehensive, as though Mother Nature meant to spit on them. Alexis alternately sulked and laughed. Gwen greeted and smiled. Bud unfolded his arms and . . . *preened?*

Riley blinked. Yep. His grandfather was actually strutting a little, puffing out his chest and putting on his most gregarious expression, the one he used while trying to sucker his doctor into letting him water-ski.

That was when Riley knew it was true. Only Jayne could have had an effect like that on Bud. Only Jayne could have had an effect like *this* on . . . him.

Spooked at the realization, Riley made himself unclench his fingers from the wheel. He couldn't just sit there like an idiot, gawping at her. Gawping at all of them. It was embarrassing. Unmanly. And still, somehow, Riley couldn't help it. His body refused to cooperate with his brain's efforts to make him behave normally.

He looked at Jayne again (to be honest, he hadn't been able to look away). What kind of cosmic "gotcha!" was this? He'd only recently reached the point where a thousand little things didn't remind him of her, didn't remind him of all they'd—

No. There was no way in hell he was heading down *that* path again. Decisively, Riley got out of the Suburban and strode toward the group.

Jayne's profile faced to the left, slightly away from him. She spoke animatedly with Bud and Gwen, saying something about how the group hadn't minded their hosts' lateness, because they'd "bonded" during the wait.

It was more than a polite excuse, Riley considered as he came closer, because the women's behavior did match his somewhat limited notions of feminine bonding. They stuck close to Jayne's side, listened avidly when she spoke, watched her with obvious fondness. Clearly, they'd fallen under her spell.

In the dozen or so steps it took him to reach her, Riley had time to notice the changes in Jayne. The longer length of her hair. The glossier look of her clothes and accessories, as though her ad agency art department work had suddenly turned more profitable. The sadder curve to her smile. For that last, he felt suddenly responsible—then remembered nearly two years had passed since their time together. By now, whatever blunted Jayne's smile owed itself to something—or someone—else.

He remembered what his grandmother had said about the self-help guru's touchy-feely "heartbreak" workshops, and guessed Jayne must be a participant. Jayne, now a woman with a hurt so deep it required special help—and seven hundred miles of travel from her home in San Francisco— to overcome it.

At the realization, two conflicting emotions struck him. First, regret—that Jayne had suffered at the hands of some thoughtless, relationship-challenged lunkhead. And second, eagerness—to pound the lunkhead until he apologized for hurting her, at the least.

He stopped beside them just as Bud demonstrated the size of his biceps for Jayne. With Gwen's permission, she squeezed it, making appropriately impressed sounds.

Riley fought an insane urge to flex.

The last thing he needed was Jayne's hands on him, he told himself. Reminding him of all they'd—

Stop it. "Welcome to the lodge," he said gruffly, offering a handshake.

Automatically, Jayne put her hand in his to accept. Riley felt the contact warm him, wend through him . . . remind him. At the same moment, she glanced upward.

Recognition swept the smile from her face. Shocked silence stretched between them. *Too much silence.*

He empathized with her inability to speak. He'd been similarly dumbstruck upon seeing her. But with Gramps and Nana and Alexis and five women watching, Riley doubted Jayne wanted to run through the whole stare-blink-gawp routine he had perfected back in the Suburban. He decided to help her out.

"Can anybody compete in this Mr. Universe contest?" He mustered what he hoped was a happy-go-lucky smile and nodded toward his grandfather's still-crooked biceps. "Or have I been outclassed?"

Joking, he extended his left arm and struck a pose. The short sleeve of the T-shirt he'd pulled on with his jeans rode up just high enough to reveal his biceps. "What do you think?"

Jayne's mouth opened and closed, but no words emerged. A spark of something dangerous glimmered in her eyes.

"Ooooh," cried one of the other women, a petite brunette with a nose ring. She rushed forward to squeeze his muscles. "Nice. *Very* nice."

As though her declaration were a signal, they all surrounded him, loosening his grasp on Jayne's hand. The gum-popping redhead admired his delts. The mousy, glasses-wearing brunette engaged him in small talk, all the while eyeballing his T-shirt hem as though wondering if he'd notice if she stripped it off for a look at his abs. The nose-ring girl murmured something encouraging about his chest. The two gray-haired, similarly featured women debated the tightness of his backside versus the width of his shoulders and came to no agreement whatsoever, which didn't stop them from urging him to turn this way and that for display.

They sounded like connoisseurs evaluating wine. *Stark, with a hint of chiseledness. Lean and cheery, almost too accessible. A smattering of just-fixed-the-radiator bouquet, with subtle washes of Safeguard for balance.*

Riley knew he should put an end to it before his intended icebreaker got out of hand . . . but he was still hoping Jayne would weigh in with an opinion too.

Familiar, but elusive; an almost-forgotten favorite.

Just as the thought crossed his mind, she straightened. He stilled, waiting to hear what her first words to him in twenty-one months would be.

Jayne's gaze swept up and down, measuring him with something between curiosity and . . . confusion?

"Imagine seeing you here," she said.

Her voice, sweet and faintly husky, sounded exactly as he remembered it. Hearing it, he wanted to smile, to shout, to develop a rare case of twenty-one-month amnesia. God, but it was good to see her.

"It's been a long time," Jayne went on. Inexplicably, she paused for the merest instant, her gaze meeting with those of the women who still clustered around him. Then she fixed him with an indecipherable look. "How have you been . . . *Riley?*"

At the sound of his name, all the women stepped back. Their expressions turned from lighthearted to revelatory to downright murderous. They shared a brief, silent communion. They nodded.

Puzzled, Riley watched as five pairs of arms crossed over five feminine chests. Five heads shook sorrowfully side to side. Five equally hostile expressions pinned him there, with his formerly cooed-over masculine assets figuratively flapping in the breeze.

"What's the matter, ladies?" With a sideways glance at his befuddled family, Riley spread out his arms. He took another stab at that happy-go-lucky smile. "Just because I already know Jayne doesn't mean the six of us can't still be friends."

The minute it left his mouth, he knew it was the wrong thing to say.

Three

She needed a fix. And she needed it fast.

Hands trembling, Jayne rummaged through her carry-on bag, the one that held all her most important possessions. Around her awaited the down-home charm of the Hideaway Lodge's private bathroom. Its plain fixtures, log cabin walls, and single lace-curtained, multipaned window said *rustic* as sure as the rooms she'd traversed to get there had.

A tube of mango body scrub tumbled to the rag rug atop the polished plank floorboards. Jayne glanced down. The economy-size tube barely missed smashing her stiletto-wearing foot. She was reminded that her cute shoes probably didn't speak Rustic either.

Heeeelp!

At her side, Gwen Davis looked on with a puzzled expression. A jar of honey smoothie lotion followed the body scrub to the floor. Various mesh scrubbers of all sizes were pushed aside. Finally, Jayne located the elixir she sought: a container of Bathing Beauty Bubbles.

Just looking at it, she felt a little better. *Calm was at hand.* Evidently, her relief showed, because her hostess turned away to finish the job she'd followed Jayne into the bathroom to accomplish.

"Towels are right here." She patted a thick stack of burgundy terry cloth. "There's extra soap beneath the sink. Plenty of hot water to fill that old tub too."

Gwen gestured toward the old-fashioned claw-footed white porcelain bathtub. At the sight of its comforting, curvy lines and pampering depth, Jayne nearly burst into tears.

It had been a very trying day.

"Just help yourself. Nobody will bother you," Gwen added, moving closer. She gave Jayne a tentative pat. As she had since she'd helped Jayne sneak away during the Riley-inspired mêlée, she gazed at her guest with concern. "Are you sure you don't want to talk about it? My grandson can be a stinker, but he's usually not—"

"Thanks, no. I really can't."

A pause. "All right, then. Whenever you're ready, I'm here."

Jayne sniffed, clutching her Bathing Beauty Bubbles. She nodded. This was awfully nice of Gwen. Offering to listen to her troubles *and* volunteering the use of the lodge's only full-fledged bathtub (the rest of the accommodations had showers) went far beyond the call of duty. She probably thought Jayne was some sort of compulsive bather, unable to hold out longer than a couple of hours without a dose of steamy suds and the honesty of 99 and 44/100 percent pure Ivory soap.

Actually, that wasn't far from the truth. Especially today.

Especially after seeing Riley.

"Thank you, Gwen. This really means a lot to me. You don't know how much. After what just happened, I—"

"There, there." Another gentle pat. A smile. "We can talk about it when you're feeling better."

Gwen went to the tub and dropped the rubber stopper in place to block the drain. Efficiently, she worked the taps. They complained with a creak, then issued forth a steady

stream of water. With a few uncertain steps, Jayne joined
her at the side of the bathtub. She sprinkled in some Bathing
Beauty Bubbles, which lathered themselves into a wonderful
froth within seconds.

Her hostess raised an eyebrow. "Impressive. I haven't
seen that much foam since the last time I tackled shaving
my legs."

"It's my favorite brand," Jayne confided. They shared a
smile. "Smells like sugar cookies, moisturizes your skin, and
makes you feel like a princess. The bubbles are practically
indestructible. Here, you can try some if you want."

She offered the container.

Gwen looked as though she'd been offered a one-way
ticket to Sin City. She shook her head. "Oh, I couldn't."

Jayne could tell she wanted to. "Sure, you can. My treat."
She nudged the Bathing Beauty Bubbles into Gwen's hand
and closed her fingers around the container. "Enjoy."

"All right. I'll try." The words sounded doubtful. But
her expression was hopeful, even a little eager. "Thank
you."

She left, having accepted a bonus packet of lavender bath
salts and a trial-size mud masque too. Five minutes later,
Jayne had taken full advantage of the resulting privacy.
She'd piled her hair in a loose knot atop her head, stripped
to her birthday suit, and lost herself in the soothing warmth
of her bath, ready to forget all about the surprise she'd just
received.

Naturally, that was when *it* happened.

Footsteps pounded down the hallway outside the bathroom. Since this part of the lodge housed the Davis family's
private living quarters, Jayne wasn't concerned—only hopeful that she hadn't inconvenienced someone with an (ahem)
urgent need. But there were plenty of additional bathrooms,

including one just off the lodge's wide-beamed, antler-decorated reception area. Surely anyone who needed—

The doorknob rattled. The door pushed open. Slapped against the opposite wall. A large body filled the opening, one both broad-shouldered and familiar. An instant later, her unexpected visitor entered the room fully and slammed the door behind him. Before she could so much as gasp in surprise, he flattened himself against it, looking vaguely panicky.

And completely gorgeous.

Riley.

How had she forgotten the impact his presence had? Tall, dark, and thoroughly at ease with the world around him (maybe a little less so today), Riley Davis had a low-key confidence that seemed contagious. It invited laughs and good times. It offered strength and masculine competence. It suggested something adventurous was right around the corner.

In this case, adventure probably *was* right around the corner. It looked as though he were being pursued.

Feminine voices sounded in the hallway outside the door. Hearing them, Riley grew alert. He canted his head to the side, listening.

His absorption gave Jayne plenty of time to recover from the shock of his unexpected intrusion—and to assess the changes in him. His hair, dark and buzz cut when she'd known him, had grown into shaggy, appealingly tousled layers. His face, all rugged angles and assertive nose, sported a new, faint scar near his squared jaw. His body, always well muscled, showed the effects of further hard use—probably in service of the adventures he'd had since they'd split. She wondered if he'd enjoyed those adventures alone . . . or if he'd had company.

Feminine company.

Not that it mattered to her, Jayne assured herself. *She was over him.* So *over him* that she could admire the width and sculpted definition of his chest dispassionately, like a student of the art of wearing a T-shirt and well-fitted jeans. So *over him* that she could trail her gaze down those jeans, sideways to the chiseled forearms Riley had flattened against the door frame, and simply savor the sight of a nicely developed man. So *over him,* in fact, that she could even take in the shoulders she used to lean her head against, the mouth that had once kissed her senseless . . . and feel nothing at all.

Okay, so she was a big fat liar. She *did* feel something. But Jayne told herself it was merely hunger for emotional closure she felt (and possibly a craving for a cheeseburger) and nothing more. Probably, once she talked things over with Riley (and had lunch), it would go away. And that would be that.

The sooner, she decided, the better. She double-checked her bubble cover, listened as the voices outside moved farther away. As they did, Riley sagged with relief.

Jayne made her move. ''We've got to stop meeting like this.''

''Aaah!''

He jerked, searching for the source of her voice. His hazel-eyed gaze found her, pinned her, *examined* her. For one frantic moment, Jayne feared her Bathing Beauty Bubbles had failed her for the first time ever and dissolved beneath the strength of his interest. Then she remembered she had the upper hand here—at least so long as he was trapped on her side of that door, hiding out. She surprised herself by feeling almost cheerful about that fact.

Riley Davis deserved everything he had coming to him for walking out on her. And more.

He'd left no real explanation, no forwarding address. And, to be fair, no promises. Only memories, and hope. Hope that he'd come back. Jayne had clung to that hope, waiting and wondering . . . until she'd finally come to her senses and gotten over him.

So over him, she reminded herself.

"What are you doing in here?" he demanded.

His voice was a raspy whisper, lest, Jayne guessed, he be heard by the women elsewhere in the lodge.

"What am *I* doing in here?" Heart pounding, she nonetheless managed to raise one bare leg from the bubbles and examine it leisurely. "I should think it would be fairly obvious. I'm bathing."

His gaze swerved away from her show of leg. "This is the family's private bathroom."

His family's, she knew now. Who'd have guessed, among all the Davises in all the world, that *his* would be her hosts for this trip? Francesca hadn't filled her in on *that* detail, among so many others.

Rugged wilderness *and* Riley. Just peachy. She didn't know how she was going to come out of all this with the research—and the breakup workbook notes—she needed.

But for now . . .

"It's the only one with a tub." Jayne shrugged. "Gwen could tell I was upset over"—*over having maybe-kinda-sorta ambushed you amid the breakup-ees*—"things, and offered to let me use it."

"So *this* is where you snuck off to." He advanced, eyes narrowed. "You set me up and then you bailed. Not very sporting of you, Jayne."

She thought it was *very* sporting, given that he'd at least had someplace to escape to afterward. She'd had nowhere to escape her broken heart when he'd left. At least, not at first. Not until she'd tested on herself the antiheartbreak strategies she'd been offering friends for years. Not until *Heartbreak 101* was born.

But honestly, "I didn't mean for any of that to happen. All I did was say your name."

"It was the *way* you said it."

"Oh?" She arched a brow, hoping he couldn't tell she wanted to shuck her hard-won dignity, drag him into the tub with her, and (under threat of serious pruney fingers and toes) extract an explanation. *Why did you leave me? Leave us?*

But that wouldn't have worked anyway. Wrinkly skin didn't scare him. Riley didn't even care what he looked like. Which probably made him twice as appealing, now that she considered it.

Jayne forced her thoughts back to the matter at hand. "Oh?" she asked again for good measure. "And what 'way' was that?"

"The 'way' that makes five pissed-off women yell at me. I barely escaped with my manhood intact."

She couldn't help it. Her gaze wandered south.

Ah, memories. Good times.

She was such an idiot.

He was waiting for her when she sent her attention upward again. He seemed affronted. "What the hell did you tell them anyway?"

"Not much." Her bubbles began to lose their loft. Casually, Jayne shored up the ta-ta territory, lest she give Riley a glimpse of what he hadn't missed. "Just that we dated for a while, a couple of years ago." *And you vanished inexplicably, just when things were getting good.* "And that it was over with now."

She shrugged, trying for nonchalance. His gaze followed her shoulders' movement . . . then slid lower, to the bubble zone. In the wake of his interest, tingles raced along her skin. Apparently, her body was having trouble remembering all she wanted here was closure. C-l-o-s-u . . . oh, heck. Did there have to be a "you" in that word?

The only "you" for her had been Riley. Once upon a time.

"All of a sudden, it doesn't *feel* over with," he said quietly.

Dangerously quietly.

"I don't know what you're talking about." More bubbles

disintegrated. Jayne reached into her cache for a pink effervescent strawberry bath bomb and dropped it into the tub. She pretended to be fascinated by the gigantic Alka-Seltzer effect it created in her bathwater.

"You don't?"

He'd come closer. Uh-oh. "Nope."

Was that a quaver in her voice? If it was, Jayne didn't have time to consider it. Because a second later, Riley called her bluff. With an ease born of well-trained muscles, he lowered to a squat that put them eye to eye. He stretched his arms along the edge of the tub, offering a contrast between his dark skin and the pristine porcelain. He nailed her with a knowing look.

"You're naked," he said, "about fourteen inches from me. Naked and wet. And bubbly." An inexplicable smile touched his lips briefly. "Really bubbly."

His expression suggested he knew exactly how fragile her bubble barrier was. But he didn't understand how fragile the rest of her was . . . and Jayne swore at that moment he never would.

"Somehow," he went on, sweeping her with a heated gaze, "this doesn't feel quite 'over with' to me. Not yet."

Jayne gulped. *Uh-oh* was right.

Experimentally, Riley trailed his fingertips in the bathwater. It swirled warmly around his skin, like the kiss of a lover.

Jayne wasn't what he'd expected to find when he'd come in there. He'd been hoping for solitude. For sanctuary from the five-woman firing squad. But, hey—he wasn't a guy to look a gift bathing beauty in the mouth. Or something like that. Seeing Jayne like this, all flushed and damp and teasing, made fools of his good intentions. Every last one.

And her smile turned him inside out.

Ahhh. Nostalgia.

"Look," she said shortly after delivering that smile, "I didn't plan this little soak for your benefit, big shot. So go take your come-ons to someone who cares."

She lobbed the pink fizzy thing at him. He ducked. It smashed against the wall and crumbled into a wet, lumpy pile.

"Awww. I think you *do* care. At least enough to practice good aim. Nice work, dead-eye. If I hadn't ducked, you'd have plastered me right in the forehead."

"Then hold still." Hefting a bar of soap, Jayne measured him. She squinted, tongue between her teeth like a marksman. *"Perfect."*

"I love it when you tell me what you want."

The soap flew. Grinning, Riley ducked again.

"Try the shampoo bottle." He angled his chin toward it.

Obligingly, Jayne sent it toward his head.

He didn't know what she was so mad about, he thought as he ducked again. After all, they were both adults. Their relationship was in the past. And *he* wasn't the dumb-ass who'd sent her packing for a heartbreak-recovery class, now, was he? Obviously, during their time apart she'd experienced worse than he'd ever dished out.

Not that Riley thought he'd treated her badly. On the contrary. He and Jayne had had an amazing time together. So amazing it had nearly tempted him to try becoming someone he wasn't.

Someone *settled.*

To him, this weird twist of fate—the two of them winding up here together—was simply the universe giving them a second chance. What they did with that second chance was up to them.

Riley voted for enjoying it. Why not?

He nodded toward the herbal conditioner. "More ammo?"

She seized the economy-size bottle. Gave it an appraising toss upward. Prepared to let it fly.

"You probably haven't noticed," he observed, "that your bubbles don't cling to a vertical surface very well."

She blinked. Frowned. "Huh?"

"Well, there *is* a reason I'm encouraging you to throw things at me."

Her arm lowered a fraction. "*What* are you talking about?"

"You." Riley gave her an admiring look, knowing the view wouldn't be his to enjoy for much longer. "And your amazing disappearing bubbles."

Jayne glanced down. Her eagerness to poleax him had raised her onto her knees in the tub, and her exertions had dislodged her foamy covering to an . . . interesting degree. She probably didn't appreciate the sight of her partially nude body, visible from the waist up in nothing but glistening wetness and a few rapidly departing bath bubbles, quite as much as he did.

"*Ooooh!*"

She hurled the bottle. To Riley's surprise, it struck its mark. He'd been so distracted by the sight of her, he'd forgotten to duck. The last thing he remembered before everything went black was Jayne's surprised face as he sank onto the rag rug beneath him. It figured . . . he ought to have known to leave the past buried, where it belonged.

No point trampling over the past. It's over with.

Hell, yes. That would be his motto from here on out.

Zzzzz.

Cold water splashed over his face. Sputtering, Riley jerked upright to the sight of Jayne standing there, wrapped in a towel, holding an empty drinking glass.

"Thank God!" she cried. "You're alive."

"No thanks to you." He caught hold of her wrist and pulled her to the rug alongside him. "Don't you know you could drown someone pulling a stunt like that? I was unconscious!''

"Only for a second. Actually, you were probably stunned, is all.''

Stunned *now,* he could only stare at her.

"I thought I'd miss you!'' Jayne went on, tucking in her towel. "I thought you'd duck again. Besides, you've always seemed pretty impervious to ordinary injuries.''

Her arch look implied she referred to more than a conk on the head. Much more. He didn't know what, and he wasn't in the mood to play guessing games. No matter how cute she looked in a two-foot-wide towel and a tousle of damp-tendrilled blonde hair.

But that didn't mean he was going to reveal any weaknesses—say, a susceptibility to head injuries via jojoba conditioner bottles—to her either. Riley sat up all the way, bracing himself on his splayed palms.

"You're right. It'd take more than thirty-two ounces of green goop to lay me low.''

"It'd take a miracle, looks like.''

Her disgruntled frown confused him. "Did I *do* something to you? Or does leaving the city always make you this peevish?''

She glared. *Leaving the city,* he decided. He'd seen it before. Die-hard urbanites and the great outdoors didn't mix very well. More than likely, Jayne had just realized out here there wouldn't be any escalators, fifty-percent-off sales, or a Starbucks around every tree trunk.

"I just didn't expect to see you here,'' she said quietly. "That's all. I didn't expect *any* of this.''

Riley dragged his gaze from the water droplets meandering across her shoulder. "I'm as surprised as you are. I only came back for a few weeks to help out my grandparents. Usually I'd be—''

"On a mountainside? Taking pictures on safari?''

"Something like that." Upon realizing how well she remembered him, he couldn't help but smile.

She did too. But her smile held a certain inscrutability. He found himself wanting to uncover her secrets, to unravel the mystery of whatever relationship had brought her here . . . to unwrap that towel. But since Jayne would probably hurl the contents of the medicine cabinet at him if he tried, he settled for conversation—and a question.

"How about you?" he asked. "You're here as part of the heartbreak recovery stuff, huh?"

Jayne nodded. Warily.

"Well, I hope it, uh, helps. I mean, I don't buy into the whole how-to-guru thing, but whatever works, right?"

An awkward silence fell. Riley had the uncomfortable sensation he hadn't chosen their topic of conversation wisely. But he couldn't very well pretend he didn't know what she was here for, could he? Whatever his other faults might be, he considered himself an up-front guy. He offered his opinions straight up and expected others to do the same.

Jayne didn't disappoint. "I hear the workshop leader is *extremely* talented," she disagreed. "Wildly popular. I guess you're not familiar with her best-selling book?"

Her raised eyebrows dared him to bluff. He couldn't.

"No. I tend to stick to the *non*-mumbo-jumbo section of the bookstore."

"Hmmph."

"But, hey"—he spread his arms—"if it helps people, I'm all for it. Obviously, there are six women here who believe in those antiheartbreak techniques." Riley tilted his head thoughtfully at her. "I just didn't think you'd be among them."

Her temper flared. "Why? Because you didn't think my heart could be broken?"

"No, because I didn't think you'd ever let yourself be more than twenty miles away from your hair colorist."

Jayne gawped at him. "These are only *highlights!*"

He'd forgotten she was touchy about her "natural blondeness."

"Look," Riley said with a conciliatory gesture. "You obviously don't want to be here. And I'm not crazy about taking out your group tomorrow—"

"*You're* our guide?"

He nodded. She muttered and turned her face heavenward, shaking her head.

"But we both have to do what we came here to do. So we might as well make the best of it. Right?"

He waited for her answer. A moment passed. Another. It occurred to him that Jayne might be considering leaving the retreat rather than deal with his antipsychobabble jibes. Had he unknowingly hurt her feelings?

Riley hunkered lower, angling his head to look into her face. "No more self-help potshots. Okay? Truce?"

Her gaze lifted. He could have lost himself in her eyes, in her nearness, in her . . . *hey. Knock it off, you mushball.*

Jayne sighed. "Truce," she agreed.

He wanted to whoop. Or at least give her a we-have-a-truce kiss to seal the deal. But before he could, she got to her feet, still clutching her wrapped towel.

"But we have some things to talk about, Riley," Jayne warned. "Some . . . issues that still aren't settled between us. Getting some closure would do us both good."

Geez, she'd already caved in to self-help speak. He stood too. "So let's talk."

"Later. I'm not talking to you dressed"—she gestured toward her towel-wrapped torso, bare feet, still-damp skin, and mostly upswept hair—"like this."

"So lose the towel." Riley waggled his eyebrows.

"That's not what I mean."

"Then I'll even the odds." He reached for the fly of his jeans. "Hand me that spare towel over there?"

"Be serious."

Feeling lighter than he had in months, he put his hands on his hips and grinned. "I am serious."

"You're never serious. Except about taking a picture. Or hitting the trail. That's part of the problem."

"What problem?"

"Nothing." Turning away, Jayne opened the bathroom door. She peeked outside, then angled her head toward the doorway. "All clear. Let's talk later. After things settle down a bit."

Riley recognized an invitation to get the hell out as well as the next guy. He headed for the door.

"How about five minutes from now?" he asked. "On the deck at the back of the lodge? We'll talk, we'll—"

"Can't. Five minutes from now I'll be talking to Gwen and Bud, asking for a reassigned trail guide."

"Ouch. You really know how to hurt a guy."

Jayne's expression sobered. "No. I don't. Maybe if I did, I wouldn't be in this predicament."

Something in her face struck him. Silenced him. He wished he could erase whatever hurts she'd suffered, however they'd come about. Intending to console her, Riley reached for her hand.

At the same moment, she shoved him into the hall.

"Hey!"

She shut the door behind him. He heard his grandmother's oak dressing table being pushed beneath the knob with a decisive jab meant to secure it against intruders.

Against him.

Riley stared at the door. He raised his fingertips to its surface. He imagined the woman on the other side of that polished wood—who was, at that moment, probably boring a hole through the pine with the force of her defensive, seminude gaze. *Let's talk later.*

Clearly, Jayne's idea of a truce and his idea of a truce were a *little* far apart. Given time, though, Riley figured he could bring them closer together.

Much closer together.

And maybe he could help restore Jayne's faith in guys like him while he was at it.

Sure, he decided as he turned away and headed down the hallway, a new eagerness to his stride. It was the least he could do, given what they'd once meant to each other. He'd show Jayne that not all men were no-good dirtbags like the one who'd sent her to Heartbreak Camp . . . and in the process cure himself once and for all of his lingering longing for blue-eyed blonde bombshells from the City by the Bay.

And his new motto? *No point trampling over the past. It's over with?* Hell, this didn't even qualify. This was just a favor for an ex. An ex Riley was going to be paired up with for the next week or so whether he liked it or not. He was only making the best of things, the way he'd suggested they both do.

So long as he could help Jayne without bringing his own vagabond ways under fire, Riley was perfectly happy to do so. Mottoes didn't come into play. Neither did an interest in rekindling things between them.

Not a damned bit.

He passed by the lodge's office. His grandfather glanced up. "You've got that foot tappin' again, son. Who you tellin' a stretcher to now?"

Hell, Riley thought. *Himself, if he didn't watch it.*

He stilled his foot and kept going all the same. He could handle it. And Jayne? Her too. Just wait and see. . . .

Four

In her room at the lodge, Alexis Davis flopped onto her bed, overwhelmed with the *unfairness* of being on the verge of womanhood, pinched by her stupid braces, and stuck in the middle of *nowhere,* all at the same time. The ruffled pink bedspread her nana always hauled out for her visits fluffed around her, obscuring the *Cosmo* she'd been reading.

If only Nana and Gramps owned one of those posh resorts in Sedona instead of this dump. Then there'd be a swimming pool. T'ai chi classes. Ayurvedic facials, like she'd read about in her mom's *Allure*. Shopping nearby—even if it *did* consist mostly of art galleries instead of the Gap. There'd be things to distract her.

Things to keep her from thinking about . . . Brendan.

Alexis still couldn't believe he'd treated her the way he had. Breaking up with her—with a note!—in front of all their friends at the Cinnabon section of the mall food court was *so* fifth-grade. *So* juvenile. So mean.

So hurtful.

Closing her eyes tight so she wouldn't cry, Alexis rolled over and grabbed the *Cosmo.* She wanted to read more of that "Fifty Ways to Look Hot" article. She wanted to return to school after spring break looking so amazing, Brendan would beg her to take him back. She wanted to make him *so* sorry.

She wished she weren't alone. She wished her friends were here. Her great-grandmother had guessed something was wrong when Alexis had arrived over the weekend, and she'd tried to help, but she didn't really understand. She'd been married to Gramps for *decades*. Nana didn't know what it was like to have a broken heart, and Alexis did.

No matter how much she wished she didn't.

Heaving herself upward, Alexis hit the play button on her CD player. The latest dance hit from J.Lo thumped its way through her room. If she closed her eyes, she could almost pretend she was back home with her mom and her stuff and her cell phone nearby.

But her cell phone didn't work reliably out here in the boonies. The canyons messed up the signal. Her stuff didn't matter as much as being without her friends did. And her mom was busy in Rocky Point, Mexico, vacationing with her latest male "friend." So that left Alexis alone, with a whole *week* of aloneness stretching ahead of her.

A movement outside her window caught her attention. Pulling aside the curtain, she peered out. The antiheartbreak-book author strode past, wearing a dress-and-heels outfit straight out of *Elle* . . . but with an attitude straight out of *Woman Power*. She kept her head high, her back straight, and her eyes on her destination—the edge of the lodge's back deck, where Gramps stood, smoking a cigar. While Alexis watched, the author—Jayne, she remembered— approached Gramps. They turned to each other, smiling and exchanging a greeting Alexis couldn't quite hear, even though her room overlooked the deck.

She let the curtain fall back and flopped onto her bed again, still feeling misunderstood. Jayne probably knew *all* about broken hearts, she reflected. She probably knew all about getting over them too.

According to Nana, *Heartbreak 101: Getting Over the Good-Bye Guys* was a pretty good book. Not that anyone had let Alexis read it for herself. Her family still treated her like a kid—look at the *Cosmo* incident. But Jayne . . . Jayne was a different story. She'd talked to Alexis in a woman-to-woman way when they'd met earlier. She'd been nice and pretty and *so* not trying to "get down" with teenager "slang." Alexis appreciated that.

She'd have bet anything Jayne had interesting things planned for those women Uncle Riley would be trail-guiding. Things to help them get over their broken hearts. Things that . . . might help Alexis too.

Hey! Filled with new energy, she sat bolt upright on her bed. The answer to her troubles was plain: She had to go on that heartbreak-cure trip. No matter what.

Jayne watched as Bud Davis tapped his cigar into the ashtray balanced atop the deck's tumbled-stone wall. He gave another thoughtful drag, then looked at her.

"I'm sorry you're havin' a problem with Riley," he said. "I've had my share of tussles with him myself, but I know he means well. If he's offended you—"

"No, it's not that." *He's seen me naked, sir. Again. And I'm mortally embarrassed that he goaded me into a show-all bath accessories battle too.* "Riley and I . . . I just think it would be better if another guide were assigned to my group."

Bud squinted toward the desert landscape. "How many people are in your group?"

"Six, including me."

"How many days will you be stayin'?"

"Six. Our flights leave next Monday morning."

"And how long did you and my grandson date?"

"Six months, give or take a—hey!"

The older man smiled. Too late, Jayne glimpsed the wili-

ness in his eyes. Until just this minute, Bud had seemed
merely a good-natured older gentleman, white-haired and
countrified in his flannel shirt. Now, all of a sudden, the rest
of the story was revealed. This was a man, she realized,
who loved a good adventure—whether it was a trek through
the wilderness or a fact-finding mission to uncover his unsus-
pecting guest's secrets.

No wonder Riley had grown into the wanderer he was.
If his grandfather were any indication, seeking out uncharted
territory was in his blood.

"I thought so," Bud said, nodding. "And how long since
you two split?"

She couldn't resist the gruff understanding in his face.
"Not quite two years. I guess Riley didn't . . . tell you and
Gwen about me?"

At the shake of Bud's head, Jayne's spirits sank. A part
of her had hoped Riley had been compelled to talk about
her, had been unable to resist confiding news of the woman
he'd met in San Francisco and the whirlwind romance they'd
shared.

"I'm sorry," Bud went on. His lined hand covered hers,
squeezed, moved away. He gazed at a distant red rock formation. "I shouldn't have pried. But the truth of the matter is,
Gwen and I are pretty close to Riley. It was obvious something about you got to him, even before the rest of your
ladies ambushed him."

At the memory of the way her breakup-ees had leapt to
her post-breakup defense, Jayne blushed. She'd have to tell
them to lay off Riley. He was her problem, and she'd handle
him her way.

By avoiding him.

Which brought her back to . . .

"I didn't mean for that to happen," she said. "Riley and
I have already talked about it." *While I was naked.* "We've
come to an understanding, believe me." *After he returned
to consciousness.* "So about that reassigned guide—"

"Can't," Bud said succinctly. "There's nobody else to go."

He seemed aggrieved by that fact. Yet strangely stoic, as though resigned to it. Jayne didn't understand his reaction.

"But surely in an outfit this size—"

He shook his head.

"My publicist led me to believe—"

"Riley's your man."

Jayne sighed. A silly, schmaltzy, impossible-to-silence part of her still wished that were true. *Riley's your man.*

At the sympathetic look Bud threw her, she forced a smile. There was no point letting this very nice man know how undone she was by this news. By being stuck, here, with Riley.

So the Hideaway Lodge wasn't the New Age spa retreat Francesca had led her to expect. So her ex-lover was about to guide her deep into the middle of nowhere. Did that mean, Jayne asked herself as Bud went back to smoking his cigar, that she had to panic?

Yes! Yes, it did.

She'd already begun doubting the wisdom of taking five distraught breakup-ees into the Arizona wilderness, far from *69, cookie-dough ice cream, and DVDs of *An Affair to Remember*. This new development—the "ex" development—cast her plan even further into question. Her antiheartbreak-workshop attendees, chosen to participate as they had been by a Snap Books publicity contest, had every right to expect a quality experience. Mitzi, Carla, Doris, Donna, and Kelly would be looking to Jayne for guidance . . . guidance she feared she couldn't give when paired up with the one man she hadn't *quite* gotten over.

The one man who, as it happened, had *inspired* her *Heartbreak 101* book and its strategies: Riley.

"Don't worry," Bud said, breaking the (panic-filled) silence. "I've never known Riley to go back on his word.

If you say you have an understanding with him, then I'm sure that's all you need."

Sure. That, and a big padlock for my heart—so Riley won't be able to slip past my defenses again. No problem.

Bud offered a reassuring pat to her shoulder, as though Jayne were a delicate woman easily bruised by life's ups and downs. She guessed he'd already seen past her tough, take-charge cover. The realization didn't engender confidence. Because while Jayne *was* perfectly capable and usually quite self-assured, the big chink in her armor was her susceptibility to Riley Davis.

When it came to him, she was on shaky ground—and her favorite pair of leopard-print marabou-trimmed mules had nothing whatsoever to do with it. Jayne had her vulnerabilities. Evidently, love-'em-and-leave-'em types like Riley were tops on the list.

Or at least *he* was.

Gathering her courage, Jayne squared her shoulders and faced her host. She'd tried to secure a trail-guide reassignment. She'd failed. The only thing to do now was move forward.

"Thanks for all your help, Bud." Impulsively, she hugged him, feeling his flannel shirt soft beneath her cheek. "I'm sure you're right about Riley. Things will be fine."

He chuckled. "Atta girl."

A bell chimed, scattering the birds who'd been pecking at the ground near the deck. It chimed again, louder.

Bud released her. "Lunch bell. We'd better get a move on. Gwen's grub doesn't last long around here."

Hungrily, Jayne followed him from the deck into the lodge again. Maybe things really *would* be fine, she told herself. She and Riley were both adults. Surely they could behave responsibly for the duration of one measly weeklong trip . . . couldn't they?

After all, her new book contract, her belief in her "gift," and her faith in herself were all at stake. If Jayne couldn't resist Riley long enough to conduct a successful series of workshops for her breakup-ees, then she certainly didn't deserve to consider herself *over him.* And she probably didn't deserve the tongue-in-cheek label of "self-help guru" bestowed so often on her either.

Not that Riley knew about her expertise, she remembered. He thought she was merely a workshop participant, not the workshop's leader. A spark of curiosity flamed to life inside her as she caught sight of him at the far end of the lodge's communal dining room. What—exactly—would he say when he learned her secret?

Shortly after lunch—a chatty exercise in diet-regimen comparisons Riley never hoped to repeat—he gathered the women in the lodge's common area, a twenty-by-thirty room furnished with Craftsman-style chairs, two sofas, assorted side tables with lamps, and a yawning fieldstone fireplace. Beside him was Alexis. Beside her, stacked on the table to the left of the fireplace, were the supplies the Hideaway Lodge provided its adventure travel guests.

"This is your gear." He gestured toward the backpacks, two-person tents, and other items, having already dispensed with a welcome and his usual pep talk about the beauty of the surrounding countryside—a pep talk Riley believed in. "These are loaner items, yours for the duration of your trip. Some of these supplies may be unfamiliar to you, so stop me if you need an explanation as I hand things out. I don't want to go too fast."

"Smart fella," Doris piped up from the second row. "A woman *likes* a man who takes it slow."

"Nonsense," Donna rebutted, shaking her steel-colored curls at her sister. "There's room for a quickie now and then too."

"Yeah!" the other women chimed in. Within seconds, the atmosphere devolved into a debate over "slow and steady" versus "hard and ready." Riley could hardly believe his ears. *This* was the fairer sex?

"Hey!" He slapped his hands over Alexis's innocent ears, lest she hear something she wasn't prepared for. His niece had volunteered to help him outfit the group—not receive an X-rated play-by-play of the various ways to get funky. "Can we get back to business, please?"

One by one, the women quieted. Carla, the last one talking, closed her mouth with an abashed look. "Sorry," she mumbled.

"Okay." He uncovered Alexis's ears. "As I was saying—"

In the front row, Jayne crossed her legs. Her baby-blue dress parted beneath its row of buttons, revealing a curvy length of bare leg. Riley lost his train of thought completely. In fact, he was pretty sure his train of thought careened into an entirely different station.

Woo, woo! Woo, woo! All aboard! Next stop: *see what you've been missing!*

He tried again. "Uh, about these supplies—"

Now she was swinging her top foot back and forth in a slow arc that called his attention to those sexy shoes of hers. Shoes that were made not so much for walking as for being seen in, as far as Riley was concerned. But when he swept his gaze upward, her face gave away nothing. Only the merest hint of an arched brow suggested Jayne realized her actions had had any effect on him.

Fine. Two could play at that game.

He cleared his throat and addressed the expectant group. "These supplies have all been field-tested and will see you through every adventure in the coming week."

Absently, Jayne ran her fingers up and down her pendant's chain, drawing his eye to the subtle cleavage it adorned. Riley watched her fingertips graze the bare skin at her throat, move lower, lower. . . .

He blinked. Desperately, he summoned up the next part

of his beginner's orientation. "There are ten essentials you'll need on the trail. First, a map."

At his side, Alexis selected a 7-1/2-minute USGS northern Arizona map and held it in front of her, gesturing toward it like a smiling game-show hostess.

"This is a topographical map," Riley explained. "Topos are the wilderness traveler's most important navigational tool. They show roads, rivers, trails, and, most important, the lay of the land. These contour lines"—Alexis unfolded the map and pointed to the series of squiggly circles and wavy lines on its face—"show cliffs, passes, mountains, ravines, canyons—you name it. If we're going to cross it, descend it, or climb into it—as in the case of Catsclaw Canyon, our primary site—it will be on this map."

Mitzi raised her hand. "It looks like my mom's wallpaper."

"I once made a tie-dyed T-shirt that had exactly that same pattern," Donna volunteered.

"Oh, it did not," Doris said. "Your T-shirt wasn't nearly so attractive as that map."

"The green is pretty," Kelly said shyly.

Riley nodded, seizing on the first comment he felt qualified to address. "Dark green indicates tree cover. Forested areas. Light green shows scrub brush cover. As we climb into the canyon, we'll see plenty of both, along with some high-desert plants like cholla and yucca."

"There's yucca in my conditioner," Carla said. "It really makes my hair feel soft."

Instantly, an animated conversation ensued about shampoo, split ends, and hair spray. Completely befuddled, Riley stared.

This was going to be a *far* different group than he usually led.

Jayne kicked off one shoe. Sensuously, she ran her bare toes along her shin. Riley looked at her abandoned pink stiletto and couldn't help but imagine her kicking off its

mate. Unbuttoning her dress. Giving him a smile while she—
stop it.

He put his thumb and middle finger in his mouth and whistled. The women quieted in surprise.

Smiling, Riley moved on. Unique as this group was, he had the patience to deal with them. *Im*patient adventure travel guides tended to wind up dead, unemployed, or both. Even though his primary career was photography, and he loved it, he loved the outdoors just the teensiest bit more. Taking pictures only subsidized his travels—kept him in trail mix and Gore-Tex.

"Next is your compass," he said as Alexis held up a basic model. "Combined with your topos it will keep you on the trail, enable you to identify landmarks, or follow a bearing. With this, you won't get lost."

"I got lost in Nordstrom once," Carla said. "They moved the cosmetics department to another floor, and it, like, totally discombobulated me."

Heads nodded all around. "The Estée Lauder counter is my touchstone," Jayne said. "I start from there and just fan out."

"Doris has no mall sense at all," Donna said, angling her head toward her sister. "She's been known to ride the escalators up and down, just hoping to catch a glimpse of whatever store she's after."

"That's not true," Doris argued. "I was checking out the mall security guard. He was cute!"

Donna shook her head, clearly unconvinced.

Riley made a mental note to consider tying the group together on the first day, chain-gang style, so they wouldn't get lost.

"I accidentally followed a UPS guy into the men's room at my office building once," Kelly said, glancing down with pinked cheeks. "He looked so good in his uniform, I forgot where I was."

They all sighed in commiseration. Even Jayne nodded.

Rolling his eyes, Riley waited for their attention to return to him. He would never in a million years understand women's fascination with UPS men. Delivery guys in ugly brown shorts and matching shirts. What was the big deal anyway?

"I don't go to the mall at all," Mitzi said. She popped her gum. "All those different entrances and color-coded parking lots confuse me, so I go to Target instead."

Okay. He was *definitely* bringing a long length of rope for the first day. This group was directionally challenged.

"Next up," he said. "Water."

Expertly, Alexis held up a liter bottle and pantomimed taking a drink. Grinning with the kind of enthusiasm only a thirteen-year-old girl could muster, she rubbed her skinny belly. Riley winked at her. "Nice job," he mouthed.

He turned toward the group of women. "You need to stay hydrated. Water is—"

"Excuse me." Jayne raised her hand. "I'm sorry. Is Evian okay? I brought some with me."

He smiled. Next she'd be asking if she could pack in an espresso machine. "It's fine. But since a gallon of water weighs about eight pounds, there's a limit to how much we can realistically haul in. So while we're on the trail, we'll use a combination of bottled water, filtered water, boiled water, and chemically treated water. I'll go into the details tomorrow."

She nodded and went back to fiddling with her necklace. *Up, down* went her hand on its gold chain. Gently, her fingers curled around the heavy pendant between her breasts. Rubbed. Riley briefly closed his eyes and made himself think about something besides how much he'd like to follow that same path.

He *definitely* had to get to the "two could play at that game" portion of this presentation.

"To go along with the water," he said, watching as Alexis held up two foil packets, Vanna-White style, "you'll need food. Hiking and camping require plenty of energy."

Alexis, who'd been listening to this spiel since the age of eight, piped up. "In wilderness-speak, 'energy' means 'calories.' He means you'll need *plenty* of calories."

All the women brightened. He had their full attention.

"Everyone will be responsible for carrying their own food, which the Hideaway Lodge will supply."

Carla raised her hand. "Is it Zone perfect? I've been eating in the Zone for two weeks now."

"Really?" Jayne asked, looking intrigued as she turned to Carla. "How much have you lost?"

"Four pounds."

"Wow! Good for you!"

They all applauded. Riley cocked his head in confusion.

"What about Weight Watchers points?" Mitzi asked. "How many in that packet?"

Alexis turned it over quizzically, peering at the nutrition information.

"We're on the Atkins diet," Donna put in. "Doris and I don't eat high-carb foods."

"Speak for yourself, Donna. This is the wilderness. We've got to eat to live."

Kelly raised her hand. "Will there be s'mores? I went to Camp Catawba when I was ten, and we had s'mores."

They all looked at him expectantly. Riley, suffering from a flashback of the lunchtime diet regime comparisons, took a minute to realize it.

"I don't know about that stuff. We'll be eating"—he squinted at the packages—"old-fashioned beef Stroganoff with mushroom sauce, and down-home vegetarian entrée with beans. Period. End of story. Now, as far as the rest of your supplies go . . ."

"Awwww."

Refusing to be suckered by their disappointed faces into revealing the Snickers bars he always added to each pack for trailside pick-me-ups, he went on to discuss the other essentials. Firestarter. Matches. An Army knife. A first-aid kit. A flashlight.

"Some of these items will be shared among teams of two—that's how we divide each group. You'll have a buddy, and the two of you will keep track of each other. Your guide—I'll be bringing in two other men—will keep track of *you*. You can choose buddies now, while I get the demo pack ready."

The women turned to each other, excitedly pairing off. Amid the camaraderie, Jayne glanced toward Riley. Their eyes met. In hers he read curiosity, interest . . . and a certain amount of "how about hooking up for old time's sake?" mischief. The same kind of mischief, he figured, that had led her to flaunt her sexy shoes, show off her cleavage, and generally make him regret he'd ever let her go.

If Jayne thought all that stuff meant he was going to want to partner with her—in every conceivable way . . . well, she was right.

But wanting to do it and actually doing it were two different things, Riley reminded himself. He might have to suffer through the former, but he was going to avoid the latter. He was going to be gentlemanly, helpful . . . an all-around good guy. He was going to show Jayne there were decent men in the world—men who *weren't* packing the raw materials for relationship disaster.

"Later," he mouthed to her, and smiled.

She nodded and rejoined the conversation.

While the group discussed trail buddies and calorific bonanzas, Riley went to the opposite side of the table and sorted through the packs arrayed there. He was feeling pretty good about things. Happy about the way this orientation was progressing, optimistic about the women's chances for good times (and survival) on the trail, and downright saintly about his plans to show Jayne the goodness of mankind. But as he lifted the pack he'd chosen, another, less welcome emotion pushed its way into his consciousness.

Uneasiness.

Along with it came the sensation that he'd forgotten something. Riley tried to tamp it down, but it refused to budge. He tried to ignore it, along with the uneasiness, but still it niggled at him. For some reason, he felt unsure about what was happening. And then it hit him—the realization of what was behind these feelings.

In the past, getting close to Jayne had only tempted him to change his ways, he remembered. Had only encouraged him to give up the vagabond life he'd chosen and stay—*stay*—with her. Would spending time with her now have the same effect?

Riley looked at her, considering. Jayne was laughing, swiveled in her chair in a classic bombshell's pose, legs crossed seductively and dress clinging in all the right places. She looked fabulous. Warm, affectionate, funny. Exactly the way a change-your-whole-life temptress *ought* to look.

He waited for that old urge to strike . . . the urge that had whispered how nice it would be to wake up in the same place, with the same woman, day after day.

It didn't strike.

Whew. For a second there, he'd been afraid he didn't even have the fortitude to get through a single day—much less a whole week—with Jayne, and still keep his traveling-adventuring-exploring goals intact.

To see, to do, to conquer, to enjoy.

If he couldn't stick to his intentions, Riley told himself, then he wasn't the man he thought he was. And that was . . . unthinkable.

Boundlessly relieved, he called an end to the chatty discussion. With the ladies' attention secured, Riley accepted a sample backpacker's pack from Alexis and held it in his arms as he addressed the group again.

"And now, for the final part of the orientation," he said, "I'll need a volunteer to help demonstrate proper fitting of a trail pack." He grinned and delivered his standard joke.

"Someone who won't mind getting close, and won't mind having a strange man's hands all over her."

Five hands shot into the air. The women waved their arms, eager to join in. As Riley had expected, Jayne wasn't one of the volunteers.

Time for the "two could play that game" portion of our show.

Sweeping the group with a speculative look, he finally settled his gaze on . . . Jayne. He took his time considering her, and was forced to admire the way she sat straight beneath his scrutiny. Obviously, she refused to be intimidated—or to admit the sense of challenge playing between them.

"Jayne, how about you?"

Five

How about *her?* Jayne thought as Riley's I-dare-you gaze settled on her. *How about having her sense of self-preservation examined, for instance?*

It looked as though she'd checked it at the doors of the Hideaway Lodge, along with her sense of normalcy and her usual city-bred certainty. Staying here where Riley could tease her with those warm hazel eyes, that devastating smile, that alert-yet-relaxed stance of his was absolutely nuts. Any sensible woman would have taken herself far away from him. Far, far, far, far—*yikes. He was coming closer.*

At his approach, she straightened in her chair, desperate to continue projecting a confident you-don't-bug-me demeanor. During Riley's presentation, it had been hard not to fidget. She'd caught herself at it a few times—nervously crossing and uncrossing her legs, playing with her pendant, wiggling in her chair—and had put a stop to it every time . . . but not before Riley had noticed, in a couple of instances.

She didn't want him to know he could still get to her. That way lay madness—and the certain failure of her Heartbreak 101 workshop. Her techniques had never faced a challenge quite like this—more than six feet of rugged male coming nearer with every second and likely to come even closer over the next few days. Good-natured Riley, with his easy ways and drifter's heart, probably didn't even realize how his nearness turned her inside out.

But Jayne did. And she couldn't afford to succumb to it.

All around her, the workshop attendees waved their arms, eager to volunteer for the duty she dreaded: having Riley's hands all over her.

One of those hands loomed in her vision as he held it toward her, palm up in invitation. Predictably, she automatically leaned nearer. It seemed her body remembered the feel of those hands—big, strong, nimble-fingered, and surprisingly gentle—and had none of the reservations her mind did.

Jayne jerked herself back. She shook her head, scrambling for an excuse. "I, um, haven't even tried wearing a backpack before. Surely Kelly's Camp Catawba experience makes her more qualified for your demonstration. I'm a rank beginner!"

"You're *perfect*," Riley said in that rumbly voice of his.

A moment later, Jayne found herself pulled to her feet, to the applause of the group. At her side, Mr. Charming Smile gave her a reassuring pat.

"This won't hurt a bit," he said.

That's what he thought. He wasn't the one who'd have to endure the now-impersonal touch of someone who'd once caressed her tenderly . . . someone who'd once kissed her sweetly . . . someone who'd once—*whoa*. Jayne started as Riley's hands lowered to her shoulders and his fingertips grazed the bare skin near her neckline. *That* wasn't so *impersonal*.

"Wearing a pack comfortably starts with what you're wearing beneath it," Riley said. "You want to avoid seams, tears, areas that might chafe. Pure cotton rubs when wet, but silk"—his palms skimmed her shoulders—"is a fine choice, as are breathable poly blends that wick moisture from the skin.''

Jayne gawped at him. She'd have sworn there wasn't a man alive who knew the difference between silk, cotton, and rayon—much less what a "poly blend" was. And Riley could identify those fabrics by touch, while advising on their proper use. Unbelievable. Grudgingly, she admitted to herself that his expertise was probably *not* limited to breaking hearts while appearing unceasingly happy-go-lucky.

The pack settled onto her back, its weight unfamiliar.

"This is an external-frame pack," Riley explained as he helped steady it. "Empty, it weighs about six pounds."

"Couldn't I just carry my purse?" Jayne squirmed beneath the awkward load. "It's lighter. And more stylish. This feels like a gigantic fanny pack."

The women made faces, nodding in sympathy. Jayne felt vindicated. *Nothing* was more unflattering than a fanny pack. Unless it was two fanny packs.

Riley shook his head. "Can you fit a sleeping bag, several days' worth of food, supplies, and extra clothes in your purse?"

Jayne thought about it. If only she'd brought her Saks drawstring hobo instead of a handbag . . .

Doris held up her purse. "I think *I* can."

"Nonsense. *I* can." Donna raised her tote. "I once fit a nineteen-pound Thanksgiving turkey in here," she said proudly.

They all murmured appreciatively at this accomplishment.

"I saw the *cutest* Kate Spade bag in a magazine last month," Carla said. "It was, like, to die for."

"Who's Kate Spade?" Mitzi asked. *Pop.*

Kelly looked dreamy and adjusted her glasses. "Does anybody else think David Spade is cute? Because ever since *Just Shoot Me* came on TV, I—"

The conversation took on a momentum of its own. Amid its topic changes and laughter, Jayne was stranded with Riley right behind her. And she did mean *right behind her*. His warmth touched her all over. His breath tickled her ear as he spoke.

"How long do you think this will go on?" he asked, the question for her alone.

She shrugged. Which was a mistake, because it brought her shoulders more firmly against his palms. An inadvisable sizzle zipped through her at the contact. "I dunno. Until we've covered Fendi, Prada, about six other actors, and, quite possibly, gardening spades as recommended by Martha Stewart."

He whistled again. Everyone quieted.

"Or," Jayne amended, "until you stop it, probably."

Riley squeezed her shoulders gently. The camaraderie they'd shared awakened at the contact, reminding her of the way they each used to know what the other was thinking without saying a word. She knew he was smiling at her comment even before she glanced over her shoulder at him.

During their time together, the two of them had created an entire language of touches, looks, laughs. Apparently, it wouldn't take long for the Berlitz version of Riley-Jayne-speak to bring them up to speed again now.

Dammit.

He winked and nodded toward the group. "Somebody's got to be in charge."

He was in charge. Although he kept his voice low so the others wouldn't overhear, Jayne knew they realized it too. The ability to lead came as naturally to Riley as broad shoulders and a wicked appreciation for a properly fitted pack.

Speaking of which . . .

"The hip belt is secured first," he said to the group. His hands skimmed down her sides to capture the dangling straps, while he levered his chest against her back to hold the pack in place. Murmuring encouragement, Riley turned Jayne to a three-quarters-facing position toward their audience. "It helps keep the pack's weight here, where it belongs."

His knuckles nudged her hips. A thousand memories rushed forward at his touch—memories of him cradling her close during a kiss, raising her hips while he entered her, tickling her while they cuddled together afterward. Didn't he realize this position was just like vertical spooning? Didn't he remember spooning was one of her favorite things?

Helplessly, Jayne glanced at Riley's profile while he looked over her shoulder to fasten the hip-belt buckle. His jaw held the merest hint of dark, late-afternoon stubble. His mouth pursed in concentration. His eyes . . . met hers as the buckle clicked into place.

He realized, all right. He remembered. And he knew exactly what he was doing to her. Unfortunately, she was trapped for the rest of the demonstration.

Her whole body quivered. Riley's voice filled the room as he went on explaining about pack fitting, but Jayne heard almost none of it. Her mind was occupied with blocking out memories of his touch, ignoring the reawakening their contact caused now, staying the course she'd set for herself.

How could she have believed herself over him?

She was, Jayne told herself firmly. The touch of any good-looking man would have caused this reaction. Especially after the several nearly celibate months she'd recently spent. Her night-table companion, Mr. Buzzy, just wasn't the same as a real live—*geez,* his touch felt good. She was only human, Jayne struggled to convince herself further, with a woman's natural susceptibility to a sexy man's—

Was *that* what she *thought* that was, grazing her backside?

Was Riley as affected by their nearness as she was?

A trickle of hope filled her. So long as he wasn't as unruffled as his carefree expression suggested, Jayne still stood a chance. She still might escape this week as confident as she'd entered it.

Having adjusted the pack's shoulder straps, Riley stepped

from behind her. Something swung free as he did. Another buckle, Jayne realized as she eyed it dispiritedly. What she'd mistaken for helpless ardor had merely been . . . a rogue fastener.

Sigh.

Waitaminute. She wasn't disappointed. Riley could keep all his . . . *buckles* to himself, for all she cared. She didn't care if she ever saw his . . . *buckle* again. Ever.

Unwanted, a risqué vision rose in her mind. Riley, wearing nothing but a pack. Riley, gloriously naked save some strategically placed belts. Riley, wearing a smile and a come-and-get-it grin as he proudly showed off the part of him that had made so many erotic adventures possible between them.

Riley, Riley—*no*.

Oblivious to her stupidly wandering thoughts, he fastened the pack's shoulder straps. His movements stirred the air between them, making her too aware of his clean masculine scent. His *familiar* scent. If she didn't free herself from this demonstration soon, Jayne realized, she just might crack.

There were only so many sensory memories a person could be expected to withstand, especially when they were all, in combination, so delicious. The strength of Riley's arms around her. The expertise of his touch. The surety of his stance as he stood nearby to explain the process. She examined his face. Any minute now she'd rise to tiptoe, purse her lips, and—

"Finished," he announced, stepping back with a flourish.

Blinking in surprise, Jayne found herself arrayed in a fully outfitted pack. Straps comfortably crisscrossed her torso. Slippery nylon whooshed softly when she moved.

"Hey! It's lighter!" she said.

He nodded. "A well-fitted pack hugs you close as a lover."

A lover. The kind of lover that love-'em-and-leave-'em Riley Davis would never be, for her. Not since he'd broken her heart. Indignation cleared her head. How dare he stand there, casually tossing around words like "lover"? Like "hugs," for that matter?

The breakup-ees leaned nearer, ooohing and whispering.

At the sound, Jayne glanced at them. To her relief, the sight of their interested faces—the sight of all the women who were relying on her for help—solidified her goals. Those goals did not include melting at Riley's every touch, but they did include showing her breakup-ees how to cope with the challenge of an ex. Starting now.

"A lover?" she repeated, arching her brow.

Riley folded his arms over his chest. He nodded.

"Well, let's hope it's more reliable than a lover," Jayne chirped. With an expertise she hadn't known she possessed—apparently, *some* part of her hadn't been absorbed in mentally undressing Riley and reliving their steamiest moments—she rapidly unfastened the buckles and straps. "Let's hope this pack is *much* more reliable. Not prone to bailing out, for instance, just when things get good."

She shoved the pack into his arms. Riley frowned. In return, Jayne felt justified in giving him her most dazzling smile. It was hard, but she did it.

"Come on, ladies," she said. "We have things to do. Broken hearts to get over. Pre-dinner primping to be done. Who's with me?"

A chorus of "me!"'s rang out. Leopard-print compacts were waved in the air. Gratified, Jayne gathered her group. The women—including teenage Alexis—headed for the door.

"Hey!" Riley gestured toward them.

She paused in the entryway. "Oh, I'm sorry. I trust you're done with the orientation? You did say the pack fitting was the final part, didn't you?"

Looking perplexed, he nodded.

"Then we'll just get on with our day." They trouped onward.

"Wait!"

She did.

"Typically, *I* dismiss the group," he told her.

Feeling stronger, Jayne considered that. "You might as well get used to something," she said at last. "We're not typical."

Then she breezed out with her ladies in tow, back straight and stilettos steady. If Riley thought he'd make her cave with mere teasing touches, she reminded herself . . . well, he'd better think again. It would take more than that to bring Jayne Murphy to her knees.

A whole lot more.

Later that night, Jayne stood again on the rock-walled lodge deck. Darkness covered the landscape. It blurred all but the most ominous rock formations, intensified the creaks of crickets and the rustlings of unknown creatures . . . worsened her fears. She was afraid of the dark, and had been for as long as she could remember.

Luckily, light shined from a few of the lodge's windows. It wasn't bright enough to fully pierce the darkness, but it did glow subtly enough to give Jayne the courage to do what she'd come here to do.

The chill of the stone wall met her palms. She leaned against it, gazing upward at the points of light overhead. From here, with no city lights to obscure them, the stars were brilliant and numerous. Their panorama arched above her like an immense sprinkling of diamonds on velvet in a Tiffany window—only better, because they were obtainable. In a way.

Breathing in, Jayne closed her eyes. When she opened them again, she fixed her gaze on the first star she saw.

"I'm afraid," she whispered, still grasping the wall for security. "Afraid to camp, afraid to hike, afraid I'll let everyone down. Please, please give me the courage to do this."

She waited, feeling a lump rise in her throat. Swallowing past it, Jayne continued to watch her chosen star. Wishes had to be made aloud to come true, and there was nothing to do but go on.

"I swear I'll give up Godiva, stop objectifying Calvin Klein poster boys, even"—she searched for something suitably kindhearted she could exchange for the enormous wish she sought—"even use the next Macy's ad to teach little kids to read, not to target the next DKNY sale. Just please, *please* let me do this."

As was her habit, Jayne stood beneath the stars a moment longer. Then, feeling as though she'd done all she could, she turned away and headed back to rejoin the group inside the lodge.

There, the brightness reassured her. Warmth seeped through the baby-blue sweater she'd thrown on over her shirtdress, comforting her. But her conscience . . . that was another story.

Jayne ran back outside. She found her star again.

"Okay, so maybe I'll target a few shoe sales before teaching the kids to read," she confessed, her face tilted upward. "But I swear I'll do everything else!"

Riley stood outside the lodge the following morning, waiting for his group to finish their post-breakfast primp and meet him for preliminary training. The fresh April air was crisp with creosote and seven-thirty chill, and the sun's new rays held little heat. But it would warm up, given time.

He wasn't sure the same philosophy applied to Jayne. After yesterday's adventures in pack fitting, Riley had realized a few things. First, that touching and teasing might not have been the best way to bring her around to his way of thinking. Second, that being touched only made her tense up. Third, that clearly much more touching would be necessary to overcome the problem.

Fourth, and most displeasing, was that all those troubles had undoubtedly been caused by the jerk who'd sent her to Heartbreak Camp. Riley resented him mightily, whoever he was. He'd taken a fun-loving, warm, affectionate woman and turned her into someone who froze at the most innocent—or, okay, not-quite-innocent—touch.

It was tragic. Unacceptable. Reprehensible.

He could hardly wait to start remedying it.

Jayne deserved a happy, carefree life. A life like the one Riley enjoyed himself, whether he was sportfishing on Baja's East Cape or dangling from an overhang while rock climbing in Canada. Sure, Jayne's city-bound days might not feel as free as Riley's days did in the wild, but he figured she could still be happy. She could heal and go forward without that bozo ex-boyfriend dogging her thoughts.

Of course, Jayne thought she was going to achieve that healing with the help of some guru's mumbo-jumbo do-it-yourself techniques. Riley knew that was ridiculous. Who needed self-help when the help of someone who cared about you was at hand?

Yep, he told himself as he worked to assemble the things he'd need for this morning's training. That was exactly right. He might not want to lead a bunch of guidance groupies into the wilderness, but at least he could rack up a few good deeds while he did. After all, like the Zen master he'd photographed in Nepal had told him—

Hubba-hubba.

Okay, so that wasn't *quite* what the Zen master had said. But it was all that went through Riley's mind as the lodge's front door opened and Jayne and her cohorts filed out.

Okay, so "filed out" was a misnomer. Shimmied out, va-va-voomed out, sashayed out ... all those were more accurate descriptions of the sight that greeted him. Evidently, the feminine bonding he'd observed yesterday had led to a morphing of body movements. All of the women had adopted

Jayne's sexy way of walking—with various degrees of effectiveness.

They descended the front steps and crossed into the patch of sandy yard designated as the training area. Carla strutted with her beringed nose held high. Mitzi popped her gum with extra sassiness. Donna and Doris jostled each other as the sisters swished their hips. Even shy Kelly put a little wiggle in her walk.

None of them, though, had mastered the elegant jubilation that defined Jayne's movements. Dressed in a baby-blue sweater, blue jeans with the legs rolled up at the ankles, a rhinestone bracelet, and strappy heels, she somehow managed to embody sex appeal and decisiveness with every long-legged stride. Watching her move was an education in femininity . . . and a distraction that made Riley nearly pitch into the tents he'd been handling.

They stopped in front of him, their highly accessorized selves at the ready. Necklaces, bracelets, and earrings gleamed in the rising sunlight. Lipstick and eye makeup defined every face. A veritable smorgasbord of perfumes wafted on the morning breeze.

Riley sneezed. "Good morning," he said with a smile. "You're all looking very . . . gussied up today."

They beamed. *Whew.* "Gussied up" was acceptable. A man could never tell. He wouldn't have thought describing a pack that fit like a lover's embrace would have caused a mass exodus yesterday, but that's what had happened. Now, suddenly, he felt on firmer footing with the group again.

Until just this minute he hadn't realized how much he'd— well, *worried* wasn't exactly the right word—*wondered* about this post-exodus encounter.

"We all had, like, mini makeovers at the slumber party last night," Carla explained.

"Jayne brought enough Velcro rollers and Bioré strips for everyone," Mitzi said, touching her hair. "She's the best!"

"If you look good, you feel good," Kelly offered.

"Yay!" they all cheered, high-fiving each other as though they'd scored three-pointers rather than beauty advice.

"Good morning," Jayne said amid the hubbub.

His world stood still.

What? His world stood still? What was with all the mooshy sentiment all of a sudden? Riley wondered. Jayne merely looked at him, and he—

"It's a little chilly out," she went on.

—wanted to offer her the shirt off his back just to keep her warm. Shaking off the notion (her sweater looked plenty warm, and plenty perfectly fitted too), Riley addressed the group.

"Is it too late for one of those makeovers?" he asked. He grasped the ends of his shirt and tugged them outward. "I just washed this shirt, and I can't do a *thing* with it."

They laughed. He grinned, tousling his hair self-consciously with his hand. Not for a million dollars would Riley have admitted to glancing twice at Gwen's blow dryer this morning, considering "gussying" *himself* up to make a good impression.

"You don't need any help, young man," Doris said, looking him up and down. "You look fine just the way you are."

"Nonsense. *Better* than fine," Donna clarified. "Shoot, if I were fifteen years younger . . ."

They waggled their eyebrows. Riley started. Had his clothes transformed into some Chippendale-type G-string ensemble when he wasn't looking? The last time he'd checked, he'd dragged on a perfectly ordinary Polarfleece hooded shirt, jeans, and Timberlands this morning. But the sisters' lascivious looks made him double-check.

Jayne caught him at it. She grinned. "Don't worry."

Their communication mojo was still functioning. She'd guessed what he'd been thinking. Remarkable.

"Your *buckle* isn't hanging out," she added.

Huh? Riley gave her a quizzical look, but she only whipped out a leopard-print compact and urgently checked her lipstick.

He examined her pinkening cheeks, wondering at the cause of her blush. But then the rest of the group crowded around him, demanding to know what was on their training agenda for the day. Riley was forced to turn his attention to the job at hand.

"We'll be spending the morning learning to set up tents." He nudged his hiking boot toward the two-person models stacked beside him. "Then a crash course in orienteering with a compass. After lunch we'll warm up with a short hike around the base of Lower Chimney Rock. We'll make sure your packs are comfortable, your hiking boots are properly broken in—"

He stopped, looking at the sandals, Hush Puppies, thongs, and—in Carla's case—purple-laced Pumas they wore. "You *did* receive the information on hiking boots Gwen and Bud sent to all new adventure travelers, didn't you?"

Everyone nodded. Riley breathed a sigh of relief.

"And you *have* been taking some easy hikes to prepare?"

Five heads nodded. Jayne raised her hand. "Does fifteen trips to the Banana Republic near Union Square count?"

Riley began to nod. Then he gave her a sharp look. "Did you take a taxi?"

"Do you think I have a death wish? I love San Francisco, but walking is the only way to go. I used to trek twenty-two blocks just to get to work."

Used to? Had her despair over her boneheaded former boyfriend caused her to lose her art department job too? Riley became more determined than ever to help her.

But since singling Jayne out for special attention would only make her feel . . . well, *singled out,* he settled for saying "In that case, yes. That counts."

She smiled. He cheered up further.

The women had had their slumber party. He'd had a good

night's sleep, plus a head-clearing sunrise hike. Everyone was feeling good, ready to embark on their adventure. Today Riley would reassert his authority over the group and get everything back on track. Only one detail remained to be settled. . . .

"So." He rubbed his hands together to warm them, glancing expectantly toward the lodge's front door as he did. "Where's your esteemed leader, the so-called self-help guru? She ought to be here for the training."

The women all ducked their heads, glancing toward one another silently. Then, to his surprise, Jayne stepped forward.

"She's right here. One so-called self-help guru, at your service."

Six

"I thought I might find you here!"

Calling the greeting to her uncle, Alexis finished the climb to his usual spot atop the mesquite-shaded rock formation near the lodge. She scrambled over slippery footholds and sat down beside him.

From here, Nana and Gramps's lodge was still visible beyond the rise, but the rocks and trees gave the place an illusion of privacy. The sun-warmed granite would *totally* make her butt go numb if she stayed very long, but for now it would be nice to hang with Uncle Riley.

He looked up. Angled his chin in welcome. "Hey."

"Whatcha doin' out here?" She brushed off her palms and gazed at him curiously. "I thought you did the *mountain man* routine only when something was bugging you."

Silently, her uncle stared out over the scenery.

Was he shutting her out? Alexis frowned. She used to *hate* the way Brendan did that whenever his friends came around.

So she probed. "You didn't even wait to see if your group came back from their orienteering test after the hike."

He shrugged. "I'm sure they did fine."

Alexis kept her mouth shut.

A moment ticked past. Uncle Riley looked at her. "Did something happen? Did you come out here to tell me something happened? I *knew* I should have hung back and trailed them."

He started to get up. A shake of her head made him lower again, a question in his eyes.

"Nothing happened," Alexis reassured him with a wave of her hand. "They're all still in Sedona."

"Sedona? They weren't supposed to go to Sedona. They were supposed to navigate their way to the Red Rock Loop trail. Then call me on the two-way radio I left at the trailhead, so I could come pick them up." He nudged the receiver at his side.

"Yeah. Well. Turns out Jayne's a natural at using a compass." Alexis shrugged. "She led them straight to downtown Sedona instead."

"And tourist row." He nodded knowingly.

"Yeah. They're probably working the Kokopelli key chains and turquoise bracelet displays pretty hard by now." Tourists *loved* that stuff, Alexis knew. "Jayne called Nana to invite us to go shopping with them. For a famous author, she is *so* nice. I mean, she's nice anyway, even without being an author, but especially considering how *amazing* her book has done. . . ."

He remained silent. Like the rocks they were sitting on.

Alexis stopped. She gave him a speculative look. "I guess you didn't expect Jayne to blow off your plan, huh?"

Uncle Riley gazed outward again. "Jayne's *full* of surprises today."

Whoa. Robo-uncle. Alexis wasn't sure what put the ominous note in his voice, but she'd heard that tone before. Usually from one of her parents when she missed her curfew. Sure, it *sounded* okay—on the surface. But underneath there was a "you're in deep doo-doo" waiting to get out.

Suddenly, she felt kind of sorry for Jayne. And curious to

know what the woman had done to bug her usually easygoing uncle.

Before Alexis had a chance to ask, though, Uncle Riley changed the subject.

"Why didn't you go with them?" he asked. "I'm sure your great-grandma would have driven you to town."

Alexis shrugged. "I decided to stick around here. My mom usually calls after lunch."

He gave her a sharp look. Alexis braced herself. Typically, a look like that came with a hefty dose of pity and was followed by a *poor, abandoned, little girl* gesture. Like a hug. Nobody seemed to realize she was an adult now and could handle this stuff. After all, she *was* as tall as her mom these days. Taller than Nana. Just because her mom's call from Mexico had lasted all of five breezy minutes, that didn't mean Alexis needed a pity hug.

But since all Uncle Riley did was give her an understanding nod and then gaze into the distance again, she felt emboldened to continue.

"I think she thinks calling me makes her look good to Gary. That's the guy she's been hooking up with since the divorce."

Alexis had her suspicions that her mom and dad had divorced *because* of Gary. Nobody had ever told her the whole story about things, but she had eyes. She'd seen her mom dressing up like a forty-something Britney Spears to go "grocery shopping." Alexis watched Jerry Springer after school sometimes. It hadn't taken a genius to know *something* was going on.

She hugged her knees to her chest. "My mom wants us to look like this perfect mother-daughter team. All we need are some credits and a little mood music, and we'll be the freakin' Gilmore Girls."

"You're better than the Gilmore Girls," Uncle Riley said loyally. "And don't say 'freakin'.' "

Alexis snorted. Sometimes her uncle was pretty old-fashioned. It was sweet.

"Some people are hung up on the family thing." He spoke gently, frowning as he picked up a pebble and turned it over in his fingertips. "Maybe your mom is one of them. Me, I don't buy it. Never have. That cozy, close-knit thing is an illusion."

"Geez, Uncle Riley! Shatter my innocence, why don't you?"

She grinned at him. He tousled her hair and grinned back.

That was one of the things Alexis liked about Uncle Riley. She could talk to him about anything, and he didn't deliver some school-citizenship style homily about being all she could be, saying no to drugs, and brushing her teeth three times a day. He treated her like a *Cosmo*-reading, shop-surfing, brain-enabled *person* . . . not a child.

Still, his views on relationships were majorly depressing.

"I think you need to come out of the wilderness more often," she said. "You know, try a date once in a while. Loosen up. Lose the *negative* aura."

He pretended to growl at her. She laughed.

"Seriously. It's like Jayne says in her book, if you're surrounded by negative triggers that keep you stuck in your—"

Uncle Riley held up his hand. "I don't want to hear about that book."

"It's good!"

"It's a bunch of hooey." Suddenly, he lowered his eyebrows and pinned her with a *you're-busted* look. "And what are *you* doing reading it?"

"Jayne gave me a copy." Alexis shrugged off her backpack and pulled out the hardbound *Heartbreak 101*. "I brought it out here to show you the *fabulous* inscription."

She held the book toward her uncle. He shook his head.

"Go on," she urged. "I want you to see it."

He looked about as willing to touch Jayne's book as

Brendan had been to hold Alexis's hand when the rest of the eighth-grade basketball team was around. That was all the more reason, she figured, for her to urge it on him. She held it closer.

Reluctantly, Uncle Riley dropped his pebble. He brushed off his hands and accepted the book.

"The inscription is on the title page."

Paper rustled. A bird called nearby. The breeze blew Alexis's hair in her eyes, making her nearly miss the moment when her uncle read what Jayne had written.

To Alexis, a diva in training: May you never know heartbreak of your own . . . or the heartbreak of missing a fifty-percent-off shoe sale. If you look good, you feel good! Hugs, Jayne Murphy

"Isn't that the *best*?" Alexis gushed, grabbing Uncle Riley's arm. "I *love* the 'diva-in-training' part, don't you? Jayne *so* understands what it's like to be a woman. She is like, my favorite person in the whole wide world right now!"

Uncle Riley frowned. He handed back the book.

His grouchy attitude was *way* beyond her. Then she realized. "Oh! Except you, Uncle Riley. You're my standing favorite person. *Unreplaceable.*"

"Irreplaceable."

"That too." She put away the book and zipped her pack shut. "Really. Aside from you, the only other person I've ever talked to like this was Brendan, and he—"

Too late, Alexis realized she'd opened her big fat mouth and nearly spilled everything. She shoved her arms through her pack's straps and slung it onto her back. Maybe if she pretended she'd never spoken . . .

"And he . . . ?"

Rats. So much for pretending. "Nothing."

Uncle Riley raised his eyebrows. "Who's Brendan?"

She ground the toe of her Skechers in a rocky crevice and shook her head.

He tried a leading comment. "If the little creep did anything besides hold your hand, I'll break his nose."

She snorted.

Uncle Riley cracked his knuckles. "And then I'll break whatever he touched you with."

Alexis envisioned that jerk Brendan begging big, tough Uncle Riley for mercy. A small smile edged onto her face.

"You don't have to do that." She sighed. "Brendan wouldn't touch me with a ten-foot pole. *Notanymore.*"

He leaned nearer. "What's that?"

Not anymore. No, she couldn't say *that* again. Then she'd have to spill her guts about the Cinnabon incident. She might even cry. Alexis couldn't risk crying in front of Uncle Riley. As understanding as he could be, she had a feeling crying would be pushing it. A guy like him might not understand, having never experienced the urge to curl up in a ball and sob, himself. He never let *anything* get to him.

Heck, he'd even sounded okay while telling her how he didn't believe in cozy, close-knit relationships. If *that* wasn't die-hard macho, she didn't know what was.

"Nothing," she mumbled, and stood. "I'd better get back. See you around."

He examined her face. Nodded. "Okay. Thanks for the company."

Alexis gave a little wave. She began climbing back down the rocky slope. Halfway through her descent, her backpack slipped. She paused to adjust it, then glanced upward.

Uncle Riley sat alone on his rock, forearms resting loosely on his thighs. He tilted his head at a thoughtful angle. A sad angle, even. While she watched, he raised his face to the breeze, eyes closed. Something about his expression, when the sunlight hit it, made her hesitate.

He looked almost . . . lonely. As though he needed her. Or needed *someone*, at least. Drawn to him but knowing that was stupid—after all, Uncle Riley hacked through jungles on wildlife photography assignments on a regular basis, so he didn't *need* anyone—Alexis watched for a moment longer.

Then the sound of car doors slamming reached her, followed by feminine voices. It had to be Jayne and the other ladies, back from shopping! Her head filled with thoughts of seeing whatever they'd bought, Alexis turned again and headed toward the lodge.

Her uncle Riley would be fine, she told herself. He always was and he always would be.

Jayne sat on the floor of the Hideaway Lodge's common area, dressed in her favorite baby-blue pajamas. Although tomorrow she faced a grueling wilderness test unlike anything she'd ever experienced, tonight she had all the essentials to fortify her.

She had newfound friends nearby. A bowl of microwave popcorn on her lap, for sharing with those friends. And a veritable film fest of special edition DVD movies starring the swoony George Clooney. Did it *get* any better than this?

Well, sure, she thought. *Not having to face potential survival issues tomorrow without so much as the solace of a Lean Cuisine nearby would have made things much better.* But aside from that, she was feeling pretty good.

Of course, Riley's reaction to her "coming out" as a self-help guru had put a crimp in her day earlier . . . but she wouldn't think about that now.

Carla, who'd been manning the hot cocoa station, nudged her. "Jayne, it's your turn. Truth or dare."

"Ummm, truth."

"Okay." Mitzi, the game's unofficial leader, leaned nearer. The movement made lamplight dance off the glittery silver stars hand painted on her knee-length sleep shirt. "Which would you rather do . . . try on bikinis in a communal dressing room or ask a man out on a first date?"

"Ooooh." The women huddled nearer, Kelly and Carla

both dressed in flannel men's-style pajamas and fuzzy slippers. They awaited her answer.

"The date," Jayne said decisively. "Potential rejection pales compared with public cellulite exposure. Besides, asking a man out on a date is a fairly low-risk activity."

They disagreed, passing around the popcorn bowl. On the TV in the corner, George delivered a dazzling smile.

"It's true!" She raised her hands to quiet the hubbub. "The average man isn't going to turn you down. Provided you don't make your move while he has a Pamela Anderson Lee clone on his arm, of course."

There was a general outcry about *Baywatch,* breast implants, and Hooters-induced male motor function impairment.

"I know, I know. Some men can't seem to simultaneously blink, walk, and avoid drooling when confronted with a bodacious blonde. But really—"

"My Paolo was like that!" Carla interrupted. "If you got him within fifty feet of a pair of breasts, his brain like, shut down. I swear, the guy couldn't ogle and chew gum at the same time. It was like, 'breast alert! breast alert!' Completely overloaded his circuits or something."

Heads nodded all around.

Jayne smiled. "Well, sometimes the breasts were *yours,* Carla. And I'll bet you enjoyed his interest in them."

With a grudging wrinkle of her ringed nose, Carla agreed. "I guess so. At least until Paolo's commitment phobia set in, we broke up, and *he* started dating a different sorority girl every few days. Then it was like, Greek of the Week club. Ugh."

Making a face, she passed two mugs of cocoa to Doris and Donna. The sisters were attired in coordinating velour track suits, having refused to appear "in public" wearing actual pajamas.

Jayne grinned. "To get back to what I was saying . . . men have their pluses too. Let's not forget that."

"Their 'pluses'?" Doris hooted. "Never heard 'em called *that* before. 'Zip it up, hon. Your 'plus' is showing.' "

Donna winked. "Almost gives me an interest in math."

Jayne smiled, wondering if the sisters realized they'd nearly agreed on something. "For instance," she said, bypassing their more ribald slant on things, "who else would squish bugs for us?"

Murmuring, the women nodded.

"Warm up the chilly side of the bed for us?"

Nods.

"Carry our heavy suitcases?"

Scattered nods.

"Sleep in the wet spot?"

Boggle.

"Your guy *does* that?" Mitzi asked.

"In the *wet spot*?" Carla clarified.

"No way," Kelly said.

Jayne thought back to her last real relationship. Yes, Riley had actually been willing to . . .

"That's beside the point," she said hastily. "The point is, we're here to get over men—*particular* men—but not to bash all men in general. Let's remember that."

Reluctantly, they agreed. The game continued with Jayne's turn.

"Mitzi, truth or dare?" she asked.

"Truth."

"How long has it been since you've thought about your ex?"

"Two days."

"Truth!" the other women yelled.

Sheepishly, Mitzi hugged her knees. "Okay, okay. I think about Rodney all the time. He left me for another waitress at the restaurant where I work, you know. It's been pretty hard to take."

Jayne knee-walked over to Mitzi's spot in front of the weathered leather sofa. She gave her a hug. "You'll be strong when all this is over with. Just coming here makes you stronger.'' She spread her arms wide. ''And that goes for all of you!''

They cheered. The game went on. Donna accepted a dare—nibbling three pieces of non-Atkins-approved popcorn. Doris accepted a truth, and revealed the simultaneous relationships she and her sister had unknowingly been having with Marty, the handyman at their senior center . . . plus the messy breakup that had ensued when they'd discovered their unwitting man-share.

''Since there are more women than men at our age,'' Doris explained, ''Marty seemed to think it was his masculine duty to service as many girlfriends as possible.''

Indignant outbursts were heard. Donna growled and grabbed another handful of popcorn.

They took a break to switch movies at Clooney Central, then went on. The next to take a turn was Kelly, who mumbled and twisted the hem of her PJs while deliberating her choice, then stunned them all by announcing, ''Dare.''

''Okay,'' Carla said. ''I dare you to . . . insult me.''

Kelly hesitated. She peered through her dark bangs at Carla, then glanced around the room before ducking her head again. She drew a deep breath.

''Ummm . . .''

''Go on,'' Carla urged.

''Well . . . okay. I guess . . . the cocoa you made had too many marshmallows in it?''

Donna smacked her forehead. Doris rolled her eyes.

''Come on, Kelly. Really hit me. Insult me!''

Kelly looked confused. ''Why would I want to do that?''

''It's a dare, silly,'' Mitzi said. ''Just to see if you'll do it. We dare you.''

Uncle! Kelly's panicky expression said. *I give up!*

''Truth!'' she blurted. ''Truth!''

Jayne stepped in, giving a reassuring smile to her most timid breakup-ee. ''Okay, truth. Why did you come to the workshop, Kelly? You're the only one who hasn't told us about your ex.''

A hush fell over the women. Bathed in the glow of flickering Clooney-vision, they waited to hear Kelly's answer. Even the popcorn came to a rest on the floor near Jayne's baby-blue plush platform slippers.

Kelly hugged a pillow to her middle. She glanced up. ''I was having a torrid affair with a married man,'' she admitted.

Everyone gasped. Sweet, shy Kelly? A home wrecker?

''I didn't know he was married until a few months ago. And the way I found out . . . oh, it's too embarrassing!''

She buried her face in her hands. Jayne went to her and hugged her too. ''You don't have to tell us if you don't want to. Not now.''

''No. No, I want to.'' Sniffling, Kelly raised her head. ''We were having a long weekend in one of Seattle's nicest hotels. We . . . couldn't keep our hands off each other. And just when Tim took off his shirt so we could, *you know*—''

Everyone nodded, listening raptly.

''Well, that was when I saw *it*.''

'' 'It'? 'It' what? What was it?'' Mitzi asked.

Kelly shook her head. ''Someone had written on his back. With a permanent marker, I guess. Tim's a very sound sleeper, so that's probably how it happened without him knowing it, and—''

''*What did it say?*'' the women shouted.

''Oh. It said, 'Property of—' '' Here Kelly paused. ''Well, to protect her identity, 'Property of *Mrs.* Tim. Hands off!' ''

They all gasped. ''And that's how you found out he was married?'' Carla asked. She stared. ''His wife, like, *booby-trapped* him for you?''

Miserably, Kelly nodded. Jayne squeezed her hand.

''That's devious,'' Mitzi said.

''Very sneaky,'' Donna agreed.

''I'm going to have to remember that,'' Doris announced with a pointed look at her sister.

"Terrible." Carla handed over a second cup of cocoa to soothe Kelly's nerves. "And that's when he dumped you? When you found his wife's lost-and-found message?"

"No," Kelly said. "That's not when he dumped me."

Everyone commiserated. "Well, we've all been in relationships that went on too long," Jayne said, "relationships we allowed to carry on until—"

"That's when *I* dumped him!"

Stunned silence fell. Kelly blushed.

Then they all cheered. "Yay, Kelly!" everyone shouted, united in respect for her gutsy move. Carla pumped her fist, Mitzi shared celebratory pieces of Bazooka, Doris and Donna chose a new DVD, and Jayne gave Kelly another hug plus all the kudos she deserved for standing up for herself.

They were six women dressed in comfy clothes, fortified by the remains of a cocoa-and-popcorn feast, and entertained by the ever-present gorgeous-Georgeness of ClooneyTV. They were sharing, growing stronger, and preparing themselves for the days ahead. After this, Jayne realized, none of them would ever be the same again.

Wilderness, watch out!

Naturally enough, that was when the men arrived on the scene . . . and changed everything.

Seven

Riley paused in the doorway of the lodge's common room. He'd come here to introduce the other guides to the women in Jayne's group, but now ... seeing the mayhem before him ... well, he wasn't too proud to admit he considered getting the hell out of there and breaking out the brewskis with the guys instead.

Unfortunately, his fellow guide, Bruce, made the decision for all of them. One minute, he was standing there placidly beside Riley, Mack, and Bruce's fifteen-year-old cousin, Lance. The next, he was taking his big blond lumberjack-style self straight into the group of women.

"It's a smorgasbord!" he announced gleefully, gazing from one surprised female to the next. "A buffet of women! I know you said you had a group here, Riley, but this ... this is an unexpected treat."

Bruce strode farther into the room, rubbing his hands together with undisguised eagerness. "Hel-*lo*, ladies!"

The women responded mostly with raised eyebrows. Riley couldn't say he blamed them. He couldn't help but notice how intrigued Mitzi seemed. She actually smiled at the big lug.

"He's harmless, really," Riley told them, slapping Bruce on the back. "Out here in the wilderness . . . well, Bruce doesn't see much action. If you know what I mean."

"Hey!"

"And this is Bruce's cousin." He urged Lance forward. The boy came, all gangly arms and legs, self-consciously gelled hair, and overly logoed clothes. "As long as no one objects, Lance here will be coming along on our trip."

"Hi, Lance!" the women said, welcoming him with smiles and waves.

"Lance's parents took a cruise to Alaska and left Bruce in charge of the poor kid." Riley grinned. "I figure he'll need some *positive* influences while they're gone."

Oblivious to the teasing, Bruce nodded. He winked at Mitzi, mouthing something to her. She blushed.

"And this is Mack." Riley encouraged the final guide to come forward. "He comes to you with fifteen years' guide experience, an unfailing knowledge of the Arizona high country—"

"And cookies." Mack held up a bag in each hand.

"Oreos!" all the women cheered. "Yay!"

They descended on a flustered Mack, chattering and sharing and munching. They took Lance beneath their collective feminine wings, encouraging the boy to join in the fun and making him feel welcome. They even included Bruce, despite his uncouth entrance, and endured his attempts to "chat them up."

Bruce was an excellent and trustworthy guide, Riley knew, having taken out several adventure travel groups with the man. But his social skills . . . well, they needed work. Bruce tended to say exactly what he thought at any given moment. His idea of small talk was "Your place or mine, baby?" And he made no efforts to control his ogle reflex no matter who noticed. Bruce claimed this made him "all man." Riley figured it made him impulse-control-challenged.

Mack was another story. Red-haired, thoughtful, and

relentlessly cheerful, Mack was like a sitcom sidekick come to life. Nothing ever got him down . . . but he never seemed to get very much screen time either. Riley had a suspicion Mack's "very special episode" was still in his future.

"Hey, Riley! Come join the fun," Bruce called. He spread his arms wide. "I can't handle all these babes by myself."

Grinning, Riley entered the cluster of women. Someone handed him a cookie. He decided to settle in.

The plan tonight was simply to let everyone get acquainted, since the group would respond better to guides they knew and trusted. The guides, in turn, would have a better understanding of the techniques to use with their group members if they knew the women personally. Satisfied that everything was satisfactorily under way, he chose a seat on the leather sofa to watch the proceedings.

An Oreo-munching Jayne sat down beside him.

"Glad to see you," she said breezily, sending a gentle waft of her perfume his way. "After the way you left this afternoon, I started to think you might not come back."

"Of course I came back. I have a responsibility here."

She seemed to consider this. "So do I. These women are depending on me, Riley. I won't let you mess things up for me."

"I don't plan to."

"Good."

"Good!"

Well. That was that. The sounds of socializing swirled around them, punctuated with laughter and the occasional risqué punch line from Bruce. Riley and Jayne sat stiffly, their apparent truce having affected nothing.

He glanced at her. In her soft oversize pajamas she seemed fragile. Vulnerable even. His heart softened.

Riley was tempted to hug her, to cheer her, to make things easier for her somehow. But he refused to give in to the feeling. Everything was different now that he knew what Jayne was really here for. Knowing she was *leading* the antiheartbreak agenda put an entirely new spin on his plans to show her how decent a man could be. He felt stupid for having thought up the idea in the first place. And he couldn't help but wonder . . .

Had she used her best-selling techniques to get over him?

The possibility hurt his pride. And it did something else too, something he refused to contemplate but that felt suspiciously like stirring up regret. He was bothered by this in ways he hadn't begun to untangle. Even his time alone today hadn't brought him closer to a resolution.

On the other hand, there was still bozo boy, Jayne's former boyfriend, to consider. Riley was sure *he* was the guy who'd inspired her book. Because after all, Riley's breakup with Jayne had been clean.

But did that really matter? *Could* a woman get over a man because of a bunch of touchy-feely antiheartbreak techniques? And if she could . . . where did that leave the men of the world when *they* were heartbroken? Because after he'd left Jayne, he'd sure as hell felt—

No. He wasn't going to turn all introspective and girly and helpless, dammit. The fact of the matter was, Riley didn't consider himself easy to get over. No man did. And nothing would make him believe Jayne's self-help stuff really worked.

"I guess you were surprised to find out I was the group's leader," Jayne said, breaking into his thoughts.

He looked at her. "Surprised isn't the half of it. I actually thought you were here because of a broken heart."

"Well . . . I am."

Riley stiffened. He *knew* he'd detected the signs in her.

"Indirectly, of course," she went on blithely. "The techniques in my book were inspired by an actual broken heart." She raised her palms. "I know, I know. You're going to say I'm not an expert or anything. But I do have a knack for helping people, Riley. I really do. Talking to the women who've read my book made me see that."

She twisted an Oreo in half. Closed her eyes while she carefully scraped off the icing with her bottom teeth. Licked her lips with delight after swallowing the sweet filling. Smiled at him when she caught him watching.

Riley experienced an intense urge to become a cookie.

"And writing my second book—my follow-up workbook," Jayne went on, "will prove it."

"Prove your knack."

"Yes." *Of course.* "That's why this trip is so important to me. And it's also why I was so concerned about your reaction to my leading the group."

"My reaction?" Uncomfortable, he shifted his shoulders. "I went for a hike after I found out. That's all."

"*Exactly!* That's *all.* That's all you did!"

"It's not a crime. It's not even that hard. You just put on some all-terrain shoes and—"

"What about talking? What about sharing? What about expressing your feelings?"

He felt trapped. "I'm trying to quit. Ha-ha."

"Oh, Riley." Sadly, Jayne shook her head. "Maybe you need some of my techniques. I think you're seriously out of touch with your emotions."

He was perfectly in touch with at least one emotion right now. Confusion.

"Let me get this straight," he said. "You're mad because I didn't *do* anything when I learned the truth this morning?"

She nodded, eyes wide. "Of course."

"I will never understand women."

"All we want is some communication!" Jayne sat straighter, waving her halved Oreo like a chocoholic relationship cheerleader deprived of her usual pompoms. "Some *reaction,* and some discussion. You *know* it drives me crazy when you do . . . that thing you do."

"When I do . . . nothing?"

"Yes!"

Riley shook his head. Gamely, even though he wasn't

sure how he was going to manage it, he said, "I'll try to do . . . something in the future."

"Excellent." Apparently satisfied, Jayne squeezed his hand. Her chipper demeanor veered toward full relationship-counselor mode.

And aggravated him. He wasn't one of her breakup-ees, and she'd damn well better remember it.

He squeezed back, leaving their fingers intertwined.

She glanced up, startled. Something sparked between them, something not forgotten but . . . delayed. All at once he wanted to lean nearer. Wanted to find out if her lips still tasted as sweet as he remembered, if her body still fit his as well as he recalled . . . if her heart would race the way his would if they came together. He felt an urge to *claim* her for his own. And he would have, if not for—

"Come on, you two! It's time to play Twister!"

Mack, Kelly, and Carla were suddenly there, grinning. They appeared to have every intention of dragging Riley and Jayne onto the plastic polka-dotted game mat spread in the center of the common room. Riley didn't know where it had come from (he sure as hell hadn't packed the thing in), but he did know one thing for certain.

He could duck faster than they could grab.

He glanced at Jayne. "Race you to the back deck?"

"You're on!"

Laughing, Jayne collapsed against the tumbled-rock wall surrounding the deck. Riley stopped beside her in the semi-darkness, not the least bit out of breath, laughing too.

A companionable feeling came to life inside her. The intimacy of the late hour, the camaraderie of having evaded the potentially embarrassing Twister game, the slightly naughty thrill of having shed their responsibilities for a while, all combined to leave Jayne with a surprising sense of togetherness. With Riley of all people.

Who'd have thunk it?

She looked at him. In the faint glow from the lodge's windows, his features took on an unfamiliar cast, one that temporarily changed him from the man who'd laid her heart bare to simply . . . a man. A man who intrigued her despite all common sense. He looked dark, a little dangerous, wholly alive.

He looked *good.*

"You're fast," she said before she could get carried away with this stuff. "I can hardly believe I beat you."

"You didn't beat me. You tripped me!"

"My slipper came off." Jayne gestured toward her plush baby-blue platforms, both of which she'd restored to her feet. "It's not the same thing."

"Then you elbowed me when I got back up."

"I was putting my slipper back on. Can I help it if you ran into my arm?"

"And when we got to the outside door, you blatantly flaunted your bogus lead by stopping."

She rolled her eyes. "How else was I supposed to let you be chivalrous? Thanks for opening the door for me, by the way."

"Cheater."

"Complainer."

They stuck their tongues out at each other. The childish gesture didn't last long though. Both of them were smiling too broadly to sustain it.

Riley slung his arm around her shoulders. "Ahhh, this feels good. Doesn't it?"

"Just like old times," Jayne agreed, snuggling closer.

Standing side by side, they gazed out into the uncivilized landscape beyond the lodge. Silently, they shared a few breaths. Companionably, their bodies eased together.

It *was* like old times. If she'd closed her eyes, Jayne could have pretended she and Riley were back home on the coast, walking along the Pacific shoreline hand in hand, talking and laughing and loving. Wistfully, she sighed . . . and closed her eyes. Only for a moment.

A sweet moment.

"You must be cold." Stepping away, Riley tugged off his Polarfleece hoodie. Clad from the waist up in his lone T-shirt, he helped her put on the hoodie over her PJ top. He pulled her close again. "There. Better?"

"Mmm-hmm." Jayne savored the leftover heat emanating from the fleece. She let the long sleeves flop past her fingertips, feeling petite and girlish and grateful. "Much warmer. Thanks."

He nodded, his arm once again secure around her shoulders. One of the things she'd always liked about Riley was his generosity. He never hesitated to share. His clothes. His time. His cheesy curly fries at lunch when she'd ordered the salad plate. He wasn't an especially sociable man, but he was a giving one. She'd almost forgotten that about him.

He cleared his throat. "How have you been, Jayne?"

"Since I got here? Oh, fine, I guess. The bathtub shortage is a little extreme, but Gwen's been nice enough to—"

"No. I mean, how have you been?"

"But I just—oh. You mean, since . . . ?"

Riley nodded. His dark gaze pierced her, intense with the need to know. Jayne realized, all of a sudden, that he'd actually worried about her.

She blew out a deep breath. Looked away. Where to begin?

"I've been . . . fine. It was rough at first—"

His arm tightened around her shoulders. She doubted he was aware of it.

"—but now I'm . . . okay." Jayne refused to reveal any more. In a gesture as brave as any she'd ever made, she turned her face up to his. Lightly, she asked, "How about you?"

"I'm—" His voice broke. For no discernable reason at

all, Riley raised his fingers to her cheek. "Better every day," he said, and kissed her.

The contact took her breath away, stole her urge to talk and her ability to do so, all at the same time. Remembrance swamped her as their mouths met, explored, reunited. Jayne turned in his arms, knowing dimly that she should resist this . . . but having no recollection of the reasons why. Riley's lips felt too good on hers, his hands too welcome on her body, for her to turn away.

A moan escaped him. The husky sound of it thrilled her even as she felt his hands delve into her hair, prepare her; even as he kissed her again. This, *this* was the reunion they should have had, the reunion Jayne had dreamed of, thanks to all her most foolish hopes.

And now Riley was giving it to her.

His hands claimed her, touched her, tenderly pulled her still closer. The scary dark night surrounding them fell away, taking Jayne's fears along with it. Being with Riley felt right. It had always felt right, so right.

Until it had ended.

Ended.

With an anguished cry she pushed away from him. She sucked in a deep breath, trembling all over. "Riley, we can't do this. It's been too long. Too much has happened, too—"

"*We can.* Why not?"

He captured her cheeks gently between his palms, making her look into his shadowed face. A kind of intensity burned there, along with what looked like . . . surprise? Was Riley as surprised as she was that he'd kissed her? Or was he surprised to have enjoyed it . . . all over again?

Jayne clasped his wrists. Tugged his arms lower, so his touch couldn't cloud her judgment. "This isn't the right time."

"What time *is* the right time? When we're apart? We have a second chance here. Let's use it."

"Use it? Are you suggesting a *fling*?"

Powerful shoulders shrugged.

"A *fling*?" she repeated, unable to believe his audacity. Riley grinned. "You know we'd both enjoy it."

"Ooooh!" She released his wrists—the better to swat him for making such an inane suggestion. "Men! You get within fifty feet of potential whoopee, and you can't think of anything else."

He stepped closer, said seriously, "I can think of how sweet you are."

"Riley—"

"I can think of how much I missed seeing your nose scrunch up when you're trying not to smile." He thumbed the telltale crinkle at the corner of her mouth. "Like right now."

He *would* have to bring up the nose-scrunch thing. She still didn't believe she did it. It sounded terribly unflattering. Like horizontally striped Capri pants.

All the same, Jayne felt herself weakening. "You make me sound like a rabbit," she groused. "A grumpy, whiskery rabbit on laughing gas."

This time Riley was the one to smile. But he didn't back down, and he didn't let up. "And I can think," he went on, "of how much I admire you—"

Awww.

"—for actually trying to help the women in your group."

Okay, he'd been doing pretty good until now. But that did it.

"*Trying?* 'Trying to help' them?" Jayne advanced on him, jabbing her finger against the hard planes of his muscular chest. "What do you mean, 'trying to help' them? Listen, Mr. lone-wolf, out-of-touch-with-his-emotions, kiss-a-girl-in-the-moonlight Davis. If you're implying that my techniques are—"

"There's no moon tonight. Just us. Together."

Momentarily distracted, Jayne glanced up. "Huh? No moon? Then what's that?"

She pointed. Riley looked.

"The glow of Gwen's bug zapper light around the corner."

"Oh." She frowned. "Poor bugs. They probably think that nice radiant shimmer is the moon, just like I did."

And other people probably think Riley is sincere. Just like I did. Once.

For the first time in her life, Jayne actually felt sorry for the creepy crawlies. "Poor bugs," she said again.

"Maybe." He lifted his shoulder. "Deluded or not, at least they die happy."

"That's a terrible thing to say!"

"Endings aren't bad in and of themselves."

"Easily said," Jayne shot back, folding her arms, "for the person who decides when they happen."

His eyebrows raised. She had to admit, Riley did a nice imitation of a guy who *didn't* follow the love-'em-and-leave-'em code of perpetual bachelorhood. But Jayne knew better.

"You're trying to sidetrack me," she said, shaking her head. "It won't work."

"You're the one who brought up the bug zapper." He spread his arms, palms up. "I was only trying to help. *I* would rather have gone on kissing you."

His gaze dropped to her lips again. The interest—the remembrance—in his expression made heat flare in her middle. That really had been some kiss. Hot. Tender. Seductive. Honestly, no one kissed as thrillingly as Riley did, Jayne thought. It was as though he devoted his whole attention to the pleasure at hand . . . and to making sure she enjoyed herself too. It was as though—

No. There was no point traipsing down the kissing aisle in the Memory Mart. She had to stay focused. Determinedly, Jayne backtracked to the subject of their initial disagreement.

"I can't *believe* you could stand there and suggest my self-help techniques don't work," she said.

"I can't believe you could believe they *would* work."

"I can't believe you could believe I could believe they *wouldn't* work!"

Riley paused. Scratched his head. "Are you sure the kissing isn't going anywhere? Because this—"

"No!"

He held up both palms. "Okay. Settle down. Or is shrieking one of your 'techniques'?"

"I wasn't shrieking. I was . . . being assertive."

"Assertively shrieking."

"Arrgh!"

"Look." Riley came nearer, all tall, strong male and charmingly concerned heartbreaker. "I understand you're hurting. But I'm trying to help."

Great. Jayne stifled a groan. *It had been a pity kiss.*

"So don't take it out on me," he went on. "I'm not that guy, all right?"

He'd had her, up until—"What guy?"

"The guy who inspired your book. Your bozo ex-boyfriend."

She gawped at him. He actually thought . . . ?

"But there are still good men in the world," Riley continued. He patted her shoulder. "Hang in there."

She didn't believe this. "I don't need to hang in there. I have proven antiheartbreak techniques—*best-selling* anti-heartbreak techniques—to see me through anything."

Riley shook his head. *Poor, deluded Jayne,* his expression said.

"What? You don't believe me?" she asked, shrugging off his sympathetic shoulder-patting. "I'll prove it!"

"Come on, Jayne. You don't have to prove anything to me."

"Oh, yes. Yes, I do, you—you—self-help skeptic!" She stamped her plush platform slipper. "I'll prove to you the techniques in my book work. By the time this trip is over, every woman in my group will be cured of her broken heart. Just like *I* am!"

"Oh, yeah?" He leaned against the wall, self-assured and blatantly masculine. "I have news for you. By the time this trip is over, *you'll* be begging *me* for that 'fling' you turned down a few minutes ago."

"A fling? With you?" Jayne looked him over, trying to seem as though nicely defined muscles, lively hazel eyes, and a killer smile had no effect on her at all. "Hah!"

"Hah?"

"Hah-*hah*!"

Slowly, Riley grinned. *Uh-oh.* That grin meant trouble. It meant he had plans—mischievous plans—along with every intention of implementing them.

"Some men aren't so easy to get over," he warned.

Men like you, Jayne finished silently for him. She couldn't help it. The rumbling sound of his voice reached right into her heart and gave her memories a shake. It was sexy, compelling, challenging. It was . . . something she'd yearned to hear for months after he'd left.

Somehow she raised her chin and found her own voice. "Some men need enlightenment. Get ready for yours."

At that, he actually laughed. "If you think your techniques are that good . . . bring them on."

"I will!"

Riley's speculative gaze settled on her. Roved lower to the places he'd revisited with his slow-moving hands earlier. Lifted again to her face. Aggravatingly, he nodded—almost as though he approved of her decision.

Was there anything worse than an adversary who couldn't wait to do battle? At that moment, Jayne didn't think so. Riley's assurance made her wonder . . . to begin with, to wonder if he knew something she didn't.

"Then you can start right now," he said, and leaned forward to deliver his opening salvo.

At the first lowering of his head, Jayne braced herself. She could withstand another kiss. Another searing union of their mouths. Another no-holds-barred entanglement of their

arms and legs and hips. What she couldn't withstand was
... the gentle press of his lips against her forehead?

The warmth of his touch faded quickly. The shock it
caused did not. Even as Riley winked and went inside the
lodge, Jayne stood unbelieving. How could it be that his
chaste kiss, so seemingly devoid of sizzle but so filled with
tenderness, made her yearn for him in ways his passionate
kiss had not?

Confused, Jayne gripped the rock wall in front of her.
She closed her eyes, then tried for help the only way she
could think of. She opened her eyes again, fixed her gaze
on a distant star, and began.

"Okay, I'll still need the courage to hike and camp and
help my breakup-ees. But if it's not too much trouble"—
she stared even more hopefully at her chosen star—"could
I please have a gigantic dose of fortitude, too, to resist Riley
with? Otherwise, I'm in big trouble here."

Eight

On the morning Uncle Riley was due to take Jayne and her Heartbreak 101 group on their adventure travel trip, Alexis awakened at dawn with a new sense of purpose . . . and a gigantic zit.

She stared disconsolately at her face in the mirror, dabbing on Clearasil. It looked like she had a boil on her forehead. A huge glow-in-the-dark, I'm-a-geek sign right between her eyes. Averting her gaze from *the thing,* she got up and got ready for her day, her mind spinning with thoughts of all she'd witnessed on the back patio last night.

Uncle Riley and Jayne. They'd dated. Had a fling. *Something.* They were (as Nana sometimes said) "an item."

Alexis was sure of it. Last night she'd been simultaneously reading *Jane* magazine, applying Urban Decay Rebel orange sparkly polish to her nails, listening to Destiny's Child, and wishing her cell phone worked, when she'd been startled by the sound of feet stomping onto the back deck. And then by the sounds of conversation between Uncle Riley and Jayne.

One (perfectly innocent) look out her window had told Alexis there was more going on with her uncle and the author than the two had let on.

Like lip-locks. Public displays of affection. And an interesting Britney-and-Justin "true love" thing that had almost made Alexis sigh with suppressed, like, *romanticism*. She'd been able to tell right away that Uncle Riley and Jayne used to be together, wanted to be together ... totally *belonged* together now.

All they needed, she figured, was someone to help them. Someone close to the situation. Someone smart. Someone with nothing *else* to do all spring-break long. Someone like her.

Grabbing a sweatshirt, Alexis left her room. Now more than ever, she *had* to go on that heartbreak-cure trip.

On the morning they were due to depart, Jayne was getting ready to leave (at an obscenely early, pre-*Today Show* hour), when Doris abandoned her packing duties in mid-Gor-Tex and edged closer.

"I think Riley still has the hots for you," she said.

Before Jayne could reply, Donna spoke up. "Nonsense. Anyone can see it's Jayne who still has the hots for Riley."

Carla, Kelly, and Mitzi gasped. Five sets of eyes swerved to Jayne, pinning her with curious gazes. All before she'd had a chance to so much as assume a nonchalant demeanor. Wake up with Matt Lauer. Or sip a nonfat triple mocha extra-whip eye opener—which she desperately needed. Facing the wilderness while decaffeinated was just cruel.

"Is that *true*?" they asked.

"We've been, like, defending your honor," Carla said, "since the first time we met Riley—"

"Right after finding out what he did to you," Mitzi added.

"But if there's still something going on between you two ... ?"

Jayne forced a laugh. "Something going on? Between me and Riley? Whatever would make you think that?"

"The smoldering, be-my-love-slave looks he's been giving you all morning," Doris said.

"The electric current sizzling between you!" Donna added.

"The fact that you, like, disappeared with him last night." Carla crossed her arms. "Instead of playing Twister."

"The sexy underwear you brought"—Mitzi eyeballed the baby-blue silk thong Jayne had unpacked—"to go camping in."

"Ummm," Kelly said, deliberately looking away from the thong. "The panicky look on your face when we brought it up?"

Geez. The quiet ones were always the most perceptive.

All right, she'd just have to deal with this. After stuffing yet another foil envelope of questionable dried food into her pack, Jayne faced them. She put her hands on her hips.

"Okay. In order. Doris, Riley doesn't want me to be his 'love slave.' If he did, he'd just say so. He's a man of action, not smoldering looks."

They glanced behind her at Riley, their brows arched. "He looks pretty smoldering to me," Doris muttered.

Jayne ignored her. "Donna, any electric current around here is just my travel blow dryer, which I'm not allowed to bring with me." She shot an accusing look at the man responsible for denying her request to bring along the very sensible battery-powered styling aid she'd purchased. "And, Carla, I didn't 'disappear' with Riley last night. I merely went outside with him to iron out some details about our trip."

Such as his imminent defeat when he discovers exactly how effective my antiheartbreak techniques really are.

"Mitzi, I brought this underwear when my publicist told me I was going to an exclusive lodge in Arizona. *Before* I found out I was really going to *antifashion boot camp*"— Jayne raised her voice on this last, sending another look toward Riley. He'd insisted she wear the uncoordinated, unstylish, uncute outdoor wear everyone else would have on—"and not a spa!"

Her breakup-ees murmured sympathetically.

But Jayne wasn't finished. She couldn't be finished. Not yet. "And, Kelly . . . the only reason I might have looked panicky at discussing all this is that it means so much to me that you all know *I'm over Riley Davis!*"

At her loud declaration, the man of the moment looked up from across the room. He stuck a finger in his ear and waggled it, pretending her outburst had damaged his hearing. Then he grinned, deliberately provoking her.

"After all," Jayne went on, presenting him with her back, "how can I help any of you if I can't even help myself? If I weren't over Riley Davis, I would be a complete fraud."

"You have a point," Donna and Doris muttered.

Carla and Kelly nodded. "You're right. We're sorry."

Mitzi agreed. "Heck, I'll bet Jayne planned to have Riley guide our group on purpose," she said, "to show how well her antiheartbreak techniques work."

They murmured at that and seemed to agree such a move was really brave. "We'll try not to doubt you again."

Jayne didn't plan to give them a reason to doubt her. And after she said as much, they shared a group hug. Her breakup-ees vowed to give Riley the cold shoulder if he made any trouble for Jayne—an offer whose loyalty-driven motivation she appreciated even as she made them promise to be nice to their guide. Then Jayne got busy with her final packing . . . keeping her back deliberately turned toward Riley every minute.

Not that it mattered. She'd have sworn he was ogling her butt the whole damned time.

Having assembled everyone, Riley stood with them at the trailhead shortly after sunrise. Already, the morning had been difficult (with the exception of the time he'd spent ogling Jayne's wonderfully shaped backside, of course). He'd just barely averted a riot when he'd announced they wouldn't have time to watch Matt Lauer ("That cutie!" according to the women) and Katie Couric before leaving. He'd also been forced to negotiate a tense oatmeal-or-eggs standoff over breakfast, with a confused Gwen standing by, waiting to prepare the food. They'd finally compromised on muffins and fruit, with yogurt on the side. Just as he'd suspected, this would be a trip like no other.

Because of the chilly springtime morning, Riley had dressed in layers—tan utility pants, Timberlands, a white T-shirt, and a lightweight moss-colored zipped Polar-fleece—and had recommended Jayne and her guidance groupies do the same. Fully outfitted in his pack, he surveyed the group.

Groups, really. They'd split into three chattering sets, each containing two women plus at least one guide: Bruce and his young cousin Lance with Mitzi and Carla, Mack with Doris and Donna, Riley with Jayne and Kelly. Keeping the groups small would lessen the impact on the wilderness area they'd be traveling through, and would allow everyone to hike at an individual pace without feeling left behind. They'd meet at designated spots for meals, trailside workshops, and to set up camp each night.

All of the women carried the appropriate gear—packs loaded with food, clothing, tents and tent poles, water, first aid supplies, compasses, maps, and more. Each was dressed in layered outdoor wear. Jayne, Riley noticed, had altered hers.

Somehow—probably by swapping with the other women—she'd managed to put together an actual ensemble. And despite the clothing requirements he'd laid out, she still wore baby blue. Her wind pants were that shade; so were her hiking socks and the tank top beneath her pastel-colored V-neck fleece. Diamond studs sparkled at her ears. They were just visible when the breeze blew back her carefully styled blond hair.

He smiled. He should have known Jayne would find a way to add glamour to utilitarian hiking clothes.

She caught him watching and raised her hand. "Do we have time for coffee before we head out? I know of a place in Sedona that makes a great mocha with chocolate shavings on top."

"Oooh, good idea," one of the women said.

"Yum." Bruce smiled, subversive as usual.

"Sounds awesome," Mack said, typically cheerful.

"No way," Mitzi objected. "A mocha is at least three or four Weight Watchers points."

"It's not Zone perfect either," Carla added.

Riley seized on the only opening he had. "I'm embarrassed to put it this way, but . . . hiking burns lots of calories. After we hit the trail and your fat cells start begging for mercy, you'll be glad you skipped the mochas."

Blank faces stared back at him. He began to think he'd agreed to guide the only women in the universe who were immune to fat-cell phobia.

Then . . . "Yay! Let's go!"

Fists pumping in the air, the women charged the trail. Their guides hurried to keep up. *Whew*. First crisis averted.

Soon the rocky high-desert landscape glowed with the rising sun. Prickly pear, yucca, and agave pierced the spaces between boulders, and creosote bushes offered spots of color with their yellow blooms. At the travelers' approach, the occasional bird took flight. Dust rose beneath their footfalls, its dry scent mingling with that of the cool air.

A half-mile in, the three groups found their unique paces. Bruce and Lance took the lead with Mitzi and Carla. Riley remained in the middle with Jayne and Kelly. Mack, listening good-naturedly to the diverse opinions of Doris and Donna, brought up the rear with the sisters assigned to him. The trail turned rocky, beginning a gentle ascent.

"We'll actually be climbing up into Catsclaw Canyon," Riley explained as Jayne and Kelly examined the upward-winding trail with identical frowns. "Picture us at the tail end of a gigantic crack in the earth's surface. It will get deeper as we go in, and we'll climb higher. We're at a lower elevation here in the desert, but by the time we reach the other lodge inside the canyon—our turning point—we'll be at about fifty-five hundred feet above sea level. Flagstaff, above the rim and about an hour north of us, is at seven thousand feet."

Kelly stopped. "Where are we right now?"

"About four thousand feet."

Jayne stopped. "We have to climb fifteen hundred feet? That's like . . . I dunno, a *gazillion* steps on the StairMaster."

Riley nodded and kept going. "It's a gradual incline. You can do it."

He glanced backward. They stood there, gawping at him. Then Jayne nudged Kelly. The two women followed him.

"Sure we can do it," Jayne called. "Of course we can do it. But do we *want* to?"

"With *you?*" Kelly added.

At the surprisingly belligerent tone in her voice, Riley stopped. Kelly was usually so calm. Almost meek. Hell, she hadn't even entered into the breakfast fracas until an aggravated Bud had suggested skipping the meal altogether.

"Is something bothering you, Kelly?" he asked. "About me?"

The woman averted her eyes. She toed the trail, refusing to look at him. "Um, sort of."

Silently, he waited.

"But we don't have to talk about it right now. Maybe not ever, if you don't want to. Or . . ."

He waited some more. Patiently.

As Riley had expected, she cracked. "Okay! Stop hounding me!" Kelly waved her arms and unbalanced herself. She'd have tipped over if Jayne hadn't helped her. "It's just that . . . you shouldn't have treated Jayne the way you did. Not—not that I know the whole story, or hold you completely responsible, of course, but Jayne is a nice person, and she doesn't deserve . . . what you did. And that's all."

She shrank into herself, her chin burrowing into her collar. She clutched her pack straps. Peeked at him through her black-framed glasses. "Okay?"

Riley, wondering exactly what he'd done, cast a questioning glance at Jayne. She shrugged, biting her lip. Hell. Maybe he'd done "nothing" again without realizing it. With no further information to go on, he was forced to improvise.

"Okay," he said quietly. He waited until Kelly raised her head to look at him, then continued. "Thank you for telling me. Most people wouldn't have dared."

A small smile edged onto her mouth.

"You're uncommonly brave, Kelly. I'm glad to have you as part of my group."

Riley meant it. He could tell that criticizing him—however obliquely and confusingly—had been difficult for her. Later he'd pin down Jayne and extract the explanation he knew must exist for Kelly's low opinion of him.

Considering how best to coax Jayne into revealing that explanation, he glanced at her. She was already watching him, something close to gratitude in her face. So . . . she approved of the way he'd talked with Kelly? Interesting. She hadn't seen the half of it yet.

"I'm—I'm glad to be part of your group," Kelly said, blushing. "Thanks, Riley. You're really understanding."

Now Jayne seemed almost disgruntled. She kicked at a clod of dirt with her all-terrain shoes and crossed her arms, the very picture of a woman enduring a minor betrayal.

"No, thank *you*." He smiled at Kelly, for the first time really seeing the complicated and caring woman beneath her hunched shoulders, lowered glances, and hesitant speech. "Tell you what. How about if you lead this section?"

Kelly gasped. "Do you really think I can?"

"Sure. You nailed the compass-and-topo navigation training. And the trail's clearly marked. Have at it."

She shared an excited glance with Jayne. "Okay! Just try and keep up!"

Then she was off, briskly trotting up the trail again, leaving Riley to follow behind with Jayne. Just the two of them. Alone but for the fifty yards separating them from Kelly. Exactly as he'd planned.

He grinned, already anticipating the process of unraveling Jayne's self-help-style resistance to him. Surely it was paltry. Not up to the challenge about to present itself—the challenge of *him*. After all, he'd never believed those hocus-pocus techniques of hers really worked in the first place.

"You planned that!" Jayne accused, watching Kelly happily blaze a trail in front of them, her pack bobbing up and down with her movements. "I don't believe it."

"Believe it. When I want something, I go after it."

"Right. And what do you want now? Kelly with a sprained ankle?"

I want you, he thought. But all he said was "Kelly will be fine. She may even be more fit than you are."

He swept a contemplative glance over Jayne's body as she navigated the trail. She caught him at it and took the bait.

"She is not! And quit looking at me to compare."

"You want me to look at Kelly instead?"

Jayne's mouth thinned. "Do whatever you want," she said stubbornly. Her gaze moved again to Kelly, and she frowned.

"I can't do that while in motion. Standing up, sure. Leaning against a boulder, okay." He pretended to consider it further. "But moving down a trail—"

"What are you blathering about?"

"Doing whatever I want." Boy, she was easy to tease.

She yawned, obviously feigning boredom. "Which would be?"

"Finding out if you still sigh in that breathy, sexy way when a man undresses you. When *I* undress you. Finding out if your skin still smells like peaches and vanilla. Finding out if you still taste like—"

"What is the *matter* with you?" Jayne grabbed his arm, giving him a perplexed look. "Last night you were Mr.-Platonic-Kiss-on-the-Forehead. Today you're Sex-You-Up Sam. Which is it?"

"Riley." He pointed to himself, smiling. "Not Sam. Maybe you need a refresher on the man you're with?"

"I'm not 'with' you. I'm hiking alongside you." She set into motion again, moving with purpose.

He followed. "You'll be 'with' me. Wait and see."

"Ha."

"Ha?" He arched an eyebrow.

"Ha-*ha!*"

There she went again with the skepticism. It was enough to make a man want to remind her—demonstratively—of all the ways they'd once been compatible. In bed. On the beach. In the shower. At the movies.

Yes, the movies. Hell, a guy couldn't spend *all* his time making love to the woman he'd fallen in . . . in*to* a relationship with. Could he?

Riley jogged forward, leaping across some flat boulders to catch up with Jayne. "I'm not afraid to admit what I want. You might try it sometime."

"Ha!"

"I still want you, Jayne."

Her chin quivered.

"You want me too."

Instead of replying, she breathed deeply and then began counting in a low voice. She stared at her feet, as though mesmerized by their movement.

He couldn't help but feel hurt by her obvious inattention. "What are you doing?" Riley asked quietly.

"Moving meditation. It will help me resist you. I mean, refocus my energies."

He considered that. "Don't resist me, Jayne. We were good together once. We can be that way again."

As he said it, Riley realized exactly how much he wanted that. A second chance with Jayne. Sure, after the way she'd challenged him, that second chance might come in the form of a short-lived fling. But that would be enough for him. Enough to get Jayne out of his system once and for all. He'd keep it physical, keep it brief . . . and enjoy the hell out of it. So, he felt certain, would she.

If that weren't true, Riley would never have pursued the reunion he had in mind. He didn't believe in long commitments, but he didn't believe in using people either. Mutual satisfaction was what mattered. That, and savoring a connection for as long as it lasted.

In his world, that was never very long.

"Twenty-nine, thirty, thirty-one," she muttered, still stepping. "Thirty-two, thirty-three—"

"You can't hold out forever," he warned.

"*Watch me*," she huffed, still climbing.

Riley had to admire her determination. Also, the baby-blue hug of her wind pants against her derrière and legs. If he just once caught Jayne admiring him the way he admired her, he could die a happy man.

Until then he'd just have to show her that nobody laid down a challenge to Riley Davis . . . without having that challenge met. In spades.

Nobody.

Jayne completely lost track of her moving meditation count when Riley grinned away her "watch-me" answer to his challenge and moved in front of her to guide the way. The view was just too distracting.

His powerful strides ably demonstrated his athletic ability, honed by years of trekking the wilderness on guide jobs and nature photography assignments. His casual grace belied his size, lending Riley a surprising ease of movement that was a pleasure to watch. And his years of experience gave him a certain undeniable quality of . . . oh, heck. There was no point in playing nice here.

His butt was absolutely the finest she'd ever seen.

Admiring it, Jayne sighed. This was going to be such a difficult trip. She'd managed to give as good as she got so far this morning, but she wasn't sure how much longer she could hold out. Riley was trying every teasing trick in the book to get a reaction out of her . . . and he knew exactly which buttons to push.

Finding out if your skin still smells like peaches and vanilla.

She couldn't believe he still remembered the scent of her perfume. Its top notes *were* peaches and vanilla, combined with a little musk and a floral base. She had it custom blended at a frightful expense, reasoning that a beautiful personal ambiance was worth it.

But Riley . . . he was more of a Safeguard-and-Speed Stick kind of guy. He didn't wear cologne, didn't to her knowledge keep up on fashion and beauty trends. Couldn't— unless her perfumer had drastically misled her about the exclusivity of her personal formula—have encountered another woman with Jayne's fragrance. Could he really have remembered her that well? That fondly?

Nah, she assured herself as she navigated around a clump of cactus. *It's been almost two years. He's bluffing.*

Which was fine, except . . . except Riley *seemed* so darn sincere. His openhearted, over-the-shoulder grin as he extended a hand to help her ascend a boulder looked genuine. His concern when she stumbled a few minutes later felt real. And his conversation, as they trekked on down the desert trail in Kelly's wake, carried every indication of authentic interest.

Riley listened carefully. He offered thoughtful comments, brief though they sometimes were, given his strong-and-silent nature. He joked and laughed, amazing Jayne with his remembrances of the times they'd spent together. It seemed Riley had savored those times too . . . and as they shared their umpteenth reminiscence of the morning, she was dying to ask him the ten-thousand-dollar question:

Why did you leave me? Leave us?

The trouble was, she couldn't ask him that. Not without, Jayne feared, destroying the delicate camaraderie that had so far enabled them to travel together without breakup-workshop-unraveling antagonism. Or—even more important—without revealing the fact that she still hadn't *quite* gotten over him. Yet. So she only continued on down the trail, focusing on causing mutiny among her fat cells and on trying not to wreck her manicure by grabbing rock handholds too quickly.

Resisting Riley was completely doable, Jayne told herself. It was only a matter of miles before she'd begin to really believe it.

Nine

About two hours into their hike, the groups rendezvoused for the first trailside workshop. They met beside a scrub brush–filled gully, beneath a brilliantly blue Arizona sky, dropping packs at their feet and sinking gratefully onto handy chair-size boulders.

Or maybe that was just Jayne. She couldn't walk another step. Her feet seemed to think she'd taken them dancing in stilettos a size too small. Her improvised hiking ensemble stuck to her sweaty skin in more places than she cared to consider. And she could positively *feel* the sunshine baking down on her head, destroying the delicate balance of her blonde highlights.

When she returned to the salon for triage, Henri would probably think she'd been seeing another (incompetent) stylist behind his back. He'd sure as heck never believe Jayne had actually been *hiking*. She'd be branded a two-timer, relegated to the unfaithful client hall of shame, given the wobbly chair for appointments. This stupid outdoor adventure stuff would be the cause of her first case of salon performance anxiety.

Determinedly, she dug out a cute baby-blue bucket hat

from her pack and plunked it on her head. At least she wouldn't go down without a fight.

Riley's shadow fell over her. She glanced up from beneath her hat brim to see him offering her a drink of water. Wearily, she accepted the pop-top bottle with thanks, trying not to let their hands touch. She didn't succeed. Boy, was his skin warm. And a little golden too—the color self-tanner was meant to replicate. Also, his forearms were very nicely muscled, with just a hint of—

"Tired?" he asked.

Yipes. Ending her reverie beneath his all-too-knowing gaze, Jayne raised her chin.

"I just need a little break, that's all." Because really, even while power shopping she stopped for the occasional strawberry smoothie or sushi snack. Everyone knew better than to simply march, grueling-journey style, from Nordstrom to Macy's. "How about you?"

"Fine." He watched as she sipped from the bottle. Then he nodded toward her feet. "Shoes holding up okay?"

"Sure. It's my nonadjustable feet that are the problem."

He frowned and hunkered down. Before she realized what he was up to, Riley caught hold of her foot and gently cradled it on the hard plane of his thigh. He bent lower, examining the fit of her unflattering brown ATSes: all-terrain shoes.

Insanely, Jayne immediately wished she were wearing something seductive on her feet. Red T-straps. Toe-cleavage pumps. Even a pair of plastic-daisy-decorated thongs. All the better to impress the love-'em-and-leave-'em hunk staring at her brown-shrouded tootsies. But that was ridiculous.

None of the sexy shoes she'd wished for would even coordinate with baby-blue wind pants.

Riley rubbed his thumb over her shoe's toe box. "Does it hurt when I do this?"

"No, it tickles."

His mouth curved into a smile. A wonderful, manly,

aren't-you-adorable smile. But he went on examining the fit of her shoes with an air of expertise, and his next words were serious.

"Did you break in these shoes like you were supposed to?"

"Yes!" She had. Back home, she'd worn them to Union Square and the Embarcadero several times. There was nothing like window-shopping in a pair of ATSes while munching a PowerBar to make a girl feel terrifically fit. "They've been fine until now. Really."

"You probably have a pebble stuck in there." Riley eased her foot onto the ground again and straightened. "You might try undressing from head to toe until you find it."

"But it's only my shoe that's the problem."

"Hey, it was worth a try." He winked, then headed across the gully to welcome Mack, Doris, and Donna, who'd just joined Bruce and Lance and Mitzi and Carla.

Shaking her head—and smiling despite herself—Jayne watched Riley talk with the other adventure travelers. There was something about him that captured her imagination. There always had been. Maybe it was the knowledge that he saw more exotic locales in a single month than most people did in a lifetime. Or the realization that he could probably MacGyver his way out of the middle of nowhere with nothing more than a roll of duct tape and a postage stamp.

Possibly, it was the good-natured way Riley accepted all his vagabond's adventures as though they were nothing more than ho-hum ordinary life to him. Or the patient way he'd been teaching her breakup-ees to sample that adventurous life themselves. Whatever it was, the fascination she'd felt upon meeting him was gradually stealing over her all over again. Jayne wasn't sure how to combat it.

Waitaminute. Yes, she was! Back at the lodge, she had the *Heartbreak 101* book to prove it. Sure, at the moment the primary copies of her best seller were stashed beside her forbidden battery-powered blow dryer, her plastic travel-ready champagne glasses, her baby-blue faux-mink mini pillow, her real wardrobe, and the latest issue of *Vogue*. But the knowledge that had enabled her to write that book was here, in her head. Jayne was fully prepared to use it.

She lunged to her feet. "Time for the first workshop, everyone!" she cried. Then, more quietly, "Ouch. I forgot to check for that pebble."

Riley crossed his arms and leaned against the Humvee-size boulder at his back. Beside him, Bruce and Lance did the same. Red-haired Mack only stared at the women just beyond them, a quizzical look on his face.

"What do you s'pose they're doing?" Bruce asked.

"Don't know." Riley shook his head. "This do-it-yourself psychobabble stuff is all new to me. All I know is, we're supposed to stop twice a day to let Jayne work her antiheartbreak voodoo."

Gathered in a circle amid the desert landscape, Jayne's guidance groupies watched her expectantly. Each woman held something small and round in her hand, something printed in a leopard pattern. While the men watched, Jayne smiled at the group.

"Ready?" she asked.

They nodded, raising the things in their hands with a practiced, synchronized gesture.

"Okay . . . primp!"

Suddenly, powder puffs were wielded. Glittery, fluffy pink powders wafted in the air like a sweet-smelling cloud. Then lipsticks came out. Mouths puckered. Shades of red and tawny pink gleamed beneath the sunlight. Minutes later, as quickly as it had begun, the confusing ritual ended.

"If you look good, you feel good!" the women shouted in unison. They levered upward, high-fived each other, then sat down in their circle again, all smiles.

The men gawked at them. Then at each other. Their open-mouthed expressions said it all. There were no words to describe the weirdness of this.

Lance was just young and cocky enough to try anyway. "That's whack," he said, and schlumped off to play the Game Boy Advance he'd insisted on packing in.

"So *that's* what they do when they disappear into the ladies' room together!" Bruce said. "Whoa. Who knew?"

"Synchronized makeup." Mack smiled, turning up his palms. "Cool! I guess you learn something new every day."

Riley felt less sanguine. He'd been watching carefully. If this was an example of Jayne's antiheartbreak techniques, they were even more incomprehensible than he'd thought. They were downright perplexing. But on the other hand . . . they couldn't possibly work either. He felt his shoulders relax.

"First up," Jayne announced, "Reverse Romeo Reflexology!"

Huh? He shook his head, in case he hadn't heard correctly. And then, just when Riley thought things couldn't get any more bizarre . . .

"Wait!" someone cried. The sound of heavy footfalls came from the creosote-bordered trail beyond their rendezvous point. There was a flash of bright-colored trail clothes, the glare of sunshine off purple braces, and then, "I want to try this one too!"

Alexis burst over the gully in a scramble of teenage arms and legs. Panting, she slung her pack to the ground. She grinned, hands on scrawny hips. Everyone stared at her.

Including Riley. "Alexis! What are you doing here?"

"Trying a heartbreak-recovery workshop, looks like." She grinned at her uncle, confident in her certainty that now, two miles away from the Hideaway Lodge, he wouldn't send her back. "Did I miss anything?"

She stepped into the circle of women, waving and greeting them. They made room for her to sit.

"You missed the turn back home," Riley said, striding forward. "You can't come on this trip. Your gramps and nana will be worried about you."

"I left 'em a note."

"Your mother will be worried about you."

"Puh-leeze." She rolled her eyes. "Nana can prop up the phone on a pillow at noon, then hang it up five minutes later. My mom will never know the difference."

Riley feared Alexis was right. Sadly. Still . . . "You don't need a heartbreak cure."

A thirteen-year-old's world-weary sigh was like none other. "And with attitudes like *that* around me, I'll never get one either."

Huh? Riley frowned. He glanced at Jayne, wondering what she thought of all this. A feminine perspective might be just what he needed.

She gazed thoughtfully at his niece, her head tilted sideways. *Uh-oh.* Riley recognized that look. It was the lost-puppy look. The same look Jayne had gotten on her face the day the two of them had discovered a scrawny, shivering, soaking-wet mutt abandoned on the beach near the Cliff House. And although this time Jayne was unlikely to wrap Alexis in her sweater and carry her on her lap all the way home for a bath and some puppy chow . . . well, she obviously meant to help all the same.

Jayne was generous to a fault. He'd almost forgotten that about her. The only thing that could whisk her out of her social whirl was someone who needed her—a friend, a stray mutt, a homeless saxophone player. She was perfectly willing to help anyone out of a tight squeeze, whether that meant giving up her time, surrendering her fur-free sofa, or tossing her last dollar bill into a hat on the street corner.

Sure, sometimes she offered the saxophone player a spritz of CK One to erase the *parfum du boulevard*. And she grilled the prospective puppy adopters pretty hard. But all in all,

Jayne was a real sucker for a hard-luck case. Alexis's dilemma looked like no exception.

"Sure, you can have a heartbreak cure if you want one," Jayne told the girl, offering a reassuring smile. From the depths of her pack, she retrieved a spare leopard-print compact and handed it to Alexis. "Welcome to the group."

His niece accepted the compact solemnly. Her eyes shined as she ran her fingers over its glossy surface. Uncertainly, she glanced sideways at the group's guru.

Jayne nodded. "Go ahead. It's yours now."

Alexis breathed out. With trembling fingers, she worked the catch of the compact as the other women watched.

Riley watched too, feeling out of his depth. They were speaking some language he didn't understand—a language made up of feminine gestures, coded compacts, and makeup. He was about to protest, to tell Alexis she had to go back to the lodge right after the workshop anyway, when his niece opened her new compact . . . and slowly smiled at herself in the mirror.

He stilled. He could just glimpse Alexis's reflection from where he stood, and she looked beautiful. Gawky and self-conscious and painfully yearning . . . but beautiful. Riley didn't have the heart to end what had so tentatively begun.

He cleared his throat. "You're carrying your own pack," he told her gruffly. "Setting up your own tent too. I know you know how."

She glanced upward. The gratitude in her eyes made him a hero. "Thanks, Uncle Riley. I *knew* you'd understand."

Riley couldn't take any more. He waved his arm in a curt gesture. "Bruce, Mack, you're in charge. I'm off to check conditions up ahead."

Then he headed for the trail, leaving everyone temporarily behind him.

* * *

When Riley returned, the rocky clearing was pretty much as he'd left it. The gully still twisted through the scrub brush awaiting a good hard rain. The boulders still baked beneath the increasingly warm sunshine. But the unexpected scent of—eucalyptus?—hung in the air. And the sight that greeted him ... the antics of his adventure travel group ... well, something bizarre was going on, that was for sure.

The women reclined on various flat-topped boulders, their packs filling in for pillows. They'd abandoned their hiking boots and all-terrain shoes; the footwear stood to the side like a row of patient brown beagles. Poly-blend hiking socks dangled from their footless uppers like lolling tongues.

Nearest to Riley, Carla sat cross-legged. She grabbed hold of her foot and eased it into what had to be an advanced yoga position, then began massaging it. "I no longer want Paolo," she chanted. "I am free of cravings for Paolo."

"Marty is history," Doris said beside her, looking as though she were concentrating fiercely. Her sister Donna's foot was propped on her knee. She massaged its sole with brisk efficiency. "We no longer need a handyman."

"*Never* needed a handyman," Donna contradicted. "Ouch! Not so hard, Doris!"

Shaking his head, Riley continued farther into their temporary camp. Near the original "primping" circle, Jayne sat demonstrating what had to be the Reverse Romeo reflexology technique to Alexis. Both of them were barefoot, slathered from the ankles down in the lotion that must have been the source of the Vicks VapoRub smell lingering in the air. They waved sticky fingers as he passed.

Had he stepped into the Twilight Zone? A place where foot rubs passed for antiheartbreak techniques and nieces got away with whatever the hell they felt like just because their uncles were too mush-hearted to turn them down? Frowning slightly, Riley headed for the Humvee-size boulder that had been the Man Zone this morning. Maybe if he found Mack and Bruce and Lance it would restore some normalcy to this moment. They could talk about football. Doritos. Big-screen TVs.

Whoa. Riley jerked to a stop. He boggled.

To his left, Bruce was massaging the feet of a chanting Mitzi. Catching Riley watching him, the rascal grinned. Probably, Bruce had been laying the moves on Mitzi all morning, and she'd given him pity foot-rub duty. Pathetic. So much for the football talk. Maybe Mack . . .

But Mack was sitting cheerfully on the ground in front of Kelly, rubbing her big toes. He hummed. Kelly chanted something about ". . . Tim. And, I guess, Mrs. Tim?" The two of them looked cozy as a manicurist and a favorite nail art junkie. Unbelievable. So much for the Doritos talk.

Feeling almost desperate now, Riley spotted Lance and strode toward the teenager. Surely he hadn't fallen victim to whatever . . . thing . . . had happened here. But when Riley reached him, he found the boy's dreamy-eyed gaze locked on—Alexis! Terrific. So much for the big-screen-TV talk.

The whole world had gone wacko.

"What the hell is this?" Riley said. "I leave you people alone for a few minutes—"

"Forty-five minutes," Jayne said, consulting her watch.

"—and—" He faltered, momentarily discombobulated by the realization that she might actually have missed him. Then, "For a few minutes, and what happens? An ankles-down orgy!"

Alexis perked up interestedly.

He took three long steps toward her and slapped his palms over her ears. "You ought to be ashamed of yourselves."

As a group, they were unabashed. Several people shrugged.

"It's not, like, just ankles-down," Carla informed him. "It's hands too. Hand reflexology."

Riley glared at Jayne. *You perpetuated this,* his frown said.

To his aggravation, she seemed to be holding back a grin. "It's just my Reverse Romeo Reflexology technique. You see, areas in the hands and feet correspond with areas in the body. Heels to intestines, mid-soles to solar plexus, big toes to brains—"

"You'd need big toes *for* brains to believe this works!"

Jayne drew herself up. "This is an ancient and respected discipline. It helps bring the body into balance by unblocking vital energy passageways. I added a new spin by including a chant designed to help release thoughts of the person who broke your heart. If you're too closed-minded to give it a chance . . . well, that's your loss, Riley."

He scoffed.

Alexis yanked his hands from her ears. "Wait till I tell Gramps you let me go on an orgy!"

Doris, Donna, and Mitzi snickered. Given a scowl from Riley, they slapped on straight faces.

"Gramps doesn't need to know about any of this," he told his niece. It might break Bud's heart to know the family's old-fashioned, tradition-driven travel adventure trips were being used for . . . *this*. His grandfather still thought ordinary therapy sessions were for "pantywaists and crybabies." Riley didn't know what he'd make of group reflexology.

A giggle came from just behind him. Riley turned. A squirming, smiling Mitzi and leering Bruce froze beneath his gaze.

"He was tickling my foot," she complained, pointing.

"You liked it, baby," Bruce said, laughing.

More giggles. *Oh, boy.*

The whole scenario reminded Riley of something else.

"And *you,*" he said, rounding on Bruce, and Mack too. "What do you think you're doing, rubbing on your travelers' feet like demented cabana boys? You're professional guides!"

They scrambled upright with satisfying speed. "Sorry, boss," they said in unison.

"We didn't have anything else to do," Mack added.

Bruce nodded. Even Lance transferred his lovesick gaze from Alexis long enough to agree. All three of them defended the scene Riley had walked in on.

Stupid as it was, to Riley their actions felt like a betrayal. It was as though they'd gone over to the other side—the feminine side—leaving him all on his own. *Alone.* He should have been used to it. Hell, he should have liked it. But instead, it bothered him.

"You need something to do during these little trailside workshop sessions?" he asked, eyes narrowed.

The three men nodded. From the sidelines, Jayne glared—probably at his use of the word "little" to describe her techniques. He wished he hadn't, but it was too late now. He'd do better next time.

"I'll give you something to do," Riley told them. "From now on, when Jayne's conducting workshops from her *bestselling book*—" *Ha!* said the raised eyebrow he offered her.

She smiled, happier.

"—we'll be . . . we'll be . . ." He searched for a big finale. "Conducting workshops of our own!"

What? Had that actually come out of his mouth?

Immediately, everyone started talking. Riley stood amid the murmurs, hands defiantly on his hips. He faced them all down. Sure, he'd come up with the idea under pressure. But now that it was out there . . . hey, it wasn't half bad.

"Counterworkshops," he explained further, speaking to be heard above the gradually quieting chatter. "*Male* workshops. Designed with the, uh, male perspective in mind."

He drew a breath and smiled, feeling better already. Sure. This could work. Why not?

This time it was Jayne's turn to scoff. "You're an amateur. You don't even know what you're doing."

"I'll learn as I go."

They all stared at him—the women dubiously, the men warily.

"It'll be fun. Like bungee jumping. Or white-water rafting."

Mack, Bruce, and Lance relaxed. The women's mouths gaped even wider.

Riley rubbed his hands together, feeling almost cheerful about this new way to pass the time while Jayne worked her magic. A few goofy, macho workshops . . . sure. What could possibly go wrong?

Alexis shook her head. "It'll never work, Uncle Riley. You're *way* too much of a loner to lead workshops."

Silence fell. He glanced at her, stricken. Okay, so maybe he spent a lot of time alone. That didn't make him a loner. He just . . . wasn't comfortable around a lot of people. That didn't mean he couldn't lead workshops if he wanted to. And yet . . .

Maybe she's right, a tiny voice whispered inside him. He'd spent so long on the outside. So long trusting movement instead of stability, believing in distance instead of closeness.

No, Riley told himself. What did Alexis know anyway? The poor kid's idea of closeness was a five-minute call to her phone-challenged divorced mother.

Yours used to be plastering your suitcase with travel decals identical to your parents', that voice prodded. *So they'd remember you belonged with them each time you moved.*

Riley shook off the memories. "I can do it," he said. "You'll see. Now let's hit the trail."

He signaled for everyone to put on their shoes or boots and load up their gear. "We've got miles to go before tonight's big campout."

Ten

Riley hadn't been kidding, Jayne realized right about the time her leg muscles began twitching to an involuntary hip-hop beat. *He actually meant for them to hike several actual miles before camping for the night.*

They'd stopped around noon for lunch—sandwiches and juice eaten amid even craggier rocks than had set the scene for her first workshop. Then they'd continued onward, their groups in the same lead-middle-rear order—this time with Alexis joining Jayne and Riley and Kelly.

For most of the day, Jayne had actually felt pretty good about things, increasingly confident in her ability to handle the hike and to be a good role model for her breakup-ees. Now that it had begun, their adventure felt easier than she'd expected. It turned out, to her relief, that she possessed stamina she hadn't even known about. Her tired feet had rebounded, thanks to the reflexology, and so had she. She could hike for hours!

In gratitude, Jayne blessed the spinning, kick boxing, and power yoga classes she'd taken for years at the gym. She vowed to kiss her treadmill when she returned to civilization.

She smugly informed Riley that maybe she *wasn't* in such bad shape after all.

But then the afternoon struck. And with it came her usual energy drag—the one Jayne typically combated with a caramel frappuccino and a flip through the latest *In Style* magazine. Out here in the dust and the cactus and the boulders, a nice relaxing Starbucks break wasn't so easy to come by.

To make matters worse, it was her turn to navigate. Craving caffeine, Jayne stopped in the shadow of a rock overhang and squinted at the scenery around them.

"Need help reading the topo?" Riley asked, stopping beside her.

His presence immediately sparked up something inside her. Something fizzy and feminine and better left ignored. It only got worse when he unfastened his pack straps, pulled off his Polarfleece, and edged nearer wearing only a close-fitting white crew neck with his trail pants. Eyeballing his muscles, that old "Wow, have you been working out?" line came to mind—except Jayne knew Riley's muscles were the real thing. The result of strenuous activity and wilderness training.

"No, I don't need help reading the topo." She frowned. Turned around the topographical map, which *may* have been upside down. It was hard to tell with all those squiggles. "I'm doing fine, thanks. How's Alexis?"

"Better now that she's blackmailed me into keeping her on the trip. She threatened to tell Gwen the 'orgy story' if I made her go back to the lodge."

Jayne smiled. She didn't believe for a second that blackmail was the reason Riley had let his niece stay with them. She'd seen the look on his face when Alexis had asked to stay—and the affection in his eyes when he'd watched her open her new leopard-print compact. No matter how hard he sometimes seemed, Riley was a real softie at heart.

Of course, he'd sooner chew Timberlands than admit it, she was sure.

"How's Kelly?" she asked, giving the map a quarter turn.

"Taking a nature break. I told her this might be a good time, since you might be a while reading that map."

Jayne made a face. She still hadn't reconciled herself to the idea of a "ladies' room" that contained dirt, rocks, and scrub brush instead of vanities, mirrors, and liquid pink soap.

"Well, I won't be *that* long," she told him, peering at her compass. She looked up. "The trail we want is that way."

She pointed. He looked. She watched his face carefully but couldn't tell from his expression whether she was within ten miles of the right trail.

She bit her lip. Pointed in another direction. "I mean, that way."

Riley looked again, his expression inscrutable. "Sure?"

Heck, no. Help me! But she'd never accepted help from the other men in her life—her father and three bossy brothers in particular. Not if she could, well, help it. She wasn't about to start now. She could do it. She'd navigated all the breakupees to downtown Sedona shopping, hadn't she?

"Of course," she said. "That's the path."

"Okay, then." He strapped on his pack again, then made a show of double-checking the fit of hers. His hands whisked over her shoulders, her arms, her waist; they curled around her chest straps and checked for snugness. "Let's go wait for Kelly."

He moved away, taking with him the warmth of his touch. Jayne felt as though she'd been flirtatiously frisked . . . and then denied the promise of a rousing strip search to follow. She didn't *want* to want Riley to continue.

But she did all the same.

Ahead Riley paused beside Alexis at the junction of the trail Jayne, as navigator, had chosen. In this part of the wilderness area, various hiking paths crisscrossed randomly. They intersected, ran parallel to each other, went their own

way, and veered into the distance, only to meet up again
later. The scenery was no help in getting oriented either.
To Jayne's Pacific-coast eye, everything looked alien and
prickly and deserty.

Kelly caught up, sheepishly wrapping a gardening trowel
in plastic and stuffing it into her pack. Jayne shuddered.
Suddenly, she longed for a posh powder room with a comfortable antiseptic commode and a jumbo roll of squeezable
Charmin. But no mirror. She didn't want to contemplate
what she looked like until she was in a position to repair
the damage.

However, she told herself, when the going got tough, the
tough . . . put on some lip gloss and soldiered on. Jayne
applied some Cranberry Crush, flipped her hair over her
shoulders, and rejoined the group. They trouped onward,
buddied up, occasionally switching conversational partners.
It was almost fun at times. Like a moving slumber party
minus the popcorn and the Clooney-vision . . . and plus the
male perspective.

Reminded of Riley's vow to conduct male-perspective
workshops concurrent with hers along the trail, Jayne shook
her head. She couldn't imagine what kinds of things he,
Bruce, Lance, and Mack would come up with. Better Bonding Through Beer, maybe. Or "I'll Call You" 101. After
all, she hadn't subtitled her book *Getting Over the Good-
Bye Guys* for nothing.

Eventually, she glimpsed a group of four hikers traveling
toward them in the opposite direction. Using her new knowledge of trail etiquette (and feeling oddly proud of it), Jayne
moved to the side to let them pass. So did Riley, Kelly, and
Alexis.

"Hey, fancy meeting you here!" At the head of the group,
Mack approached, trailed by Lance, Doris, and Donna. As
usual, he looked positively merry, if a little confused. "How
come you're going the wrong way?"

Oh, no. "Wrong way?"

"Yeah. We've been trailing you for the past hour or so. I figured we'd catch up, but not this soon." He turned to his group and high-fived them. "We rock!"

"We're ... *sight-seeing*," Riley told his fellow guide. "You'd better take the middle position. We'll be right behind you."

Mack nodded.

"Hi, Alexis," Lance said shyly.

Alexis stuck her hands in her pockets, elbows turned out crookedly. She nodded. "Hey."

"Your, um, braces look nice and purple today."

Alexis's brow furrowed. "Like, *huh*?"

Jayne saw an amused look pass between Riley and Mack.

"Come on, sport," Mack said as though that shared look had been a signal of some kind. He slung his arm around Lance's skinny shoulders. "No sense using up all your best lines right off."

They hiked away, Lance casting backward looks at Alexis. Alexis rolled her eyes and stared at the ground, blushing.

Watching them leave, Jayne drooped. "How long have you known?" she demanded, turning to Riley.

"That you were going the wrong way?" He shrugged. "From the minute you mistook that gully for a butte on the topo and veered onto the parallel trail. I knew you'd figure it out eventually."

She goggled. "You let me lead us in circles on purpose?"

"You weren't doing it on purpose."

"I meant *you!* You purposely let me screw up."

He put his hand on her shoulder. "It's okay. You did fine. Really. This is the only way to learn."

Alexis and Kelly nodded sympathetically. "We didn't mind," Kelly said.

"Yeah." Alexis nodded. "Once I navigated me and Uncle Riley into a cow pasture up near Munds Park. Trust me, he was *way* madder to step in cow doo than he is right now."

They gave her compassionate smiles. Compassionate, she-doesn't-know-any-better smiles. Jayne felt like crying. In fact, she *was* crying. On the inside. Her throat tightened and her eyes watered. She had to blink like a wanna-be mascara model to keep from letting the tears fall.

She had to explain. Riley's "we were sight-seeing" attempt to cover for her was sweet, but Jayne couldn't allow him to let her off the hook.

"Thanks. It's just that"—she swallowed hard, her hand fisted on the useless (to her) topographical map—"there aren't any landmarks out here. Everything looks the same without a Gap on this corner and a McDonald's on that corner and a bunch of street signs in between. You know?"

They all nodded.

"I'm sorry, everybody," Jayne said. This time, a few tears did fall. She brushed them away with the back of her hand, then glanced up. "I thought I could do it. I didn't mean to put us behind."

"It's not a race," Riley told her.

"I don't care *where* I am as long as I don't miss your next workshop," Alexis added. "They can't start without you."

"I enjoyed the scenery," Kelly insisted loyally. "Twice."

"Oh, you guys!" Gratefully, Jayne sniffed. She waved her arms, urging everyone forward for a thank-you hug—even Riley, with his stiff what's-a-group-hug shoulders. "I'm so glad we're all together! You're the best!"

They blubbered companionably for a few minutes, being mutually empathetic and sharing "when I got lost" stories. All except Riley, of course. He ducked out of the group hug as soon as the initial contact ended.

When Jayne looked up, he stood near a patch of cactus, his shoulders rigid. His lonesome profile turned outward. He looked hard as stone, competent and strong and . . . alone. Alone in a way that tugged at Jayne's heart and made her want to go to him.

She held herself steady, knowing she was only kidding herself to think Riley needed her.

Once upon a time he hadn't been alone. He'd been with her, and he'd been happy—or at least Jayne had believed he was. What, she wondered now, was the real story?

Riley slung his pack to the ground, grateful to release its weight from his back for a while. He'd never have allowed any of the women to carry as much as he did, not because he believed women were any less competent, but just because he was trained for this and they weren't. Also because his mother (ardent environmental activist that she was) had taken the time to ensure her son understood cultural concerns as well—chivalry toward women chief among them.

Riley still opened doors for ladies. He still held out their chairs, and he wasn't opposed to letting a woman have the last word either. He still carried the heaviest load, and he watched out for the women in his care. Even, sometimes, when they didn't want him to . . . like Jayne.

He'd known damn well she wouldn't let him help her read the topos today. He'd known it the same way he'd known she'd catch her breath when he touched her. The same way he'd known she'd kiss him back when he kissed her. He knew *her.* Jayne was stubborn. Independent-minded. Proud.

In those ways, Riley figured she was a lot like him. She needed to live her mistakes before their risks turned real for her. He didn't mind a couple of extra miles of trail-walking. It was all part of being a guide. He only wished she hadn't felt so upset about it in the end.

But that was over with now. Now the other guides and adventure travelers milled around the rocky clearing just beyond Riley's spot. Now it was almost time for another antiheartbreak-workshop session. Now wind snaked down his neck and lifted his shirt from his sweaty back. He relished the cooling sensation.

He would not, Riley thought, relish the next workshop quite as much.

Idly, he surveyed the obligatory pre-workshop "primp" session. It had to serve some purpose, but he was clueless as to what it was. Was it workshop foreplay?

"Okay, ladies." When she'd finished her lipstick, Jayne stepped to the middle of the clearing with an air of purpose. "It's time for the Memorabilia Mash Mambo!"

Eagerly, the women put away their leopard-print compacts. Intrigued in spite of himself, Riley watched. The other men did too. They drifted toward his place gradually, their gazes fixed on the workshop group.

Jayne perched on a rock, somehow managing to look like a leggy blonde pinup girl despite the trail dust and rustic setting. It was in her attitude. She wore carefree glamour cheerfully, the way other women wore new shoes. Her girly-girl ways charmed him. They always had, even when they puzzled the hell out of him.

"Did each of you bring a memento of the relationship you're here to get over?" she asked. "Something representative of your good-bye guy?"

The women nodded. They brandished various items—a ring, a letter, a dried flower, movie ticket stubs, a music CD.

" 'Best of the Do-Wop Hits'?" Jayne raised her eyebrows at Mitzi. "Really?"

Mitzi popped her gum. She nodded. "Me and Rodney's 'song' was 'Shoo Doo Be Doo.' We worked in one of those fifties-style diners together." She gave the CD a longing look.

"Okay. A CD is just fine." Jayne patted her hand. "Here's what we're going to do," she told the group. "The purpose of this workshop is to remember your relationship, celebrate your relationship, and then put it in its place. I'm handing each of you a waterproof, rip-proof Tyvek envelope. You'll use these later.''

They each accepted their envelopes solemnly.

''After we finish this technique, remember that I want your feedback, okay? These are all potential chapters in my upcoming hands-on breakup guide workbook. I need to know how well each of the techniques work. All your opinions are important to me.''

They nodded. Even Alexis, who'd withdrawn . . . a Cinnabon wrapper? . . . from her pack. Riley cocked his head, curious.

''We're all set, then.'' Jayne stood, her movements purposeful and her attitude professional. Riley couldn't help being impressed. ''I wanted to bring a CD player for this particular workshop, but *somebody*''—her meaningful gaze pinned him as the nefarious *somebody*—''wouldn't let me pack in a boom box. So I guess we'll just have to hum some mambo music. First, I'll demonstrate the technique. I just need a—oh, shoot! I forgot to bring my demonstration memento.''

She bit her lip, looking around—evidently for a substitute breakup ''memento.'' Ever willing to help, Riley stepped forward. ''Here,'' he called, grabbing the first thing that came to mind and tossing it to her.

His Swiss Army knife.

Jayne caught it. She fumbled it first, like a shortstop bobbling an infield bunt, but she caught it. Then she peered into her cupped palms to see what it was.

That was the moment Riley remembered. He remembered using his knife's corkscrew to open wine on a date with Jayne. Remembered using the wood-saw blade to slice French bread on their oceanside picnics. Remembered Jayne using the nail file to repair her chipped manicure . . . remembered kissing her and then carrying her to bed, all because she'd looked so cute while concentrating on the repair job.

Too late, he remembered that that knife had been a part of too many damned memories of their time together.

He remembered using the magnifying glass to find a lost sequin from Jayne's dress. He remembered using it to cut off clothing tags for her after she returned home all flushed and excited after a shopping spree. He remembered using the built-in ballpoint . . . to tell her good-bye.

Hell. How could he have been so stupid?

She gazed across the distance separating them. Remembrance filled her face. That, and sadness. Riley felt like the biggest kind of jerk. A thoughtless jerk. He stepped forward to apologize.

Just then Jayne tossed the folded knife in the air. She caught it with a jaunty gesture, a wobbly smile on her face.

"Thanks, Riley." Above her forced smile, her gaze flashed over him, blue and dangerous. "This will be perfect."

Uh-oh. He was pretty sure his Swiss Army knife was indestructible. But then, it had never come up against an ex-girlfriend with a point to prove either.

He offered a carefree wave and a nod. Jayne didn't need to know he sort of cherished that knife. Just like she didn't need to know exactly how few possessions he owned. Riley didn't care about *things*. He cared about experiences. About the adrenaline rush of adventure and the reassuring familiarity of staying on the move. She couldn't take *those* things away from him.

He'd already proven that by leaving her, hadn't he? *Before* she'd fully tempted him into settling down, trusting, changing.

"First, the celebration," Jayne told her guidance groupies, who watched avidly. "Hold your piece of relationship memorabilia, and then . . . mambo."

Unselfconsciously, she started humming. Holding his army knife in her hand, she began to dance. Her hips swayed in the mambo, her feet kicked up little puffs of dust, her eyes closed as her head fell back. Her baby-blue hat tumbled to the ground. Jayne lost herself in her demonstration. Her body moved lithely, her lush honey-colored hair flowing in the breeze.

"She's an excellent dancer," Mack told Riley in a low voice, nodding. "Very uninhibited."

"Yeah." Bruce nudged him. "Hey, this workshop stuff could be pretty good."

Even Lance looked up from his Game Boy. "Whoa."

It was hard for Riley to drag his gaze from Jayne's sassy little hip thrusts, but he did it. All for the sake of scowling them into submission.

"Sorry," they mumbled, then went back to watching.

After less than a minute, the dance ended. Jayne opened her eyes to retrieve her fallen hat, and all the women applauded. Bruce stuck his fingers in his mouth to whistle. Riley deterred him with a jab to his rib cage.

"Thanks," she said when the applause died down, cheeks pink with pleasure. "That was just a demonstration, of course. Your own personal mambos can go on as long as needed. Then the next step." Jayne brandished her Tyvek envelope. "Mashing."

With enthusiasm, she thrust the knife into the bag. She ripped the protective strip from the adhesive, dropped the bag onto the ground, and closed the envelope with a stomp from her shoe. She bent over to retrieve it.

Bruce nodded, grinning. His ogling reflexes seemed to be having a field day. "This workshop is awesome. Wait'll they're *all* doing it!"

Riley considered punching him in the nose. He settled for telling him to shut up, then began planning his first macho counterworkshop. After all, he'd said he'd do it. He was a man of his word.

Jayne raised the sealed envelope over her head. *"Voilà!* By the time your memorabilia is stowed in your envelope, you'll have put to rest a big chunk of your memories too.

And when you're ready to revisit them someday, they'll be there for you. Safe and sound.''

"Yay!" All the women lunged to their feet, ready to mambo and mash their memorabilia.

"This is our cue to exit." Riley angled his head sideways, motioning for the men to follow him. "We've got our own workshop to conduct."

They trouped toward a distant set of boulders. Bruce cast a longing glance backward. "Will our workshop have dancing women?"

Riley shook his head. "Eyes front and center, mambo boy. Let's give the ladies some privacy."

"Did you bring one of your super-duper cameras, by any chance?" Bruce persisted. "One with a telephoto lens and a tripod and crystal-clear imaging?"

Riley always carried a camera. Leaving it with his gear in his battered Suburban home-on-wheels was like leaving a chunk of himself behind.

"No," he said, foot tapping helplessly in a way Bud would have had a field day with. "I'm not here to take pictures."

"Shit, Riley. I thought you were my friend!"

"I am." He grinned at Bruce's disgruntled expression. "That's why I'm not taking pictures of the women for you. I'd like you to make it back from this trip alive."

Lance and Mack chuckled. Then they all picked up the pace toward their chosen spot, ready to workshop themselves into complete Riley-led macho-ness.

Eleven

The sunshine made Jayne squint and pull her Gap hat lower as she approached the place she'd seen Riley and the men disappear to. She'd finished her workshop and had helped all the women pack up their gear afterward. All that remained now was finding their guides. And accomplishing one additional solo task that she wasn't quite looking forward to.

As she rounded a tall boulder, a lizard scurried away. Jayne shrieked and stopped dead, her heart pounding. She searched her mind for any wildlife shows she might have seen on TV, shows that explained whether or not lizards were carnivorous, poisonous, or in any other way dangerous.

Nothing came to mind. She remembered that she avoided wildlife shows because she couldn't stand watching the big critters munch the little critters while a TV host yammered on about "the circle of life." That, in Jayne's opinion, was just plain mean.

Movement to the right, just above her head, caught her eye.

"You probably gave that poor little gecko a heart attack," Riley said, looking down from the top of the rocky overhang beside her. "Come on up—if you can spare the time from terrorizing innocent lizards."

"Is it gone?" She searched the ground.

"It's gone." His head and torso disappeared from view, and his voice sounded farther away. "There are some foot- and handholds off to your right."

Jayne frowned. His teasing reminded her of things. Things she'd rather forget. *Had forgotten.* Like her widowed father's laughter when ten-year-old Jayne had baited her hook with gummy worms on the annual family fishing trip. Like her older brothers' hoots and hollers when she'd failed to dribble, bat, or catch a ball.

Well, she'd caught Riley's Swiss Army knife today, that was for sure. And that was what had brought her here. The sooner she finished what she had to do, the better.

She found the crevices and helper boulders Riley had mentioned. With a little effort, Jayne made it to the top of his gigantic rock. There, she clutched the knife she intended to return to him . . . and stared.

Bathed in sunlight and completely shirtless, Riley lay sprawled on the slablike surface of the rock. He'd pillowed his head with his discarded shirt and fleece. His attitude was relaxed, his finely muscled body amazing, his expression peaceful, as though he were asleep and dreaming a fabulous dream.

He cracked open one eye and caught her gawking. "Nice view, huh?"

It was horribly arrogant of him. She'd be the first to admit that. But he did have a point. Jayne whisked her gaze from the intriguing span of nakedness visible between his rippled abs and the waistband of his low-slung pants. *Wow.* Would fanning herself with her hat be too obvious?

"Your pants are a little wrinkly," she said, trying to sound nonchalant. "But otherwise I guess you look—"

His grin was all too knowing. "I meant the view of the countryside."

"Oh. That's nice too." *Too? Arrgh!*

Riley's grin broadened. His watchful patience was as much a part of him as his thick dark hair, wicked hazel eyes, and body made for mischief. She wished she were immune to all of those things. Starting now.

But she wasn't. Obviously. She had to save face.

"So, where are the rest of the guys?" Jayne put her hands in the back pockets of her wind pants and looked around for the other guides. "Aren't you supposed to be conducting some macho guy workshop for them right now?"

"I am."

His body remained relaxed. He closed his eyes again, seeming to enjoy the whisper of the breeze against his skin. Probably, he was. Riley had always been a sensualist. She couldn't help but imagine how the sun felt on his partially nude body, how the wind tickled, how the rocks provided a rough counterpoint against his back. How *she* would feel lowering herself to straddle him, taking off her shirt to rub her breasts against his naked chest . . . kissing him until they both were breathless.

She blinked. "You are?"

"Yes. This is a distance workshop. Power Napping. Useful for football game halftimes, waiting on line at the DMV, and killing time while your girlfriend changes outfits for the tenth time." He opened his eyes and levered upward on his elbow. "Impressed?"

"Wildly."

"I don't believe you when your eyes don't get in on the smile."

"Riley—" She shook her head, helplessly grinning.

"That's better. You have a beautiful smile, you know. It makes me think you're smiling just for me. A guy could melt under a smile like that. It's unforgettable."

" 'A guy'? Not you?"

He paused. His foot tapped. He shrugged one shoulder and finally said, "This isn't about me. It's about *you*. You begging me for that fling we talked about." His gaze held her, his eyes sparkling with mischief. "Remember?"

"Don't hold your breath." Jayne began to feel drawn in, bedazzled by his interest. How was it that Riley could affect her this way, when she didn't even have the power to keep him interested in a relationship he'd seemed happy with? She held the army knife toward him. "I just came to return this. Thanks for the loan."

Their fingers touched. Riley used the contact to hold her in position, crouched amid lonely rocks and endless skies. A fierce longing swept through her. Why did things have to be this way? Why couldn't she get over him? Why hadn't she thought to comb her hair before coming here?

"I thought this would still be bagged in Tyvek," he said.

"I cut it out of the bag for you."

He nodded. Looked at her seriously. "Did it work?"

"Cutting it out of the bag? Of course it worked. You can see that it's right there—"

"That's not what I mean."

Jayne tilted her head. Their fingers still touched, and she wished he'd just accept the knife and be done with it. Looking at it had raised memories of all the times Riley had used it to help her in some way or another. She didn't want to be reminded anymore. Not when there was no future in it.

"What do you mean?" she asked.

"The Memorabilia Mash Mambo. Did it crush whatever memories you had of us?"

" 'Crush?' Geez, that's putting it kind of harshly. Don't you think so?"

She looked at him and saw that he did not, in fact, "think so." His expression was wary, his gaze direct. Jayne blinked with surprise. A person would almost think . . . he didn't want their memories "mashed."

"My workshop techniques aren't meant to be therapeutic for *me,*" she told him, pushing the folded knife into his palm at last. She stood, brushing dust from her pants.

"They're meant to help my breakup-ees get over the hurts in their lives."

"What about your hurts? What about your bozo ex-boyfriend?"

"Truthfully?" Jayne crossed her arms. "The more time goes by, the more I wonder if I really knew him at all. What we had . . . wasn't what I thought we had."

Riley nodded sagely. She couldn't *believe* he didn't know she was really talking about him. About their relationship. She decided to change the subject.

"What about you? What are your plans after this guide job is finished?"

"I'm up for a *National Explorer* photography assignment in Antigua. After that a potential story on swimming with whales in Patagonia." Idly, he examined a bank of fluffy clouds scuttling overhead. "I don't think about the future much though. When you're dangling from a cliff in Peru, there's not a lot of time to worry about next week. You take care of right now, the rest takes care of itself."

For the first time, she understood his philosophy. It was a revelatory moment, given how opposite they'd seemed at times.

"You know, I found that out myself," Jayne said excitedly, "when I was writing my book. It was a huge project. Impossible to finish all in one day. I just had to take it page by page."

"And you finished it. To great acclaim."

She nodded. "Imagine that, huh? The woman who could hardly wait for her manicure to dry, hitting it big by being patient. Until now, my book was my greatest achievement."

"And now?"

"Well, now I need *another* book. My breakup work-book."

He make a face. "Sounds grueling. Sure you don't want to escape to Antigua with me and get away from it all?"

The friendly atmosphere between them froze. She'd been

humming along, finally relating to Riley's day-by-day philosophy for the first time, and then . . . *bam*.

She couldn't look at him. Couldn't look and see the ear-
nestness in his face—before he remembered he liked to
travel alone.

"Tell you what," Jayne managed to say. "I'll run off to
the tropics with you right *after* I fall for that fling you keep
dreaming about between us. Okay?"

Since she had no intention of doing *that*, it seemed a safe
statement to make. And since Riley was likely to move on
to the next adventure before fulfilling his end of the challenge
they'd issued each other, he seemed likely to agree.

He did. "You're on," he said, then got up and headed
alongside her, back to their temporary camp—just as though
he meant to get started on it right away.

Alexis ducked behind a creosote bush as Uncle Riley and
Jayne passed by. Hidden behind its wiry branches and tiny
blossoms, she watched them stride side by side back to the
campsite.

*So . . . Uncle Riley wanted to have a fling with Jayne,
huh?* Thoughtfully, Alexis pondered all she'd overheard. It
sounded like her uncle was *crazy* about the book author.
And like the book author was fighting a pretty major
attraction herself. Not that Alexis could blame Jayne. Uncle
Riley *was* pretty awesome.

He was tall. Strong enough to go mountain climbing,
scuba diving, and white-water rafting. Funny enough to
make even so-serious Nana and Gramps laugh over dinner.
Honest enough not to dish out fake sympathy to Alexis over
her mom's embarrassing second-teenager-hood with Gary
the Loser. Yeah, all in all, she figured her uncle was probably
a catch.

And Jayne . . . heck, she looked like a model or something.
Not that she looked *perfect*. But she did have a way of

walking and talking and just *being* that gave her an extra little glow. Plus, she was totally nice, and had offered to show Alexis how to tweeze her eyebrows later too. Also, she seemed to have lots of friends.

Uncle Riley needed friends. Alexis worried about him sometimes, worried about the way he spent months on assignment in the middle of nowhere. He wasn't getting any younger. She was pretty sure he'd already made the transition from MTV to VH-1, a sign of impending senior citizen status for sure.

She had to do something. After checking to see that the coast was clear, Alexis emerged from behind the creosote bush. She jogged down the trail, going fast enough to keep Uncle Riley and Jayne in her sights. As soon as she caught one of them alone, she'd get started on her plan.

Someone stepped out from behind a boulder and onto the path. Alexis shrieked, and smacked right into him.

Lance.

"Ooof!"

He blushed from the collar of his T-shirt all the way to the hairline of his boy-band-wanna-be haircut. The redness in his face made a zit turn Day-Glo on his forehead. She shook her head.

"Haven't you ever been hiking before, doofus?" she asked, disentangling her feet from his. She put her hands on her hips. "You're not supposed to just charge out onto the trail like that. You could, like, *maim* someone."

Her killer glare seemed unable to penetrate the geek force field around him. "Uh, sorry. I didn't mean—I mean, are you okay?"

"What do you think, flop-feet?"

He ducked his head. "I guess your mouth survived okay."

"What?"

"I mean . . ."

Lance was staring at her braces. She just *knew* it.

"Your, uh, hair looks interesting."

''You creep! Take that back!''

''Make me!'' He ran down the path, his lumbering body leaping around boulders and clumps of cacti. He stopped a few yards away and looked over his shoulder.

''This is *so* juvenile,'' Alexis said, faking a yawn.

''Chicken,'' he goaded.

''Start smokin', you big weirdo. 'Cause you're *toast!*''

She sprinted down the path after him, ready to make him eat dust.

Over the course of the next few hours, the high-desert began to give way to the forested canyon's outermost edge. Gentle slopes took the place of boulders; tall wild grasses grew instead of prickly pear and cholla. A cool breeze tossed the branches of the trailside juniper bushes. The temperature dropped steadily, a harbinger of the coming night.

Riley squinted up at the sunset's streaks of orange and pink. They'd stopped to make camp almost an hour ago. So far, only he, his guides, Lance, and Alexis had managed to pitch their tents. His niece sat next to him now, watching the new adventure travelers struggle with nylon taffeta, aluminum poles, and zip-up rain flies.

''Shouldn't you help them?'' Alexis asked.

He shook his head and took another sip of coffee. ''You were there. We ran through this several times at the lodge. They all know how to do this. They're just a little nervous right now.''

Riley glimpsed a flustered Jayne, staring at the heap of her tent as though it were a particularly recalcitrant hairstyle on date night. She seemed to be having the most difficult time of all. After her adventures in navigating, he guessed he shouldn't have been surprised. Jayne belonged in the great outdoors like klieg lights belonged in a darkroom. Not at all.

Although he'd suspected as much, Riley was disappointed. A part of him had hoped Jayne would love the wilderness. It would have been something in common, something besides a tendency to talk around the truth.

He didn't really believe she meant to go to Antigua with him. She probably didn't really believe he meant to seduce her. One of them was wrong. Only time would tell which one.

Alexis nudged him. "You and Jayne make an *awesome* couple, Uncle Riley. You should have told me about you two."

He choked on his coffee. "What?"

"I saw you on the trailside this afternoon. You're having a fling with Jayne, right? Doing the mattress mambo?"

"I'm *not* having a fling with Jayne." Yet. "And don't say 'mattress mambo.' "

His niece grinned. "Well, I think you should. You need someone like her in your life. Someone *nice*. With *friends*. And a makeup kit the size of Wisconsin."

Was it just him, or did that last sound a little self-serving? He should let the whole matter drop, he told himself.

"What makes you think that?" he asked instead.

"That you guys should be a couple? I dunno." Alexis picked at her glittery nail polish. She flopped the heels of the sport sandals she'd changed into upon making camp. "Maybe it's the way Jayne talks about you. And looks at you."

Suspiciously, Riley frowned. Then he snuck a glance at Jayne, still swamped amid her tent. *She was watching him!* Feeling a completely idiotic surge of excitement, he averted his gaze.

"She talks about me?" he asked in a low voice.

Alexis nodded. "All the time."

All the time! "What does she say?"

His niece shrugged. "Girl stuff. I can't say."

"Could you say for—" He reached for his wallet. "A ten spot?"

"Uncle Riley! Do you think I can be *bought?*"

"Do aspens grow at seven thousand feet?"

"Uhhh . . ."

"Yes." Making a goofy face, he handed her the money. "So what does she say about me?"

"Well . . ." Alexis looked both ways, then leaned nearer to cup her hand around his ear. "She says . . ."

Listening, Riley felt his eyes grow wide. He *knew* he'd been right about Jayne. There *were* still feelings between them.

And it *wasn't* just him.

"And you've seen her watching me?"

Alexis nodded knowingly. "Like Nana watches Gramps eat ice cream."

"Huh?"

"When she's on a diet."

"Ahhh." He nodded, unreasonably pleased by this news—and unwilling to reveal as much to Alexis. Riley hunkered forward on the hillside they were seated on and caught her eye. "So, since we're already talking about this stuff . . . how are things with you and Lance?"

"Lance?" She made a face. "He's a jerk."

"He's a nice boy."

"*All* boys are jerks," Alexis said. Then she got up, grabbed a jacket, and headed for the edge of camp.

Riley couldn't help but wonder which *particular* jerk had convinced her of that. The Brendan she'd mentioned, maybe? He didn't know, but he did know who could help him find out.

"I need your help," Riley said.

Jayne paused in the middle of wrestling her two-person tent into submission. She glanced up, panting. Her hair was in her eyes, a crazed expression was on her face, and she didn't exactly look like a woman who was ready to help someone. Nevertheless, she nodded.

"What can I do for you?"

"It's Alexis. I think she has . . . issues with boys."

"Every thirteen-year-old girl has issues with boys. Do they like her? Does she like them? Will a nice one ask her to the dance on Friday? It's normal. But I think it's really *very* sweet of you to be concerned."

Jayne flashed him a sappy smile. Riley rubbed the back of his neck, uncomfortable with her sentimental assessment of him.

"She says all boys are jerks."

"Don't worry." She wrestled her tent poles, trying to make their shock-corded joints snap into position. "In a few years she'll upgrade her opinion to 'all men are bozos.' "

He frowned. "As a former boy—and current man—I resent that."

She shrugged, then went back to glaring at the collapsed heap of the geometric dome tent she'd later share with Kelly. "You guys reap what you sow, big boy."

"It's wrong to let one bad apple spoil the whole bunch." Reminded of the lame-ass loser who'd sent Jayne to heartbreak camp, Riley let his frown deepen. "There are lots of decent men out there. Men who are trustworthy. Fun to be around." He followed her around her tent's edge as she prepared for another assault on it. "*Teeming* with sexual prowess."

She glanced over her shoulder. "I thought we were talking about Alexis's boy problems."

"Uh, we are."

Her brow arched. "You really want her to hook up with a kid who's 'teeming with sexual prowess'? I'm not sure I can help you with that."

"Look, all I know is, it kills me to know she's hurting. She's too young to be this jaded. There must be something that would help." Absently, Riley glanced around the campsite, where the other guidance groupies were crawling inside their now fully assembled tents or setting up camp stoves. A series of electronic beeps drew his gaze to Lance, who was playing Game Boy Advance. "I've got it!"

"I wish I had it." Jayne stared dispiritedly at her tent as it sank onto itself. "I *suck* at camping."

"You need practice, that's all," Riley assured her. He'd had an idea, and he felt better already. "And *we* need . . . to set up Lance and Alexis. It's perfect. They'll have a little teenage trailside romance, it will have a natural ending when the trip ends, Alexis will feel better about boys, and nobody will get hurt."

"Are you serious?"

"Sure. Nothing cures a broken heart faster than getting wrapped up in a new relationship. No matter how short-lived. So long as it's good."

He waggled his eyebrows teasingly, thinking of how good their rekindled fling would be once Jayne let down her guard a little. Once he'd shown her all men weren't heartbreakers.

She gawped at him, mouth open. "Maybe I should just talk to Alexis," she disagreed.

"Yes." Riley nodded, giving her a grateful shoulder squeeze. "Talk to Alexis. Good idea. I'd really appreciate that. Talk up moving on. Talk up Lance. Hell, talk up the good qualities of mankind while you're at it."

Feeling almost jubilant, he prepared to make his first round of the campsite. He needed to make sure things were set up properly, offer help where it was needed. Now that he had a plan of action in mind, he was ready to move forward.

"I'll do what I can," Jayne said doubtfully.

"Great!" Relieved, Riley leaned forward and planted a quick kiss on the silky hair at the top of her head. She seemed stunned when he released her, staring up at him silently. "Good luck with that tent!"

Then he headed onward, ready to do his duty.

Twelve

That night, Jayne lay in her tent—finally erected after about a million attempts—beside a snoring Kelly. All around her, blackness closed in. She'd never been anyplace so dark, except maybe a movie theater in the few seconds after the lights went down but before the feature rolled. It was spooky. And scary. And it was keeping her awake—frightfully awake.

She palmed her key-chain flashlight. Keeping it aimed away from Kelly's side of the tent, she carefully flicked it on. Its small beam of light illuminated her fingers and created a comforting circle on the red nylon of her tent. Jayne breathed a sigh of relief.

No horror-movie creature lurked in the few inches between her sleeping bag and the tent wall. Nothing had morphed in the night, no critters had crept inside, all was well. Girding her courage, she turned off the light.

Uneasiness gripped her. She flicked the flashlight back on. Then off. On. Off. On, just for a few more minutes, until she felt sleepy . . .

A rustling at her tent's zippered entrance made Jayne freeze. A bear! A crazed serial killer! Another lizard!

"Psst. Jayne, it's me."

"Riley?"

She squeezed out of her sleeping bag, the air mattress tucked beneath squeaking in protest. Careful not to wake Kelly, Jayne knee-walked over her slippery "bed" and unzipped the tent's outside flap. Then she fluffed up her hair, pinched her cheeks for emergency color, and poked her head outside.

Riley was kneeling there in the moonlight, dressed in the same kind of head-to-toe insulated gear she had on to combat the evening chill. She'd resented its necessity. She'd never before worn a week's worth of wardrobe to bed. But somehow, on him the layered clothes looked natural and rugged and appealing. *He* looked appealing.

"I saw your light," he said in a low voice. "Can't sleep?"

His voice comforted her to a ridiculous degree. His *presence* comforted her even though she couldn't see his features clearly in the darkness. Jayne was embarrassed to feel so cowardly, especially when she was supposed to be providing a positive role model for her breakup-ees.

She shook her head. Unwilling to reveal any weaknesses to a man who'd once left her behind, she searched for a believable insomniac's excuse. "It's the quiet. It's just so . . . quiet."

His grin warmed her. "It's not all *that* quiet. Maybe you should listen harder."

Intrigued, she did. She heard the breeze as it swooshed through the bushes and grasses nearby, heard crickets call, heard an owl hoot. A small smile edged onto her lips. "Hey, that's kind of nice. Like one of those 'nature sounds' CDs, only free."

Kelly's next snuffling snore all but vibrated the tent walls.

"And with interesting sound effects too," Riley joked.

They shared a smile. A cozy feeling enveloped them, a feeling both familiar and, alone here in the dark, very welcome. Then Riley's gaze dropped to the flashlight still gripped in Jayne's palm. A thoughtful expression passed over his face.

He knew! Deeply embarrassed to be caught in a fear so childish as hers, Jayne bit her lip. In this, she couldn't stand teasing. There had to be some excuse she could offer him, some rationalization, some—

He sent his gaze upward, then returned it to her face. "Well, I just stopped by to make sure you were okay. Since you are, I'll just be . . . going back to my tent."

Gratitude—and longing—filled her. They were so close. . . . "Wait."

In the midst of his turning-away crouch, Riley paused. He kept one hand on her tent's outer flap. "What's the matter?"

I want to talk to you. To touch you. To catch hold of the magic we had once, and keep it safe this time.

"Um, will our next campsite have bathing facilities?"

His eyes sparkled. "I can rig up something for you if you want."

"I meant a bathtub." She dreamed of hot water, clean porcelain, lots and lots of Bathing Beauty Bubbles. She *craved* them. Jayne hadn't gone more than a day without a bath in years, and this stressful trip made her yearn for her restorative routine more than ever. "A real bathtub."

"Sorry," Riley said. "I can teach you survival skills, hike you all over the wilderness, even show you the things I love about being out here. But I can't deliver Mr. Bubble and company."

It was nearly the same thing he'd told her when she'd pined for a bath earlier this evening. Jayne's shoulders slumped.

"Thanks anyway," she said. After all, it wasn't his fault her publicist had sent her on this deprivation detail. Somewhere in Manhattan, Francesca was probably holding a martini in one hand and a decent pillow in the other, laughing her head off. "And thanks for stopping by."

"You're welcome." Another thoughtful look. "You know, I *can* make your sleeping arrangements a little more comfortable for you."

Riley stood. Unzipping sounds followed, then the whoosh of nylon against nylon. Overhead, the tent's mesh "skylight" flipped open to offer a breathtaking view of the stars. Jayne crooked her neck to see them, and felt a little better. She already knew which one she'd choose for her next wish.

"Thanks, Riley," she said when he lowered near the tent's entrance again. "I thought the zipper was stuck. It was impossible to open."

"Nothing's impossible if you want it bad enough." He winked, then cupped his hand over her flashlight-grasping fingers. "Good night, Jayne. Sleep well."

He strode into the darkness, leaving her alone.

"Psst, Jayne. Wake up," Kelly said.

Jayne heard her but felt too groggy to respond. In her sleep-drugged mind, Kelly's repeated "Psst, Jayne" transformed into Riley's greeting from last night. It meshed with the dream she'd been enjoying, a dream frothy with soapsuds and steamy with a naked man rising from the bubbles. He held out his hand to her, inviting her closer. Her dream self drew nearer. She recognized Riley, slick and strong and sensitive enough to make sure she had stars to fall asleep beneath.

"Jayne," he said. "Jayne . . . you're a fraud. You're not over me. You know you're not."

"*Arrgh!*" She wrenched awake and found herself mummified in what felt like her apartment's comforter, only slipperier. She thrashed around, identified several mysterious muscle aches, and stilled in confusion.

"What's happened to me?" she wailed. "I think somebody beat me all over with a long-handled body loofah!"

Beside her, Kelly smiled. She brushed her bangs away

from her glasses. "We all feel that way. It's the hiking, I think. We're not used to it yet."

The hiking. Everything came flooding back to Jayne. The fact that she wasn't in her familiar apartment. The trail. The going in circles, the rehydrated beef Stroganoff she'd been too hungry to refuse at dinner last night, the lack of a soak in a hot tub or even a shower. She remembered sitting beside the small campfire Mack had built, dozing off with exhaustion, lying rigidly awake afterward in the inky scariness of her tent.

She remembered Riley . . . opening up the stars to her.

No. Better not to dwell on Riley's kindness, Jayne told herself firmly. She was supposed to be resisting him.

She yawned. Peered into the reddish light caused by the sun struggling to penetrate their tent's nylon walls. "What time is it?"

"Just after sunrise. The guides say we have to get an early start if we want to make it to the halfway point between the Hideaway Lodge and the canyon lodge by this afternoon."

Ugh. A predawn wakeup call had almost been tolerable yesterday, when the excitement of beginning their trip had livened things up a little. But two days of crawling out of bed before the sun had reached a reasonable skyscraper-height was pushing it.

Jayne flopped onto her sleeping bag again. "I'll catch up."

"Come on, sleepyhead." Kelly tugged at her arm. "I hear the guys are making breakfast."

Mmmm. Breakfast. Pancakes, waffles, omelets . . . even cornflakes. Okay, so getting up might not be so bad. She was starving. Yesterday's hike must have offered up plenty of those fat-burning benefits Riley had promised, so she had some room to splurge. Picturing a nice morning meal al fresco, Jayne pushed upward.

"Atta girl," Kelly said.

Jayne rubbed the sleep from her eyes, straightened her abundance of layered outdoor wear, and then whipped her hair into a ponytail at the top of her head. She stuffed her stockinged feet into her unlaced ATSes. Trailed by Kelly, she crawled from the tent and shuffled into the chilly campsite.

" 'Morning, ladies." Red-haired Mack smiled and waved from his position crouched beside three compact camp stoves. He had an oven mitt on his waving hand. "Breakfast will be ready in a jiffy."

He was so sweet, Jayne thought. And—even though he wasn't her hazel-eyed, dark-haired, constantly teasing type—so darn cute too. She turned to say so to Kelly, and saw that Kelly apparently already agreed. Wearing an eager expression, she approached Mack with hesitant steps. "Need any help?"

The guide's smile broadened. His gaze softened when he looked at Kelly, and Mack gestured for her to sit beside him. "Sure! I could use some company. Why don't you join me?"

Jayne lingered a moment. Kelly sat beside Mack. They looked companionable, snatches of their conversation drifting on the *non*-pancake-scented breeze.

Where were those pancakes anyway?

Wanting to be ready for them, and assured that Kelly was in dependable hands, Jayne headed into the bushes. A few minutes later, she'd performed her most basic morning duties. Muscles gradually unkinking, she trudged sleepily back to the campsite. She wished she had a nice triple latte. A nice chocolate-chip scone. A nice roof and walls and central heating, and a nice old-fashioned bathtub and—

"Good morning," Riley said, interrupting her thoughts. He strolled across the clearing with a handful of plastic bowls and spoons, looking bright-eyed and happy. "Sleep well?"

"Like the dead, thanks to you." Her smile was split with another yawn. She stretched, feeling the pull of post-hiking soreness all over her body. "Those stars were just what I needed."

He nodded, his gaze lifting from its appreciative perusal of her stretch. "There's nothing like being out in the great outdoors for a good night's sleep. I can hardly manage it in the city these days. It seems twice as noisy to me now."

Jayne thought of the typical sounds she awakened to. Traffic, auto alarms, her neighbor's TV, a car stereo booming rap music on the street below. She had to admit, birdcalls were much nicer. While doing her duty amid the twitter of wild birds this morning, she'd felt almost like a Disney cartoon heroine. The ones who set bluebirds chirping and bunnies hopping and all manner of cute woodland creatures following them. *Tra-la-la-la-la.*

"Nature has its appeal." Jayne wrinkled her nose. "I guess."

Riley smiled as though delighted by her opinion. Why that should be, she didn't know. Obviously, he'd never intended to share "the great outdoors" with *her*. This joint expedition had been an accident.

She wondered if he'd ever taken a girlfriend on one of his adventure photography expeditions. Probably, he'd taken someone tomboyish. Someone capable, like him. Someone eager to test her mettle against squirrels, sand, slimy fish, and civilization deprivation.

Someone, Jayne thought morosely, like the person her father and brothers must have hoped *she'd* become.

"I'm glad to hear you say that," Riley told her, "because we'll be in the thick of it today."

At her blank look, he elaborated. "Nature, that is. We'll be climbing more this morning, doing some fishing, making our way up into the canyon. By this time tomorrow, we'll be two thirds of the way to the canyon lodge."

"Does it have a bathtub?" she asked hopefully.

"Yes." He looked at her—leisurely, as though mentally

stripping away her multiple layers of clothing and sliding her naked body into said bathtub. "It does."

Nirvana. She could hardly wait. She said as much, only to see Riley's interested expression grow even more ... interested. She couldn't resist adding, "How big is it? Big enough for two?"

His gaze rose from her midsection, lingered for the merest instant where her breasts were shrouded in Polarfleece, and stopped on her face. She tried not to show how his attention made her tingle, even as he cocked an eyebrow.

"Is that an invitation?"

Damn. She should have known better than to flirt with him. *She* halfway meant what she said, but he ... didn't. "It's an innocent inquiry. I have a bottle of Bathing Beauty Bubbles, two wild-berry bath bombs, a tin of honey body balm, and a whole assortment of herbal bath beads, all going to waste in my pack."

Thoughtfully, Riley stepped nearer, close enough for her to catch the mingled scents of fresh air and ... soap? ... clinging to his skin. Soap, in the wilderness. How had he managed that, when she couldn't hunt down a bath to save her life?

She angled her chin for a closer view, and realized the slightly antiseptic fragrance she'd detected was shaving cream. There was an overlooked scrap of it still visible just beneath the rugged edge of his jaw. For some reason, that tiny sign that Riley did, indeed, sometimes miss a detail reassured her.

Maybe that meant he wouldn't realize she was succumbing to his love-'em-and-leave-'em appeal all over again.

Jayne stifled a tender urge to thumb that shaving cream away. Instead, she stood steady as he spoke. She had to be strong. Ignore his nearness and its effect on her. Especially since Riley was probably coming closer just to deliver another lecture on packing in only essential items.

He hesitated, as though reluctant to spoil their early-morning repartee with serious adventure travel business. Or maybe as though trying to fathom why one woman needed the equivalent of a bath shop in her backpack. Then Riley lowered his head intimately.

"What, *exactly*," he asked, "does a person do with honey body balm?"

The husky note of intrigue in his voice made her shiver. *Rub it all over me,* she thought instantly, crazily. *Rub it all over you. Rub it all over each other, until we're sweet and soft and hard and needful . . .*

Boy, would she never learn?

"I guess that's for me to know and you to find out," Jayne said saucily.

With luck, her teasing would divert his attention long enough for her to escape with her pride intact. She *did* thumb the shaving cream from his jaw with a hopefully lighthearted gesture. Then she straightened her fleece and trouped to her tent to finish getting ready for her day . . . this time leaving Riley staring after *her*.

Holding a packet of premoistened towelettes, Riley strode through the campsite. He passed Lance and Mack and Bruce, each of them diligently working either to prepare the morning meal or to teach one of Jayne's guidance groupies how to operate her camp stove. He shook his head at Bruce's continued (and obvious) flirtation with Mitzi, as the guide tried to talk her into skinny-dipping in a nearby creek.

"Are you nuts?" Mitzi asked. "It's forty-five degrees out. I'm a woman, not a Popsicle."

Bruce chuckled. "A Popsicle, huh? Well, if you *were* . . ."

Riley didn't want to hear whatever ribald rejoinder his buddy would come up with. He quickened his pace. He approached Jayne's tent at the far edge of the campsite, thinking about his plans to give her the on-the-trail towelettes as a bath-time substitute. The disposable towelettes wouldn't be as enjoyable as, say, honey body butter, but Riley figured they'd satisfy Jayne's bath-junkie mania better than nothing.

He neared the tent. Suddenly, Alexis's voice came from inside the domed red nylon. He stopped with the greeting he'd been about to call out still on his lips.

Maybe Jayne was talking with Alexis, he thought. Telling his niece all the things Riley and Jayne had discussed yesterday—about how boys *could* be trustworthy and fun and nonheartbreaking. Maybe she was helping Alexis already. Not wanting to disturb them, he turned and prepared to move quietly away. What he heard next, though, stopped him.

"So you never—*ouch*—even knew your mom?" Alexis asked, her voice drifting through the tent's mesh skylight. "That's, like, *totally* sad. Ouch!"

"I knew her," Jayne said. "Just not for very long. She died when I was three. So it was sad losing her . . . but I recovered. I still had my dad and my brothers." There was a pause. "Please hold still. I don't want to poke you with the tweezers."

Ahh, Riley realized. *Another primp session*. Probably, Jayne was using that girly beauty talk to get closer to Alexis. Very smart of her. His respect for her touchy-feely methods rose another grudging notch.

"Anyway, my childhood is beside the point," Jayne went on as he listened. "All I did was ask if you wanted to let your mother teach you how to tweeze your eyebrows. I know *I* would've liked that."

Alexis snorted. "My mom thinks racking up a big AT&T bill qualifies as mother-daughter bonding. She wouldn't be interested. Besides, she—*ouch*—gets her eyebrows waxed at the salon."

Jayne murmured something in reply. Riley decided again to leave them be. Their conversation had veered from the

If the Free Book Certificate is missing, call 1-800-770-1963 to place your order.
Be sure to visit our website at www.kensingtonbooks.com.

To start your membership, simply complete and return the Free Book Certificate. You'll receive your Introductory Shipment of FREE Zebra Contemporary Romances. Then, each month as long as your account is in good standing, you will receive the 3 newest Zebra Contemporary Romances. Each shipment will be yours to examine for 10 days. If you decide to keep the books, you'll pay the preferred book club member price of $15.95 – a savings of up to 20% off the cover price! (plus $1.99 to offset the cost of shipping and handling.) If you want us to stop sending books, just say the word… it's that simple.

BOOK CERTIFICATE

Yes! Please send me FREE Zebra Contemporary romance novels. I only pay for shipping and handling. I understand I am under no obligation to purchase any books, as explained on this card.

Name _____

Address _____ Apt. _____

City _____ State _____ Zip _____

Telephone (____) _____

Signature _____

(If under 18, parent or guardian must sign)

Offer limited to one per household and not valid to current subscribers.
All orders subject to approval. Terms, offer, and price subject to change. Offer valid only in the U.S.

CN102A

Thank You!

THE BENEFITS
OF BOOK CLUB
MEMBERSHIP

- You'll get your books hot off the press, usually before they appear in bookstores.
- You'll ALWAYS save up to 20% off the cover price.
- You'll get our FREE monthly newsletter filled with author interviews, book previews, special offers, and MORE!
- There's no obligation — you can cancel at any time and you have no minimum number of books to buy.
- And — if you decide you don't like the books you receive, you can return them. (You always have ten days to decide.)

llı..lı..lll...ıllılıl..lıl..lı..llıl..lll..l

Zebra Contemporary Romance Book Club

Zebra Home Subscription Service, Inc.

P.O. Box 5214

Clifton , NJ 07015-5214

interesting subject of Jayne's girlhood to feminine masochism, and he didn't know how much of that he could take. If they started talking about bikini waxes, he might have to run.

Then Alexis said, "It costs my mom a *huge* amount of money every month to go to that salon too. My dad used to *totally* have temper tantrums when he saw the bills."

Riley nodded reluctantly, eyebrows raised. Knowing his younger brother, he could believe it.

"Sometimes," his niece went on with a sigh, "I don't think looking good is worth it."

"Oh, but it is!" Jayne disagreed. Her silhouette wasn't visible through the nylon tent wall, but she had to be nodding. "Good grooming is important. After all, makeup, tweezers, and the judicious use of hairstyling products are all that separate us from men. Also, cute shoes. Hold still!"

"*Yeow!*" Alexis sniffled. "Is it supposed to hurt like this? I feel like my forehead is on fire."

"We can wait a minute if you want. But, yes, beauty hurts sometimes." A pause. "Especially when nobody notices it."

"When nobody notices it?"

An awkward moment passed, as though Jayne regretted having made the comment. Then, offhandedly, "Right. Or when nobody appreciates the effort that goes into it."

"I'll bet everyone notices *you*."

Silence. Jayne had to be shaking her head. The realization stilled him. How anyone could fail to notice—and appreciate—her was beyond him.

"That's whack," Alexis said.

Riley grinned, recognizing Lance's lingo. It seemed Alexis didn't think Lance was quite as much of a "jerk" as she claimed.

"*Everyone* must notice you!" his niece continued indignantly. "You look like a model or something. I can't *believe*—"

"Not everyone values looking good," Jayne said gently.

"Like who?"

"Well . . . like my family, for instance." Jayne's voice had quieted. A muffled *ouch* from Alexis told him Jayne still worked the tweezers. "My dad and my brothers. I always thought—oh, never mind. You don't want to hear this."

Riley did. Intensely interested, he lowered to a hunk of rock behind the tent Jayne and Alexis occupied.

"Sure, I do!" his niece said. "Come on, spill."

"Well . . ."

Jayne's hesitant voice betrayed pain she was reluctant to speak of. It made him ache to comfort her. To tell her *he* thought she was beautiful, inside and out. To erase whatever indifference her family had hurt her with. But he couldn't. Not now. Not until he knew the whole story.

He'd met her gruff father and three brothers while in San Francisco—for brunch, a Giants game, and an ill-advised just-us-men trip to Hooters (there was nothing more awkward, Riley had discovered, than watching your current fling's father ogle a busty waitress). But his interactions with Jayne's family had been brief, relatively impersonal, or both. He didn't really know much about them . . . or about Jayne's relationship with them.

He'd left before things had gotten that far.

Now, he listened.

"I grew up in a house full of men," Jayne said. "The toilet seat was always raised, 'the game' was always on TV, and the closest anybody ever came to being affectionate was high-fiving each other after a touchdown. My dad wasn't cold—don't get me wrong—he was just . . . clueless. He had no idea how to raise a girl. Especially one like me."

"One like you?"

A wistful sigh. "One who begged for a baby-blue bedroom. One who worshipped every cartoon princess, who outfitted Barbie from head to toe, who considered slumber parties a weekend necessity. I'm afraid I was always a girly-girl. In my family I couldn't have been more of a square peg in a round hole.''

"They should have thought you were unique, then,'' Alexis insisted. *"Extra special.''*

Riley recognized Gwen's philosophy in that statement and felt proud of Alexis. His grandmother had her old-fashioned moments, but she knew what was important. Apparently, she'd passed that knowledge on to her great-granddaughter too.

"Extra special?'' Jayne repeated. There was amusement in her voice . . . amusement covering something else, something like longstanding hurt. "That's what I'd always hoped, I guess. It didn't quite turn out that way. But by the time I discovered that, it was too late. I was hooked on beauty products. Hot for hair spray. Bananas for bath accessories. I couldn't quit.''

At her attempt to lighten the conversation, to turn it away from her disappointing past to the moment at hand, Riley felt a wave of tenderness. Jayne might have been hurt. *Had* been hurt. But she wasn't bitter, and she didn't blame anyone for that hurt. Instead, she bravely moved on, being the only kind of woman she knew how to be.

"Well, I'm *glad* you couldn't quit,'' Alexis said, evidently wise enough to realize when a sad moment needed glossing over. "So is my baby unibrow. And so are all your workshop women. They're looking better every day.'' There was a shuffle against the tent floor. *"Prrriimp!''* she mimicked.

They both laughed.

"The only thing more important than looking good and feeling good is having good friends,'' Jayne said. "Remember that, okay? Because being alone—being lonely—is just about the worst thing there is.''

A solemn silence fell. Riley imagined Alexis nodding, her brows puffy but well groomed. He imagined Jayne giving his niece an affectionate hug, the two women bonded forever in familial misery and tweezer trauma. More than likely, Alexis shared Jayne's dread of being alone, having experienced it more than a thirteen-year-old ought to have since her parents' divorce.

"I'll bet *you're* hardly ever alone," Alexis said after another murmured *ouch*. "You have tons of friends."

"I'm alone sometimes," Jayne confided. "It's hard."

She'd been alone after her bozo ex-boyfriend bailed, Riley thought. *Alone, and hurting.* Silently, he cursed the jerk who'd left Jayne lonely. His determination to make up for that loser's shortcomings grew twice as strong.

Then a terrible thought occurred to him, blotting out the rest of Jayne and Alexis's conversation. Had *he* left Jayne alone and hurting too?

He'd always believed theirs had been a casual affair, steamy and sexy and filled with good times. He'd always believed she'd viewed their relationship the same way he had—temporary and enjoyable. What if, Riley wondered for the first time, she hadn't? What if Jayne had wanted more?

Shaken by the question, he stood. His fingers trembled on the packet of towelettes. After one last glance toward Jayne's tent, Riley made himself start moving. He could deliver the towelettes to her anytime. Right now he felt an overpowering urge to do something else. Anything else.

Anything that didn't involve staying still. Wondering. Or feeling the confusion that coursed through him like river water past a kayak's smooth hull.

What if Jayne had wanted more?

He needed to move, that was all. His only mistake had been staying and eavesdropping on something that was none of his business in the first place. Determinedly, Riley tossed the towelettes into his tent as he passed and then just kept going. There were plans to be made, equipment checks to be performed. The sooner he got this group to the canyon lodge—where rendezvous Jeeps were scheduled to return everyone to the main Hideaway Lodge—the sooner this trip would be over with.

The sooner he could head on to Antigua and return to the life he understood.

Thirteen

The wilderness was out to get her.

So was this trip.

Jayne came to those conclusions naturally enough, after a morning filled with one calamity after another. First, there'd been no pancakes. Or waffles. Or even cornflakes. Instead, for breakfast there'd been gluey reconstituted oatmeal, coffee made with treated water, and dried apple slices. Not even pretending she was eating muesli at an exclusive Swiss spa had been enough to convince Jayne the stuff was palatable. And this, after having earned a real, honest-to-God *splurge* with all that hiking? It was some kind of cruel outdoorsy joke. Her thighs might have appreciated it, but she did *not*.

Second, there'd been the guide switch. Riley had announced that the hiking groups would be shuffled—this time he would lead Doris, Donna, and Lance. Mack would lead Kelly, Alexis, and Mitzi. And Bruce (with his double entendres and cheerful ribaldry) would lead Carla and Jayne. That might not have been so bad in itself . . . except Bruce seemed determined to set a land-speed record for distance hiking. He wouldn't settle for anything less than the equivalent of a level eight on Jayne's health club treadmill.

Then there were the bugs, the bug bites, the dirt, the constant incline, her sore, overworked muscles . . . clearly this whole scheme was insane. She was trying to make the best of it. Honestly. But if not for the necessity of researching her techniques' effectiveness for her antiheartbreak workbook, Jayne would have turned around and used her last remaining energy to hike back to civilization, where she belonged.

However, if her group reentered civilization now, it could be disastrous. Civilization meant her breakup-ees would have easy access to their exes—*and* to resolve-destroying "our place" drive-bys, "our song" replays, and "our past" remembrance wallows. For the sake of all the women in her care, she had to carry on.

Dreaming of gardenia-scented body powder, she trudged onward in Bruce and Carla's wake. Longing to test the effectiveness of her peppermint tranquility bath set with a good scrubdown, she navigated past the increasingly tall pines and twisty oaks. Craving a movie, a shopping spree, a research trip that didn't require getting slapped in the face with evergreen boughs and tripping over half-buried fallen trees, Jayne kept going.

She hadn't had time to do anything more with her hair beyond a basic ponytail. She hadn't had the resources to put together more than a rudimentary, mostly baby-blue hiking ensemble, and today wore soft track pants, a camisole with a fleece top, and her ATSes. Her makeup consisted of mascara, an all-in-one emergency color stick, and lip gloss. This was probably the worst she'd looked since emerging from awkward teenagerdom, and Riley was partly to blame for it.

He'd appeared suddenly at the campsite after a mysterious absence, his expression rough and his eyes evasive. Gone had been the teasingly seductive man she'd flounced away from after their morning conversation. In his place had been a brisk and professional guide ... a stranger. He'd announced his plans for the day's hike, asked everyone to be ready to leave in ten minutes, and then had stonily spent their remaining time helping the women pack up.

He hadn't helped Jayne. Instead, he'd avoided her. She didn't know why. She'd caught him watching her once, a speculative tilt to his head. Upon noticing she'd noticed, though, he'd instantly averted his gaze, his face tightening.

She should have been relieved. Glad, even. If Riley kept his distance, avoiding the temptation of rekindling their relationship would be that much easier. Even so, Jayne wasn't relieved. She was concerned, and distracted, and even a little disappointed. It seemed a part of her had enjoyed wrangling with him, had looked forward to testing her resist-the-hunk skills against Riley's disarming smile, merry eyes, and undeniable charisma.

She probably just missed the challenge, Jayne told herself. She detected the sound of running water nearby and cocked her head to listen more closely. She missed proving to herself that she could resist Riley. It had been good for her self-confidence to resist him, a balm to her pride to confront him and sometimes emerge the victor. Sure, that was it.

Right. And wedgies would be back in style any minute now.

They came to a bank overgrown with tall grasses, studded with wildflowers. It sloped sharply downward to a stream-fed pool of clear water, the source of the sound she'd heard. Just above it, Bruce and Carla paused.

"Time for fishing!" her guide said.

Fishing. Great. Belatedly, Jayne remembered Riley saying something about hiking, fishing, and getting deeper into nature today. Probably, she'd blocked out the memory.

Unfortunately, she'd also forgotten her gummy worms.

She glanced around the perimeter of the water. The other groups had stopped too. The other guides—like Bruce—

efficiently unpacked the fishing gear. They assembled rods with practiced motions, set out bait, surveyed the lazily swirling water with eyes that probably saw more than a postcard-perfect view.

And it *was* perfect, Jayne realized. Serene and bucolic, with sunshine splashing over the water and leaves rustling in the breeze. She could almost begin to ... appreciate this. Grudgingly, Jayne forgave Mother Nature for the potty ambush she'd suffered this morning (after having forgotten to pee downhill), and sat on the bank to watch the action.

A few yards away, Doris and Donna stood beside Riley and Lance, arguing in low voices about something Jayne couldn't make out. The sisters had vowed before hitting the trail this morning to make life difficult for their new guide, and none of Jayne's protestations had changed their minds. Driven by loyalty to their antiheartbreak coach, the two women seemed determined to punish Riley for what they saw as his months-old abandonment of Jayne.

She didn't approve. But she did understand. And a teeny-tiny part of her appreciated the thought behind Doris and Donna's plan too. Misguided as it was, her breakup-ees' faithfulness made Jayne feel she'd truly forged new friendships here. There was no *way* Riley would get past those two. Not when they had mayhem on their minds.

Of course, Riley had changed Kelly's mind about him pretty quickly, she remembered. *I'm glad to be part of your group,* Kelly had said shyly yesterday. *Thanks, Riley. You're really understanding.*

Well, that didn't mean he could work similar magic on Doris and Donna. Those two were determined, their fidelity unshakable.

"Come on down, Jayne." Bruce waved his arm, indicating the fishing pole and bait he'd set out beside Carla's. "Time to catch some lunch."

She shuddered but gamely made her way down the rock-and grass-studded slope. The rushing water grew louder. A fresh fragrance rose from the banks, tinged with a hint of mossy green. Bruce explained that the plan was to catch some fish, then the guides would clean them while Jayne conducted her next antiheartbreak workshop. Afterward, they'd all enjoy grilled fish for lunch and head on their way.

Within no time, Jayne was gripping a pole. She dangled her line in the pool of water, watching skeptically as the bait Bruce had hooked for her eddied in the current. Some poor fish was about to have the shock of its life. And it would be all her fault. Poor fish. She enjoyed a tasty plate of sea bass with miso glaze as much as the next girl, but this . . . well, it was too much.

She yanked her pole from the water.

Suddenly, Riley was right beside her. "Problem?"

"Yes. I just became a vegetarian."

"Anything to do with that fishing pole in your hands?"

"Of course! How can I dupe some poor fish into snacking on my bait and then . . . and then . . ."

"Club it over the head and eat it?"

Jayne felt her eyes widen. "Do you really do that?"

"Only when shark fishing." He examined the fishing pole in his own hands, then expertly cast his line into the water. He tapped his foot. "The rainbow trout we'll catch here require only a small punch."

She gasped. "That's barbaric!"

"It's the way of the wild." A grin played about his lips as he teased the line in the current. He shrugged. "You'll get used to it."

"No, I won't. That's like . . . like luring a person into Macy's with the promise of fifty percent off leather pants, then bashing her with a hundred-pound mannequin when she isn't looking!"

Riley cast her a skeptical glance. "I doubt those mannequins weigh an entire hundred pounds. They look underfed to me. Their plastic hipbones stick out." He shuddered. "Ugh."

She stared at him. "I'm a vegetarian now," Jayne repeated. "I'll eat granola bars for lunch."

"Eat two. Or three. I don't want you to look like one of those mannequins."

He rotated his shoulders as though releasing some pent-up tension. All at once, cheerfulness emanated from him—that, and competency. He capably handled his fishing rod, confidently watched the water for signs of the fish he'd undoubtedly catch with hardly any effort at all. She'd bet Riley had never had second thoughts about anything in his life.

Including leaving her behind.

Unwilling to dwell on that, Jayne cast her line again, the way Bruce had shown her. It snagged on a partly submerged log.

Riley noticed. "Need help?"

"No." She gritted her teeth and yanked. "I can do it."

So what if it had taken twelve tries and twice as many swear words from Bruce to learn the technique? She had it now. Jayne bit her lip and pulled harder.

The line came free. With a determined swing of her arm, she tried again. Again the line snagged—this time on a clump of mushy leaves trapped between two rocks. Frustrated, she gave a mighty tug.

"Easy." Riley's hand covered hers, guiding her into the motion required to free her line. "Save your energy for clobbering those fish."

Her line loosened. It went slack as Jayne watched Riley's profile, noticing that grin of his again.

"We're not really going to bash the fish, are we?" she asked, eyes narrowed.

"You're not. I think you've had enough for one day."

She felt like clapping her hands with glee. Instead, she arched an eyebrow. "I have?"

He nodded. Gathering up their poles, Riley gestured for her to follow him to the outcropping of rocks where Mack was showing Kelly and Alexis how to reel in their catch. Farther along the water's edge, Lance proficiently strung together the fish Doris and Donna had snagged. Tellingly, none of the fish were being clubbed. Jayne frowned.

Sometimes—especially where Riley was concerned—she was much too gullible. Next he'd have her convinced she and her breakup-ees really were going to cook their dinners on the camp stoves by themselves tonight.

"This ought to suffice for my share—and Jayne's," Riley told Mack, handing the redheaded guide a string of fish Jayne hadn't noticed before.

He set down the poles and bait. She noticed his foot tapping again and considered the movement. This wasn't the first time she'd noticed it.

"You're in charge for a while," he went on to tell Mack. "I promised Jayne some private tutelage in wilderness survival."

She gawped. "You did no such—"

"Oh." He feigned surprise. "Did you want to do some more fishing first?"

Gulp. He had her there. Mutely, she shook her head.

"Then come on," Riley said, and took her hand to lead her away from the water's edge.

Pine trees rose all around, interspersed with ash and mountain oak. Dried needles crunched underfoot, mixing with fallen leaves and soil. A peaceful breeze wended between the thick-barked trees. It combined with the springtime Arizona sunshine to make the day pleasantly warm.

Riley led Jayne from their fishing spot. The sound of burbling water fell away quickly. So did the murmur of adventure travelers' and guides' voices, replaced by birdcalls and wind song. Soon they were alone.

Jayne turned to him, her ponytail swinging. Her face, without its usual gloss of color and glimmer, glowed nonetheless with fresh-scrubbed beauty. Riley loved the way she looked, perfectly free and open. He'd almost have believed he loved *her*—all except for the conclusion he'd come to while fishing over the past hour.

"What's this all about?" she demanded, hands on her hips. "You know darn well I'm a hopeless case when it comes to wilderness survival skills, so—"

"*This* is what it's about," Riley said, and kissed her.

She jerked in surprise. Their mouths met—his purposefully, hers in the midst of a protest he didn't want to accept. He held her against him, one hand at her waist and another behind her neck, silently urging her to listen to all the things he could say only this way . . . only through this kiss.

Please hear me, he thought, crazily desperate and equally determined. And in a magical moment he knew he'd always remember, Jayne did. Her protest gave way to acceptance, then eagerness. Riley relaxed. A sense of rightness filled him. He pushed farther, moving them both up against the wide trunk of a sheltering pine.

He held her hips, steadying her against the tree at her back. With a moan, Jayne wrapped her arms around his neck and went on kissing him exactly as he'd dreamed. Willingly. Passionately. Needfully. Losing himself in their joining, Riley felt his senses reel with the wonder of holding Jayne again, here, now. She was sweet and good and always remembered. All the most relentless parts of him insisted he get closer. *Closer.*

He raised his arms, cupped her head with trembling hands. Silky strands brushed past his palms. His fingertips encountered the ponytail holder binding her hair, then moved onward to caress her cheek. He urged her to open wider to him, and she did. With a hungry groan, Riley bent his head to take what Jayne offered.

Their kiss went on and on. Their wilderness clothes clung together, forging a new relationship between Gore-Tex and baby-blue fleece. Their bodies did the same, moving to a remembered rhythm. As the sun warmed their faces and the wind whispered its secrets, their breathing rose in the stillness, unified in shared need. Riley gasped as their mouths broke, came together; he braced his legs and held Jayne close as their bodies shook, arched as one.

This was what he wanted, what he'd dreamed of. *This* was what Riley had realized lay unfinished between them, as he'd fished today with thoughts of Jayne rambling relentlessly through his head. He'd spent the morning over the puzzle of having disappointed her, over the possibility of having left her lonely. In the end he'd come to only one conclusion.

A true ending was what they needed.

Not a note left on the morning of a new assignment's departure. Not a silent good-bye as he bent over a sleeping Jayne and memorized her features before leaving. A *real* ending, a parting as understood as it was certain—those were the things he owed Jayne, Riley knew now. Those were the things she needed. The things he'd give her . . . this time.

It was all so damned simple. So obvious. He couldn't believe he hadn't realized it before. He'd never gotten over her because he needed to give Jayne a good-bye. To give them *both* a good-bye.

But that didn't mean they couldn't enjoy each other in the meantime.

Now, with Jayne in his arms and her kiss on his lips, a new hope—a new purposefulness—filled Riley. It energized him anew. He all but crackled with enthusiasm, and with the relief of having solved the puzzle of his continued thoughts of her. Now he knew how to set things right between them once and for all.

Reluctantly, he ended their kiss. Smiling, he bent his knees until their foreheads gently touched. He gazed into her eyes.

"I'm sorry, Jayne," he said, his voice roughened with regret. "I'm sorry for hurting you. I didn't know."

Her body went rigid. She pushed away. *"What?"*

"I didn't know I'd hurt you. But I figured it out today—"

"Who have you been talking to?"

"What? Nobody. I've been thinking, and—"

"Thinking?" She turned in a circle, her arms wide with apparent disbelief. "About me?"

Riley nodded.

"Ha! Don't do me any favors."

He stepped toward her, intending to take her hand. She turned away before he could. Somehow, things had gone awry. Again. He had to explain before Jayne misunderstood. Too late.

"What were you thinking anyway?" she asked, spinning to face him. She trod through the fallen leaves, crunching their dried surfaces beneath her all-terrain shoes. "That you'd haul me out here, kiss me, and make me forget all the—all the *things* that happened between us?"

"Well . . . sort of." Actually, that was pretty much what *had* happened. "You didn't seem to mind."

His grin faded beneath the glare she threw him.

"You can't say you didn't enjoy it," he added.

She folded her arms. "I didn't enjoy it."

"Liar. You enjoyed it as much as I did. As far as I'm concerned, that's just more proof I'm right about this."

"What?"

She kept *saying* that. "Like I said before, I'm sorry. But I'll do better this time. *We'll* do better. We have a second chance here. Let's use it. Together, for as long as it lasts."

At the word *together* a haunted look filled her eyes. Jayne gazed up at him, momentarily silent. Riley regretted all the more having let her down. This time, this second chance, he'd make things clearer. Was already making things clearer—he hoped.

"And this is what you brought me out here to tell me?"

He nodded.

"I already told you I'm not having a fling with you,"

she warned. Her chin tilted at a determined angle. "I'm not. You can't make me."

"Actually . . . I can." Riley couldn't help but grin as he considered all the myriad ways to do so. "I can make you forget every objection you have."

"No, you—"

"I can." He stepped nearer, letting his gaze rove over her. As always, the sight of her warmed him . . . everywhere. "I will. But this time I'll do it right. I'll do everything right, the way I should have before." He added the ultimate incentive. "It'll be fun."

"No." She hesitated, as though weakening. "No fling. I'd have to be crazy to—"

"I'm not talking about a fling. I'm talking about finishing what we started all those months ago."

Apparent disbelief widened her eyes. He nodded, making sure she understood he was serious. About this. About her. About giving Jayne the—hell, he couldn't believe he was even *thinking* this—*closure* she needed.

She tilted her head sideways, examining him. "Riley, you can't do this to me. You can't. I'm over you now."

Ouch. That hurt. He didn't believe her, but it hurt.

"Give me this," he urged. "Let me make everything right. I owe it to you."

"You owe it to me? Damn right you owe it to me, after the way you—" She broke off, drawing in a deep breath as she visibly calmed herself. His smile was brittle. "Gee, I never thought I'd hear you admit it. It's a miracle."

He decided to overlook her cynicism. So she was skeptical of him. That was understandable. They'd attempted a casual fling once before, and Riley had ended it badly. This time he would do everything right—including saying good-bye fairly when the time came.

"Please," he said. "Please let me make things up to you. I can't promise forever—"

"You never could."

"—but I swear I want to make you happy."

Jayne wavered, biting her lip. She glanced up at him, her lovely blue eyes uncertain.

Riley experienced a moment's uncertainty himself. Had he made things clear enough? Had he explained properly?

Sure he had. He'd said "for as long as it lasts," hadn't he? Had warned he couldn't promise her forever. That was fair. Just to be sure, Riley clarified.

"When this trip is over, our relationship will be—-"

"There's one thing I want," she interrupted, as though unable to remain silent any longer. Her serious look deepened, became even more earnest. More determined.

"Anything."

"This time," Jayne said, "*I* want to be the one to say good-bye."

Surprise rooted him in place. That was the *last* thing he'd expected from her.

He should have been glad, Riley knew. He'd never been good at good-byes—not since childhood. Usually he avoided them. He distrusted a sappy good-bye the same way he distrusted stability. The same way he distrusted the close-knit families and long-term friendships he'd glimpsed—but had never been a part of—growing up as the son of globe-trotting parents. Those things didn't fit in with his experiences. They never had.

But this meant, he reminded himself, that Jayne understood his intentions; accepted them. Relief warred with disquiet inside him. If the truth were told, her desire to be the one to end things between them hurt.

Riley nodded and stepped nearer. "All right."

She flinched. "And—and this has to be a secret between us. If my antiheartbreak ladies find out we're . . . involved again, my credibility will be destroyed."

"Understood."

"One more thing." Her chin rose another notch. "I want to be the one to say how far this goes."

He pretended to deliberate. "That's three things."

"Take it or leave it. Those are my terms."

"I can accept that." With a smile, he slipped his hand to her cheek, loving the softness of her skin against his palm. He'd missed touching her. "Only what you want," he promised. "*Everything* you want."

Jayne tilted her head and closed her eyes briefly, as though enjoying the feel of his hand cradling her. When she looked up at him again, her gaze was decisive.

"Right now I want you to kiss me," she murmured. "Again and again and aga—"

He did, cutting off her words with a kiss as tender and fierce as he could make it. As their lips came together, as their bodies reunited in a way their hearts had yet to retry, Riley couldn't shake the sensation there was something he'd forgotten in all this . . . something important.

Something like . . . he was still in love with Jayne.

Oh, hell, he thought, and lost himself in their kiss with unmatched fervor. *One or both of them was crazy to be doing this. And it was probably him.*

Fourteen

Alexis tromped through the lightly forested area beyond the fishing hole, looking for Jayne and Uncle Riley—and determinedly *avoiding* Lance, who'd volunteered to help her. Although he was a high school sophomore and therefore an automatically desirable *older man,* she refused to be tempted into something that would only end in Cinnabon disaster. After all, she was older herself now. And wiser.

Next time she'd follow Jayne's advice from the *Heartbreak 101* book. She'd evaluate her options, make an informed decision, and engage her heart only when she was sure.

Confident that she'd made terrific progress in getting over Brendan already, Alexis ducked beneath a pine bough. She straightened, scanning the landscape. "Uncle Riley? Jayne? Oh, *there* you are, Jayne."

She smiled as the author emerged from behind a clump of baby oak trees, wearing hiking clothes and a curiously dreamy expression. Alexis waited as Jayne picked her way past pinecones and over fallen logs, calling a greeting as she came.

"Where's Uncle Riley?"

"I, uh—" Jayne glanced backward, then quickly faced front again. She shrugged. "I guess he beat me back to camp. We were . . . having a wilderness survival tutorial."

"Ugh. When *we* did that, Uncle Riley made me eat moss."

"I didn't have to eat moss," Jayne assured her, an odd smile quirking her lips. She hugged herself.

"Good. Well, anyway, Mack sent me to look for you." Alexis admired the way Jayne had managed to coordinate and accessorize her outdoor wear and vowed to do the same. "He says you'd better come start your next workshop before the women start throwing fish guts at Bruce."

Jayne made a face. "That bad, huh?"

"He volunteered to teach nude rock climbing if you weren't back within half an hour. *With* all the appropriate harnesses."

Jayne shuddered. They both laughed.

"In that case," she said, "I'd better hurry up."

She caught up to Alexis, then passed her while cheerfully gesturing for Alexis to follow.

Ten yards out, Jayne stopped. "I'm already lost. I think I have a mental block about the wilderness."

"This way." Alexis offered to take the lead, having memorized much of this area during previous hikes. Doing so, she came closer. Peered at something caught in Jayne's ponytail. "You have something in your hair."

She plucked it out. Held it toward Jayne.

"A leaf." Jayne gave a nervous laugh, snatching the crispy dried leaf from Alexis's fingers. "Wonder how that got there?"

"Some bark too." She removed a slender, piney scrap.

Jayne grabbed it. With another awkward chuckle, she tossed it over her shoulder, then brushed her hands clean. "Ha! I guess I ought to leave some of the woods *in* the woods, huh? Let's go."

Suspiciously, Alexis squinted as Jayne passed by. The last time she'd seen so many leaves and bark in a person's hair, her mom and dad had been trying out techniques from their *Making Whoopie in the Wilderness* book. In the backyard. In a tent. In the *backyard*. It had been totally *gross*.

But this time . . . *hmmm*.

Alexis hurried to catch up. She turned Jayne in the correct direction, then moved on. "I've been wondering . . . did I ever mention the way Uncle Riley looks at you?"

"Me?" Jayne stopped dead. "Riley looks at me?"

"All the time. In this *really* lovestruck way. He talks about you too."

"Really?"

Alexis nodded. Jayne was already hooked. She could tell. And Uncle Riley had been a slam dunk yesterday. Sheesh, this stuff was easy. Alexis realized she had major potential as a matchmaker. She could set up shop in the school cafeteria, start taking applications after spring break, maybe even charge a fee. Why not?

Alexis smiled. "You bet. And you won't *believe* what he told me yesterday. . . ."

Riley was in love with her.

Jayne still couldn't believe it. She conducted one more antiheartbreak workshop (shiatsu trigger banishment). She ate fresh fried trout for lunch (shamefully delicious). She even hiked another several miles into the canyon (gorgeous, truly). But even after all that, Jayne marveled over what she'd learned.

Of course, Alexis hadn't come right out and said it. She hadn't said *Uncle Riley's in love with you*. But she might as well have. The things she'd described . . . well, obviously *love* was the most reasonable conclusion to be drawn from the behavior Alexis had detailed with teenage enthusiasm.

Immense satisfaction filled her. Jayne knew she'd been right about Riley. There were still feelings between them.

And it wasn't just her.

Giddy with the knowledge, Jayne trouped after Bruce and Carla. Her feet no longer hurt, her legs no longer ached. Her heart was light, and her steps were too. Riley's kiss-ambush earlier made twice as much sense now. So did his amazing invitation. The words he'd used would linger in her memory forever, she was sure.

I'm talking about finishing what we started all those months ago.

Okay, so she'd caved in the face of his sincerity. She'd relented when he'd kissed her and kissed her and . . . she'd relented. Period. She'd made the decision to take Riley up on his offer, but looking back on it now, Jayne felt fine with that.

She had her antiheartbreak techniques. She had almost two years' worth of separation from Riley, two years' worth of personal growth and confidence. Her heart was safe. She could pick up where they'd left off, enjoy herself, and move on. She could date like a man.

Date like a man. Hey! That could be a fabulous follow-up book, after her *Heartbreak 101* hands-on workbook was published. *Date Like a Man: Dazzle Like a Woman.* It could work. She had to get a proposal to her editor right away.

Newly excited about both her personal life and her professional life, Jayne bounded over a fallen log. She kept her eyes on Bruce and Carla up ahead, but her thoughts raced onward. So long as her clandestine reunions with Riley weren't discovered by her breakup-ees . . .

The possibility gave her pause. It made her remember something that had been pushed aside by the surprise of Riley's suggestion and the heat of his kiss. Something important.

Something like . . . oh, yeah. She was still in love with him.

Oh, boy, Jayne thought. She picked up the pace, as though she could outrun her doubts along with her outdoorsy inexperience. It was no use though. This put their rekindled romance in a whole new light. *A crazy light.*

One or both of them had to be nuts to try this again, to finish what they'd started. It was probably her.

When Jayne reached the rendezvous point to conduct her next workshop, Mack's group wasn't there yet, but Riley's was. She didn't know how he'd managed to outmatch drill sergeant Bruce's punishing pace, but he had. While Bruce vanished to "hang a leak" and Carla shook her head at him in disgust, Jayne held back to catch her breath. To her right rose the forest they'd been hiking through. To her left soared a magnificent red rock cliff. And in front of her lay the space allotted for her upcoming antiheartbreak workshop.

Doris, Donna, and Lance worked good-naturedly to set up the temporary camp they would inhabit for the next hour or so. Riley worked too, hauling fallen logs for seating amid the forested area's less rocky terrain. He would drag the logs back to their original locations when they'd finished with them, Jayne knew, having watched him follow the backpacker's "leave no trace" dictum several times on this trip already.

His outdoorsman's conscientiousness was something she admired about Riley. His outdoorsman's strength, she considered now, was another. He'd removed his fleece outer garment to work in his close-fitting crew neck shirt, and the sight of all those chiseled muscles in action was breathtaking.

Riley moved with natural grace, with purposeful motions and innate male agility. His forearms flexed as he sought purchase on a thick-barked fallen pine log. His biceps strained as he freed the log, then began dragging its six-foot length to join the others he'd moved into the clearing just beyond Jayne's vantage point.

Riley sighted another, final log and matter-of-factly pulled it too. He seemed unfazed by the thigh-high rounded length of wood, unbothered by the exertion required to move its undoubtedly considerable weight. Watching him, a tiny thrill passed through Jayne . . . which was ridiculous, really. She'd never been much for the he-man type, had never been overly impressed by machismo. But this . . . this was different.

It wasn't as though Riley were doing something particularly meaningful—say, building a shelter for them. But Jayne had the sense he could have if he'd needed to. He could have cared for them all expertly and indefinitely. Despite the dangers he posed to her heart, with Riley she felt safe. Protected. As alien as the feeling was, she enjoyed it.

Doris and Donna approached him. "We're finished," the first sister said. "And I wanted to tell you again, Riley, how grateful we are to you. If you hadn't showed us how to pad our feet with that moleskin, Donna and I would have been crippled with blisters by now."

"Nonsense, Doris. What really did the trick were those telescoping walking sticks Riley loaned us."

"My feet hurt more than your stupid knees."

"My knees are worse than your big ol' feet any day."

"Crybaby."

"Bigfoot!"

Doris opened her mouth to rebut. Riley's raised palms and gruff expression stopped her. "You're both welcome."

They quit bickering, turning to him with identical worshipful grins. Riley was oblivious. He began slapping away the worst of the dirt and spiderwebs from the logs he'd arranged. It was a concession to cleanliness, Jayne knew, designed partly with her in mind. She'd been ridiculously grateful when he'd initiated it, despite his jokes about her "princessy posterior."

Riley glanced over his shoulder at Doris and Donna. "You two need more work to do?"

"Oh, no."

"We've got plenty."

The sisters hurried away, not noticing Jayne watching,

openmouthed, from the edge of the campsite. "... Really is so sweet" drifted past and "quite a hunk. If I were fifteen years younger ..."

Jayne couldn't believe it. *He'd conquered Doris and Donna too!* First Kelly, now the squabbling sisters. Jayne's he-done-me-wrong allies were melting like cherry Sno-Kones in a puddle of sunlight. Was there no end to the magic Riley Davis could work?

He glanced up and saw her standing there. A glad-to-see-you smile broke over his handsome, square-jawed face. "Jayne! I was hoping you'd get here soon."

Girlish delight filled her. *Nope, there was no end to the magic.* Jayne spread her arms. "Yup, here I am."

"Good. Because Lance needs help sharpening the sticks for toasting marshmallows with. He's over in that stand of trees."

He tossed her the damned Swiss Army knife again. She couldn't catch it, and it landed with a thud at her feet. Memories of her brothers laughing as she missed Frisbee toss after Frisbee toss ("The dog catches better than you do!") assaulted her as Jayne looked at the knife taunting her from the ground.

Indignantly, she bent over and snatched it from the dried needles underfoot. "Fine. Stick sharpening? I can do that. Anything else?"

"Nope. Thanks."

Jayne turned. Riley's voice followed her:

"You'll need the big blade."

She glanced at the knife in her fist. "I knew that."

"It folds out. And don't cut off your finger. I don't have any spares." He paused. "Spare fingers, that is."

"Har-har."

"They need to be big sticks," he warned. "Long ones."

Jayne envisioned bashing a certain bossy trail guide over the head with a *big, long* stick. "Of course," she said.

Then, raising her head high, she stalked off to show know-

it-all Riley exactly what she could accomplish when moti-
vated.

Shaking his head, Riley watched the feminine swish of
Jayne's hips as she huffed off in her baby-blue ensemble.
He felt a little guilty for sending her to do something she
was undoubtedly ill equipped to do, so he decided to throw
out a peace offering.

"Lance has probably finished most of them by now. There
won't be much for you to do."

"Don't worry about me."

"Be careful not to slice off *Lance's* finger either."

"Bite me. I can do it."

Her cocky swagger carried her all the way into the woods
and out of his vision. Riley laughed. He'd almost forgotten
how bawdy Jayne could be when ruffled. Beneath her high-
heels-and-lipstick exterior beat the heart of a bona fide
wanna-be tough girl.

Chattering voices drifted toward him. An instant later,
Mack entered the clearing with Mitzi, Kelly, and Alexis.
Mitzi immediately located Bruce and went to flirt with the
guide (making the source of the hearts drawn in arranged
leaves and "M + B" spelled out in stones he'd seen along
the trail immediately obvious). Kelly waved cheerfully to
Riley and then began purifying some water through a filter.
His niece looked for Lance, caught a glimpse of him through
the pine branches, and deliberately swerved toward Riley
instead.

That worked for him. He had a bone to pick with Alexis
and had since early this morning.

He looked up as she passed. "Hey. I never made you eat
moss, dammit. Stop spreading that around."

She paused. Frowned over her shoulder. "Made me eat . . . ?"
Alexis echoed, then comprehension dawned. "You *were*

fooling around in the woods with Jayne!'' she crowed. ''I *knew* it!''

He stiffened. *Whoops.* Too late, Riley remembered he'd been ducking behind a tree, waiting for Jayne to get a head start on him so they wouldn't reveal the truth about their temporary reconciliation, when he'd overheard that aggravating tidbit fall from his niece's lips.

''Don't you have some chores to do?'' he asked, frowning as he leaned forward to finish dusting the logs. ''Fish to clean? Tent poles to straighten? Somebody *else* to pester?''

''You're getting lucky with Jayne,'' Alexis sang. She pumped her hips and pushed her palms in the air in some kind of demented whoopee-celebration dance. ''You're getting lucky with Jayne.''

''I am not.'' But it hadn't been for lack of trying. At a crucial juncture amid the fallen leaves, Jayne had remembered that amour al fresco might include actual bugs and had bolted upright. Riley could still feel the sizzle inside him caused by their preceding kisses though. Not that his innocent niece needed to know that. ''It's none of your damned business.''

Alexis went on dancing. She stopped singing long enough to peer at his head. ''I'll bet you have leaves in *your* hair too. Jayne did. No *wonder* she looked all dreamy.''

Dreamy? His heart softened. He *wanted* Jayne to feel dreamy, wanted her to . . . Hang on. He was getting sidetracked.

''It must be the mall deprivation making you loony,'' he told Alexis firmly. ''You're imagining things.''

''Oh, yeah? Did I imagine the goo-goo-eyed look you were giving Jayne when I got here? Huh? Huh?''

Riley shoved a hand through his hair. *Hell.* All of a sudden, this was looking like a very long trip. Still prodding—literally now—Alexis jabbed him in the shoulder.

''Huh? Huh? Huh?''

''I have a workshop to get ready for,'' he told her with

dignity, raising his jaw. Then he strode away before he could get himself into even more trouble.

Alexis sat on a bunch of logs with the other women that afternoon, waiting for the next antiheartbreak workshop to begin. Beside her, Carla, Kelly, Mitzi, Doris, and Donna all held the hairbrushes Jayne had requested they bring. So did Alexis. She could hardly wait for things to get started. She needed a break. That loser Lance had been following her around the campsite almost from the moment she'd gotten there.

He'd even tried to impress her by showing her some stupid tree branches he'd whittled. *As if.* Alexis had told him she preferred Jayne's ribbon-wrapped, polka-dotted (with red nail polish) marshmallow-toasting sticks. Which was true. Jayne's sticks had *style.* Even Uncle Riley had agreed— once he'd recovered from an inexplicable laughing attack.

But once Jayne's workshop began, the guys' workshop would begin too—which meant Lance would leave her alone for a while. Alexis waited impatiently for Jayne to take her place in the center of their group.

Finally, she did. The breeze tossed her ponytail and the sun glinted off her blonde highlights (Alexis *had* to get highlights exactly like those, she decided), and from somewhere she'd produced her leopard-print compact. Alexis palmed her identical compact tightly in her non-hairbrush-holding hand. It felt good to be part of the group.

At the camp's edge, Uncle Riley quietly led Lance, Bruce, and Mack beyond some trees to another nearby clearing. With a knowing nod Alexis watched him go. His innocent act hadn't fooled her a bit. She knew darn well neither he nor Jayne had been able to resist her superior matchmaking skills.

At Jayne's call, they primped. Alexis spent most of her primping time trying to cover a monster zit. Then all the women yelled out, "If you look good, you feel good!" and high-fived each other. The whole thing gave Alexis a warm and fuzzy feeling, sort of like the last five minutes of *7th Heaven*. Only this was better, because this wasn't TV—it was real.

"This workshop is based on one of my original techniques— shampoo therapy," Jayne said. "It's called *Really Wash That Man out of Your Hair*."

Everyone hooted and hollered. Alexis did too. *Take that, Brendan!*

"Now, since *somebody* wouldn't let me bring actual shampoo bottles on the trail," Jayne continued, shooting a disgruntled frown in the direction the men had gone, "and the bathing facilities here leave so much to be desired—"

"I *heard* that!" came Uncle Riley's voice from within the trees.

"—we're going to have to improvise. I have one container of dry shampoo, and I'm going to share it. What you do is—"

She went on to explain the technique. Before long, the dry shampoo had been passed, the hairbrushes were being wielded, and everyone was muttering the mantra Jayne had given them.

"Get out of my head, Brendan, you *weasel,*" Alexis said. The scent of cinnamon still gave her twinges of heartbreak-by-association, and she'd had enough. "Get out, get out, get out!"

"Get lost, Marty," Doris and Donna chanted as they vigorously massaged the dry shampoo through their graying curls.

"You can't, like, hurt me anymore, Paolo," Carla said, rubbing her scalp.

"I'm over you, Rodney," Mitzi recited. Her gaze drifted to the men's location. She spotted Bruce in the distance and winked at him, as though proving the technique miraculously effective.

"Bye-bye, Tim," Kelly said. "You're no good for me." Beneath her shampoo-squeezing hands, faint tears rolled down her cheeks. Her voice broke. "Sorry . . . Mrs. Tim."

Witnessing Kelly's heartbreak, Alexis couldn't help but feel sorry for her. Tim had obviously been a scumbag. She scooted nearer to Kelly and gave her a hug.

"It'll be okay," she whispered. "And your hair looks *amazing.*"

Kelly brightened. "You think so? Thanks!"

Alexis felt better already.

Jayne walked among them, offering encouragement, demonstrations, and effectiveness boosters. "Coming clean" was good for body and soul, she told the breakup-ees.

Jayne looked sad as she said it, Alexis noticed. Almost as though she believed she might never be squeaky clean again. Being on the trail had that effect on some people, but it seemed doubly tough for Jayne. She was a regular bathaholic.

All the same, the author rallied. "Who's feeling better?" she asked when everyone had finished.

Alexis instantly raised her hand. "Me!"

Mitzi did the same. So did Doris and Donna.

Carla only hung her head, but Kelly sniffled and raised her hand partway.

"Excellent!" Jayne beamed at them. Then she swept a compassionate gaze over Carla and Kelly. "The rest of you, take heart. There are more techniques on the way. I'll be with you for every step. Remember, I've been there. I understand what you're going through, and I'm here to help."

Everyone cheered. In the center of the group, Jayne blushed and stared at her shoes. Alexis felt a surge of affection for her so strong, it was startling. Yes, she decided, Jayne could definitely become her aunt. Definitely.

She'd be perfect.

And she even came with a bonus makeup kit to share, Alexis reflected. What could be better?

Fifteen

After her workshop, Jayne found Riley and the other men sitting in a nearby clearing with their backs against several thick-trunked pines. They held out their arms in front of them, palms turned partway up and fingers slightly curled, and gazed determinedly into the distance. Flickers of movement caught her eye. Their thumbs, she realized. Every last man was wiggling his upraised thumb.

She frowned in puzzlement. "Riley?"

"Shhh. I'm conducting a workshop here."

"A workshop for what?" she whispered.

"Thumb development. I call it the Remote Control Relay. Useful for when you need to whip through a hundred and fifty channels while your girlfriend gets another diet Coke."

Jayne rolled her eyes. "Unbelievable."

His smile was boyish. *Appealingly* boyish. "Thanks."

He kept his profile toward her, apparently concentrating on his *technique*. She let her gaze travel over the beard-shadowed edge of his jaw, the assertive line of his nose, the amused quirk in his lips. A sigh nearly escaped her. He'd kissed her with those lips. He'd kissed her, eased her onto the pine needles, trailed his mouth down her neck as he slipped his hands beneath her multitudes of outdoor-wear layers to unerringly cup her breasts. He'd stroked her there, making her dizzy. If she hadn't remembered the buggy hazards surrounding them, Jayne wasn't sure what would have happened.

But she *was* sure she would have enjoyed it.

"I'm considering a BarcaLounger-Fridge Beer Dash next," Riley said, breaking into her thoughts. "The guys and I can run up the trail with boulder-size beer can stand-ins in each hand for training."

She pictured it. "Gee, Riley. The potential usefulness of that . . . well, I can hardly describe it."

His grin widened.

"You should think about writing your own book," Jayne went on mock seriously, giving him a teasing nod.

"Nah. That would mean staying in one place." He frowned. "Working on one thing."

She considered his dual careers as nature photographer and trail guide. Both fit perfectly into his stay-on-the-move lifestyle. "But you already work hard," she said, deliberately misunderstanding. "You could do it."

"Thanks." Riley swept her with a hasty grateful glance as he got to his feet. "I appreciate your vote of confidence, but the settled life isn't for me."

There was nothing to say to that.

"I'll be back in a few minutes. If you're done with your workshop, we'll head out after that."

Jayne agreed, wondering what she'd said to cause Riley's rapid exit. She watched him stride away, his shoulders straight and his movements steady. He nodded at the other guides as he passed them but didn't stop to talk. For the first time, it struck her that Riley spent a lot of time away from the group. Alone. On purpose. He isolated himself *on purpose*.

The very idea was alien to Jayne, who did everything she could to avoid feeling as lonely and out of place as she had while growing up. It wasn't as though Riley was unpopular with the other adventure travelers or guides—on the contrary. Bruce and Mack, for instance, obviously liked and respected him. So what, she wondered, was the rest of the story?

Curious now, Jayne resolved to find out. And she knew exactly how to begin.

That evening Riley hunkered down beside Mitzi's Coleman stove, watching the frizzy-haired waitress maneuver its fold out supports into position. Performing the steps he'd shown her, she connected the fuel line. She struck a match. In the center of the stove's supports, a tiny blue flame burst into life.

"I did it!" she cried. Exuberantly, she hugged him. Bubble gum popped in his ear. "Thank you so much!"

"You're welcome."

"And after only six tries this time too. I swear, I thought you might give up on me after that whole water-purifying mix-up—"

Riley remembered his struggles to explain the filtering process to Mitzi, after Bruce had gotten too frustrated to go on. With an effort, he kept the smile on his face so her feelings wouldn't be hurt.

"—but you didn't. You're the greatest, Riley!"

Her hug tightened. Tentatively, he patted one hand on her back. Then he leaned away quickly, feeling awkward but pleased to have helped. Adventure travelers needed to trust their guides—and he'd detected some serious antagonism coming from a few of the group members. Now Riley was making progress with them.

Mitzi, for instance, beamed at him.

A muffled "hmmph" came from nearby.

He turned his head. The only person close enough to have spoken that loudly was Jayne, who sat on a folded tarp beside her own camp stove, looking mildly betrayed. She caught him watching her and went back to waiting for the water to boil for her instant macaroni and cheese.

The vaguely disgruntled pucker of her lips remained though. Riley wondered at its cause.

"How are things coming along for you?" he asked, cocking an eyebrow. "Need any help?"

She lifted her chin. "You *would* have to ask that, wouldn't you?"

"Huh?"

"It's not nice to gloat, you know."

Again, "Huh?"

"I'm doing fine." She folded her arms over her chest, glaring into her pan of water as though her angry gaze could boil it. "Just fine. In fact, I've never needed less help than I do right now. Never, ever."

Was she upset because he hadn't helped her work her camp stove? He didn't think so. And yet ... no. It was probably best not to think about it too deeply. Thinking about it would only lead to talking about it—which, with women, often devolved into a Serious Discussion About Things.

Riley nodded. "You're probably right. You're getting the hang of things," he told Jayne. "Bruce told me you navigated him and Mitzi all the way here—"

"With only one tiny detour," Mitzi put in.

"—and with no help from him at all." He gave Mitzi a not-now look. "And you set up your tent much faster today too."

Jayne's skeptical gaze collided with his. "I poked a hole in my air mattress with a bivvy sack."

Riley still didn't know how she'd managed that. He suspected she'd brought along contraband stilettos inside the soft fabric bag, but confronting her about it now was pointless.

"Easily fixed," he assured her, "with some duct tape."

"I dunked my flashlight in the wash-up pail."

"That's what waterproof casings are for."

"I screamed when a squirrel came near my tent."

"They're sometimes fairly ferocious looking."

"I got lost coming back from a nature break."

He kept as straight a face as he could. "You found a little extra privacy, that's all."

"Oh, what's the use?" Jayne flung her hands in the air. "I'm terrible at outdoors stuff!"

Okay. This required further intervention. With a keep-up-the-good-work nod for Mitzi, Riley moved closer to Jayne. He sat on his haunches in silence, hands loosely clasped between his knees. He waited.

"I've never been able to get the hang of 'guy things,' " she complained, going on just as he'd known she would. "My dad knew it, my brothers knew it, and now . . . everyone else knows it too!"

She buried her face in her palms, shaking her head. "I want to do *girl* things," Jayne said defiantly. "I'm *good* at girl things. Really good."

He hated seeing her upset. But in an odd way, the fact that Jayne was bothered by her difficulties reassured him. That meant mastering those skills had begun to matter to her. A little. It was a start . . . a start to forging a potential love of the outdoors they could share.

"Camping and hiking aren't guy things. They're fun things. I promise." He put a hand to her knee. "You just need more wilderness training."

Jayne's head came up. She regarded him through suspiciously moist blue eyes. She sniffled. A cautious hopefulness edged onto her expression.

"Wilderness training?"

Riley nodded. "That's right. With your wilderness instructor." He pointed at himself, then pitched his voice to a husky, private timbre. "I know things about . . . nature . . . I can hardly wait to show you."

Comprehension dawned. A small smile curved her mouth.
"I'd like that."

So would he. "Okay, then. Come on."

They stood together, Jayne wiping her eyes with her fingers. She followed him to the edge of the evening's campsite.

"Hey," Mitzi called from behind them. "What about
your boiling water? What about dinner?"

"You can have it. I'm not hungry," Jayne shouted over
her shoulder, waving to Mitzi. The conspiratorial smile she
gave Riley made his blood run hot. Her gaze never left his
as she yelled out, "I'll have a little something later."

"I've got a *big* something for you right now," Riley
promised in a low voice.

She laughed with delight over his teasing. Her attention
whisked past his chest and lower, in an assessing, deliberately provocative arc. There was one thing about Jayne—
she could give back as good as she got.

"I'll just *bet* you do," she said. "I can't wait to see it."

"I can't wait to show you."

Caught up in the connectedness their bantering engen-
dered, warmed by it, Riley took her hand. Moments later,
they'd entered the privacy of the wooded area far beyond
the camp. Riley shook out the thing he'd tucked beneath
his elbow before leaving.

"My tarp?" she asked, looking puzzled.

"You bet." He spread it over a soft carpet of fallen leaves,
then gestured toward it as anticipation simmered through
him. "Your bug-free haven awaits."

Jayne bit her lip, staring downward. "But . . . can't the
bugs just crawl on top of the tarp and get me that way?"

"Not if we work fast," Riley said, and carried her down.

Jayne giggled as he kissed her, then moaned as their
familiar union deepened. They rolled over. In an instant,
Riley had playfully pinned her arms over her head.

"I guess you caught me," Jayne said, smirking. "What
are you going to do with me now?"

"Make up for lost time," he promised. He wedged his knee between her parted track-pant-covered thighs, then lowered until his chest barely grazed her breasts. Riley looked deeply into her eyes, overcome with tenderness for the woman lying so trustingly in his arms. "And make you regret every minute you won't be spending right here. With me."

She sighed. "Oh, Riley."

"Save your breath," he instructed with a kiss. "You'll need it for screaming with pleasure later."

And with that he began . . . making time irrelevant to both of them.

Later, Jayne trudged dispiritedly back to the campsite, running her fingers through her bedraggled hair in an attempt to lose her involuntary "big-haired crazy woman" look. Recognizing the effort was futile, she gathered the strands in a fresh ponytail and snapped her covered elastic over it.

She sighed. She should have been lying blissfully in Riley's arms right now, enjoying the afterglow of fabulous spontaneous lovemaking. She should have been snuggled against his blast-furnace heat, complimenting him on a job well done. She should have been prostrate with satisfaction, unable to move a muscle except to grin. But no. She wasn't. And why not?

Because she was a girly-girl, that's why.

Riley hadn't said as much. In fact he'd been very considerate, very understanding about the sudden mood-wrecking realization Jayne had had partway through their "wilderness training." But the truth was, they hadn't come together in the intimate way they'd both hoped for. And it was all Jayne's fault. She was disappointed . . . but it had to be this way.

After all—how could she *possibly* make love with him, when she hadn't bathed for two whole days now?

During those two days, she'd hiked. She'd labored to set up tents and blow up injured air mattresses. She'd even climbed a tree (sort of, to the lowest branch), to try to discover her navigation error today. She *had* to be stinky, or at least less than fresh. And although Riley's frequent use of the premoistened towelettes he'd introduced her to seemed to have left him clean and appealing, Jayne couldn't say she felt as confident about herself.

Then too, they'd been apart for so long. Was it a crime to want things to be nice for their first time in a long time?

Riley hadn't acted as though it was, even though Jayne knew he had to have felt as frustrated and disappointed as she did. Instead, he'd held her hand. He'd talked. He'd made her laugh with squirrel jokes and moose impressions and stories of hikes gone comically awry.

He'd cared for her.

And on a practical level, Jayne recalled, he'd even managed to make good use of their stolen time together. He'd actually taught her a few facts about wilderness survival.

Sure, she hadn't made whoopee, she told herself. But now she knew how to tie a wicked square knot.

Disgruntled, Jayne tromped farther. The sounds of the nearby camp grew louder. It was just past sunset now, and everyone would be gathered around the small rock-encircled fire. As she passed between two trees, Jayne glimpsed Mack and Bruce standing a short distance beyond Lance and the breakup-ees.

The sight of the guides niggled at her. They could help her with . . . something . . . she'd been meaning to do. Something she'd planned to do before getting caught up in the defection of yet another breakup-ee to the Riley Fan Club.

Riley. That was it! She remembered her earlier curiosity about the way Riley frequently left everyone behind, remembered her resolve to discover the reasons behind it. Who better to explain Riley's tendency toward aloneness, Jayne thought now, than his longtime friends Mack and Bruce?

Decisively, she stepped forward. With her erstwhile clandestine lover still in the forest to give her a head start, this might be her best chance to dig into his secrets.

"Hey, Mack!" she called. "Bruce!"

They turned at the sound of her voice. Within moments, she'd caught up to them. Self-consciously, Jayne checked her fleece for more telltale dried leaves, then addressed them both.

"I have some questions for you two," she said. "I'm really hoping you can help me out."

Beneath a stand of aspens that glowed ghostly white in the light from the campfire a few yards distant, Jayne leaned her shoulder against a tree. She resisted an urge to check her hair, and fought back the need to swipe on some lip gloss before unsightly chapping set in. She'd been trying to act like one of the guys in the hope such behavior would relax Mack and Bruce enough to cut loose some secrets. She'd even tried to spit. The resulting dribble of drool hadn't been pretty.

"About fifteen years now, I guess," Bruce was saying in response to her last question—how long each of them had known Riley. Casually, he reached down and adjusted something in his pants—something that required a funny hip wiggle and a wince. "My folks moved next door to his grandparents when I was going into high school. Riley usually spent the summers there."

Jayne nodded. She considered scratching her butt but couldn't manage such out-and-out fake machismo.

"Almost as long for me," Mack said, his expression open and Howdy-Doody cheerful. "We wound up working the same cross-country ski trip nine or ten years ago. We hit it off, I guess." He shrugged. "We've guided lots of groups together since then. There's nobody I'd rather hit the trail with."

"Except a Playmate." Bruce gave a *huh-huh* laugh. "Or one of those Victoria's Secret lingerie models."

"I meant that in a professional sense."

"Hey, so did I. Those girls *are* professionals. Professional hotties! Yowsa!"

Bruce pantomimed burning his fingers. Jayne shook her head and reminded herself the man meant well. He was just a little . . . juvenile when it came to women. In all other ways he was a devoted and capable guide. And he knew Riley thoroughly.

"So you'd say you both know Riley pretty well?" she asked.

They nodded. Mack stuck his hands in his pockets and cast a glance toward the group of travelers around the campfire. Was she mistaken, or did his gaze linger just a bit longingly on Kelly's bespectacled face?

" 'Bout as well as anybody, I guess," Bruce said.

"Yeah," Mack agreed, swerving his attention back to Jayne.

"What does that mean?"

They hesitated. Finally, Mack spoke again. "Well, you've seen Riley." He spread his arms wide. "Riley comes . . . and he goes. I don't think he has many close ties."

"Not even to his family?"

They gave her blank looks.

"His parents? They're Greenpeace volunteers?"

"No kidding?" Mack asked.

"Huh." Bruce scratched his head. Then *he* spit.

Jayne pretended he hadn't. "Don't tell me neither of you know anything about Riley's family."

They shrugged. "He doesn't talk about himself."

"And you've never *asked* him? Not in ten, fifteen years?"

Mack and Bruce shared a perplexed glance.

"You call yourself *friends?*" Jayne prodded.

"Sure."

" 'Course."

"The subject hasn't come up in our weekly knitting circle," Bruce cracked. Mack grinned.

This wasn't going at all as she'd hoped. Regrouping, Jayne offered up a hopefully masculine-seeming sniff. She waggled her own hips but couldn't go so far as a crotch grab. "What about girlfriends? Surely you guys talk about those."

Bruce frowned. "Did you just jab me in the ribs?"

She backed off, chagrined. "I meant it in a camaraderie-building sense." Jayne waggled her eyebrows encouragingly. "You know, man-to-man talk about the ladies."

Mack shook his head. "Nice men don't drag the women they care about through the conversational mud." Again, his gaze drifted to Kelly.

"Come *on*, you guys! Give me the dirt!"

"Look," Bruce said. "Riley is different. He's ... the one-night stand of friendships. He's lots of fun when he's around, but in the morning he usually has someplace else to be."

"Good analogy," Mack said approvingly. "Way to go."

Bruce beamed. Jayne felt like tearing her hair out.

"Maybe you two aren't the people I should be talking to about this."

They disagreed. "Like we said before," Bruce told her, "we know Riley as well as anyone."

"Maybe better," Mack said. "But he's a hard man to buddy up to. He's alone most of the time. I think he likes it that way."

"Yeah. Riley's fun when he's around, but ..." Bruce shrugged, making his meaning plain. *But he's not around much.*

"Then he doesn't let *anyone* get close to him?" Jayne asked, frustrated. Riley could return any minute now, and she didn't have much time.

Bruce concentrated. "Well, there *was* that one girl ..."

"The one in . . ." Mack snapped his fingers. "San Francisco."

Everything inside Jayne went still. *San Francisco.* Where she'd met Riley. Where she'd loved Riley. Where he'd left her, inexplicably, behind.

The two men sighed like lovesick sailors on a two-day pass. "That was somethin' else," Bruce said. "He fell for her hard."

"Really loved her, I think," Mack agreed.

She hardly dared to breathe, but she had to know. "What was her name?"

Another blank look from Bruce. "Dunno."

Jayne stared expectantly at Mack. He shook his head.

Still, it had to be her. She hardly dared hope, and yet . . . *it had to be.*

"But if you don't even know her name," Jayne asked gently, "how do you know Riley was in love with her?"

"Simple," Bruce said. "He never talked about her."

Okay, she was losing it. They were making no sense at all. Maybe pretending to be macho was affecting her strangely. But it was her only hope of keeping the conversation going, so she had to keep it up. Jayne lifted her arm and scratched her fleece-clad armpit.

Apparently, Mack took pity on her, because he offered an explanation: "The only thing Riley would ever tell us about the woman from San Francisco was that he'd met her," he said, "and that he missed her."

Missed her. Yearning welled inside Jayne. If only that were true. If only Riley had missed her. Missed her enough to come back.

"Yeah," Bruce agreed. He raised his eyebrows as Jayne tried to carry on her just-us-guys cover by belching. Only a small "peep" emerged. "See, with an ordinary girl, a guy talks about her with his buddies. But with a special girl . . . well, he clams up. He doesn't want to risk blowing it."

"*And* he doesn't want to risk having his buddies make

fun of her *perfectly harmless* pet name for him,'' Mack added, looking stormy for the first time.

"Quiet, Piggly-Wiggly. I'm trying to talk to the lady."

Mack glared at Bruce, then transferred his gaze to Jayne. Deliberately ignoring the other man, he continued. "Also, with Riley and the San Francisco woman, it was the *way* he talked about her. The way he looked when he remembered her."

At the reverent tone in his voice, Jayne held her breath. Both men grew silent for a moment. It felt almost as though they were paying respect to the mysterious ideal of true love. Jayne was touched. Deep down, they were sweet, really.

Bruce hawked a loogie. "It was a beautiful thing."

"Yeah."

Oh, brother. Jayne recoiled, all pretense of being rough and ready gone. She was nothing like a man, and it was useless to pretend. She loved baby blue and kittens, shoe shopping and chocolate. She was a *girl*.

A girl with a mission—a mission to end Riley's loneliness. Hearing about his self-imposed exile just about broke her heart. If there was anything Jayne was better at than girly-girl stuff, it was making friends. Before this trip was through, she vowed, she'd show Riley how wonderful being close with other people could really be.

Sixteen

Riley entered the campsite from the opposite side he fig-ured Jayne had come. As he did, his gaze was instantly drawn to the campfire circle and the people sitting on logs around it. They looked cozy. As cozy as they'd looked together every night so far. The firelight flickered on their smiling faces as they talked in voices too low to carry clearly to his position. Sparks snapped into the night sky above them.

Go over there, a part of him urged. But a lifetime of being on the outside kept Riley where he stood. He'd always been the new kid, the American curiosity in a foreign land. He'd never hung out at the mall, cruised through suburbia with a newly minted driver's license, bruised his thumbs playing video games with pals. Thanks to his parents' dedication, from the moment he could hug a tree, Riley had been involved in more "meaningful" environmental and cultural pursuits.

He'd been good at them. He didn't regret his expertise in outdoor skills and wilderness sports. He didn't feel sorry for himself. But he had . . . once.

Photography had saved him. It had changed him. Seen

through his camera's lens, the world took on a personal light. Captured through that lens, the world became his. Riley had loved photography instantly. He'd begun taking pictures in Norway, Chile, Turkey—and shortly afterward, a chance encounter with a *National Explorer* magazine editor had changed his life. Since then, he'd divided his time between photography assignments and guided travel work, comfortable with the movement and change both required.

But now . . . now he felt inexplicably lured by the gathering in front of him. It didn't make sense. Riley had never experienced such a powerful longing before—except as a boy. And that had been before he'd learned to accept things the way they were. Hell, aside from his weird settling-down yearnings in San Francisco with Jayne . . .

Jayne. Of course. He felt this way only because of Jayne. Probably because of their rendezvous in the woods. They hadn't come together the way he'd hoped, and that explained this feeling.

Satisfied, Riley squared his shoulders. He wasn't changing. He wasn't craving something so unreliable as stability. He was merely sorry to have missed another opportunity with Jayne. *Whew.* He headed toward the opposite end of camp, intent on double-checking the tents and water supplies. He'd almost made it past the crackling fire, when Jayne called out to him.

"Riley! I'm so glad you're here." She hurried toward him, a welcoming smile on her heat-flushed face. She took his arm and began dragging him toward the fire. "Look, everyone! It's Riley, come to join us!"

They turned interested faces toward him. Riley blanched.

"Nah, I have things to do." He gestured vaguely toward the dark, safe edge of camp. His stupid foot began a telltale tap. "Equipment to check. Routes to plan."

"Marshmallows to toast." Jayne pressed one of her silly "designer" sticks in his hand. The ribbons tied to it fluttered in the breeze and tickled his fingers. "Yum-yum."

"Uhhh—"

"Look, here's your first marshmallow." She poked one onto the end of his stick with exaggerated care. Her upward glance implored him to toast it.

Well, if it meant that much to her . . . "Okay. One marshmallow won't kill me."

"Yay!" the women cried, as they often did. Riley couldn't *believe* he'd actually agreed to do this. Campfire gatherings were for other people . . . people who needed people, or some psychobabble crap like that.

He reluctantly edged nearer. Everyone called out greetings. They shifted to make room on the nearest log. Jayne pushed his shoulders downward, shoving him into place. Within seconds, Riley found himself somewhere he'd never been—inside the circle. Travelers pressed close on all sides, getting resituated. The conversation resumed, this time to include him.

Uncomfortable, he rotated his tense shoulders.

"Isn't this nice?" Jayne asked chirpily beside him. She covered his hand with hers, guiding his stick into position above the fire. She kept it there with a gentle pressure.

He grunted. What was he supposed to say now? There was no purpose to this gathering. There were no instructions to be given, no training to be offered, no plans to be made. Riley felt at loose ends, and he hated it.

Maybe he could take a cue from Jayne. She was never at a loss for friendly behavior. He cleared his throat and began with her.

"Your, uh, hair looks nice. New style?"

She patted the strands, which stuck out from the clip at her nape in a way that seemed purposefully haphazard. "Just a little something I worked up until I can wash it properly," she said, looking pleased. "I saw it on a woman at the gym a few weeks ago, and just remembered how to do it."

"It's cute."

"Thanks, I—" Jayne's eyes narrowed suddenly, as

though she'd just remembered she was talking to a man with no previous interest in hairstyles, cute or otherwise. She opened her mouth, obviously intending to ask him about it. Riley took a deep breath and moved on.

"That, uh, color suits you, Kelly."

Kelly blushed and patted the collar of her bulky pink sweater. "Gee, thanks, Riley. It's nice of you to notice."

He pushed his luck and went for broke. "That neckline is great. Very, um, Bogey."

Beside him, Jayne frowned. "You mean *Vogue*-y?"

"Sure. Okay."

Her look of suspicion deepened. Riley concentrated on turning his marshmallow, watching it puff as it toasted. When it was done, he raised it to his mouth and blew. A brilliant Jayne-style maneuver struck him, and he spoke to Doris, Donna, and Carla next.

"Ladies, is this marshmallow Atkins-approved? Is it Zone perfect?"

Carla raised her brows.

The sisters gawped. "Well, I think so," Donna said, recovering first. "I don't have my book with me, but—"

"Nonsense," Doris argued. "With all that sugar? That marshmallow's got high carb written all over it."

"Hmmph. That hasn't stopped *you* from pigging out."

"I resent that! Who lost two pounds last month, and who didn't?"

Clearly *not* the two-pound loser, Donna crossed her arms over her chest and sulked. Riley regretted having mentioned anything at all. This group togetherness stuff was tricky.

He regrouped. "Mitzi, what's life like at the restaurant?"

She launched into a story about one of her regular customers, a man who'd ordered a double bacon cheeseburger and fries delivered to his hospital room after having bypass surgery. Told with Mitzi's usual wisecracks, the tale had everyone laughing. Feeling a little more at ease, Riley jabbed another marshmallow onto his stick. He offered one to Jayne too. She took it, still watching him with a speculative expression.

The night deepened. Conversation flowed freely around the campfire. When Riley got stuck or panicky, he considered what Jayne would have done, and tried that. In the process, he learned more about press-on nails, sushi bars, and self-help hoo-ha than he'd ever imagined. He also learned that Alexis didn't think Lance was too much of a jerk to be sat next to. And that his good buddy Mack had a major thing going for Kelly. The two of them shyly traded glances all night.

Gradually, the tightness in Riley's chest began to loosen. Even Jayne relaxed beside him, seeming to accept his new chattiness at face value. She guffawed at his tentative jokes, smoothed over his occasional oddball question, and generally beamed at him as though he were a prize pupil and she the tenacious teacher. He found her proprietary attitude a little strange, but he didn't mind. Riley had the sense he was pleasing her, and that was all he really wanted.

Encouraged, he asked Carla about piercings and Lance about Limp Bizkit. He started a discussion about Bruce's secret cross-stitch hobby, and stifled a grin at his buddy's insistence that it was "totally Zen, dude." By the time the small fire was reduced to embers and he was packed with toasted marshmallows, Riley began to believe he'd misled himself all along. He could be part of a group. He could fit in. Hell, he could even enjoy it.

Then the unthinkable happened.

"How about you, Riley?" Doris said. "You've asked us all about ourselves, but we've heard nothing about you. What made you want to become an adventure guide?"

"Oh, don't stop there," Donna disagreed with a wave of her lined hand. "Tell us *all* about yourself." She leaned forward. "We want to know *everything*. Absolutely everything."

Instantly, the group quieted. Everyone looked at Riley.

The air turned heavy. The night pressed in. A hard band of ... *something*, some feeling he didn't want to name, clamped around his chest. Trapped beneath it, Riley clutched his marshmallow-toasting stick. He swallowed.

He couldn't do it.

"Some other time," he muttered. "I've got work to do."

Then he threw his stick into the fire in a shower of sparks and headed off into the darkness again.

Jayne looked from the smoldering stick to the man pushing through the group. She watched Riley turn away, his face grim. His shoulders stiffened as he met the darkness at the edge of the campfire's lighted circle, then he melted into the night.

Disappointment filled her. He'd been so close! He'd talked, he'd laughed ... he'd done those things with ten other people, all at the same time. Riley had enjoyed himself; she knew he had. Jayne had watched him. She'd seen his wary, elbows-on-knees posture slowly give way to open, arm-waving interest. She'd seen his gaze slide from troubled to relieved. She'd witnessed his transformation from determined outsider to cautious joiner. In a single night, Riley had stepped far beyond the boundaries he'd set for himself.

And then things had gone too far. He'd retreated.

Helplessly, Jayne searched the murky tree-filled landscape for signs of him, looking for any glimpse of the strong, elusive man who'd captured her heart. She wondered if she should follow him. Riley had to be ... lonely, out there. Loneliness was the worst thing she could imagine.

That decided it. Jayne got to her feet and said her good nights. Alone, she grabbed another fleece from her tent, then went in search.

*   *   *

After a scary, flashlight-guided trek past some trees, she found him. Riley sat atop a boulder, gazing up at the night sky. For a moment, she let herself admire the stillness of his posture, the silent strength of his features . . . the courage that let him confront the darkness this way. He really was amazing. Stillness and silence were not Jayne's personal strong suits. And courage? Heck, her idea of courage was braving a bikini wax without a triple-strength Tylenol before-hand.

She stepped closer. "Are you wishing on a star too?"

A pause.

"Don't need to." His voice sounded unsurprised, as though he'd known she was there all along. Riley looked over his shoulder leisurely, his face shadowed. "My wish just came true."

In the darkness, intimacy laced his plainspoken words. Jayne felt herself warmed by it even as she clambered onto the chilly rock beside him. She settled there, with Riley's help, and cradled her flashlight securely between her palms.

"Oh, you couldn't possibly have wished for me," she said with a shrug, secretly pleased. "I mean, I was right there beside you. At the campfire, all along."

"The campfire." He exhaled. "Right."

"What? It wasn't that bad, was it?"

"Define 'bad.' "

"Riley—"

"It doesn't matter." He squeezed her knee, giving her a smile in the glow of the flashlight's upright illumination. "What matters is that you're here now."

Awww. Jayne smiled. But still . . . "Everyone loved you! You were witty and charming and *interested,* which is even more important than interest*ing,* in my book. I mean, almost anybody can be fascinating, even if it's only because they're a little weird—"

"Weird? Are you trying to tell me something?"

She rolled her eyes. "But almost *nobody* is *interested* these days. With some people, you can't get a word in edgewise because they're so busy talking about themselves."

His lips quirked.

"And that's not a problem with you!" Jayne hugged his arm, trying to transmit some enthusiasm to him. His warmth instantly chased away the chill. "Really, I'm very proud of you."

His reply was a self-conscious *hmmph*. She leaned sideways, hoping to jostle him into good cheer. "Come on. I am! I'm proud of you."

"I'm proud you're proud."

"Admit it. It was a little fun, wasn't it?"

He hesitated. Clearly, stronger measures were called for here. Like a tickle attack. Jayne jabbed the flashlight between her knees and lunged sideways. "Admit it! It was fun!"

"Hey!"

Her fingers probed his ribs, his flat abdomen, his sides. Riley gawped at her, automatically doubling over. She kept at it until his laughter overrode the crickets' songs, until Riley wrestled both her wrists into his grasp and stopped her.

"It was a little fun," he said grudgingly.

"And you enjoyed it."

"Always have to push, don't you?"

"Well?"

"Okay." His smile widened. "The marshmallows were good."

That was probably all she'd get out of him tonight, Jayne decided. "That'll do. Tomorrow we'll tackle your side of the story. You can tell us all about your photography expeditions."

He went still. Then he released her wrists. "I'd rather hear about what you've been doing for the past two years."

Missing you. Wildly unwilling to say *that,* Jayne wrinkled her nose. She studied the trees silhouetted against the starry sky. "Writing a book. Going out with friends. Scouring shoe sales. The usual."

Riley shook his head. "You know, after I left San Francisco, it was months before I could pass a shoe store and not automatically slow down . . . so you could have a look."

His admission surprised her. "Good thing there aren't many shoe stores in the Congo."

"Yeah." His gaze searched hers, igniting something forbidden and long denied. "Good thing."

"Yeah," she repeated in a whisper, feeling herself melt into the attraction he'd always held for her. "Really good."

I missed you, she read in his eyes. *I still do.* Jayne felt the same. Remembrances swirled between them. A hush fell over the forested landscape, as though the night itself waited to see what would happen. She held her breath. When she'd agreed to pick up where they'd left off, she hadn't expected their reunion to pack such a wallop. And she hadn't expected to like him again either.

But she did.

She thought of Riley slowing down at a shoe store. Glancing over his shoulder. Realizing she wasn't there. She'd had those moments too. Moments when their braided lives had unraveled before her eyes, over and over again.

If she wasn't careful, she'd stop dating like a man and start surrendering her heart like a woman.

"But I guess I should save all the best stories for tomorrow, right?" Briskly she sat straighter lest she leave herself vulnerable to the subtle seduction of Riley's body warming hers . . . to the pull of his companionship. Kissing amid the trees she could handle. Rekindling a friendship was trickier. "So . . . what do you usually do for fun on your adventure travel trips?"

"Fun?" He spread his arms. "This is it."

"No, I mean—when you've hiked as far as you're going

to for the day, and you've finished all the work to be done, what do you do just for fun? If you don't hang out by the campfire—''

"This. Is. It.''

"You spend time *alone?*'' She'd seen it, but she hadn't believed it. "On purpose? For *fun?*''

"It's not a crime. It's . . . peaceful.''

Jayne shook her head. "Don't you ever get lonely?''

At that, Riley seemed genuinely puzzled. He shrugged. "Alone isn't lonely.''

"Of course it is!'' He must be in denial. "If you're alone, it means nobody wants to be with you.''

He made a wry face, then pretended to perform an underarm body odor check. "I hope not.''

Undeterred by his lightheartedness, she said seriously, "If you're alone, it means you don't fit in.''

"It means you're alone. By yourself. Period.''

"No!'' Sure, he could pretend to be stoic about it, but Jayne couldn't bear to think of him forever on the outskirts of life's big campfire. Riley deserved more warmth than that. "Trust me, I know what I'm talking about. If you could only see—''

"It's okay. I like it. Most of the time.''

Ah-hah! she thought, grasping onto the tiny confession he'd offered. He *was* lonely. And she couldn't bear it. She'd spent too many years being on the outside herself, never fitting in with her family, to let Riley suffer a similar fate.

'' *'Most* of the time,' '' Jayne repeated. "See? You need me. I can help you. I know I can. I know all kinds of ways to avoid being alone. Take a party, for instance. You might find yourself alone on the way to the ladies' room—''

"Not very often.''

''—but if you take a friend, share your lipstick—''

"Again, that may be a problem for me.''

''—even offer to guard the stall door, you won't be!''

He looked at her as though she were crazy. "I'm *used* to being alone. You don't have to cure me of this."

She did. She knew she did. Now that she recognized the extent of Riley's un-admitted-to loneliness, Jayne knew she had to do something to help him.

"Let's role-play some conversation," she suggested.

His crazy-woman expression deepened. "Let's not."

"Okay. Let's practice cocktail party chitchat, then. It helps if you're prepared with some subjects at hand. Like current events. Book-group opinions. Canapé recipes."

He raised his brows at her hopeful expression. "You can't be serious." He apparently saw that she was, and balked. "I don't even know what a canapé *is.*"

"See? That's why you need a recipe! Now let me think about this . . . first we need a good opener." She considered a few, then brightened. "Like 'I love your dress!' Or 'How do you know the host?' " She smiled at him. "Now your turn."

"This is ridiculous."

"No, that might offend your host."

"Jayne, snap out of it."

"That might offend *me!*"

"I mean it." Riley slipped his hand to her cheek, gently turning her face toward his. Her demonstration party face met his solemn expression, and she felt her features droop.

"Being alone isn't that bad," he said. "I'll show you."

He shifted on their shared rock, as though preparing to get up. Panicked, Jayne grabbed his arm. "Just don't take the flashlight with you."

"I'm not leaving you here alone. I'm . . . demonstrating."

Confused, she watched through the dimness as Riley found a new position on the boulder. The next thing she knew, they were sitting back to back, not touching. She started to turn around.

His touch stopped her. "Hold still. Pretend you're alone."

"I don't want to."

"Do it for me."

At the thought, her whole body tensed. But she didn't want Riley to think she was a coward any more than she wanted him to think she *wasn't* over him. So Jayne nodded. "Okay."

"Good." His deep voice, so familiar and so welcome, comforted her. "Now relax and look up."

Hesitantly, she did.

"See the stars? All you have to do is look at them."

Jayne almost scoffed. She could do that. She'd been wishing on stars her whole life. She craned her neck and complied. A glittery panorama met her view.

"Wow."

"Don't talk. You're alone."

"Of course I'm not alone. You're right—"

He cleared his throat. She piped down.

Several minutes later, a night breeze rustled the tree branches and pulled her attention from the stars. This "alone" thing sure felt real, Jayne realized. For all she knew, Riley had snuck off while she'd been stargazing, and . . .

Yikes! She grabbed for his hand.

"I'm right here," he said, linking his fingers with hers. He didn't turn around, didn't scoot nearer so their backs touched. He didn't have to. His presence was all she needed.

"That was ten minutes straight," Riley announced over the sound of her pounding heart. "You survived. I'm proud of you."

"Great." Jayne sagged with relief. "Can I stop now?"

"If you want to."

She did stop. Gratefully. When she turned, it was to see Riley's beaming face. She didn't have the heart to remind him this hadn't been a genuine "alone" experience. Not when she'd known he was with her every minute. But he was sweet to care about her all the same.

Jayne told him so. He shook his head and muttered some-

thing subject-changing about the stars. Before she could so
much as explain her feelings in more depth, Riley launched
into a story about what the ancient Mayans had believed
about the night sky. She found herself diverted. He pointed
out constellations and galaxies, outlined the Milky Way with
sure movements of his hands, handed her a knit hat for
warmth.

In return Jayne showed him the star formations she'd
discovered during her "alone time." The lipstick galaxy,
slender and sparkly. The powder-perfect circle of moon. The
PMS black hole. Riley laughed and nodded as she pointed
them out, and in the end, things turned out nicely. Really
nicely.

They stayed that way too. At least they did until Jayne
returned to camp . . . and found the javelina waiting in her
tent.

Seventeen

Morning dawned *totally* too early on the trail, in Alexis's opinion. Before the sun had finished crawling above the cliff near their campsite, she was awakened by the sound of pots clanking and water being poured. It was as if some demented Galloping Gourmet had taken the place of a normal alarm clock. Alexis would have preferred waking up to her radio blaring dance remixes.

Sleepily, she checked to see if her boobs had magically grown bigger overnight. She prayed her feet hadn't managed the same thing. Everything was the same. Depending on how you looked at it, that was okay.

Wiggling as wakefulness slipped through her, Alexis wondered how her mom was doing in Mexico. She wondered if Gary the Geek was still there too. She wondered if any phone calls had come to Nana and Gramps's place while she'd been gone, and if her mom was sorry she'd missed talking to Alexis.

Fiercely, Alexis hoped so. It would serve her mom right. Maybe then she'd realize her "little girl" wouldn't care about lame phone calls forever. Soon Alexis would be going away to college. She'd be too busy to think about things like sometimes wanting a hug from her mom.

Ugh. It was *way* too early to be so bummed out. Alexis crawled out from the solitary nylon dome she'd pitched beside Carla and Mitzi's shared tent.

The cold fresh air made her skin tingle. She gulped in a big lungful, pretending she was an experienced older woman camping out with her gorgeous boyfriend. *Her famous recording-artist boyfriend.* Yeah, that was it. He'd been so blown away by Alexis's hot bod, personal charm, and overall babeishness that he'd ditched his personal touring jet to spend time with—

"Coffee?" Lance asked.

Sucked from her daydream by his reedy voice, Alexis frowned. How had he managed to sneak up on her like that? Worse, had he actually seen her . . . *pretending,* like a kid?

"Coffee stunts your growth, dodohead. Don't you know anything?"

"It's really good." He waved the cup beneath her nose, obviously trying to tantalize her. "I made it myself."

She exhaled. "If I take it, will you quit *pestering* me?"

His answer was a grin. A grin that reached all the way inside her. A grin that seemed to say *you're terrific.* Startled by it, Alexis stared.

The next thing she knew, Lance was wrapping her fingers around the stupid coffee cup. "It'll keep you warm," he said.

His touch jolted her. She gawped.

"You, uh, look pretty with your hair like that."

He was copying Uncle Riley. Uncle Riley had said almost the same thing to Jayne around the campfire last night. Not that Alexis cared right now. For some reason, she felt like giggling. Or maybe batting her eyelashes.

She looked around to make sure no one was nearby to witness this embarrassing turn of events. "Thanks." She couldn't prevent a smile and suddenly wished she'd brushed her teeth.

"No prob." Lance puffed out his chest. He studied his shoes, then glanced up at her with his head still partly ducked. "Hey, you want to join up in the same group today? I know a spot where there's some cool wildflowers. I could show it to you."

Alexis knew that spot. But for some reason, she didn't want to say so. "Uh, okay. I guess."

Still feeling giggly, she slurped her coffee. It burned her tongue and seared all the way down. But she didn't want to hurt Lance's feelings, so she stifled a wince. Determined to finish her coffee, she took a smaller sip and stared at the sunrise as it filtered between the trees.

Beside her, Lance stared at the sunrise too. A little of the awkwardness between them dissolved. He edged closer, and their shoulders touched.

Giddiness shot through Alexis, followed rapidly by a *whoosh* of excitement. Lance smiled at her. That was when she knew—the trouble with Brendan had been that he was a *boy*. Lance was a *man*. Almost, anyway. This time she was positive everything would be different.

Riley reached Jayne's tent that morning just as she shoved aside the flap and crawled out. He watched fondly as she pushed to her feet and ran a hand through her long blonde hair. Then he swept his gaze over the rest of her. He frowned.

It looked as though Jayne had gotten dressed in the dark. There wasn't a scrap of baby blue in sight. Her trail pants had a hole in the knee. And he was pretty sure her fleece top was on backward, judging by the way the zippered collar fluffed up behind her head like a lion's ruff. He strode nearer.

Her red-rimmed eyes bugged at the movement.

"It's okay," he said, making a calming gesture. "It's just me."

"Whew! For a second there, I thought you were the javelina again." Jayne shifted her gaze warily from side to side. "I've been up most of the night waiting for it to come back."

"You missed it that much, huh?"

"Right. We really bonded. I love things with shaggy hair, piggy little eyes, and a stench that hits you from a mile away."

He smiled, relieved that she could joke about it. "You just described Bruce."

She made a face. "That thing creeped me out."

"Don't worry, it's gone now," Riley reminded her. Upon hearing Jayne's scream last night, he'd come at a run. A few minutes' patient coaxing had had the confused (and hearing damaged) javelina on its way. "I shooed it away. It didn't mean any harm though. Probably, it got separated from its herd and was looking for some food."

"Well, it obviously knew it would find an easy mark with me. The back-to-nature neophyte."

"It wasn't personal."

"Yeah, right. Those were *my* shoes serving as its appetizer."

He shrugged. "Your tent must have been left unzipped."

"Like I said . . . back-to-nature neophyte. After everything else, I should have known something like this would happen. Why wouldn't I be javelina bait too?"

"Jayne, it was a *baby* javelina. It couldn't have hurt you. Everyone else thought it looked kind of cute."

"It looked *grouchy*." Jayne squinted her makeup-free eyes, appearing to think about it. "Grouchy, hungry, and ready to stomp all over anybody who got in the way of a midnight snack."

"Again, just like Bruce."

She made a face. "I'm serious. It *knew* I was an easy target. It knew! I don't belong out here, Riley."

"Sure, you do." He smiled. "You're just lucky it wasn't

a raccoon in your tent, rifling through your stuff. Trying on your hats. Wearing your nail polish.''

"They can *do* that?"

"Only the big ones. Big enough to gnaw through the tent.''

Her eyes grew wide. "I want a steel tent."

"Then you get the *really* big ones. The raccoons who like a challenge.''

"Oh, my God."

"You'll probably need to share my sleeping bag until we're safely out of raccoon country.''

"Ahhh." Jayne crossed her arms. It was obvious she'd caught on to his teasing. "That won't be necessary. If I see any raccoons, I'll just whack them with my fishing club.''

"Good." He looked her over, reassured to hear some of the feistiness reenter her voice. "Better now?"

"I'm fine," she said blithely—just as though her body *weren't* probably going into shock from hair-spray withdrawal right now. "Fine and dandy.''

Fine and dandy? She sounded like Mary Poppins. Now Riley was really worried. "Are you sure? Because you look—''

He paused, nodding meaningfully toward her clothes.

Her brow arched. "Yes? I look . . . ?"

Uh-oh. But he was too worried not to continue. "You look sort of—well, shorter, for one thing." Riley tilted his head, examining her, distracted from his original mission by the realization. "I knew there'd been something different about you lately, but until now I hadn't put my finger on it. Yes, you're definitely shorter.''

She glared.

"More petite?" he tried, thinking that might sound better.

"Shorter." Jayne's mouth turned down in a glum line. She indicated her feet. "It's the shoes. I lost a good three inches going from stilettos to ATSes. I'm usually much taller. Everything looks so . . . ordinary from down here.''

She didn't sound happy about it. Given that, Riley should have left well enough alone. But the sight of her clothes wouldn't let him. Now that he was closer, he saw that Jayne's shirt tag stuck up in the back—and Jayne was a militant tucker-inner. He'd lost track of the times her fingers had slipped deftly inside his collar to hide his tag when they'd been together. If she was ignoring her own tag now . . . well, something was definitely wrong.

He couldn't believe such a change could come about just because of a javelina encounter. After all, the baby piglike creature hadn't actually hurt anything or anyone—including Jayne herself. There had to be something else going on here.

He scrutinized her, trying to figure it out. Oblivious to his concerns, she yawned again and ruffled her hair, leaving several strands sticking up on one side. *She didn't even smooth them down.* Her leopard-print "primping" compact didn't magically appear either. Riley became convinced trouble was afoot. Maybe the javelina incident, harmless as it seemed to him, had been the last straw for Jayne.

Either that, or he'd slipped up and done "nothing" again.

He hoped it wasn't that. "Nothing" was so hard to fix.

Riley squinted, trying to figure her out. "You're okay, then?"

Jayne nodded, giving him a quizzical look.

He was going to have to come right out with it. "I'm worried about . . . how you look. Your clothes."

And your hair, your ragged thumbnail, your shoes—which were, he noticed, on the wrong feet and unlaced. It wasn't that Riley was shallow. He knew there were more important things than surface beauty. Jayne's looks didn't matter that much to him. But they *did* matter to Jayne. Usually.

"Oh." Comprehension filled her features. "Well, it's simple." She waved her hand. "Ever since last night, I've lost my will to accessorize."

"Your will to—"

"Accessorize. Right. Also, I've lost all interest in coordinating. I mean, does any of it really matter? When it comes right down to it, does looking good *really* matter—especially out here in the wild? Does *anything* matter at all?"

He paused. "You're not a morning person, are you?"

In reply, Jayne shook her head. The motion messed up her hair even further. She *still* didn't fix it. This was not good.

"But—if you look good, you feel good," Riley said, so worried, he felt compelled to dredge up her self-help mantra. "If you look good, you—feel—good."

She shrugged. "I feel okay. I'm going to go gather some sticks and bark for breakfast. Cut out the middleman in my All-Bran. See you on the trail."

Jayne waved halfheartedly, like a beauty queen in a parade. Then she schlepped away with her shoelaces flapping, her pants dragging, her fleece backward and inside out, and her derrière—Riley saw with a wince—decorated with a hiking sock that must have clung by static electricity. It plastered her right cheek like a foot-shaped white flag.

He shook his head, worried but uncertain what to do. Jayne didn't seem concerned about her condition—but then, people in trouble often didn't.

In all his years guiding adventure travel trips, Riley had seem some pretty strange things. Successful CEOs who broke down halfway up a mountain summit, defeated by a storm that defied their schedules. Hypothermia victims who fought against the dry clothes and warm shoes that ultimately saved them. Competitive couples whose refusal to cooperate doomed them to shared failure.

But *I've lost my will to accessorize? I've lost all interest in coordinating?* Those were new to him.

Behind him, Kelly shuffled out from her tent. She caught him watching Jayne and shook her head.

"I'm worried," Kelly said. "I think Jayne's in trouble. After the javelina left, I caught her trying to sleep with her cache of bath products. Do you know how hard it is to get forty winks with bath beads and Bathing Beauty Bubbles clanking beside you all night?''

Jayne *had* been restless. "No," he said.

"Well, I do." Kelly crossed her arms. "Baths are Jayne's primary form of stress relief, you know. And now, being on the trail . . ."

"No baths," Riley finished, beginning to understand.

"Right. I think it's pretty hard on her dealing with all of us in her group. And all the nature stuff. And the javelina. Plus, well—" Hesitating, Kelly bit her lip. She gave him a pointed look.

"Me? Plus dealing with *me?''*

Kelly nodded. "Sorry."

"No point shooting the messenger," he told her, suddenly remembering what Jayne had said when they'd met at the Hideaway Lodge.

These women are depending on me, Riley. I won't let you mess things up for me.

Riley folded his arms, still watching Jayne in the distance. Now she had a clump of wet leaves on her shoe, and it dragged along in her wake. Her guidance groupies looked askance when she passed by in all her disheveled glory, but Jayne waved at them and continued onward. Her butt sock swished perkily from side to side with every step.

Riley groaned. "I've got to do something to help her."

"I'm not sure what you *can* do. She's stressed out, and she's staying that way. Unless you can turn up a bathtub somehow." Kelly frowned doubtfully.

"I can. There's a bathtub at the canyon lodge!" It was a little . . . rustic, sure. But it was a bathtub, the cure for everything that ailed Jayne. "It's only a few hours away. We'll be there by this afternoon."

Relief filled him. Unified in newfound hopefulness, he and Kelly watched Jayne. Soon she would get the relaxing bath she needed. Everything would be all right again. She'd bathe, she'd recover her will to accessorize, she'd . . . pause at the campsite's edge and roll up her trail pants? Two mismatched socks flashed as Jayne strode into the trees.

"A few hours might be too late," Kelly said worriedly.

"I'll think of something," Riley said. Then he headed out to do exactly that.

"It's time for the next workshop," Jayne said that afternoon. She'd hiked all morning, had soaked her shoes during a creek crossing everyone else had navigated easily, and had finally devolved to the point where she actually considered beef jerky "a treat." Now she just wanted to get on with things. "The title of this workshop is—"

"Wait!" Mitzi said from within the group gathered around Jayne. "What about the primping?"

Murmurs of assent were heard. Alexis waved her leopard-print compact overhead, clearly ready for the usual preworkshop ritual. Kelly put her chin in her hand and cast a worried glance toward the men, who were leaving for their own workshop.

"Oh, all right." Halfheartedly, Jayne withdrew her compact. "Is everyone ready? Okay . . . primp. I guess."

They all fluffed and powdered and lipsticked. She rolled her eyes and snapped her compact shut. She just didn't have the energy to primp today. Not after last night. Not after . . . everything.

Jayne thought she'd been hanging on pretty well—but the javelina had obliterated the last of her back-to-nature courage. All she wanted to do now was get finished, get to the lodge, and get back to civilization.

As soon as the lipsticks were recapped, she began. "Again, the title of this workshop is—"

"Hey!" Her breakup-ees' disappointed gazes stopped her. They all frowned. Well, all except Carla—who'd said she wasn't feeling well, and had opted out of this particular workshop. She was resting nearby.

"Oh, all right." To make them happy, Jayne formed a weak upraised fist and finished their usual ritual. "What's our motto?"

They all shouted happily, "If you look good, you feel—"

"Okay, okay, that'll do." Everyone drooped. Well, that was just too bad, Jayne told herself. It was time for them all to get serious. "Now, the title of this workshop is Karaoke 'Your Song' into Submission. Its purpose is to desensitize you to that special song you and your ex shared."

"Me and Rodney's song was 'Shoo Doo Be Doo,'" Mitzi volunteered. "But I'm working on a *new* song these days."

Her sideways glance caught Bruce as he walked to the clearing where Riley's "macho" workshop would be held. The guide saw Mitzi wave. He blew her a kiss. She giggled.

Kelly cleared her throat. "Tim and I first danced to 'Your Cheating Heart' at a Patsy Cline soundalike contest. Come to think of it . . . that should have been my first clue."

They all commiserated.

"Brendan once burned a mix-CD of Lenny Kravitz songs for me," Alexis told them. "I guess that's *pretty* romantic. Does that qualify?"

"Sure it does," Jayne said, mustering a smile.

"Marty dedicated 'The Way You Look Tonight' to me on Buster Boogaloo's radio show," Doris said. "The Sinatra version, of course. Marty was a traditionalist."

"Nonsense," Donna disagreed. "Marty was a happening dude. And he dedicated that song to *me!*"

"You never even listen to Buster Boogaloo."

"I might if you weren't always hogging the radio!"

"Hogging?"

"Ladies . . ." Jayne brought them both around to the subject at hand. "Let's get started."

They practiced the various songs once quickly, so everyone would be familiar with the lyrics and melodies. Then Jayne began her demonstration of the technique.

She cleared her throat. "Now, the romantic song I'm going to karaoke into submission is—"

"—'your song' with Uncle Riley?" Alexis asked.

That got everyone's attention.

Jayne nodded. That was what she'd planned. But now, suddenly, she didn't want to destroy her fondness for that song. Her techniques were effective. She believed in them. She didn't want to use them to sever the link "their song" made between her and Riley.

She was probably strong enough to skip this step, Jayne assured herself. What could it hurt?

Switching gears, she mentioned the first song that came to mind. "Umm, 'Born to Be Wild.' "

"Cool!" Alexis said.

"Really?" Doris and Donna put in, squinting skeptically. "*That's* your special romantic song?"

"Is there something *wrong* with that song?" Jayne asked. When they all shook their heads, muttering *I guess not*'s,' she knew she'd successfully convinced them. "So, here goes. Is everyone familiar with this one?"

She hummed a few bars. Everyone nodded.

"Good. Since we couldn't bring an actual karaoke machine on the trail, your job—when you're not holding the 'mic' "—she indicated the hairbrush in her hand—"is to be the background music. Just hum, sing do-wops, do whatever comes naturally to you. Okay?"

The group members nodded. Alexis looked a little concerned, but she nodded too. More than likely the girl was worried Jayne would ruin her uncle's special romantic song—and this, after Alexis had revealed Riley's feelings for Jayne. Reminded of that, Jayne felt reassured about her decision to switch songs. Given how Riley had reformed so far, it wouldn't be fair to do a search-and-destroy mission on their favorite ballad.

Standing up, "mic" in hand, Jayne launched into "Born to Be Wild." She rumbled on the bass, reached for the high notes, and emoted as much as was possible with a song that urged her to "get her motor running." She gestured wildly. Clenched her hairbrush mic. Hunched over with musical passion during the "yeah, I got to go make it happen," parts. Even jumped onto a boulder for her grand finale.

Strangely enough, the song made her feel invigorated for the first time that day. Singing felt good. Moving felt good. Pretending she could actually be "wild" in any sense felt good. The rest of the women did their parts too, pretending to play electric guitars and acting as backup singers.

"Ta-da!" Jayne said when she'd finished, slightly out of breath. She flung her hair back and took a dramatic bow.

The women applauded. The men at their nearby workshop site hooted and hollered. Jayne blushed and squeezed her "mic."

"And that's how it's done," she explained. "You exaggerate the sad parts, parody the dramatic parts, and repeat the process as often as necessary to rob 'your song' of its power." She sat down again, leaning closer to confide in them. "And to give *yourself* power. After you've karaoked your song into submission, you'll never be at the mercy of a radio blaring love ballads, or a mushy Muzak elevator ambush, ever again."

"Yay!" they yelled, applauding some more.

They launched into their individual karaoke sessions. Within minutes, the clearing rang with the sounds of "Shoo Doo Be Doo" sung as sappily and as crazily as possible. With the strains of "The Way You Look Tonight," à la the Squabble Sisters. With the groove of assorted Lenny Kravitz melodies. And finally with a shouted, over-the-top rendition of "Your Cheating Heart," which was sung with particular gusto by every woman there.

Watching them, joining them, Jayne felt a cozy sense of sisterhood steal over her. This was what it was all about. Helping people. Making a difference to them. Proving—to

Francesca and to the world and to herself—that her self-help techniques really worked.

That her "gift" really existed.

Being with Riley hadn't derailed her, she realized. It hadn't hurt her research—and her breakup-ees hadn't found out about it either. Now her wilderness trip was almost over. Even though she hadn't exactly become *Hiking Monthly*'s new centerfold girl, she'd survived.

Jayne's spirits lifted a little. Her posture did, too. As it did she felt a telltale prickle at the back of her neck. Automatically, she felt behind her for the sticking-up clothing tag she knew would be there.

She tucked it in. Her gaze fell to the hole in her pants. To her shoes, with their toes pointing awkwardly—and uncomfortably, Jayne realized suddenly—in the wrong direction. To her fleece top, which was inside out and . . . backward?

With a sense of awakening, she felt the wind whoosh over her lip-gloss-free lips. She felt the sunshine beat down on her uncombed, un-hat-protected hair. She felt the unaccustomed-to lightness of un-made-up eyes, and remembered tossing her mascara into a bivvy sack with desperate laissez-faire that morning.

Aaack! What had she done?

She'd abandoned every principle of self-respect she'd ever espoused. Beautification. Fragrance application. Hair stylization. She'd become the *before* in a Before-and-after makeover shot. She'd become . . . ordinary.

Panicked by the realization, Jayne grabbed for her pack. Too late, she realized it was stowed several feet away, along with everyone else's.

Around her, the women continued to sing. Apparently, Kelly needed another round of "Your Cheating Heart" for her song to be properly karaoked into submission. Joining in to keep everyone on track, Jayne glanced sideways, hoping to see that her pack—and the essentials-only makeup kit inside it—was within reach after all.

Instead, to her horror she saw Riley . . . headed straight toward her. Straight toward her *ordinary* self.

Eighteen

Riley strode nearer, bemused by the women's enthusiastic singing. They'd chorused together so loudly, all the guys had started humming along from a distance. Of course, he was still confused by Jayne's "Born to Be Wild" routine—having heard the subject of the workshop—but he figured that must have been her and Bozo Boy's "song." It would be just like that heartbreak-camp loser to saddle Jayne with an unromantic "romantic" song. *He* and Jayne had shared a *much* more romantic tune.

He stood to the side until they'd finished singing. As the group started to break up, Riley approached Jayne. Despite her impromptu Steppenwolf routine, he wasn't convinced she was okay.

He'd seen her skip the primping, after all.

"Never knew you were so 'wild,' " he said, grinning.

She looked away, as though distracted. "It's just a song. And I'm, uh, pretty busy right now, Riley. Don't you have a workshop of your own to do?"

"I'm tag-teaming with Bruce. My session was Perfect Poker Faces. His was Catcalls, Hoots, and Hooters: Impress

Her with Streetwise Sweet Talk. I aced wolf whistles, but I'd had all I could take after the *hey, baby*s started.''

Jayne nodded seriously. Then she seemed to remember something. Rapidly, she visored her hand over her eyes to shield them.

"Well, uh, good for you," she said, looking down at the ground as though searching for something. "See you around."

"I came to make sure you're okay."

"Fine! Fine." She tugged her hair with her free hand, smoothing it. "I'm fine. Just busy."

Riley hunkered down, trying to look into her face. "Are you sure you're all right? Because this morning—"

"I'm great. Just peachy. So you can go . . . do whatever you were planning to do. Thanks for stopping by!"

She shooed him away with her hands. The motion seemed to remind her that she'd left her eyes unshaded and her hair unsmoothed, because Jayne jerked her hands back into place. If possible, she huddled even more into herself.

Now he was *really* worried. She was acting so strangely. Riley took her hands gently in his and tugged. Jayne yelped, and moved them back into place.

"What's wrong?" he asked, frowning.

"My eyes! I . . . I have something in them."

"Both of them?"

"Ow! Ow! You'd better . . . leave, right away."

She swiveled on her log seat, turning away from him. He examined her. Having apparently decided to leave her hair alone, she'd covered her entire face with her hands.

"Let me see," he urged. "Maybe I can help."

"No!"

Riley rocked backward slightly on his heels. Recovering from her vehement refusal, he said, "I don't mind. Come on."

"Don't look at me!"

"I'll *have* to look at you," he said reasonably, "to help you."

"Not now!" Jayne surged to her feet, hands still over her face. She moved them to fix her hair, to tug her shirt, then to cover her face again, all in rapid succession. Nearly jumping with frustration—or was it pain?—she clapped her palms over her eyes again. "I'll take care of this. You . . . go find Carla and see if you can help her, okay? She's not feeling well."

"Ooookay."

The minute he agreed, she galumphed to the pile of backpacks, pulled hers free with an expression of profound relief, and then scurried to the edge of the trail. Riley would have sworn Jayne muttered something about "Can't *believe* I'm a 'before'!" but that didn't make sense. Did it?

He got to his feet and went to find Carla.

The air was cooler high in Catsclaw Canyon. The surrounding territory felt remote, even though it was closer to a settled area. Riley rounded a stand of trees and found Carla exactly where the other guidance groupies had said he would—alone on a boulder.

She had her feet propped on a pile of rocks. Her nose ring gleamed in the early-afternoon sun. Her hiking clothes were ripped, layered, and twisted in unique ways that lent them a punk edge. As he watched, she stuck the end of a pen in her mouth and stared thoughtfully at the tablet of paper on her lap.

"I brought you some instant chicken soup," Riley said, approaching. He eyed her carefully, noting the wariness in her gaze. Carla was the only group member he hadn't been able to win over yet. It didn't sit well with him. "Here. It's not bad if you put enough Tabasco in it."

He produced the miniature bottle that was always part of

his gear and handed it to her along with the cardboard carton of hot soup. "Every camper's best friend."

She accepted both with a nod and a distinct lack of eye contact. "Thanks. See you around."

Riley frowned as he watched Carla balance the soup and Tabasco on her lap. What *was* it with women today? Every one he encountered told him to get lost. Surreptitiously, he checked his breath. *That* wasn't the problem. He tried another tactic.

"That's a cute nose ring."

"Save it. Men think my nose ring blows."

"Well, isn't it kind of tough to blow with a nose ring? I once photographed a Kikuyu tribesman who said—"

Interrupting his joke, Carla shook her head. She actually paused in her Tabasco-ing of the soup too. "Look, I'm, like, trying to have a little privacy here. So if you don't mind . . . ?"

He did mind. He was going to earn her trust, dammit! Now, what else could he do?

Riley rubbed his hands together. "I'll bring you a blanket to cushion that boulder. Jayne said you're not feeling well."

"Don't bother."

"Some water?" He offered the bottle strapped at his hip. "Not thirsty."

He frowned. "Soup taste okay? I made it myself."

Pointedly, Carla set down the carton. As ridiculous as it was, Riley's feelings were hurt.

"Could you just, like, leave me alone, please?" she asked.

"I could." He sat down beside her instead.

"But you're not going to. It figures." She threw up her hands. "The one man I want to pay attention to me won't, but I'm a magnet for everybody else."

"Not everybody. Just me."

She sighed. "You don't really want to be here."

"Neither do you, I'm guessing. Why'd you skip Jayne's workshop?"

"I'm sick. See?" Carla gave a feeble cough.

"I'm not buying it," Riley said. "You look fine to me."

Wondering what was going on, he glanced at the pad of paper on her lap. "Who's the letter to?"

She hesitated. "My Paolo."

"I thought the workshop participants weren't supposed to contact their exes."

"We're not." She raised her chin defiantly. "But I only signed onto the workshop to, like, bother my Paolo. I thought as soon as he knew where I was going, he'd realize what he'd done to me and—"

"And take you back?"

Carla nodded. "But he didn't. He only shrugged and said, 'Whatever you've gotta do, Carla.'" Her gaze shifted from her forbidden letter to his face, pleading with Riley to understand. "Not everybody is strong like Jayne, you know! The rest of us could never buddy up to an ex, like she's done with you, and be okay with it. She knows how to keep things casual, so she doesn't get hurt."

Casual. Then Jayne *was* fine with things as they stood. She didn't want more from him. Didn't want him to settle down. Didn't want him to change. Not that she'd asked him to before, really. It had been implied in their increasingly serious relationship though.

He waited for the relief he expected to strike. Oddly enough, it didn't. In its place came a sense of . . . disappointment?

Dismissing it, he said, "I guess that's why she's the author."

"Yeah." Carla picked up her soup. She began spooning it into her mouth. "Jayne's really smart. And totally strong. I really admire her."

"Me too."

Carla gawped.

"It's true. Coming here has been a challenge for her. But she's tackled things head-on."

Beside him, Carla's expression turned thoughtful. She squinted up at him. "Are you sure there's not something more serious going on between you and Jayne? Because when you talk about her, you look sorta dreamy and—"

"Me? And Jayne?" He made a dismissive sound. "We tried it once, and it didn't work. Remember?"

"Same thing goes for me and my Paolo. That doesn't mean it might not happen again."

They both looked down at her letter. Filled with large loopy script and heart-dotted i's, it covered the entire page.

"Do you want it to?" Riley asked quietly.

"Well, I do and I don't." Carla took a deep breath. She wiggled on the boulder, as though settling in for a long talk. "See, Paolo and me were meant to be together from the start. It was all, like, a misunderstanding when we split. See, it's—hey, are you sure you want to hear all this?"

Riley smiled at her eagerness, at the flood of words that had spilled the minute he'd expressed more than a passing interest. Clearly, Carla needed to be heard. Even though socializing wasn't his strong suit, he was the one she'd chosen to talk to. He couldn't bail out now.

"I'm sure," he said.

"Okay. Well, like I was saying—"

Carla's words tumbled out, coming faster as she warmed up to her topic—and her audience. Riley smiled and nodded. He almost regretted not taking Jayne up on her "conversation lessons." But what Carla really needed, it seemed, was someone to listen. He figured he could do that as well as anyone.

"Then what happened?" he asked when she paused.

"Oh, boy," Carla said. "You'll never believe it!"

It was ten more minutes before he got another word in edgewise.

*   *   *

That afternoon, more hiking followed. A trailside lunch came and went. Striking out again with her pack strapped on, Jayne tried to focus on the path that brought her closer to the canyon lodge—and the end of her journey—with every step. Instead, she was continually distracted by Riley.

He'd been acting strangely all day. Especially since returning to the workshop campsite with Carla. They'd strode in together arm in arm—Riley nodding, Carla beaming and talkative. *Another member of the Riley Davis fan club,* Jayne had thought at the time. But now she wondered if something else was going on with Riley. Because he hadn't left her alone for a minute.

When he'd gone to help Carla, Jayne had managed to fix herself up a bit. She'd had time to slick on some lip gloss, brush on mascara, and bundle her hair into a ponytail. But before she could do more than turn her fleece top right side out, Alexis had come to her for advice about Lance. After that, she'd had no opportunity to improve the way she looked.

Well, she *had* tied her shoelaces. But beyond that—*nada.* And Jayne didn't want Riley to realize it.

She tried ditching him by joining Mack's trail group. Riley rearranged the matchups. She tried avoiding him by lagging behind. Riley waited for her, a concerned look on his face. She tried jogging ahead, turning her collar up, and staring at the scenery instead of at him whenever he spoke to her. None of it worked. Wherever she went, whatever she did, Riley was there.

It was almost as though he was worried about her. Almost as though he was shadowing her on purpose, like a private detective with a specialty in makeover wanna-bes. If she hadn't been so preoccupied with trying to avoid showing Riley her worst side, Jayne would have thought his diligence was sweet. As it was, the way he looked at her—as though nothing had changed—just gave her the heebie-jeebies.

Couldn't he tell she needed a good blowout? A facial? A manicure?

As though she'd cued him to resume his efforts, Riley matched his pace more closely to hers. He pulled something from his pocket and handed it to her.

"A bandanna?" Jayne asked, puzzling at the square of soft cotton she'd accepted.

"Not just any bandanna. A *baby-blue* bandanna."

He looked incredibly pleased by this. Why, she didn't know.

"What's it for?"

"Well, I pack it in as part of my regular supplies, but I figure it qualifies as an *accessory*." Riley's eager hazel-eyed gaze searched her face. "I thought you might want to wear it."

Still mystified by his continued watchfulness, she shrugged. "Well, I guess it *would* protect my highlights from the sun. Thanks."

They both stopped beside a juniper bush, letting Mitzi and Alexis take the lead in their small group. Jayne folded the bandanna, then wrapped and tied it around her head in a way she'd once seen in *In Style*. She modeled the effect for Riley.

"Beautiful."

Jayne snorted and started walking again.

"I mean it." He caught up, matching her pace with no visible effort at all. "You're beautiful to me no matter what you wear."

"You don't have to sweet-talk me, Riley."

"It's the truth."

"Come on, I—"

"We didn't exactly meet under the most glamorous of circumstances, remember? You pushed me—and my camera—out of the path of an incoming wave, and wound up on the pier soaked yourself."

Jayne remembered. The cold, salty seawater had drenched her from head to foot. "My stiletto got stuck between the planks in the pier."

"It's probably what kept you from being washed away." Riley gave her a fond smile. "I like stilettos."

"And then you gave me your coat and bought me a cup of coffee. Remember the look on that woman's face when you snuck into the ladies' room at that café to help me dry off with the hot air dryer?"

"It was like she'd never seen a man before."

"Not a man trying to talk a woman he'd just met into accepting his pants and shirt—and socks!—until hers dried."

He grinned. "I'd have given you anything just to hear you laugh again the way you did when that wave surprised you."

"And *I* would've happily seen you naked while you switched clothes." Boy, *would* she have. Riley was then—like today—a major hunk. "But your pants would never have fit—"

"I still would do anything for you, Jayne. Especially today."

"—and I wouldn't have been caught dead in a muscle T, however nice it looked on you."

What he'd said registered. It was so surprising that Jayne risked exposing her pallid, no-blush face to peek at him. "Today?" she managed. "Why especially today?"

"Because I think you need it. You've been through a lot. And because—" At a shout from Alexis up ahead, Riley paused. He scanned the landscape. "Never mind. I'll show you what I mean instead. We're here."

Then he grabbed her by the hand and hustled them both along the trail toward the log lodge just visible between the trees.

* * *

At the canyon lodge, a sense of celebration zinged through the air. Jayne felt it too. They'd made it to the end of their journey, and from here on, their survival was assured. Jeeps were scheduled to pick up everyone for transport back to the Hideaway Lodge, but since the group was ahead of schedule, they wouldn't arrive for another day. Until then there was nothing to do but relax.

With relieved smiles, the women collapsed on the rustic upholstered furniture in the lodge's common room, unshouldering their backpacks and groaning as they removed their ATSes. The men set about their duties, checking the firewood, fuel oil, and water supplies, inventorying groceries, and scouting the bedrooms on seek-and-destroy missions against marauding spiders. Jayne made a special request that they keep their eyes open for any possible javelinas in her assigned room, then fell into an armchair beside the unlit fieldstone fireplace.

Soon, a rag rug cushioned her stockinged feet against the cold hardwood floors. A cup of coffee—courtesy of Mitzi and Bruce, who'd disappeared into the kitchen together, ostensibly to brew the stuff—warmed her hands. A grandfather clock ticked off the length of her blessed indoor sanctuary.

Alexis and Lance left the group and, fortified by the knowledge that the lodge had electricity, went on the hunt for a radio so they could tune in some "decent music." The breakup-ees gradually scattered. Kelly agreed to let Mack demonstrate the lodge's solar panels for her, in a move Jayne figured had to be the granola-and-Timberlands version of "want to see my etchings?" Doris and Donna argued over the best way to assemble a jigsaw puzzle they'd found. Mitzi and Bruce returned to the kitchen to "make toast." Carla announced she needed to think things over, and planned to do it on the lodge's wide front porch.

Within a half hour of arriving, Jayne found herself alone. Spooked by how quickly everyone had abandoned her, she got up. She paced. She worried.

Sure, she'd told her breakup-ees that the workshops were finished. And she'd explained that their final get-together would be an informal session tomorrow, geared toward gathering feedback about her techniques. But just because they weren't officially required to spend time with her, did that mean they didn't want to?

Apparently so. The realization disheartened her.

Frowning, Jayne went to the window. She had to do something about this. She just had to.

"I'd have thought you'd have had enough of the view," Riley said from behind her.

"I'm not looking at the view."

"That's pretty much all that's out there."

"I'm looking for neighbors. People to chat with. People to borrow a cup of sugar from. People to invite over for a kaffeeklatsch."

"People who haven't deserted you?"

She wheeled around. Riley was watching her perceptively. Maybe too perceptively. "I never said that."

His hands settled on her shoulders. He smiled. "You didn't have to. But you're missing something important here. The reason everyone left is because of *you.*"

"Great. I feel *loads* better now."

"No. Let me try again." His fingers squeezed her shoulders gently. "What I mean is—"

"That I don't fit in. It's okay. You don't have to shield me from it. I can take it."

But not very well. She turned her face to the window again, only to catch her reflection in the glass. Pale eyes, undefined lips, and straggly, bandannaed hair met her gaze. She really should have fixed herself up while she'd had the chance. Now it was too late. Self-pity swamped her.

"The way I look," Jayne couldn't help but moan, "that javelina wouldn't even want me for company."

In the glass, Riley's puzzled face loomed over hers. Then realization swept his features, and he turned her around again. "Yes! You look terrible! You've realized it!"

"You don't have to sound so happy about it. I look like Mother Nature after a really bad bender."

"It must have been the bandanna," Riley said inexplicably.

Even more inexplicably, he hugged her. He didn't release her either. He kept her locked in his arms, where Jayne was forced to confront the flex of his muscles, the scent of wood smoke on his clothes . . . the beloved familiarity of his body pressing against hers. Riley put both palms to her cheeks and cradled her face, beaming down at her with delight and . . . pride?

"Yeah. It's a magic bandanna," she agreed, feeling confused but unwilling to ruin his good mood.

"*My* magic bandanna," Riley said. He straightened, then seemed to remember something. "And all I meant to say earlier was that the only reason your guidance groupies feel free to do their own thing is because you've empowered them. You've cured their broken hearts so well that some of them are even ready to try again. *You did it.*"

Well, looked at that way . . . "I *did* do it!"

Riley nodded. "You did. And now that you're finished with that, there's only one more thing you have to do."

"Actually, there are tons more things." Jayne ticked them off on her fingers, feeling encouraged again. "I need to shampoo my hair, fix my pedicure, wash my clothes . . . does the lodge have an ironing board by any chance?"

"It's got something even better." A devilish glint heightened the green in his eyes, and made his smile look twice as inviting. "And it's especially for you. Come on."

Nineteen

The canyon lodge's master bedroom suite was at the far end of the two-story structure, having been added on several years after the first log had been notched. It possessed a four-poster bed, assorted furniture, an attached bathroom, and the most privacy to be had in the entire lodge. It was this last that concerned Riley as he led Jayne there to reveal his surprise.

"Wow!" she said, whirling one-handed from the bedpost. She landed on the pillow-piled mattress. "My bunk is 'Camp Catawba.' Yours is 'Camp Eddie Bauer.' This is great!"

"Glad you like it."

She gazed at him seriously from atop the deep green-and-white comforter. "If you've brought me here to switch sleeping accommodations, I accept."

Before he'd even blinked, Jayne began bouncing. For a moment, Riley watched in surprise as she bounced to her knees, then to her feet, then leapt nearly ceiling high. The bed's plain net top fluttered. Something inside him did, too, at witnessing her unbridled enthusiasm.

"A mattress!" she said as she bounced. "Real sheets! Pillows! I'm in heaven."

"That's not the surprise," he called through cupped hands.

"It's not?" She stopped, bandanna loosened on her hair. She straightened it with one hand, then accepted his help getting down from the bed. "What is it, then?"

"This way." Riley headed for the short hallway—edged by a closet—that connected the bedroom and bathroom. Halfway there, he stopped Jayne. He untied her bandanna, then held it in front of her face. "May I?"

Jayne blinked. "Blindfold me?"

He nodded.

She swallowed. Curiosity—and interest—brightened her eyes. "Okay."

With gentle motions, he tied the bandanna over her closed eyes. He made sure it wasn't too tight, made sure she couldn't peek . . . made sure his body nudged up against hers as he did so. This surprise may have been for Jayne, but Riley realized it was starting to thrill him too.

They progressed to the bathroom doorway. The scents of soap and roses teased them inside the rustic log-walled space. There, it was warmer. Steam clouded the room's mirrors and made the air moist to breathe. The soft rug he'd laid padded their footsteps as they drew nearer to Riley's surprise.

"Can I look yet?" Jayne asked, suppressed excitement in her voice. She jiggled a little. She'd always loved surprises.

"Are you ready?"

She nodded. Suddenly, Riley wasn't sure *he* was ready. It meant a lot to him that she be happy. He took one last look at everything he'd arranged, making sure every detail was perfect for her. His fingers shook as he untied the bandanna.

Jayne gasped. She clasped her hands over her heart. "A *bath!*"

She gave him an unreadable over-the-shoulder look. "So *this* is what you've been doing since we got here."

He shrugged. "Well, this . . . and raccoon-proofing the place."

Smiling, she stepped nearer the old zinc washtub he'd scrubbed and polished and filled with hot soapy water. Reverently, like the bath fanatic she was, Jayne knelt and dipped her hand to the froth.

"I couldn't find any of the deluxe bath products you like," he said, wishing the freestanding tub were bigger and fancier, "but Gwen always keeps Mr. Bubble on hand."

"Mr. Bubble is perfect." She stood to blow soapsuds from her fingers, then laughed. "What do you think got me hooked in the first place?"

"If a storm hits and the power goes out, we're screwed," Riley told her, gesturing toward the dozens of white candles he'd arranged and lit on every stable horizontal surface. There were short, squat candles and tall, thin tapers and multiwick extravaganzas and everything in between. "This includes the lodge's entire emergency supply."

"In that case, I'll pray for clear weather." She turned to him in the wavering candlelight, her features warmed by the glow. "It's beautiful."

So was she. *Beautiful.*

"Sorry the tub isn't a traditional model. I scrubbed the hell out of it though, so you don't have to worry about—"

"I'm not worried." Jayne edged nearer, pressing her thumb to his lips to silence him. She angled her head, nudged her thumb past his lower lip, and softly kissed him. "I'm grateful. I don't know how you knew I needed this. Thank you."

He felt encouraged. And relieved. He nodded toward the vanity, where several teakettles waited atop a bath towel. "There's extra hot water in case you get cold."

"Oh, I won't get cold." Meaningfully, she ran her hands down the front of his fleece, then slipped them to its hem. Moments later the garment whisked over his head. She dropped it. "I'll have *you* to keep me warm."

"You make it hard for a man to be chivalrous." He shook his head. "This bath is supposed to be just for you."

She eyeballed the tub. Shrugged. "It looks big enough for both of us to me."

"I had a shower while I waited for the tub to fill." He'd set up a hose system to pipe hot water from the sink to the old-fashioned washtub. For aesthetics' sake, he'd removed it before bringing her here though. Women cared about things like that. "You go ahead. Get in. I have some chores I should—"

"Oh, no, you don't." Jayne grabbed his T-shirt as he turned away. She tugged him nearer, then pulled his shirt off altogether. She tossed it away, her expression daring him to disagree . . . and urging him to join her. Again.

Riley couldn't say he regretted her single-mindedness. He did, however, begin to feel things were unequal between them. Here he stood, bare chested and barefooted, while his intended bath-ee was still completely dressed.

"As an invitation, ripping off my clothes is a little ambiguous," Riley said. "What if birthday parties were run that way?" With a grin, he unzipped Jayne's fleece top in demonstration. " 'Please, drop by my party, won't you?' "

He raised the garment over her head and tossed it onto a nearby chair. "Tonight. All night."

She smiled. He continued, lightly running his hands over the form-fitting T she had on underneath. He slipped his fingers along the hem, teasing the warm skin just beneath. "I'd love to see you there."

At his mock-serious tone, Jayne raised her eyebrows. "Gee, I wonder how a person RSVPs to an invitation like yours? I suppose . . ." She tucked her fingertips into the front of his pants and deftly thumbed open the top button. "Oh! Why, look at that. Will this do?"

Her blue eyes sparkled. Her disingenuous grin warmed him all over. Her hips swayed, inviting his touch as she teased him with another up-and-down sweep of her hands on his chest.

Riley cupped her derrière in his palms and drew her against him. "That'll do," he said, and lowered his head.

Their kiss was hungry, familiar, utterly necessary. Their mouths met in the steamy heat, sliding and tasting and searching. After days of never being truly alone, they luxuriated in the privacy of a room to themselves—with Jayne doubtless thrilled to have four walls and a ceiling too.

"I don't know if I should stay," she murmured, frowning slightly, when their kiss ended. "My breakup-ees might need—"

"They're fine for now. Your workshops are finished, right? Bruce and Mack can handle anything else that comes up."

She bit her lip, thinking.

"Jayne?"

In reply, she crossed her arms and took off her shirt. Her bra was utilitarian and white. Riley couldn't help but think it was the sexiest thing he'd ever seen.

"Is that a yes?" he asked. "You're okay with this?"

"Boy, you've obviously been out in the wilderness too long." She delivered a nibbling, sexy kiss that had him groping for her when she pulled away. "If you can't recognize a seminaked woman as a yes—"

"I can." Lightheartedness filled him. He unsnapped her bra's front clasp with a pinch of his fingers. "That's a 'yippee!'" he informed her mock seriously.

"Oh, good." Shucking the white cotton straps from her shoulders, Jayne smiled. "I'm so glad we're on the same page."

"Shimmy some more, and I'll read you the whole book."

She did. Naked. Riley didn't think his life could get any better. Unless maybe Jayne stayed, or he . . . no. He'd be damned if he'd start down *that* path. Besides, Jayne had her fingers on his fly again. She was either taking off his pants or measuring him for a jockstrap. Either way, he stood cooperatively still, enjoying every inch of the task.

"See anything you like?" he asked, biting back a groan.

"I like everything I see." She leaned back, gauging the effect. "Now, if I can just ease past this . . . obstruction. . . ."

"Obstruction? Nice way to talk about—"

"You like the way I talk, and you know it."

She was right. He liked her surprising bawdiness, her open interest, her dexterity with a button fly. But Riley didn't have the words to say so. He didn't even have the ability to tease. Jayne's touch had stolen his will to do anything more than breathe—and love her.

She opened his fly wider. She slipped his pants lower, past his straining erection. Her fingers whisked over the soft cotton that still covered him. He throbbed. There was something wicked in the glance she gave him next, something expectant and heated and loving. He wanted to laugh with joy—but that would be too much for a simple one-night reunion, wouldn't it? So instead he only grinned like a goofball, and began kissing her.

He pressed his lips to her mouth, her neck, her palm. He nibbled her earlobe, delighting in the way she wiggled with pleasure. After kicking away his discarded clothes, Riley started in on Jayne's trail wear. Her socks were first (he tickled her toes), then her pants whisked to the floor.

Wearing only his white boxer briefs, he took a moment to savor the sight of Jayne dressed in nothing but her skimpy polka-dotted panties. Noticing his interest, she turned in a circle, modeling them for him. They were yellow and baby blue, a combination that unreasonably cheered him. It turned out she'd been wearing her signature color all along.

"Those will have to go, of course," he said, nodding toward her panties. On her, they were sexy enough to require a warning label. "Better hurry. Your water's getting cold."

She raised an eyebrow. "You first."

Her pointed glance indicated his briefs. The sassy gleam

in her eyes made it plain she found his appearance every bit as appealing as he did hers. It was just like old times, Riley thought. Each of them hungry for the other . . . each of them daring the other to make the first move.

He shook his head and pulled her into his arms again. The press of her bare breasts against his chest made it hard to form a coherent thought, much less speak. But he did it. "It's your bath. I insist you go first."

"Ever the gentleman, hmmm?"

"You've got it." He smiled. "Chivalry has its rewards."

Slowly, Jayne gyrated against him. A moan escaped him. *There was one of those rewards now.* Nothing had ever felt this good. He tipped her head up and kissed her, then urged her toward the foamy tub. Rose petals floated in the water, barely visible amid the mounds of bubbles.

She abandoned their kiss reluctantly, her eyes heavy-lidded and dark with desire. Hooking her thumbs in the waistband of her panties, she bent at the waist and whisked them off. Riley saw a flash of thigh, a delectable glimpse of derrière, and then the water splashed. Jayne sat in the tub, beckoning him in.

"Come on. The water's wonderful."

Doubtfully, he surveyed the tub. It would be a tight squeeze. To make room, she drew up her knees. She gave him an inviting smile.

Riley couldn't resist. "You know, you have a way of making bubbles look awfully sexy."

"How sexy?"

"I'll show you."

Fifteen minutes later, they'd successfully tested the limits of the washtub. It seemed two people *could* fit in the bath . . . so long as they were willing to be close. Very close. Luckily for Riley, there was nothing he wanted more than to be close with Jayne. Now. All night. Forever.

Hang on a minute . . . *forever?*

Hesitating with the soap in his hand and Jayne's about-to-be-scrubbed back within reach, Riley balked. *He* didn't want forever. He wasn't a forever kind of guy. So what the hell?

Clearly, his feelings were being confused by all this closeness, by the pleasure of being with Jayne again. That was all. Feelings didn't change what he knew to be true. Feelings didn't change a *person*. After tonight he'd return to his old self again. In the morning he'd be eager to leave, ready to hit the trail, anxious for adventure.

To see, to do, to conquer, to enjoy.

Hell, yes.

And Jayne understood that too. Hadn't Carla just told him how skillfully Jayne was handling her temporary relationship with him?

Relieved, Riley went on soaping Jayne's soft, smooth skin. Her little sigh of enjoyment as he slid slick fingers over her shoulder blades brought him all the way back to the moment at hand. This was going to be a night to remember, he reminded himself. It had to be. It was the night he would say good-bye to Jayne—for the last time, the way he should have long ago.

Tonight he would give all he could to her. Because tomorrow . . . well, tomorrow didn't exist for them. Tonight was everything.

Jayne fell backward onto the bed, laughing as Riley carried her down. The plush comforter pouffed around her. Her long wet hair (shampooed at last!) puddled beneath her head and shoulders. Her damp skin prickled with goose bumps as the air stirred by their movements washed over her naked body.

She felt no embarrassment at her nudity, no shyness or self-consciousness. Because she was with Riley. She'd always been comfortable with him. With him she felt beautiful. Desirable. From the moment he'd unveiled his Mr. Bubbley surprise, being with him had felt right . . . just like old times.

"Hold still," Riley instructed huskily. "I'm not done with you yet."

Naked too, he wielded a towel. Grinning, he wedged his knee between her thighs for balance, then dexterously dried her hair. He smoothed every strand, touched her face tenderly with his hands, cradled her close for a kiss like all the others they'd shared. Passionate. Skillful. Loving.

Through it all, he was fully aroused, and the restraint he practiced drove her wild. What other man would have ignored an erection hard enough to hit a home run with just for the sake of making sure her hair was untangled? What man except Riley would have even understood her well enough to try?

Heedless of her unstyled tresses, Jayne writhed as he patted a terry-cloth path down her body. He took his time, diligently absorbing every errant drop of water, every gleaming trace of soapsuds. She watched his face as he cared for her. His expression was intent, his eyes dark with desire and appreciation. His beard stubble had begun its nightly appearance, and its shadow lent his features a ruggedness and masculinity she loved.

Jayne ran her hand along his jaw, enjoying the faint prickly texture beneath her palm. She trailed her fingers lower, to his wide shoulders and chest. Apparently, adventure travel guiding provided a fierce workout, because Riley's body was formed of the lean, solid muscle only real labor could endow. His chest and arms were perfect, his abdominals and thighs powerfully carved . . . exactly as she'd remembered. Possibly even better.

Giddy with the joy of being with him again, Jayne dipped her thumbs into the sexy hollow just below the tattoo at his hipbones, then lower in a teasing stroke. She admired Riley as he moved, taking in every dreamed-of inch of him. This night was *hers*, a reward for her bravery, a bonus for curing her own broken heart. Now that she was safe from falling for Riley, she meant to savor every single minute of time with him.

She'd earned it, hadn't she? And if she happened to wish for more, for a future together? Well, she *wouldn't,* and that was that. She'd reformed, Jayne assured herself. No matter how her feelings urged her to give herself to Riley, her body understood this was only one night. Tomorrow didn't exist for them.

Satisfied with that for now, Jayne arched beneath Riley's crouched body and tugged him to her for a kiss. She lost herself in the meeting of their mouths, in the heat of their bodies coming together. Her skin burned. Pleasure wended its way through her middle, leaving her limbs heavy and her thoughts muddled. Riley kissed like a man who'd decided to claim his woman, and for this one glorious night, Jayne luxuriated in being that woman. In his arms, she felt safe and warm and *wanted.* For now nothing else was necessary.

His breathing quickening, Riley rolled them over so that Jayne straddled him. His gaze touched her face, lowered to her breasts, lingered. His hands followed suit.

Closing her eyes, she threw back her head and moaned as he cupped her, stroked her, lightly teased her. He thumbed her rigid nipples and she shivered . . . he levered upward with her in his lap to kiss her breasts and she cried out loud with pleasure. This, *this* was what she needed. Riley's hands on her body, his lips on her skin . . . his husky murmurs of enjoyment in her ears.

His arms cradled her waist, keeping her upright. That hottest, hardest part of him nudged between her thighs, and her slick heat welcomed him. He felt huge and ready and gratifyingly aroused, and it was all Jayne could do not to nudge herself the slightest fraction to the right and . . .

"Whoa," Riley breathed. "Not yet. There's more of you still needing attention."

She protested as he turned them yet again, this time so

that Jayne lay on her belly against the soft comforter. With tender kisses and whispered promises, Riley made sure she would agree with the leisurely pace he apparently meant to set. He kissed from the back of her neck downward, tickled the undersides of her knees, and emerged from a foray to the back of her thigh with a rose petal clenched between his teeth.

"Not as soft as your skin," he announced as he plucked it out. He let the bath-time-flower remnant drift to the floor. "Not as tasty either."

"How can you be sure?" She turned over, reaching for him. "You haven't tasted all of me yet."

"Easily remedied."

With that hoarsely voiced promise, Riley eased down the bed. He smiled wickedly and parted her thighs. Moments later Jayne found herself desperately holding his head as he delivered a *very* intimate kiss. Her whole focus narrowed to the thick strands of hair in her fingers, the delicate rasp of his tongue, the heat of his breath against her most sensitive places. With an expertise both reverent and wonderfully wild, Riley loved her with his mouth and hands and murmured encouragement until Jayne couldn't stand any more. She came unraveled, clutching the comforter for support, trembling and moaning and begging. Her orgasm swept powerfully over her, and when she finally dared to open her eyes again, it was to see Riley . . . grinning.

She arched a brow. Truthfully, it was the largest part of her still capable of movement. "You look proud of yourself."

"And you look amazing." He crawled up her body, pulled her into his arms. "I love making love to you."

"Spoken like a man who thinks he's finished."

"Not by a long shot. I'm keeping you here all night."

"Then I'd say it's my turn."

Rediscovering her energy, Jayne rose and pushed on his chest. He fell backward willingly, bringing her with him for a kiss. She let her hands rove lower, let her fingers rediscover the tautness of his middle ... the silken steeliness of his penis. She stroked him with her palm, feeling a rush of feminine power at her ability to arouse him. Riley moaned and lifted his hips at her touch, his eyes bright as he watched her.

"I ... like ... your ... turn," he said.

"You'll like this even more," she promised, and gave him an intimate kiss of her own. She trailed her lips down the length of him and back again, offering a tongue-swirling embellishment at the end. "You taste like Mr. Bubble. And roses."

"You talk like a woman who isn't driving me wild. Please, Jayne. Please, don't stop."

She didn't. Instead, she loved him as thoroughly and as well as she could—and if affectionate enthusiasm counted for anything at all, Jayne decided, then she was definitely the best he'd ever had. Her theory was proven when he groaned and urged her upward again.

"Please, you have to stop," Riley said.

She paused. Licked. Paused again. "Gee, make up your mind."

Her suggestion seemed to stump him. "Mind? I still have a mind?" He rumbled with wholly masculine pleasure as she circled him with kisses. "I think it's broken."

"It's otherwise occupied."

Thoroughly enjoying herself, Jayne did her best to torment him. She knew he intended to make love to her, and she wanted that too. But for now ...

"Hey!"

Riley grabbed her and spun. He panted, possibly from the exertion of having executed yet another Kama Sutra–style move. Jayne found herself sprawled beneath his big, strong body ... and fascinated by his big, wide smile.

"My turn," he said.

She pretended to acquiesce and fluttered a hand. "Oh, all right. Have your wicked way with me."

"I intend to."

He did. Long moments swept past, during which Riley did love her, meticulously and well. He touched her with a care that warmed her heart, and when she looked at him, she saw something unexpectedly serious in his expression. Although he purposefully kept their lovemaking playful, Jayne glimpsed something new in his eyes. As he touched her, the poignancy in his face stirred her in ways she'd never experienced.

This went beyond a casual encounter, Jayne realized all at once. And she couldn't deny it any longer.

She couldn't deny it as Riley held her hips in his hands, gazing at her with wonderment. She couldn't deny it as he entered her, and the pleasure of being reunited with him soared through her. She couldn't deny it as he began a tender dance of slide and retreat, thrust and kiss, shudder and moan. She loved him . . . both seriously and endlessly. She always had, and there was no doubt now that she always would.

Losing herself to their joining, Jayne held Riley to her. She loved him, loved him . . . but he only made love to her. He did it remarkably, it was true, but now she wanted more. More of him. More of them. More of the things she could never have.

She couldn't date like a man. She couldn't. No matter how hard she tried. She could only love like a woman— something she wished she'd realized before now.

A tear squeezed from the corner of her eye and streaked a trail across her temple. As it soaked into her pillow, Riley lifted his hand to her face. Jayne opened her eyes to find him watching her, his expression indescribably gentle.

"It's always been you, Jayne," he said. "Always."

"Oh, Riley." More tears threatened, but she managed to hold them back. Instead of weeping over what they couldn't share, she wanted to revel in what they could. She rocked her hips closer. She wrapped both arms around him, her hands cupping the taut muscles of his backside to urge him onward. "Please, don't stop."

"Never."

He didn't stop. He didn't look away either. Riley kept his gaze locked with hers as their bodies came together, and the intimacy of it all stole Jayne's breath. They were so good together, so perfect ... even their heartbeats took on a unique synchronicity as they both raced toward a climax. She panted and arched upward; he moaned and drove onward. Closer, closer Jayne came—and when she did, Riley was right there with her. He savored the long, blissful moments when her body hugged him nearer, then stilled as pleasure roared through him too. Shouting hoarsely, he united them for a final time.

Sinking back into the comforter and pillows, Jayne flung her arms outward. Her heart thundered. Her breathing panted. Her ears even rang. Despite her melancholy mood only moments earlier, she couldn't help but grin.

Riley slumped for an instant with an enormous "ahhh" of pleasure that only made her grin wider. Then he rolled to the side with her in his arms.

"I think my kneecaps are numb," he said, smiling.

I think my heart is lost. To you. No, she couldn't say that.

"I think my teeth were vibrating," Jayne told him.

"Mine too!"

"My toes did a rumba," she elaborated.

Riley glanced downward. "Mine cha-chaed."

"I've never felt better."

He cuddled her closer and kissed the tip of her nose. "Didn't you know? This is what love feels like."

She knew now. For a nanosecond, she regretted it.

Catching her, Riley gave her a puzzled look. Then he lowered his gaze to her lips and kissed her again. "If you look that puzzled, you obviously need a remedial course." His hands slipped past her waist. "Allow me ..."

"Again?"

"Again."

"Now?"

"I've waited a long time for you," he explained as he languorously slid against her. He cupped her breast, his fingers caressing the delicate skin at her side. "I can't think of a better time."

A few minutes later, neither could Jayne. In fact, it was a very long time before she thought of much of anything at all . . . except Riley, loving her.

Just for tonight.

Twenty

Sometime past midnight, Riley realized things had changed between him and Jayne. They'd changed, and for the better too.

It had happened so sneakily, amid lovemaking and bed jumping and snack smuggling. He hadn't realized it until just this minute. But now, with the luxury of time—and an armful of warm, wonderful woman—he considered the ways things were different . . . and how those differences had come about.

More than likely, they'd started when he'd seen Jayne again all those days ago, and his body had gotten freeze-framed in his Suburban. Probably, they'd continued when he'd found himself tutoring her girly-girl self in outdoors survival—and had picked up speed when he'd begun hoping she'd love that same outdoors as much as he did. Definitely, they'd taken hold completely when he'd watched Jayne welcome him into her bathtub . . . and now there was no escape.

Not that Riley wanted an escape. Making love with Jayne, he'd realized how much he'd missed her. They were perfect together. And now that Jayne was better equipped to handle a casual relationship, there was no reason they couldn't be together. He didn't need that long good-bye he'd planned, Riley told himself. He didn't need to say good-bye to Jayne at all. He could say hello instead . . . whenever he was in town.

There'd be no more avoiding Bay Area photojournalism assignments. No more turning away from any mention of San Francisco. From here on out, he'd purposefully visit the city by the bay, because that was where Jayne would be, waiting for him.

For an instant he frowned, thinking of the times when she *wouldn't* be waiting for him. After all, he couldn't expect her to put her whole life on hold just for his occasional vagabond visits. There would be other men. But he could handle that. He could—

"Hey!" Jayne said. "You're squeezing the life out of that pillow!"

He blinked and saw that he had the fluffy goose down in a fisted stranglehold. Okay, so maybe he couldn't handle the thought of Jayne with another man as maturely as he thought he could. He'd work on it. The future looked too bright not to.

Riley smiled at her and released the pillow. He made a dismissive gesture. "I was just thinking."

"About . . . ?"

About making our future permanently temporary. On the verge of suggesting the arrangement he had in mind, he reconsidered. "About intimidating that pillow into multiplying. We need more. We've squashed all ours into pancakes."

Jayne gave him a sassy look. "Oh, but the *way* we squashed them. What fun."

"I'll say." He smoothed her hair. Kissed the top of her head. Gazed thoughtfully at their nude bodies, entwined together amid the tangled sheets. How should he broach the topic? "In fact—"

*In fact, let's get together for some more of that fun when-
ever I'm within a hundred miles of you.* What do you say?

No, he couldn't say that. He needed something more
suave. More persuasive. Riley didn't think he could take it
if she turned him down. Not now that they'd rediscovered
each other. Not now that Jayne had learned to accept the
impermanence that was as much a part of him as his Timberlands, tackle boxes, and photography lenses.

Curled up coquettishly beside him, Jayne ran her hand
over his chest. She slipped it over his abdomen. " 'In fact'
what?"

"In fact, I can't believe you have the energy for that,"
he sidestepped, deciding to save the discussion for later . . .
later, when she *wasn't* touching him so stirringly. "Wow."

"Well, you *did* feed me Twinkies and coffee." She
winked. "Blame it on the sugar and caffeine."

"It was all I could grab from the kitchen. You made me
promise not to be seen."

Remembering his disgruntlement at her request, Riley
scowled. What the hell was up with that?

"And I appreciate it too," she purred. "Thank you."

Her hand moved. A few seconds later, his latest hard-on
tented the sheet. He forgot all about being annoyed and
began thinking about being Super-Endurance Man . . . for
her.

She drew away the sheet, uncovering him. "Hmmm.
Looks like you're ready for your reward."

Riley nodded, pleasure uncoiling beneath her continued
touch. Jayne could arouse him with a look, a whisper, a
breath. As near as he could tell, that was just more proof
they were meant to be together . . . or at least as together
as a man like him could manage.

"I've been meaning to ask you," Jayne said suddenly,
peering at his midsection. "What's this mean?"

Her fingers had found his tattoo. Imprinted just above and

to the right of his pelvis, it formed an ancient black ink symbol in a place where only he would see it.

"It's a tribal language. I had it done about two years ago."

Her gaze lifted to his. *Two years ago,* he saw reflected there. *After we broke up.* But the recriminations he might have expected weren't there. Jayne only nodded and stroked his tattoo, once. "It's sexy."

He owed her the truth. The truth he'd told no one else.

"It means 'to remember,' " Riley said. "But I never needed it. Not the way I thought I might."

She scrunched her nose, looking perplexed.

"I always remembered," he added. "I always *wanted.*"

"Wanted?"

"You. I always wanted you. Remembered you."

At his revelation, something passed over her face, something curious and intent and almost hopeful. But then a certain stubbornness took hold, and Jayne caressed him again.

"Well, tonight you've got me," she said lightly. "So we'd better make the most of it."

"Anything you say." He smiled and waggled his eyebrows teasingly. "I live to please."

And then, not long afterward, he did.

Jayne awakened in the morning with a smile in her heart and a pounding in her head. Wincing at the sensation, she put her hand to her brow. Maybe she had post-incredible-sex disorder. Or a Twinkie hangover. It had been days since she'd noshed with such abandon, after all. And even longer since she'd *loved* with such abandon. *Ahhh.*

Rolling over in bed to snuggle closer to Riley, Jayne gave him a one-armed hug. He reciprocated sleepily. Even conked out, he remembered to be affectionate. Could he *be* any more wonderful?

His lovemaking last night—and the intimate talks they'd shared over junk food and sugared java in between—had surpassed everything she'd remembered. And that was saying a lot. She and Riley had reconnected in every way. They'd rebuilt a trust that was rock solid. Now their relationship felt more real and more remarkable than ever before.

Riley must have felt it too, Jayne told herself. He must have felt things shift, must have felt their lives fall into sync. This time she dared to believe things might actually work between them. This time they'd find a way to be together. No matter what.

Her usual optimism returned. Here, in Riley's sunshiny bedroom at the lodge, Jayne felt cozy and hopeful. Here, as her body shared heat with his and their toes mingled beneath the sheets, she felt *right*. Happily, she gazed at Riley's sleeping profile, delighting in the rugged slope of his nose, the rowdy angle of his jaw, the sensual slant of his mouth. He really was a gorgeous man. Not even another Clooney-vision film fest could have put him to shame.

Smiling, she pushed aside the bedding. His shoulders came farther into view, along with his chest and arms—one of which cradled her close. She trailed her fingertips along the center of his torso, then swept them lower to his exotic tattoo.

I always remembered. I always wanted you.

His revelation had stunned her. Pleased her. Most of all, it had encouraged her. Despite his leaving, he must have fallen for her every bit as hard as Jayne had fallen for him. Why else would Riley want to tattoo a permanent reminder of her on his skin? For a guy who claimed to avoid all commitments, that was a pretty telling gesture.

It could mean only one thing.

"I love you too," she whispered, gazing into his sleeping face. "I always have."

He shifted. Had he heard her? Breath held, she waited for him to open his eyes. She hadn't meant to wake him, but if she had . . . maybe Riley would finally say he loved her. Maybe he would say he'd decided to stay.

He slept on. Disappointment nudged at her. Oh, but she'd fallen hard this time, Jayne knew in that moment. Harder than ever before, for Riley. But really, they were both adults. Both willing. Both free to be together. So what was the harm in that?

A sudden knock at the door made her remember what the harm was in that.

A second knock made her panic.

Her breakup-ees! They couldn't discover her here! If they did, they'd realize Jayne was a fraud. If they found her cavorting with her forbidden ex, they'd realize her techniques were phony . . . and her "gift" was nonexistent. Which must be true, she thought dispiritedly. Just look at her.

Picking up where she'd left off with Riley after her breakup-ee trip was one thing. Canoodling with him during the trip was something else again. The distinction between the two was something she'd forgotten in the heat of the post-bath moment. What had she been thinking?

Mobilized into action by a third knock, she groped for the frothy pink nightie she'd been modeling last night for Riley (before he'd deliciously divested her of it). Their luggage had been delivered to the canyon lodge by Gwen and Bud, and now Jayne had her full travel wardrobe—for all the good it did her. Once her breakup-ees knew she was a useless broken-heart curer, they were unlikely to be impressed by coordinating shoes and a cute miniskirt.

"Riley! Wake up!" she whispered. "Someone's at the door."

That someone knocked again. Jayne struggled into her nightie, reasoning it was the best cover she'd manage on short notice. Shoving her feet into marabou-trimmed pink bedroom slippers, she tottered to the other side of the bed.

She kicked all their discarded clothes beneath, then shook Riley's shoulder.

He barely budged. Apparently, hot, steamy lovemaking could work to a girl's disadvantage ... if it left her hot, steamy fella too exhausted to be manhandled out of his incriminating position on the morning after. Arms fluttering, Jayne bent over so her face was right beside his ear.

"Riley, wake up! I need—"

"I've got what you need, baby," he teased in a sexy, drowsy voice. His arm dangled from the mattress and found her leg. He slid his palm up her thigh, then cracked open one eye. "Just let me get a bowl of Wheaties and a spoonful of coffee grounds first, and I'll make you soooo happy—"

"No! That's not what I mean."

He opened both eyes. Then widened them as he centered his gaze on her cleavage—revealed to advantage in her nightie. "Hey, good morning! You wake up real nice."

Riley smiled broadly. Jayne preened. "You wake up nicely too," she said, distracted from the emergency at hand by the sheer novelty of having a thousand-proof hunk at her disposal. "*Really* nicely. Maybe we've still got time for—"

Another knock—a louder one—jolted her to attention. She grabbed his biceps and tugged. She had to get him out of sight.

At the same moment, he quirked his eyebrows. "Is someone at the door? I'd better go see who it is."

He disengaged himself from the tangled sheets, then stood in glorious nudity. Sunlight glowed over his muscles, casting them in golden perfection. Oh, but to be a ray of sunshine free to roam over that face, those shoulders, that butt—*hang on, here*. She was getting distracted again.

Thump, thump, thump came from the lodge hallway. The door rattled.

Riley started toward it. He stopped, dragged some of the sheet around his waist, and began walking again.

"Stop!" Jayne tackled him partway there. "I'll get it."

"Don't be silly." He wobbled, stumbling on the trailing bedding. "It's my room."

"That's the whole point." If *he* answered the door, he might blow her cover.

Shoving, pulling, and coaxing, she urged him away from the bedroom door and toward the room where they'd shared their bath. She kept up a constant stream of murmured encouragement, desperate to get Riley out of the way.

Once they were near enough, she opened the louvered closet door. "I'll be right back, I promise."

Using her best fifty-percent-off-sale move, she shouldered him inside the closet. Another final-clearance heave-ho landed him all the way inside.

"Hey!" Off balance, he clawed at the hanging clothes.

"I'm sorry! Just please, *stay* in here," Jayne begged, then she shut the closet and went to answer the door.

Frowning in the closet, Riley pushed aside a musty blanket that had fallen on his shoulder. In retaliation, something pungent smelling and hard whacked him on the side of the head.

A cedar moth-proofing block, he realized as he squinted groggily at it in the bars of light struggling through the louvered door. A minute and a half ago he'd been getting reacquainted with Jayne's silky thigh, preparing to strip off her filmy nightie with his teeth. Now he was getting clobbered by Martha Stewartish housekeeping paraphernalia.

What the hell was going on?

Irritated, he tried the doorknob. It didn't turn, and he boggled at it. Had Jayne actually *locked* him in?

When a second try yielded the same results, Riley knew she had. This perplexed him even more than the linebacker-style maneuvers she'd used to shove him in here in the first place. Why would Jayne want to lock him in the damned closet?

For a bleary instant, he tried to comfort himself. Maybe he'd pleasured her so well she couldn't bear to let him get away. Riley brightened, standing taller as he clutched the sheet to his naked middle. Maybe Jayne had enjoyed their mushy-gushy reunion conversations so thoroughly, she wanted to make sure they shared more of them. He knew he did. In fact, he'd begun reconsidering his plans for the future. All at once, settling down didn't sound so bad. Especially with Jayne.

Then another, less cheerful thought struck him. Maybe someone . . . in *particular* was at the door. Someone Jayne didn't want to know about their rekindled affair.

But who?

Mack? Bruce? Bozo Boy, who'd inspired her book *and* sent her to heartbreak camp? Riley would send him to Broken Nose Camp if he dared to try hurting Jayne again, he vowed. If he could just get out of this closet . . . he was next to useless amid the sweaters and forgotten hats.

"Alexis!" came Jayne's voice from across the room— from the *nonimprisoned* side of the room. She sounded surprised. "What are you doing here?"

"Jayne? But isn't this . . . Uncle Riley's room?"

A pause. "We . . . switched. Riley let me use his room last night, and he . . . was more than welcome to use mine."

Jayne couldn't even lie properly, he noticed. She was probably too softhearted to tell a fib to Alexis.

"Hmmm. Well, *anyway,*" his niece said, "I guess you could probably give a message to him if you see him?"

There was another pause. Riley imagined Alexis in her purple braces and thirteen-year-old-diva's clothes, then pictured Jayne in her nightie and ridiculous feathered shoes. He'd be damned if he'd stay in here like a cast-off gigolo, waiting for his lover's beck and call. He felt unwanted. Discarded. Used. He rattled the closet doorknob.

Jayne coughed to cover the sound. "Sure, I'll give him a message."

"Okay." A pop of bubble gum. "Just tell him his driver radioed ahead, and his Suburban will be here in like, half an hour. So he'll have plenty of time to make it to Sedona for his flight to Antigua."

Riley froze. *Damn! Antigua.* He'd meant to explain all that to Jayne this morning, when they woke up. But they hadn't actually slept much last night. And afterward, probably because of all the hiking they'd done over the past few days, or maybe because he'd finally had Jayne peacefully in his arms . . . well, afterward he guessed he'd just crashed. Nothing short of Full Pink Nightie had had the power to awaken him.

"Antigua?" Jayne asked. "Riley's going to Antigua?"

He yearned to open the stupid closet door to stop this disaster before it went any further. But when he rattled the bars of his impromptu cage, Jayne only buried the sound in another, fiercer cough. When he started to call out, her voice overrode his.

"I didn't know that," she said slowly. "I thought he'd changed his mind."

"Nope." He could well imagine Alexis's shrug. "He's got some *National Explorer* assignment there. Photographing emus or something."

"Emus."

"Yeah. So you'll tell Uncle Riley? 'Cause I don't want to have to track him down to give him the message. Lance is waiting for me."

"Right. Okay." Jayne sounded dazed. "I'll *absolutely* give Riley the message. As it turns out, I've got a few things I want to say to him too."

Uh-oh. Mad. She was definitely mad. At the realization, Riley felt trapped. There was nothing that made him feel more helpless, more useless, than when Jayne was mad at him. She'd want to talk and talk and talk, and he'd be tongue-tied with only his prepared statement for defense.

I've planned this trip to Antigua for months now. It's a good opportunity. I'll see you when I get back.

Okay, his statement sucked. He needed more time. Turning, Riley pushed past the clothes hanging on the closet rod. If he could only find a trapdoor in here. A secret passageway. An escape hatch, from the—

Outside the closet, the women said their good-byes. The bedroom door closed with a decisive clunk. Feminine footsteps trod across the floor.

Jayne was coming. *Think,* he commanded himself. *Explain this so she understands.*

The closet door swooshed open. A warm block of sunlight fell into the space, illuminating the dire lack of emergency exits. Feeling the heat on his back, Riley turned, the cedar block he'd been using to shove clothes out of his way still in hand.

Jayne stood there, arms crossed and high-heeled-slippered foot tapping. She raised a brow. "Antigua?"

He should have expected it but he hadn't. The minute he saw Jayne, every syllable of Riley's prepared "statement" flew right out of his head.

Twenty-One

Alexis strode down the lodge's hallway toward the dining room, where Lance was waiting. Already this morning she'd fixed her hair twice, shaved her legs once, and *totally* gone wild with the makeup Jayne had lent her yesterday. She wondered if Lance would notice the way her eye shadow coordinated with the jeans from her restored luggage, and if he'd like the CK One she'd spritzed on.

Jayne had. She'd complimented Alexis on her eye shadow and her perfume . . . before she'd gone all schizo about the Antigua thing, that is. The shock on her face when she'd learned about Uncle Riley's trip had been *obvious.* Alexis wondered if Jayne and Uncle Riley had hooked up last night and decided they probably had. After all, they were totally in love.

Just like her and Lance. Alexis spotted him near the break-fast-piled sideboard in the dining room. She performed a last-minute breath check, then happily headed toward him.

He glanced up with a PowerBar in one hand and a shelf-stable chocolate soy milk in the other. A wide smile spread over his face—a smile that was for *her* alone. The sight of it made Alexis feel kind of giddy—sort of like when she watched 'N Sync on *Total Request Live*. He handed her the food, then chose some for himself.

"You, uh, look great today," Lance said. "That makeup makes you look sort of like Mandy Moore."

Mandy Moore was *totally* cute! Psyched by his compliment, Alexis chirped out a thank-you and followed him to the dining table. All around them, various adventure travelers and guides sipped coffee, ate toast and oatmeal, and talked. The hum of the different conversations was comforting. It made Alexis feel less conspicuous—although she did notice Doris and Donna nod approvingly when Lance pulled out a chair for her. He even waited until she sat down to take a seat across from her.

Lance was a gentleman. Unlike Brendan. He was sweet too. She hadn't done a thing to make him like her, Alexis thought as he unwrapped her breakfast and handed it across the table, and still he *did* like her. In fact, she considered further as she chewed, she'd pretty much been as obnoxious as possible to Lance, and it hadn't made a bit of difference. He'd liked her all the same.

With Brendan, she'd had to change her whole schedule around to be with him—occasionally even ditching her Spanish Club meetings to spend time with him. With Brendan, she'd had to watch what she said so he wouldn't think she was a geek. With Brendan, it hadn't mattered *what* Alexis had done—in the end he still *hadn't* liked her. Not enough anyway.

Puzzled by the difference, she peered at Lance. He smiled at her and shyly inched his hand closer along the tabletop. His fingers closed tentatively around hers, and a jolt of excitement whooshed through her. Lance didn't even care who was watching when he held her hand! He didn't complain that hand holding was for wusses, or pretend to hold her hand then ask her to pull his finger. (Gross.) Instead, Lance just . . . touched her in the nicest way. Like he wanted to be nearer to her.

Halfway through her soy milk (she and Lance were considering becoming vegetarians together), Alexis had a revelation. Maybe it didn't matter what she did—people would like her (or not) for all kinds of reasons. Because of who *they* were. Not because of who she was (or wasn't). Some people were loving, like Uncle Riley and Nana and Gramps. Some were sweet, like Jayne and Lance. Some were immature, Cinnabon-wielding buttheads with gold chains, an Xbox fixation, and no neck . . . like you-know-who.

Wow. All this time she'd thought she needed to change herself. She'd thought she needed the "Fifty Ways to Look Smokin' Hot" article in *Cosmo,* and maybe a personality transplant too. Now Alexis realized she didn't. She was fine! If someone didn't realize exactly how *fine* she was . . . well, that was their problem, not hers.

It all made perfect sense. Feeling immensely better, Alexis finished her PowerBar. She started to rise to get another one, but Lance beat her to it.

"Still hungry?" he asked. "I saw one of the chocolate-peanut butter bars over there. I'll go get you one."

"Okay, thanks."

Propping her chin in her hand, Alexis watched Lance lumber over to the sideboard. He took his time choosing another PowerBar for her, his big hands hovering over the selection. He obviously wanted hers to be the *ideal* PowerBar.

She wished her mom would put that much thought into what Alexis wanted. Sadly, she considered what it would be like to have a mother who cared about the details, who asked about homework and enforced a curfew and *noticed* things about her daughter. Instead, her mom was too busy running off to Mexico with the boyfriend du jour.

Feeling discouraged again, Alexis moped as Lance made his selection. He waved it in the air with a smile, which she returned halfheartedly. Her mom was the *worst.*

And then it hit her. Her mom was . . . just who she was.

A globe-trotting, divorced, forty-something Britney wanna-be who liked lots of boyfriends. The fact that she rarely spent more than ten minutes on the phone with her only daughter didn't mean there was something wrong with that *daughter*. Maybe her mom *didn't* dislike her the way Alexis had secretly feared. Maybe she simply wasn't good on the phone.

To be fair, Alexis thought a little squirmily, she hadn't exactly been Miss 411, either. She'd been mad about being left out of the Mexico trip, and she'd wanted to make her mom pay. Maybe if she hadn't limited her end of the phone calls to "uh-huh," "no," and "whatever," things would have been different.

Well, they would be different. When spring break was over, Alexis vowed, she'd make a better effort. Heck, she might even offer to give her mom a makeover. Britney's look was getting *so* last year. Her mom deserved a better role model.

Like Mandy Moore.

Alexis was smiling when Lance stopped beside her chair. He handed over the PowerBar. After she took it, he squeezed her shoulder manfully—then paused.

"Hey, you smell great. Is that new perfume?"

Yup, things were looking better and better, all the time, Alexis decided smugly. Before she knew it, she'd be driving *herself* to the mall. She was just *that* mature these days. Look out, world! Alexis Davis was on her way!

Still stunned, Jayne stared at Riley, waiting for his answer. Waiting for him to say this was a mistake, he'd cancelled his plans, he wanted to stay. But he didn't. A few minutes ago, she thought crazily, he'd looked sort of cute amid the coats and sweaters. Now he only looked like the man who'd betrayed her trust.

Again.

She was so stupid to have gotten herself in this mess.

"Antigua?" she asked. "But I thought—after what we— well, since we've . . . *Antigua?*"

"I'm not talking about this in here." Frowning, Riley pushed past the things in his way. He stepped out from the closet, trailing the sheet around his waist.

Jayne followed. "You're not talking about this, period! I can't believe you've ambushed me with this. I thought you'd changed your mind. I thought things were different now."

"They are different."

"How? Because it's taken you only six days to decide to leave instead of six months? I have to tell you, Riley, that's not—"

"That's not it." He gritted his teeth. "Look, I've planned this trip to Antigua for months now."

That was *it?* She was disrupting his *plans?* Hot with fury, Jayne stalked toward him. "Not good enough."

Looking trapped, Riley ran a hand over his bristly jaw. "It's a good opportunity."

"So am I, dammit."

His smoky gaze swerved to her face. In his eyes, Jayne glimpsed both stubbornness and . . . anguish? What the hell did he have to feel anguished about? She was the one who'd been misled here. She'd trusted him. Loved him. Believed she was important to him. And how had he repaid her? By treating her like a *fling*.

She'd thrown away her "gift." Risked ruining her research and disillusioning her breakup-ees. Jeopardized her book contract. For this. Would she never learn?

"Well?" she prodded. She desperately wanted to give Riley the benefit of the doubt. But how could he not be explaining himself? In his shoes, she'd have been talking her head off. "Well?"

"I'll see you when I get back," he said confidently.

"Ha!"

"Jayne—"

Too infuriated and hurt to speak, she tottered to the edge of the bed in search of her discarded clothes. She had to sweep her arm furiously under the frame—then get on her hands and knees—to retrieve those items that had the audacity to elude her.

"You'd better not be ogling my butt!" she yelled, her voice muffled by the bed ruffle.

"I always ogle your butt." He sounded hurt.

"Not anymore." Jayne hurled a hiking boot over her shoulder, not caring if she clobbered him in the head with it. With dignity she added, "It's not your butt to enjoy anymore."

She got to her feet with an armload of clothes and yesterday's shoes, feeling energized by the activity. Riley's hurriedly averted glance told her he *had* been ogling her. At the realization, all sorts of mixed emotions assaulted her. Anger that her erstwhile reunited lover dared to lay claim to her in that way. Pride that her butt was ogle worthy. Embarrassment at her juvenile proclamation.

She raised her chin. "You can go find some . . . some *Antiguan* butt to ogle!"

"I don't want Antiguan butt." His voice was gentle. Shaking his head, Riley came to her. He raised one hand to caress her upper arm, leaving the other clutching his sheet. "I don't. I don't want that."

"Too bad." Wrenching from his grasp, she crossed the room and pulled out her luggage. She stuffed her things inside the topmost piece. "Because you can't have *me*."

"Jayne—"

Finally! Finally he was going to explain himself. She paused, not looking at him. When a moment passed and Riley remained silent, she looked over her shoulder. "Yes?"

"I—" Looking frustrated, he gave her a beseeching look. She straightened and crossed her arms. "What, Riley?" His frustration only seemed to increase. "I'm out of prepared statements! Damn.'' He stomped to the four-poster and kicked it. Grimacing in pain, he hopped on one foot for an instant. ''Nope, this isn't a nightmare. Shit.''

He hoped she was a nightmare? Now Jayne was really hurt.

'' 'Prepared statements'?'' she repeated, going back to her packing. ''What am I? A political problem? A messy scandal? A pending personal-injury lawsuit?''

''No.''

She waited for more. Nothing came. ''That's it? 'No'?''

Riley stood nearby; she could feel him. ''I'm trying, Jayne,'' he said huskily. ''I just woke up, I'm not even dressed yet—''

''Gee, and already you've broken my heart. Nice work.''

Silence descended, heavy with hurt. This time, though, Riley did more than fumble over an explanation. He strode to her decisively, the floorboards thundering beneath his feet. He grabbed both her arms, spinning her away from her luggage, and stared down at her.

''I did *not* break your heart!''

''Oh? And who would know about that?''

''Not you, obviously.''

''*I'm* the expert!''

''Sure.'' Riley nodded. ''The heartbreak expert. How could I have forgotten your famous techniques?''

He released her angrily, and Jayne hurled down the T-shirt she'd been packing. ''They work! They helped me, and lots of other people.''

He shook his head. ''They taught you to stuff men in closets. I'd hate to see the kinds of losers you must have dated for your research.''

This was too much. She was too hurt to keep the truth inside anymore, too hurt to hide her feelings. ''It was *you,* all right? You!''

Riley looked puzzled. ''Me? Me what?''

''You were the 'loser' I dated for research,'' Jayne said.

Just for a moment she triumphed in the surprise in his eyes. "You were the one who broke my heart. The one who inspired my antiheartbreak book. The one—the only one—I could never quite get over. It was you, you, you—"

You, who I fell in love with again. She stopped herself just in time. Tears choked off her voice before she could reveal the most hurtful truth of all. *You, who I need.*

"It was you," she whispered.

Suddenly, Riley was there. He pulled her into his arms, but Jayne struggled. The last thing she wanted was his pity.

"Ow!" he yelled. "You kicked me in the shin!"

"Consider it a 'keep away' sign."

"I don't want to. Jayne—" He followed her to the end of the bed, where she'd stomped to stack her luggage. "Jayne, listen to me. I was starting to change my mind about Antigua. I'd almost decided to look for an assignment closer to home."

Almost? Almost decided? That was the best he could do? How, exactly, had "sweet talk" like that duped her? "I don't want your pity," she said stubbornly.

"It's not—oh, Jayne." Riley's lips pressed against her forehead, her hair, her cheek, as he tried to turn her sideways to face him. His hands were everywhere, encouraging her to let him hold her. "It's not pity. Look, I should have said this before, but . . . I had an idea."

"Wow, alert the media." She sniffled, wiped her eyes with the heel of her hand. She unloaded some clothes for today. She yanked open the zipper of her backpack and surveyed its contents through teary eyes. "Riley Davis has been thinking."

"I've been thinking about *you*, dammit!"

He spread his arms wide in an emphatic gesture. The motion called Jayne's attention to his sheet—the lack of it. He stood there completely nude, and completely unbothered by that fact. She guessed if she were a man with a wonderfully carved torso, broad shoulders, and powerful thighs, she might not care either, if—

No! Riley wasn't hers to ogle anymore either.

Suddenly, Jayne felt awfully naked. Glancing down at herself, she realized she'd never changed from her sheer pink nightie and slippers.

"Don't think about me," she told him as she reached for her clothes. "You're already on your way to Antigua, remember?"

Geez, she'd really believed he'd changed his mind. Feeling like the biggest idiot who'd ever fallen for a charming ex, Jayne kicked off her slippers, watching the marabou trim flutter as they sailed across the room. She stepped into a pair of trail pants. Some jumping up and down and a little wriggling later, she was tucking her nightie into her waistband. Its top and matching panties would have to stand in for underwear. She was in no mood to get naked in front of the man who'd just let it be known she wasn't good enough to stick around for.

"Listen to me," Riley said. "About my traveling—"

"Save it." She pulled on a fleece top and socks, then reached for her ATSes. "It's none of my business. Obviously."

"But it *is* your business. I've been thinking, we could make our future permanently temporary. Like an arrangement. You know, whenever I'm in town, we could get together. Come on, Jayne. It will be fun."

Jayne glanced up from her shoes. Riley actually looked hopeful. "Have you lost your mind?"

"I've lost my heart."

"*Stop it.*" Some things hurt too much to hear.

"We're perfect together. You liked the hiking!"

As if *that* explained anything. "I was *forced* to hike."

Again that hurt expression from him. She didn't get it.

"You're better at 'temporary' now," Riley insisted doggedly. "I know it could work."

Blinking back tears, she finished tying her shoes. She looked up. "I don't want temporary, Riley. I want permanent."

His jaw literally dropped. He frowned.

"I want stability. Companionship. Lifelong passion."

He shoved a hand through his hair, seeming confused.

"I can see you don't want the same things," Jayne went on. "I guess I should have already known it, but—"

"Damn right you should have known it! You *did* know it! I never pretended to be anything but what I am."

"No, but I let myself pretend." Feeling indescribably sad, Jayne stood. "I'm sorry. I just can't date like a man."

Huh? asked his expression. Riley rallied. "Good thing. I want a woman. I want you."

She shouldn't ask it. She shouldn't. But somehow Jayne just couldn't resist. "Enough to skip Antigua?"

He hesitated, and that was it.

"I can't stay here," she said, hefting her pack.

"You are *not* leaving." His fierce expression dared her to disagree.

She did. She also tried to explain. "Remember when we played hooky from fishing and we agreed to try again?"

He nodded reluctantly.

"I told you something then," Jayne said, working to strap on her backpack. "I told you that this time *I* wanted to be the one to say good-bye."

Riley glared at her. He gave a grudging nod. "I remember. But I'll be damned if I'll let you—"

"For the first time in my life," she whispered, "I think I need to be alone." She couldn't believe it, but it was true. Drawing in a deep, fortifying breath, Jayne rose on tiptoed ATSes. She pressed a salty kiss to his lips. "This is it. Good-bye, Riley."

Then, while she still had the strength to do it, Jayne turned away from Riley for the last time, and left him behind.

Twenty-Two

Riley stared at the open doorway, hardly able to believe what had just happened. Jayne had actually gone. The door creaked as it swung a few inches inward, stirred by her passage. For the first time in his life, *he* was the one who'd been left behind.

It was horrible.

Listening to her footsteps echo down the hallway, he had the uncomfortable sensation of hearing his future change irrevocably. At that moment Riley realized exactly how much he'd been hoping things would work out between him and Jayne. He realized exactly how much he loved her.

It was you. You were the one who broke my heart. The one who inspired my antiheartbreak book. The one—the only one—I could never quite get over.

Still stunned by her revelation, Riley put a hand to his head and frowned. He was a good-bye guy. A guy who sent women to heartbreak camp. *He* was Bozo Boy.

The knowledge put every one of Jayne's kooky antiheartbreak techniques in a whole new light. It made him see her and all her guidance groupies in an entirely different way.

Without meaning to, he'd inspired a whole damned best-selling *movement*. It was a hell of a lot to make up for.

It was too much to make up for. He'd never promised Jayne anything more than he'd given her, Riley told himself angrily. He'd never offered tomorrow, because he'd always known it wasn't his to give. It never had been.

But this ... this was like every outsider moment he'd ever had, magnified a gazillion times and served up in Technicolor. With surround sound. Left behind by someone he cared about, Riley suddenly knew that loneliness cut both ways. Geography was irrelevant when it came to feeling empty.

He'd always imagined the people he'd left behind carrying on with their lives, instantly obliterating the gap left by his leaving. Now he wondered. Was it possible they'd hurt? Just like this?

God, he hoped not. This was the worst feeling in the world. It poured through him like cold on an Arctic peak, silent and irrevocable. He might never feel warm again.

He didn't know what to do. He'd always escaped before this point, had always been on the move before his feelings caught up with him. Now Riley had the damnable sense there wasn't a journey long enough to drive back everything inside him.

The blare of an auto horn split the quiet peacefulness outside the lodge. Another blast followed, jolting Riley from his thoughts. *His Suburban.* The Hideaway Lodge employee who'd agreed to meet him here with it must have arrived.

Automatically, he moved to the corner where he'd tossed his pack. He dressed, putting on his trail pants, a long-sleeved T-shirt, socks, and boots. He shoved his hands through his hair and rubbed his gritty eyes, noticing the achiness behind them and then determinedly ignoring it. Numbness edged into the Arctic chill inside him and found a perfect fit.

All he knew how to do was keep moving. Riley didn't know if the journeying that had always saved him would be enough this time . . . but it was all he had. Bleakly, he shouldered his pack. He took one last look at the room—the room where he'd loved Jayne.

The room where he'd lost her.

Then, drawing in a deep breath, Riley headed outside, back to the life he'd known and no longer missed. Back to the life he'd so blithely summed up only a few hours before. *To see, to do, to conquer, to enjoy.*

To grieve.

Damn. With a mighty effort he swallowed the lump that rose to his throat. He closed the door on the togetherness he'd found with Jayne, brushed the wood with his fingertips one final time. Riley tapped a decisive beat on the hard painted pine, then stepped away. Leaving wasn't much, but there was still a chance it could save him. Without Jayne he knew for sure that nothing else would.

Tromping around the forested area beyond the canyon lodge, Jayne lost track of how many steps she took. She lost track of how many logs she scrambled over, how many leafy oaks she passed beneath, how many trails crisscrossed her path. All she could think about was her need to get away.

Right now the great outdoors seemed as good a place as any to fulfill that need.

She'd stopped by the lodge dining room before leaving to ask a surprised Mack to take charge of her breakup-ees until she got back. They'd need someone to lean on until it came time to return to the Hideaway Lodge, Jayne had told him—someone responsible.

She hadn't told him exactly how poorly she herself fit the bill . . . but more than likely her red-rimmed eyes and bed-head hair had spoken for themselves. Jayne was a woman out of her element. She wasn't sure how she would ever find herself again.

Sick with regret, weak with loss, she just kept going. She

ascended a hill dotted with green ferns and forest grass, crab-walked sideways with ATS-ensured steadiness down into a gully shaded by pines. Strange as it was, the rugged terrain felt almost comforting to her now—quiet but for the whoosh of the wind, still but for the occasional rustle of a bird, warm but for the icy disappointment inside her. Within it, Jayne walked and walked. Eventually, she came to a place that fit the criteria she'd so recently been trained to look for (sheltered on one side, relatively flat, bare of animal tracks, and a short distance from a stream), and dropped her pack.

She needed to think. To plan. To recover. Broken hearts took time to heal, and hers felt more shattered than most. She didn't think she could face her breakup-ees until she'd come to terms with that, at least a little bit.

Riley's eagerness to be on his way without her had hurt Jayne deeply. His unchanged plans to leave for Antigua had been a slap in the face to her hopefulness, her vulnerability, her love. Once again she'd obviously been judged and found wanting . . . only this time the stakes were much more serious than a family fishing trip or a touch football game.

Unlike her family's occasional rejections, Riley's felt deliberate and precise. She couldn't make the same excuses for him that she made for her father and brothers. Riley did know better.

At least, she'd thought he did.

I didn't know I'd hurt you, he'd said on the day they'd snuck away from fishing duty together. *I'm sorry.*

But not sorry enough to avoid repeating the process, Jayne thought as she went about the business of setting up a small camp for herself. Not sorry enough to stay.

Many minutes later she'd finished the necessary preparations. Guided by the coaching Riley had given her, she'd laid out her standard-issue Hideaway Lodge sleeping bag and inflatable mattress, prepped her camp stove, erected her tent, and laid out a one-person stone-encircled campfire in case it got cold.

She didn't know how long she'd need to stay here. Until the impulse to call Francesca to confess her status as a fraud passed, maybe. Or maybe until her impulse to beg Riley to stay went away.

Nah. There was no *way* she had provisions to last that long.

Sinking to a seated position atop her sleeping bag, Jayne surveyed her little campsite with a mixture of surprise and pride. She was struck, all at once, by how easily she'd accomplished it. A person would think she'd spent her formative years whittling tent stakes rather than perfecting her mascara technique and constructing the ultimate girly-girl philosophy. She guessed some of this nature stuff had sunk in. She felt almost . . . competent at it now.

But feelings didn't change what she knew to be true, Jayne reminded herself sternly. Feelings didn't change a person. After she left here, she'd be the same old Jayne—helpless to fit in, always on the outside, *un*special.

Dispirited, she grabbed her backpack and dragged it toward her. Unzipping it, she reached inside to retrieve the extra copy of *Heartbreak 101: Getting Over the Good-Bye Guys* she always kept with her. Usually, seeing the tangible proof of what she'd accomplished cheered her. If anyone needed cheering right now, it was her.

Her fingers fumbled, encountering nothing that felt like the familiar spine of her hardcover book. Opening the pack wider, Jayne peered into it and realized what was wrong.

This wasn't her pack.

Oh, no. What had she done? Driven by the need to find out exactly what she'd brought with her into the wild—exactly what she'd be forced to rely on (to wear!) until she returned—Jayne explored further. She unearthed a series of things she recognized from her adventure travel orientation sessions. One by one, she lay them on the sleeping bag beside her.

An ordinary flashlight. Matches. Topos. A water treatment

kit. Professional digital camera. First aid kit. Two Snickers bars—

Camera?

Hurriedly, Jayne dug deeper. She found a familiar-looking fleece. A shaving kit. A pack of premoistened towelettes like the ones Riley had given her to—

Riley. This was Riley's pack. In her haste to get away before she blubbered and begged him to reconsider, she'd grabbed the wrong pack from the bedroom floor.

Jayne smacked her forehead and stared at the supplies spread before her. She'd been too teary-eyed earlier to differentiate between their identical-on-the-outside packs, she figured. But now she saw clearly. And at the sight of the fleece Riley had lent her that night on the balcony while wishing on a star . . . yearning pushed through her.

She missed him already, the commitment-phobic, wanderlust-crazed jerk.

Well, that was just how pathetic she was, Jayne told herself. Clearly, she needed to get stronger. She needed to do something to empower herself, something that would prove she could handle whatever life threw at her—in spite of the fiasco with Riley. Otherwise there was no telling how she'd get through this.

She needed a crash course. The overnight equivalent of the Buttmaster 2000, designed not to eliminate cellulite but to eliminate weakness. If she could just tackle something really scary, that would do it. Something like . . . never plucking her eyebrows again. Cutting up her Macy's card. Staying at her campsite all night, alone.

Alone. That was it! The very thought gave Jayne shivers. Until just this moment she'd been too caught up in her pain to realize exactly how alone she already was.

How alone she already was. Yikes! What had she done?

She bolted upright, eyes peeled for rogue raccoons or marauding javelinas. The wind blew her hair in her eyes, seeming to murmur sinisterly. Clouds covered the sun with evil portent, and—okay, so maybe it already *had* been a little cloudy. But that didn't matter. What mattered was, Jayne had gotten herself in a fix again. The question was, could she handle it?

Heck, no! Dark, scary, do-it-yourself stuff coexisted with Jayne Murphy about as well as stripes coordinated with plaids. Who was she kidding? She had to be reasonable.

But still . . . this just might be her only way to salvage her future. Her career. Her pride. Those were all she had left now, Jayne reminded herself. Without Riley, she was on her own. So she'd better make it good.

Newly determined, Jayne brushed off the leaves that had drifted onto her sleeping bag and daintily sat on it. She grabbed Riley's pack to refill it with his things—and that was when it happened.

She discovered the most surprising thing of all.

Inside the canyon lodge's common room, Alexis glanced toward the wide windows overlooking the forest. There, seven of the eight adventure travelers still remaining at the secondary lodge stared out at the sight that had held them transfixed for the past two hours.

Jayne. Wilderness adventure Jayne, to be exact.

"What's she doing now?" Alexis asked, pushing a checkers piece across the board toward Lance. He countered her move.

"She appears to be constructing something," Mack answered, squinting. "I think it's a primitive hanger for her clothes."

"It is!" Beside him at the window, Bruce scoffed. "Next she'll be weaving a purse out of aspen bark."

Mitzi perked up. "Would that work? Neat!"

"I don't know, Mitzi," Kelly said. "I wouldn't recommend it. A bark purse would be a definite *Glamour* don't."

"I once made a purse out of a Quaker Oats carton covered with wallpaper," Doris offered. "It looked very mod."

"Like something Twiggy or The Shrimp would have carried," Donna agreed. "I remember that." The two women smiled at each other.

"I'm, like, never going to carry a purse again," Carla volunteered. "I just decided it last night. A purse is nothing but excess baggage. It, like, lets you hold on to things you don't need anymore. Like my . . . I mean, like Paolo."

All the women, including Alexis, stared at her.

" 'Paolo?' Not 'my Paolo'? Just 'Paolo'? Does that mean you've given up on that loser?" Doris asked.

Decisively, Carla nodded. "I, like, deserve better. Being here with all of you has made me realize that."

"Awww." The women clustered together for a group hug. Alexis told Lance to king her, then joined in.

"Now she's dragging over a huge fallen branch," Bruce said, breaking in with the latest wilderness adventure Jayne update. "What the . . . ? She's already got a camp-fire, so—"

"A weapon," Mitzi said knowledgeably. "She just wants to protect herself in case another javelina comes along."

"Or something *worse,*" Kelly added. All the women nodded.

Lance frowned. "Doesn't she know she's within a quarter mile of the lodge? Within sight?"

"I'm sure she thinks she walked farther than she did," Donna said. "She looked pretty upset when she started. I doubt Jayne knows exactly how far she went."

"Right," Doris agreed. "She was going in circles around the perimeter of the lodge for a while there. And those trees probably block her view of us. We can only see Jayne so clearly because she's up on that hill."

"Somebody should go after her," Lance announced.

They all looked at each other. A moment ticked past.

"Mitzi and I will," Bruce announced, tugging a blushing

Mitzi nearer by the hand. "We'll reconnoiter Jayne out of the—"

"You'll reconnoiter *yourselves* into the nearest secluded spot for a little nature nooky," Donna said, shaking her head.

"Something wrong with that?" Bruce asked.

Everyone rolled their eyes.

"Well, I can't go," Lance said. "Jayne left me in charge. With Riley gone, I'm it."

"I'll go," Alexis announced. Sheesh, older people took *forever* to decide stuff. She made a quick hoppity move that ended her checkers game with Lance, then pushed back from the table. "I'll make sure Jayne's all right."

"You'd better hurry. It's almost lunchtime," Bruce said, looking out the window again. "And I think—" He glanced down at Mitzi with a worried expression. "I think she just started crying."

As far as Riley was concerned, airports were part of an alternate reality.

Inside an airport, time crawled or raced, depending on if you were early for your flight or fifteen minutes late. Logic vanished, replaced by a kill-or-be-killed mentality that insisted it was okay to trample the other travelers if they dawdled at the wrong speed. All roads led to uncomfortable chairs, and second-grade knowledge of sequential numbers went by the wayside when staring at a too-high boarding pass number. Human kindnesses and courtesy mostly disappeared, brought low by layover tussles in the Wiener King hot dog line.

Not that any of those factors affected Riley in particular. No, his usual M.O. was to arrive early, sleep as much as possible to pass the time, and carry on everything. In keeping with that philosophy, he arrived at the small Sedona airport still numb from his confrontation with Jayne, completed the check-in procedure, and promptly napped.

He placed his backpack on the seat beside him, then turned sideways so his knees rested on its bulk. He wadded up the fleece he'd grabbed and tucked it beneath his cheek. With his body spanning two chairs in the nearly-empty waiting area, he leaned his head to the right and took a shuddering breath.

The next thing Riley knew, someone was shaking him.

He awakened to find a gray-haired sixtyish man peering into his face. Blinking at the man's lined face and turquoise-studded string tie, Riley shook his head to clear it.

"I said, are you all right?" the man asked.

He had the impression the man had been trying to wake him for some time. Was his flight leaving? Riley had set his watch alarm to awaken him in time, but there was always a chance it was broken. He jerked his wrist upward. The time indicated more than forty-five minutes remained until boarding.

"You were crying in your sleep," the man explained in a low voice. "Not blubbering, mind you," he added at the doubtlessly alarmed look Riley shot him, "just sad, silent tears. Nightmare?"

Slowly, Riley raised his hand to his cheek. His fingertips came back wet.

Jesus. His freaking emotions had ambushed him while he'd slept. Exactly when he'd been at his most defenseless, they'd snuck in and *bam!* Helpless bawling. What was happening to him? He couldn't remember the details of what he'd been dreaming, but he felt sure it had been about Jayne.

He missed her. Already.

"It's okay, you know," the man said, sitting down in the chair across from Riley. He gave him a wise look. "Catches up to us sooner or later. Nightmares are just our brain's way of giving us a big smack upside the head, telling us to pay attention. You don't have to be embarrassed."

"I'm not embarrassed," Riley lied. He swiveled, ducking his head to wipe away the tears as he did. He dried his hands on his pants. "But thanks for waking me."

The man nodded. "You don't look like a fella who takes easy to being caught off guard. I figured you'd want to know."

He didn't want to know. He wanted to *never* know. When it came to being helpless against his feelings, Riley wanted nothing to do with it. But it looked as though the rest of him had other ideas. Scary, touchy-feely, *emotional* ideas.

As a result, he was afraid to try napping again.

Instead, after sniffing away the last of his tears, he cleared his throat as manfully as he could. He deepened his voice. Extended his hand. "Riley Davis. Buy you a cup of coffee?"

Ten minutes later, he and K.C. Logan were on the road to becoming friends, unlikely as it was. They slurped scalding coffee in the waiting area, chatting about the weather and the Diamondbacks and photography. Somehow, talking with K.C. felt natural to Riley—and so did bringing some other travelers into their conversation when they sat down nearby. Hell, if he'd known passing the time with gabbing worked this well, he'd have quit napping years before this.

Maybe, Riley thought uncomfortably, *there was something to Jayne's theories about being with people.* Maybe Alexis had been right and he *was* a loner. The thought depressed him. Was it too late for him?

If it was, Riley told himself, then he didn't want to know. Determined to forget his past—and Jayne—as easily as she'd tossed him into a damned closet and hidden him, he went on talking. Faster than he'd have thought possible, more than an hour swept past, punctuated by two flight-delay announcements.

"I wish this damned thing would get going. I'm only headed as far as Dallas," K.C. said, naming the city that would be Riley's second stopover once the Sedona-to-

Phoenix flight got under way. "Got grandkids I'm visiting there."

"Oooh, grandbabies!" Everyone in their small group brightened and talked faster. Wallets were produced, snapshots were unfolded in arrays of clear plastic, and one grandmotherly type even passed around her camcorder with footage of "the little darlings."

Instantly, Riley felt shut out. Cast aside. Forgotten. It occurred to him that this kind of shutting out was—literally—what Jayne had done to him this morning. Being left behind was what he'd always dreaded most. No wonder he'd instantly gone on the offensive. No wonder he'd pretended he'd never changed his mind about going to Antigua.

No wonder he was alone now.

Miserably, he looked at the faces of the people grouped around him. Older and younger, they all glowed with happiness while sharing images of the people they loved.

He had people, Riley told himself defiantly. He had photographs too. Personal ones. Although it went against his every instinct, he grabbed his backpack and made ready to share some of his photos with K.C. and the gang.

He reached inside. "Look, everybody! Here's my—"

"Self-help book?" K.C. interrupted.

Their stunned expressions gathered on the hardbound book in his hand. Not the thing he'd expected at all, it was instead a . . . copy of *Heartbreak 101: Getting Over the Good-Bye Guys*?

Riley frowned. Jayne must have slipped the book into his backpack at some point during their trip. Probably, she'd been hoping he'd absorb some of her techniques through osmosis and become a "sensitive guy." He almost would have tried it if it would have kept her from pushing him away this morning. He almost would have done it, if . . . awww, the hell with it. It was too late anyway. He crammed the book back into his pack.

"Don't be embarrassed," the grandmotherly type cooed, trying to stop him.

"He's prone to that," K.C. confided, "but he'll tell you he's not." He offered a sympathetic look.

"It's okay. I loved that book!" said another of the group. She tugged his arm until Riley relented, then took the book from him. Exclaiming over how the techniques inside had helped her divorced daughter overcome heartbreak, she showed it to her husband. "It's a runaway best seller, you know. I'm hoping the author goes on *Oprah* someday."

Riley rubbed his palms on his thighs. "It's not my book— it's a . . . friend's. I don't read that kind of stuff. Real men don't need to. Right, K.C.?"

The older man looked doubtful. "If it would make my Ada happy, I'd read the dictionary. Twice. Standing on my head."

They all nodded. "Me, too's" were heard. Riley couldn't believe it. Shoving their protests from his mind, he decided to stick with his original plan. He reached into his backpack. His fingers groped for the familiar item he sought. Instead, he touched something smooth and cool and round, and withdrew it.

A leopard-print compact.

Jayne's leopard-print compact.

He had the wrong backpack, he realized, scanning the contents for the first time since leaving. How had he taken the wrong pack? Sure, they were identical on the outside. Sure, Riley hadn't exactly been thinking clearly when he'd left the lodge this morning. Sure . . . sure, he could believe it.

While the others talked and passed around Jayne's book, he sat in his chair and examined the compact in his hand. He ran his fingers over its glossy surface, remembering Jayne's "primp!" battle cry. He rubbed his thumb over the catch, thinking of Jayne perched on a rock, bombshell style, fixing her makeup. He opened the catch and peeked inside.

Geez, he looked like hell. His face was pale, his eyes red-rimmed, his features miserable. Was this what love did to him?

No, he answered himself instantly. *This was what the lack of love did to him.* He'd really believed Jayne was the one.

Angrily, he snapped the compact closed and put it away. At the same moment, the grandmotherly traveler turned to him.

"It's going to be a while till our flight gets here," she said. "We're all going to get a bite to eat at Taco Tillie's. Would you like to join us?"

The others had risen. They waited expectantly. K.C. met Riley's gaze and nodded in encouragement.

"No, thanks," Riley said. "I'm . . . not hungry. You all go ahead. Enjoy yourselves."

"Sure?" asked the man Riley recognized as the divorced daughter's dad. "They've got an enchilada plate that's only four ninety-nine."

"You've got to keep up your strength, you know," said another woman. She patted his arm, apparently not noticing Riley's biceps was twice as big as her hand. "You don't want to get too thin now."

"I'll get something later, I promise," he said. "First I have to take this book back to my Suburban"—Riley indicated the copy of *Heartbreak 101* that had just been handed back to him—"and rustle up some traveling supplies. It turns out I've got the wrong pack."

He'd already shipped some equipment to the Antigua site—cameras, tripods, lenses, basic essentials—and with the additional clothes to be found in his Suburban, he could manage. Anything else he could buy on location. After a walk to the long-term-parking area, he'd call Mack and ask him to send someone from the Hideaway Lodge to pick up Jayne's pack and deliver it to her.

"I'll bring you back a doggie bag," K.C. said with a wink.

"Okay. Thanks." Riley watched as, after more assurances from him that he wouldn't starve to death, the group headed for the airport restaurant. Then he gathered up his—okay, *Jayne's*—pack with every intention of taking a walk himself.

He made it only as far as the next row. There Riley sank into a chair and pulled out the book again. Drawn by some mysterious but powerful impulse, he gazed at the author photo on the back. He touched the name embossed in pink script on the front and ruffled through the pages. A sentence caught his eye, and Riley began reading.

It was exactly like talking to Jayne, he discovered—minus the flirty looks, the warm touches, the smiles. Still, it was closer than he was likely to ever come again, and Riley had time to burn.

Assuring himself that reading this self-help book did not make him an official "sensitive guy," he turned to the first page and read the introduction. Two paragraphs in, he realized he was getting sucked into Jayne's prose. Riley glanced up worriedly to make sure no one was staring at him strangely. Apparently, he hadn't grown a sweater with leather elbow patches, a couples-therapist-style beard, or an intense urge to redecorate. Relieved, Riley dove back into page two.

It was a very long time before he glanced up again.

Twenty-Three

Perched atop her sleeping bag, Jayne let her campfire die down. All her attention was for the thing she'd found in Riley's backpack—the thing in her lap right now.

She'd been stunned to find it. Especially in Riley's pack, since he was the epitome of an essentials-only guy. According to his own philosophy, he should have been carrying only those things required for basic survival. From the looks of it, though, he'd considered *this* item essential for a very long time.

It was a photo album. Protected by a zippered waterproof outer covering and about an inch thick, it was small enough that Jayne could hold it easily. Inside, it was bound in leather. At first she'd thought it was some kind of professional portfolio, meant to display his photography work.

Her initial tentative glance at the pictures inside had made her realize the truth. This was a personal collection, one not meant for any eyes except Riley's.

The first photo was a slightly yellowed one. In it a long-haired man and woman stood side by side, dressed in late-seventies clothes—Earth shoes, flared jeans, and ponchos. A small heap of mismatched luggage rested at their feet, plastered in travel stickers depicting exotic locales. Jayne had never met Riley's parents, but this had to be them ... just as the dark-haired boy at the edge of the frame had to be Riley himself.

She leaned closer to peer at his image. He'd had longer hair then, its side-parted over-the-ears style badly in need of a trim. His little face looked serious as he confronted the camera. In one fist, little Riley clutched his own luggage, covered in decals identical to those of his parents'—right down to their placement on his bag.

If not for the matching luggage, Jayne mused, it would have been hard to tell Riley and his parents belonged together. They stood so far apart, *seemed* so far apart. The same was true in the subsequent picture, a snapshot taken on what looked like a fishing boat. Again Riley stood separate while his parents put their arms around each other and smiled for the camera.

Studying the pictures that followed, Jayne developed a new understanding of what Riley's childhood must have been like. His parents, while friendly-looking and undoubtedly engaged in worthwhile environmental and cultural pursuits, seemed to have refused to let a child change their life. It looked as though they'd simply picked up baby Riley after he'd been born and carried on with what they'd been doing, leaving Riley to keep up ... or be left behind.

At the thought, Jayne's heart ached for him. She knew only too well what it was like to feel on the outside in your own family. What it was like to feel like an imposition, a hanger-on in someone else's plans. In all the time she'd known him, Riley had never confided in her much about his childhood, but suddenly, so many things made sense.

His traveling. His unease with groups of people. His need to stay on the move. More than likely, globe-trotting felt like home to him ... just like getting lost in her social whirl felt like home to Jayne. She and Riley were alike underneath, she realized. Both struggling to avoid their loneliness. Both veering, in the process, too far in the wrong direction.

Wiping away a few sad tears, Jayne cleared her throat and looked through the photos again. Within them she saw a collage of all that was most important to Riley—snapshots of Alexis, black-and-white prints of Gwen and Bud, images of a dark-haired man who must be Alexis's father—Riley's younger brother. There were photos of Mack and Bruce together with Riley on a mountain peak. Photos of Riley with other guides, on other adventures. And on the last page . . .

A photo of her.

Jayne blinked. She stared at the picture, finally recognizing it as a shot of her getting dressed for one of the nights out they'd shared. She'd paused amid putting on lipstick— the tube was still in one hand—and her hair was wild from her mousse-and-blow-dryer routine. Her eyes sparkled. She remembered Riley having caught her off guard for that photo—she'd been puckering up to blow him a kiss when he'd snapped it. When she'd complained about not being photo ready, he'd shrugged and claimed there wasn't any film in the camera anyway.

Liar, Jayne thought now, impossibly moved by the fact that he'd carried an image of her all this time. There were no other women (save Gwen and Alexis) in the album. No other women except her. Did that mean what she hoped it meant? That there were no other women in Riley's *life* either?

Swallowing hard to bring her tumultuous emotions under control, Jayne stared up at the tree branches overhead. This had been such a difficult day. If this revelation had come earlier, if Riley had explained a little further . . . maybe things would have been different between them. As it was, all she could do now was put away the photo album, gather up Riley's pack, and return everything to Gwen and Bud when she got back to the Hideaway Lodge.

Except Jayne didn't want to. Her gaze lingered on the pictures as she flipped through them again. Her imagination took flight as she peered at the images one more time. Truth be told, she had her own secret mementos of Riley. Movie-ticket stubs. Flower-delivery cards. Matchbooks from clubs. And (most prized of all) a cast-off T-shirt he'd lent her to sleep in, which Jayne had never returned because it reminded her of him. *She* had never fully let go either. Not even when she'd decided to write her book, using herself as the ultimate example of how to overcome a broken heart.

A part of her had always felt she and Riley were meant to be together. That same part of her had been defeated twice now by Riley's leaving.

A sudden sound in the nearby bushes interrupted her thoughts and put Jayne on full alert. Before she could so much as grab her self-defense stick and guard her territory, though, the intruder tramped into her campsite.

Alexis.

"Hey, Jayne," she said cheerily, waving as she took in the embers-only campfire, the tent, the fluffed-up sleeping bag . . . the photo album in Jayne's hands. "How about some company?"

Jayne boggled. "How did you know I was here?"

The girl hesitated. "I followed your trail." She hunkered down, perfectly at ease in the outdoors, and shucked her backpack. She withdrew a pair of sandwiches from inside it and offered one to Jayne. "PBJ?"

"No, thanks. I'm not hungry." *I'm on the heartbreak diet. Nothing but salty tears, tart regrets, and sweet-and-sour memories.* "You go ahead."

"You need to eat, you know. To keep up your strength. That's what my mom always says. 'Don't let the bastards get you down,' she says."

"I have strength." She was here, wasn't she? Braving the great outdoors all alone? "And don't say 'bastards.' "

Alexis shook her head, smiling. "You sound just like Uncle Riley."

"*You* sound like you're feeling better about your mom." It hadn't escaped Jayne's notice over the past few days that the girl had certain . . . issues . . . with her mother. The fact that she'd repeated her mother's advice—and fondly too— was an encouraging sign. "How'd that happen?"

With a shrug, Alexis finished chewing a bite of her sandwich. "I just realized some stuff. Partly, it was getting to know Lance that helped. And partly, it was your workshops that did it. All that primping made me feel like I was worth spending time on, you know?"

Jayne blinked. She did know. Invariably, she felt better about things if she took the time to fix her hair and put on some mascara. It was unexpectedly heartening to realize she'd helped Alexis understand that too. Sometimes the little things mattered more than they seemed to. That was why Jayne never felt her interests were shallow, even when other people did.

"Well, if you look good, you feel good," Jayne said, and cracked a smile for the first time in hours.

"Totally." Picking up the other half of her sandwich, Alexis nodded toward the album in Jayne's hands. "So, whatcha doing with that?"

"I accidentally picked up the wrong pack. This is Riley's, and I—" Jayne stopped, suddenly realizing the significance of Alexis's casual question. "You *knew* about this? This album?"

"Sure. Uncle Riley's just a big mushball at heart. I've been begging him to take out that *stupid* sixth-grade picture of me for, like, *forever,* though, and he won't do it."

Jayne's mouth dropped open. Stymied by Alexis's easy acceptance of her uncle's softer side, she frowned. Now that Alexis had revealed that Riley's album wasn't a deep, dark secret, there was something about it that bugged her. Something she couldn't put her finger on.

"Do you know what this *means?*" Jayne asked.

"That Uncle Riley thinks I look cute with pigtails?"

"No! Although of course you do."

Alexis grimaced. "What, then?"

"I don't know." Jayne looked at the album again, bothered by a realization that was just on the tip of her mind. Then she had it. "It means Riley can make a commitment! He's committed to keeping *all* these people in his life."

She waved the album, feeling hope soar within her. "You, your grandparents, his friends. *Riley can commit!* That's why he comes here to help Gwen and Bud. That's why he lets you come on trips with him. That's why he hired Bruce and Mack. That's why he's done *all* of it!"

Wrinkling her nose, Alexis put down her PBJ. "So?"

"So? So this is great!" Every fear she'd ever had that Riley was a lost cause, incapable of commitment and unable to be depended upon, became tangible to Jayne in that moment. In the next, they all whooshed away. Now that she had proof in hand of Riley's true nature, she could rest easy. "This means—this means—oh, God. This means Riley *can* commit . . . but not to *me.*"

As quickly as it had come, her elation vanished. Jayne drooped. The only thing worse than a commitment-phobic man, she realized, was a man whose commitment phobia was activated only by *you.*

"What do you mean?" Alexis asked. "You're in that album too. Remember? Look!"

"But *I'm* not in his life. Riley left me this morning. Left me! He'd had it planned for weeks, and even though I thought he'd changed his mind, he hadn't. He went to Antigua without me. Twice he's left me now. *Twice.*"

"He leaves us too."

"Oh, Alexis. That's not the same. Not really," Jayne said gently. "Besides, he comes back to you, right? That matters."

Alexis nodded. She stared out into the green landscape

beyond them, thinking. Then she gave Jayne a sharp look. "Why didn't you go with him?" she asked.

The simplicity of the question gave Jayne pause. Why *hadn't* she ever tried to go with him? "Be—because Riley never asked me to go, that's why."

"Did you ever ask him to take you?"

"Uhh—"

"Or ask him to stay?"

"I shouldn't have to!" Jayne exclaimed, raising her arms. "He should want to all on his own."

"And my mom should want to spend more than ten minutes with me on the phone," Alexis pointed out. "But she doesn't."

"Oh, Alexis—"

"Nope, don't feel sorry for me," Alexis said, palms out to forestall the hug Jayne moved to give her. "I've worked it all out. I'm okay."

Skeptically, Jayne examined her. But she did seem okay. Imagine that.

"Anyway, back to you and Uncle Riley." Alexis straightened her Hello Kitty T-shirt with glittery-painted nails and appeared to give the problem some thought. "Maybe it isn't about you," she finally said with all the wisdom of a person who'd been down this road before—however impossible *that* was. "Maybe it's about *him*. Maybe if you'd asked Uncle Riley, he'd have stayed with you. Forever even."

Stayed. Hardly daring to hope, Jayne thought about it. What would Riley have said if she'd asked him to stay with her?

"No, he'd never be happy," she said. "He doesn't like cities, doesn't like being around lots of people—"

"He spent the past week with lots of people!"

"—doesn't like to shop—"

"He would with you!"

At Alexis's insistence, something Riley had said resurfaced in her mind. *It was months before I could pass a shoe store and not automatically slow down . . . so you could have a look.* Maybe he wouldn't mind too much after all.

Leery of hoping, Jayne tried another tactic. "Then there's *me*. I don't like to be alone, don't like the wilderness—"

"You just spent a whole week in the wilderness," Alexis cried. She flung her arms outward, indicating the campsite surrounding them. "You've become travel adventure Jayne!"

"I still don't like to fish—"

"So eat at restaurants! Sheesh. Jayne, you and Uncle Riley are perfect for each other. You belong together."

That was exactly the belief Jayne held closest. But after all that had happened . . . "No, it's better this way," she said stubbornly, wanting to convince herself even more than Alexis. "If my breakup-ees had found out about me and Riley—if my *publisher* had found out, if the press had found out—I'd have been a laughingstock. A get-over-him guru who can't get over him? How ridiculous is that?"

"No more ridiculous than ignoring true love when it's right beneath your nose."

"Alexis . . ." Jayne breathed out, frustrated by the girl's staunch insistence. "You don't understand. Riley and I are just too different. *Way* too different. And—"

"Opposites attract," Alexis chimed.

"—and I'm too afraid."

Alexis's eyes widened. So did Jayne's.

What had she just said?

It was true, though, she realized in that moment. She *was* afraid. Afraid of failing, afraid of not being good enough, afraid of being laughed at. Even though she was decades away from her father's "careless dad of a daughter" routine and her brothers' constant teasing, their opinions of her had colored her world. Maybe they always would.

"How can *you* be afraid?" Alexis asked, looking genuinely confused. "You must be the bravest person I know."

Jayne scoffed.

"You are! Did you know that Bruce wanted to make a

bet with Lance and Mack about how long it would take before you ordered a helicopter airlift back to civilization? That Gramps made Riley promise to keep the pace slow so you wouldn't get discouraged? Jayne, we all knew this adventure travel trip was *so* not your thing. But you did it anyway. You made it. That's brave.''

"A bet. Ha!" Jayne grumbled, offended. "Remind me to put Tabasco sauce in Bruce's beer when we get back."

"Don't worry. Uncle Riley wouldn't let them do it. I shouldn't have said anything." But Alexis grinned, probably at the notion of Jayne getting revenge via hot sauce.

"I wouldn't really do that," Jayne confided.

"I know. But I might tell Bruce I told you about it just to watch him squirm while waiting for your revenge."

"That's evil!" They both laughed, feeling even closer than before. Jayne was so glad she'd met Alexis. Beneath all the glitter and attitude, she was a sweet girl.

"So . . ." Jayne shored up her courage and glanced sideways at her newest—and youngest—confidante. "Do you really think I'm brave?"

"The bravest."

"Because I'm thinking about doing something that will require a lot of bravery."

Alexis gasped. "Stay here all night? *Alone?*"

At that, Jayne smiled. "No. I was going to because I thought I had something to prove to myself. But now, thanks to you, I know I don't. At least not that way."

Giving her a canny look, Alexis brushed off her PBJ fingers. "Does this have anything to do with Uncle Riley?"

"If it's not too late, it does," Jayne said, jumping to her feet. It would mean risking her future . . . but all of a sudden she knew she had to try. "Come on, help me pack up."

The airport grew more crowded as the day wore on. A hum rose from the conversations of dozens of travelers, and the fragrances of hot coffee and . . . enchiladas? . . . wafted toward Riley as he read. He finished his final passage and looked up.

K.C. stood there, waving a Taco Tillie's doggie bag. "Good book?" he asked.

"Excellent book," Riley said, closing it with a thoughtful feeling. He hadn't read the whole thing—only the parts most relevant to Jayne's personal struggles—but he'd read enough to be enlightened. "I know all about women now. From here on out, I'll never be clueless about what women want again."

K.C. frowned. "Somebody dropped that book on your head, son. Nobody'll *ever* know what women want."

But Riley did. He knew what Jayne wanted, and that was what mattered. After his initial interest in her book, he'd come to an important realization, one that had kept him reading. If he ever wanted to make things work between him and Jayne, he needed to know what had gone wrong in the past. Now he did. He was ready.

"I know what *my* woman wants," he told K.C. "As soon as I get back from Antigua, I'm going to give it to her."

Sitting down across from him again, K.C. shook his head. "Why not do it now? If you want to be with her—"

"Now's a bad time." Riley felt his foot begin to tap. He stilled it with a hand to his knee. "Things ended . . . badly."

"All the more reason to straighten things out," K.C. said. "Women aren't like us. They stew on things, piling more and more stuff into the pot until the whole mess boils over. Then we're left to clean it up, wondering what the hell happened. Nope, I say if you need this woman—"

"I don't need her." *Tap, tap* went his foot.

"—you go on and get her. Hell, this flight's been delayed so many times, it might never come in."

Riley crossed his arms. "I don't need anybody." *Tap, tap.*

K.C. gave him a speculative look. His gaze dropped to

Riley's tapping foot. "You know, I had a son who used to fidget around like that whenever he was tryin' to get out of telling me something. I wonder . . . what're *you* hiding, Riley? 'Cause you're not fooling anybody but yourself.''

Stunned, Riley gawked at him. He remembered Bud saying something similar to him back at the lodge. Remembered other instances when he'd suffered this uncontrollable foot-tapping tic. Remembered how he'd felt, just a minute ago, claiming not to need Jayne.

"Holy shit!" Riley surged to his feet. "K.C., you're right!"

The older man only sat there placidly and nodded.

"I *do* need Jayne! She's funny and sweet and wild. She wishes on stars and really means it. She doesn't let me push her around, and she—" He thought of her bravely tackling the wilderness, determinedly helping her antiheartbreak ladies, wholeheartedly welcoming Alexis into the group. He thought of her pulling him into the campfire circle with the promise of a toasted marshmallow, and encouraging him to spend time with all the travelers. "She makes me a better person, K.C. I know that sounds stupid, but it's true."

"It only sounds stupid if you ignore it."

"Right." Giddily, Riley contemplated his future. Him and Jayne together. Little Jaynes, little Rileys, maybe even a dog.

He'd never had a dog. He'd never been in one place long enough to take care of one. He pictured a cocker spaniel, a German shepherd, a mutt that would catch a Frisbee. Jayne might want something girly, like a poodle. They would work it out.

"Attention, all passengers," an airline employee said over the loudspeaker. "Flight 352 to Dallas is now boarding at Gate 2."

"That's me." K.C. hefted his luggage.

It was them. Their shared flight. At the realization, Riley

felt bombarded. Feelings pushed at him, tugging him in all directions. Automatically, he shouldered his backpack.

"We must've missed the arrival announcement," he said, walking toward the boarding gate.

K.C. touched his shoulder. "You're still going? What about your girl?"

"I'll think about that on the plane." Riley frowned, focusing on the task at hand the way he usually did. "I can always come back for her."

K.C.'s eyebrows rose. "What if she's not waiting for you?"

"Not waiting for . . . of *course* she'll be waiting for me!"

But . . . what if she wasn't *waiting for him?* Dread nailed him to the spot. Typically, when faced with a problem, Riley took action first and deliberated later. He acted on instinct. In the wilderness, slow contemplation got a person in trouble— sometimes lethal trouble. It didn't pay to be Mr. Thoughtful when confronting a rock slide or battling rapids. His whole life had bowed to that philosophy.

He frowned. "You think she'll wait for me, don't you?"

"Dunno. Do you want to take that chance?"

Hmmm. Making amends later, after Jayne was calmed down and had gained some perspective—versus crawling back to her now, while she was still mad. Keeping his *National Explorer* commitment—versus potentially losing this and future assignments. It shouldn't have been a difficult choice.

But it was.

Filled with good intentions but uncertain how best to realize them, Riley wavered. He glanced at the boarding gate, at K.C. waiting for his decision. He looked at Jayne's book, and her photo on the back. *Damn.* What was he going to do?

Twenty-Four

Everything was quiet when Jayne reached the canyon lodge with Alexis in tow. Birds twittered in the trees, a gentle breeze blew, and sunshine sparkled from the two Hideaway Lodge vans parked in front of the log-cabin-style structure.

The return-trip vans, Jayne realized. *Here to take everyone back to civilization.* The adventure travel trip she hadn't wanted—but which had given her so much—had already come to an end.

Feeling unexpectedly melancholy at the realization, she stopped for a moment. This might be her last trip here to Arizona. The last trip she'd be able to afford for a very long time if things went badly in the next few minutes. She was risking a lot by coming here this way.

But she was risking it all for Riley.

With a defiant lift of her shoulders, Jayne began walking again. She caught up to Alexis just as the girl ascended the lodge porch and reached for the door. No sounds came from inside, no laughter or conversation. Jayne imagined all her breakup-ees, all the guides, *everyone,* simultaneously frowning with their arms crossed as they waited to hear her explanation for having disappeared this morning.

They were supposed to have had their final antiheartbreak-technique feedback session today. Everyone had been expecting it. In her turmoil, Jayne had forgotten it until just now. She quavered.

The screen door creaked open. "It'll be okay," Alexis whispered. "Whatever you have planned, it can't be *that* drastic."

Oh, but it was. Jayne knew it just as she knew there'd be no avoiding it. Not now that she'd made her decision. Nervously, she swept her hair from her eyes, then licked her lips in lieu of lip gloss.

"I'm ready," she said, and stepped inside.

Within, the common room held the sort of energy that told Jayne everyone had been watching her approach from the window—and had scurried for their seats when she'd ascended the steps. Curtains fluttered, rugs were ruffled from the passage of hasty feet, and chairs teetered with the impact of having been all but dove into. Now, though, everyone sat quietly, being studiously nonchalant as Jayne entered the room.

Doris and Donna glanced up from a crossword puzzle, seeming surprisingly at peace with each other. Bruce and Lance frowned at the checkerboard between them, while Mack stood nearby pretending to study the game. Carla read a book—upside down—while Mitzi brushed her hair. Only Kelly happened to look at Jayne directly, and that was because she was very *obviously* interested in the time displayed on the wall clock behind Jayne's head.

The time. She didn't have much of that to lose. According to the information Alexis had given her, Riley's flight had left over two hours ago.

"Hi, everyone," Jayne said, waving awkwardly.

Two men she didn't recognize but who she assumed were the return-trip van drivers peeked around the kitchen corner, then disappeared. They'd obviously been drawn by the tension in the air. And scared off by it too. Too bad. Their help could be important to her later.

"Hi?" she repeated.

"Oh, hi!" One by one, her breakup-ees and guides looked up from their individual activities. Each person feigned surprise.

She guessed they did it to spare her feelings. Their faces confirmed it—and she was touched by their concern. Jayne hoped they wouldn't be sorry for it once they learned the truth about her. The last thing she wanted was to be a disappointment to even more of the people in her life. It looked as though there might be no help for it though. She might as well forge on ahead and get this over with.

"I . . . have something to tell you," she said, dropping her backpack to the floor. Nervousness assailed her, and Jayne fisted her hands tightly. "It's not going to be easy, but I hope you'll all keep open minds."

In his creaky Suburban, Riley bounced over the unimproved northern Arizona dirt roads, hands fisted on the steering wheel. He'd left the Sedona airport a short while ago, encouraged by shouted wishes from K.C. and the gang. After a short stop in town, he'd motored on toward the canyon lodge with only one thought in mind.

Jayne.

He hoped he wasn't too late. She hadn't been there this morning when he'd found Bruce and Mack to tell them he was leaving, and he had no idea where she'd gone—only that she'd, incredibly, decided to hike there. By now Jayne might be miles down the trail.

Well, if she was, he'd just have to follow her, Riley decided. At a run. With that thought in mind, he patted the container housing the surprise he'd brought for her and drove a little faster. It would be tough to bring his surprise on the trail, but he'd do it if that's what it took.

Fifteen minutes later, Riley parked his Suburban in a cloud of dust outside the canyon lodge. He eyeballed the waiting vans with an acute sense of relief. At least the whole crew hadn't already left. That meant—maybe—that Jayne was still there too.

He hefted his surprise and carried it toward the lodge. All around him it seemed mysteriously quiet. No music from Alexis and Lance's radio wafted past on the breeze. No giggling came from Mitzi and Bruce. No laughter from Carla and Kelly. No bickering from Doris and Donna.

Something was definitely wrong. Had Jayne gotten hurt on the trail? Were they all huddled worriedly around her, waiting for an airlift helicopter to arrive? He never should have let her go on her own no matter how proficient she'd become at wilderness skills. Worried now about more than reaching her in time, Riley quickened his pace.

As he ascended the porch steps, awkwardly holding his surprise, Jayne's voice came from inside the lodge's common room. To his relief, she sounded fine. Better than fine. Remarkable. Her voice drifted strong and firm through the screen door that opened onto the common room, and she was saying something about . . . her book?

Frowning, Riley paused with his hand on the screen door's metal handle. He listened, not wanting to barge in if she was conducting important antiheartbreak-book business. If there was one thing he was sure about, it was that Jayne's work was important to her. Maybe the most important thing to her.

"I know you all came here to learn how to cure your broken hearts," he heard her say. "I wanted nothing more than to teach you. Heck, my whole hands-on workshop-in-a-book concept was designed so people like you could learn what to do! And I'm so grateful to you all for coming here. For listening to me. For giving me your ideas. They were all wonderful. I can't tell you what a fabulous second book they would have made.''

Would have made? Riley thought. What was she talking about?

He heard Jayne clear her throat as though she was getting choked up about something. Curious, he edged sideways on the porch silently, until she came into view through the screen. Her shoulders were straight, her hands clasped, her head momentarily bowed. All the guidance groupies, all the travel guides, Lance and Alexis . . . everyone sat with their gazes fixed on her as she stood, hesitating, in the center of the room.

"I say 'would have made,' " Jayne continued, "because there won't be a second book. There won't be a *Heartbreak 202: Hands-on Help*. I'm so sorry to disappoint all of you, but I'd be the wrong person to write that book. I was the wrong person to write *Heartbreak 101!* When I tell you what I'm going to do, you'll understand why."

There were murmurs of surprise, sounds of people shifting in their chairs. Needing to fidget off tension himself, Riley instead stood still to hear more clearly. He shifted the surprise in his arms, then tilted his head and waited. Jayne's success as a self-help guru meant everything to her. What could possibly have convinced her she needed to sacrifice it?

"It turns out," Jayne said clearly, "that I've violated the most basic tenet of *Heartbreak 101*. I've fallen in love with one of my exes. Again."

Fallen in love? Riley clenched his surprise harder, stunned by this news. *With who?* Bozo Boy? Someone else?

Then he realized *he* was Bozo Boy, according to the revelation she'd given him this morning. It was possible Jayne meant him, meant that she'd fallen in love with *him*. A rush of hope filled him as Riley went on listening. He didn't *want* to be Bozo Boy. But if he had to be, he wanted to be the Bozo Boy she loved.

"No, not really 'again,' " Jayne was saying. "The truth

is, I've loved Riley Davis since the day he saw me get soaked by a runaway wave and did everything he could short of barricading the ladies' room to get me dry. I've loved him since he left me, and all the time he was gone. I've even loved him since we got thrown together on this crazy trip.''

Riley blinked, an unbelievable happiness soaring through him. *Jayne loved him.* She really loved him. In spite of everything, she loved him.

Damn, he was a lucky man.

''I know this makes me a fraud,'' Jayne went on, her voice quavering. ''I'm sorry. But Riley means more to me than any book, any job, ever could. I love him and I don't think I'll ever stop. So even though it means leaving you all before we've had a chance to conduct the final technique-feedback session we'd planned for today . . . I'm going after him. I have to.''

In the silence that followed, she grabbed her pack from the floor. Riley saw Alexis give Jayne a two-thumbs-up sign, and they exchanged teary-eyed smiles. The rest of the group only sat there, probably too astonished to speak, as Jayne headed for the door.

''I'm going to Antigua,'' she announced as she did, ''providing the van drivers will take me to the airport so I can catch a flight. Otherwise, I'll walk! I have ATSes. I can do it! And when I get to Antigua, I'm going to track down Riley. And if he'll have me—''

''Hell, yes,'' Riley said loudly, opening the door at last. He stepped into the common room, bowled over by the beautiful, longed-for sight of Jayne in his path. *''He'll have you.''*

Okay, she was going to pass out, Jayne realized. She was going to keel over right there in the lodge's common room in front of everyone and spoil this movie-perfect moment.

"Riley?" she asked, gaping at him. "What are you— how did you—how much of what I said did you—"

"*Enough,*" he said, and came to her.

He looked big and strong and beloved. Also worn and battered and broad. His dark hair was mussed. His clothes looked slept in. But when she gazed into his eyes, Jayne saw love there, and that was all she needed.

"*I'll* have you," Riley went on. "Thank God you still want me. I'm so, so sorry for everything. For hassling you about your book—which is excellent, by the way. I just read it. And for not helping you more on this trip when I knew it was hard for you. And for botching my explanation this morning. I just froze, Jayne. It happens. It doesn't mean I don't need you to forgive me. And most of all"—he set down the thing in his hands, which looked like a plastic-and-wire carrier of some sort—"I'm sorry for leaving you. I was an idiot. Please, please forgive me."

Stunned, Jayne gawked at him. Vaguely, she became aware of all her breakup-ees, all the travel guides, even Alexis and Lance, turning their heads back and forth like spectators at a tennis match, following her conversation with Riley. Now they all turned expectant faces toward her.

"I'm sorry too," she said. "For everything. Oh, Riley, I would go anywhere with you. I would survive nature breaks and fish whacking and tent building. I would go places with you that didn't even have a *Nordstrom.* That's how much I want to be with you."

He grinned. "Is that an 'I forgive you'?"

"Yes," Jayne said, smiling back. "If you forgive me." Then something else occurred to her. "But aren't you supposed to be in Antigua?" she asked. "You were supposed to have left already. I was supposed to run after you and make a dramatic appearance. It was my plan. My insanely romantic plan."

He smiled. "I couldn't leave without you. I couldn't leave without setting this right."

"Well, I have to say, I feel a little gypped," Jayne told him lightly, still grappling with what all this meant. "My big dramatic gesture was going to be really spectacular for you, and—hey, what about your *National Explorer* assignment?"

"Reassigned."

"What about your job?"

"I'll handle it. Nothing matters more than you."

"Oh, Riley." Tentatively, Jayne took his hands. They wove their fingers together, and a giddy feeling filled her like bubbles of happiness. "Do you mean it?"

"Do I *mean* it?" Riley lowered his brows, gazing down at her seriously. His hands felt warm and steady in hers, and wonderfully familiar. "Jayne, I need you. I need you like I need a tarp in a mountain rainstorm, like I need a paddle for my kayak, like I need . . . like I need friends gathered around on the happiest day of my life."

Everyone around them sucked in a surprised breath. Jayne only snuggled closer, having already fully understood the truth. Riley was just a big mushball at heart.

"Please," Jayne said, "say we can try again."

"Please," Riley said at the same moment, "say we can try again."

"*Yes!*" they both yelled, laughing aloud with happiness. "Yes, yes, yes!" Riley pulled her into his arms and kissed her, and the instant their lips met, everyone in the room shouted out.

"Yay!" they yelled, feminine voices mingling with gruff male ones, younger with older and loud with quiet. "Yay!"

Apparently not a man to be dissuaded by a little thing like the overwhelming approval of their friends, Riley tilted up Jayne's chin with his hand and deepened their kiss. It felt like a homecoming, like a reunion of the best kind . . . like a promise to never be separated again.

And this time, Jayne knew, they'd both learned enough to keep that promise. Forever.

Finally Riley raised his head. He bracketed her face in his hands and gazed down at her with remarkable tenderness. "I love you, Jayne. I always have, and I always will."

"I love you too. So much."

The cheering resumed. Their friends surrounded them, the men slapping Riley on the back and the women hugging Jayne with squeals of joy. Thoroughly taken aback, Jayne shook her head. They really approved? She couldn't believe it. She'd been so sure they'd be disappointed in her.

Another thought occurred to her, and Jayne squeezed Riley's hand to get his attention. Instantly, he gave it to her.

"Riley," she began quietly, "are you sure you want me? Even if I don't have a 'gift'? Even if I can't help people with a second book?"

He frowned. Everyone grew silent, including Jayne. She bit her lip, waiting nervously for his answer.

"You do have a gift," he said. "A gift for caring about people, and a gift for helping people. A gift for making me a better man. That'll never go away."

Jayne promptly burst into tears. He was so sweet.

"Besides, we'll have none of this 'no second book' nonsense," Doris interrupted, giving Jayne a stern look. "There's got to be a second book, and I don't mean your workbook, although we want that too. It's already in great demand among *certain* circles. Like right here."

She nodded, exchanging a meaningful glance with her sister. Donna spoke up next. "Yes, I agree with Doris," she said to Jayne's utter astonishment. "We can't wait to read it. The workshop one *and* the other one. We need that book, so you can't stop now, Jayne."

"What do you mean?" Mystified, Jayne dabbed her eyes, then searched the faces of everyone around them. "What book?"

"Hell, *True Love 303: Living Happily Ever After,* of course," Bruce said, slinging an arm around a smiling Mitzi.

"With the two of you for an example, what else could it be?"

Hey, that wasn't a bad idea, Jayne thought, reassured that her breakup-ees seemed to have happier futures ahead of them, just like she did. Maybe she *had* done some good here, like Riley had said.

She just might consider that *True Love 303* book idea further, she decided. Later. *After* she and Riley had done some more *personal* celebrating. She gazed into his face and found him already watching her. A smile tipped his lips. It probably matched the one she wore. Their gazes caught and held, united in rediscovered love.

"I almost forgot," Riley said suddenly. "My surprise."

He bent to the container he'd brought, a container nearly knee-high and almost perfectly square. A faint scuffling sound came from inside it as Riley worked at the latches.

"I wanted to make sure you knew I was serious about this 'forever' stuff," he said as he crouched. He hesitated and directed a meaningful look at Jayne. "I wanted you to know I had plans for our future already. So I brought you . . . this."

He unfastened the latch all the way and reached inside. Riley stood, cradling something small and tan against his chest. He turned to face her, and . . .

"A puppy!" Jayne stared at the tiny, wriggling bundle of furry puppyhood in Riley's big hands. Her heart melted. "You got a puppy?"

"For us. To raise together." He stepped nearer so she could pet its soft fur. He raised his eager gaze to her face. "Someone at the airport recommended a private breeder to me when I asked where I could get one. Once I saw this little guy—"

"He's adorable!" Jayne cried, still petting the puppy. Her breakup-ees gathered around too, exclaiming over his floppy ears and wavy fur.

"You like him?" Riley asked. "He's a cockapoo. Half

cocker spaniel, half poodle. But we can get a plain old poodle too," he added hurriedly, "if you'd rather."

She didn't understand the vulnerability in his worried, hopeful look. But she did want to ease it.

"I love him! I can't wait to raise him together," she said, nuzzling the puppy's nose. "You know," Jayne added, "I've been thinking about this, and I could write anywhere. I could travel with you, and so could he."

"I could take pictures anywhere," Riley countered, "even in San Francisco. I'll walk little Primp every day."

"Primp?" Jayne raised her eyebrows. "We can't call him that. It's one letter away from being a criminal offense."

"Well, Leopard-Print Compact just sounds stupid." Riley pet the puppy, making googly eyes at him. "But you inspired me to get him, so his name will have to remind me of you."

"He's a boy. 'Primp' will turn him into a sissy dog."

"With a rhinestone collar like the one they gave me, he's already on his way."

"Never mind. We'll think of something."

They huddled together over the puppy, their fingers touching as they got acquainted with "family life." Then Jayne and Riley smiled. An unspoken accord traveled between them. As one, they turned together to their friends.

"We'd better go walk the dog," Jayne said.

"Yeah, right away," Riley agreed, grabbing the leash from the corner of the pet carrier. "I'll take Jayne back to the other lodge in my Suburban, if you all want to rendezvous there."

"For the technique-feedback session we missed," Jayne clarified, instantly catching on. "And for the final celebration dinner Bud and Gwen promised us before we catch our flights tomorrow."

Everyone looked skeptical. Jayne and Riley didn't care. The outdoors waited—and along with it, privacy. After a few good-byes (and a promise to meet later at the Hideaway Lodge), they carried the puppy and leash outside. They breathed deeply of the fresh air surrounding them. They smiled.

Jayne glanced at Riley. "So . . . you wanna sneak back inside after they leave and have a real reunion?"

"Wouldn't miss it for the world," Riley said, grinning.

"After all, we have a reputation to protect," Jayne went on. "If I'm going to write that *True Love 303* book—"

"Which, of course, you should."

"Then we're going to have to live it. We're going to have to live true love every minute of every day."

"That'll be easy," Riley said, and kissed her. "Because I truly love you. Every minute of every day."

"And I love you. Every minute of every day."

They put on their puppy's leash, linked hands, and started walking. This time their steps fell perfectly in sync.

"It's the only right thing to do," Jayne told the man she loved, shrugging playfully as she considered their future together. "We have to fulfill our destiny after all."

Riley agreed with another kiss to seal the deal. And then, for every minute of every day afterward . . . they did share true love.

Hiking, shopping, and one *completely* cute puppy included.

Dear Reader,

The first time I went camping, at the age of seven, I was dismayed to realize the entire endeavor would take place *outdoors,* where there weren't any books to keep me company. I was disillusioned when, despite my sharp-eyed watch, Yogi Bear never turned up to steal my family's picnic basket. And I was sure that, the minute I turned my back, a squirrel would gnaw through my pup tent and gobble up my M&Ms. The trauma!

I've since recovered—and have happily gone on to trek all over Arizona's untamed, out-of-the-way spots. I didn't mind a bit drawing on those experiences— plus a little research—to write this story. It was such fun tossing Jayne, the ultimate city girl, out of her urban comfort zone and into the arms of her rugged adventure travel guide, Riley. These two were made for each other! I couldn't wait to see what would happen when they were reunited in *Reconsidering Riley,* and I *really* couldn't wait to share their happily-ever-after with you.

I'm currently working on my next Zebra Books contemporary romance, *Perfect Together,* and I hope you'll look for it when it hits the shelves in 2003. Until next time . . . I'd love to hear from you! Please write to me at P.O. Box 7105, Chandler, AZ 85246-7105, send e-mail to *lisa@lisaplumley.com,* or visit my Web site, *www.lisaplumley.com* for previews, reviews, my reader newsletter, sneak peeks of upcoming books, and more.

In love and laughter,
Lisa Plumley

P.S. If you're looking for more fun and romance, please watch for my story ''Merry, Merry Mischief'' in the Zebra Books Christmas anthology *Santa, Baby.* Featuring holiday stories by Lisa Jackson, Elaine Coffman, and Kylie Adams, *Santa, Baby* is a fun way to get in the spirit of the season—and it's on bookstore shelves right now!

Contemporary Romance by
Kasey Michaels